Straight Flies the Arrow

A novel of love, loyalty, and wonder

Timon,

I rejoice in the ways the Lord is working in your life! Sydney Tooman Betts

Sydney Tooman Betts

Copyright ©2017 Sydney Tooman Betts

No part of this book may be reproduced, stored in a retrieval system or transmitted by any means without the written permission of the author.

Cover photo: Carolina Bouldin

Cover model: Jay Tavare

Cover design: Rob Trahan

ISBN 13: 978-1-7329079-2-8 Softback

For I-Am-Savior,

my romantic hero and

ever-faithful friend;

&

for my son,

who inspired one of my

favorite characters

The People of the Book
By Sydney Tooman Betts

A River Too Deep
A novel of loss, love, and faithfulness

Light Bird's Song
A novel of fear, love, and longing

Straight Flies the Arrow
A novel of love, loyalty, and wonder

Dear Reader,

Although the story contained in Straight Flies the Arrow is not dependent on the first two novels in this series, several reviewers have expressed the characters are best enjoyed by reading all three in order. The protagonists of A River Too Deep became the supporting cast of Light Bird's Song, and this third and final book continues their story. You will find an alphabetical list of primary characters separated by tribe on the following pages.

As this is the last book in this series, I will dearly miss this fictional family of friends. I hope you grow to love them as much as I do.

Happy reading!

Sydney

Sparrow Hawks

Among-the-Pines: Pacing Wolf's seven-year-old daughter

Bites-With-Dog: Pacing Wolf's Lumpwood war-society brother

Braids-His-Tail: Otter Woman's Lumpwood husband

Bull-Will-Not-Fall: Good Man belonging to the Fox war-society

Falling Bear: Wild Dog shamed and murdered his woman

Held-Back-the-Enemy: Bites-With-Dog's son, adopted into the Lumpwood war-society by Pacing Wolf

Hopping Owl: Bites-With-Dog's short, round wife

Hunts-For-Death: The Sparrow Hawk's Real Chief

Jackrabbit: Among-the-Pines' sharp-tongued grandmother

Kept-Us-Alive: A new name for Small Doe, Pacing Wolf's wife. The Allies know her as Light Bird

Last Son: a Blackfoot friend of Wolf-Who-Lays-Down. He is three

Last Woman: Kept-Us-Alive's closest friend

Little Blackfoot: Last Woman's eight-year-old daughter

Otter Woman: A clanswoman who befriended Kept-Us-Alive

Pacing Wolf: The Lumpwood leader of the Many Lodges clan

Paints-His-Shirt-Yellow: the eldest follower of I-Am-Savior

White Belly: Paints-His-Shirt-Yellow's middle-aged son

Wolf-Who-Lays-Down: Pacing Wolf and Kept-Us-Alive's toddler son

Allies

Angry Man: Surly man who desires Plays-With-Her-Earrings

Brought-Us-the-Book: Kept-Us-Alive's white mother

Elk-Dog Man: Preying Eagle's keen-sighted youngest brother

Follows-In-His-Shadow: Preying Eagle's youngest son. He is eight

Light Bird: Small Doe's given name, also Kept-Us-Alive

Little Turtle: An excellent tracker who is Preying Eagle's brother

Old Many Feathers: The Allies' esteemed and influential elder

Plays-With-Her-Earrings: Pretty Face's childhood tag-a-long

Pretty Face: Preying Eagle's second son

Preying Eagle: Allied leader who married Brought-Us-the-Book

Red Fox: Swallow Woman's husband and Wild Dog's father

Running Deer: Two Doves' husband and Preying Eagle's father

Straight Arrows: Preying Eagle's eldest son. Kept-Us-Alive's brother

Swallow Woman: Red Fox's beautiful but bitter woman

Two Bears: Preying Eagle's brother and Running Deer's second son

Two Doves: Running Deer's regal silver-haired wife

Walks-Behind-Them: Wild Dog's cousin and constant companion

Wild Dog: Red Fox and Swallow Woman's evil son

Young Deer: 14-year-old who longs to run his older brothers' path

Chapter 1

PACING WOLF SILENTLY EDGED out from under the buffalo robes he shared with his sleeping woman and pulled a hunting shirt over his head. In the dim morning light, her face appeared as smooth and her expression as childlike as it had the morning he had stolen her from an enemy village, but the slight mound raising the buffalo robe atop her mid-section belied the impression. She had already borne him one son, who was nestling peacefully against her far shoulder. He hoped the small-thing growing within her now would be another—this was no time for daughters. Tucking his sharpened knife into his belt, he caressed them both with his eyes.

I do not like leaving them.

The Women-Who-Talk-Against-Each-Other-Without-Fear had long accepted her, most calling her by a new name: The-Woman-Who-Returned-To-Keep-Us-Alive or just Kept-Us-Alive. He still thought of her as Small Doe, the name his heart had begun dubbing her while she gathered firewood with her poor-sighted grandmother. What he had yet to work out was how he might soften her fate if he failed against the Shamer of Our Women.

In the days before he walked within I-Am-Savior's shadow, he would have entrusted her to Hunts-For-Death, his adoptive Lumpwood father, whom the Good Men had chosen as Real Chief once old Hair-Up-Top had traveled to the Mystery Land. As he now considered doing so, though, he could not rid himself of a vague but niggling anxiety.

Hunts-for-Death would provide for her well, he reasoned, running his thumb along his ax-head to make sure it too was sharp, *but she would not be happy. Her graceful form and features might awaken his attention.*

Although his adoptive father was far past his first vigor, many women still admired him. He kept three wives already, along with the Blackfoot captive old Hair-Up-Top left with him before he died. To this later woman, Small Doe was more sister than friend, but if Hunts-for-Death decided to take her into his bed, jealousy might compel the other three to treat her cruelly. At best, they would allot her the most grueling chores.

As his little son shifted, pushing aside the gleaming black hair that had hidden his diminutive features, additional misgivings crept over Pacing Wolf's heart. A cleft had begun forming in the ground he had always shared with his Lumpwood father. It had been barely perceptible at first—a slight crack in a grassless patch of prairie that had drunk little rain—offering Pacing Wolf hope that Hunts-for-Death might yet walk beside him along his new path. Lately, it had widened to a gaping ravine. Several Men-Who-Lead-the-Moving-Bands held the Creator's Book in contempt, not only because a daughter of a hated enemy introduced it to their tribe, but also because it condemned some of their traditions, causing divisions among the people.

Glancing fondly at his daughter, Among-the-Pines, curled in a ball beneath her own covers, Pacing Wolf wished she had already lived through enough summers to draw a warrior's interest. If so, he could easily secure her a place to dwell if he did not return, and she was sure to offer a home to her young stepmother and toddling brother. Kept-Us-Alive and she had formed an unmistakable bond, though his dead woman's mother, Jackrabbit, had fought mightily to destroy it. Pretty as his daughter was, however, a girl of seven summers was of little use to a man. She needed twice that many—and more summers were exactly what Pacing Wolf lacked.

As he wound down the river path to bathe, a gust of bitter wind set the fringes of his hunting shirt a flutter. The leafless trees provided little protection, reminding him again of the Old Ones' warnings: the approaching winter would be severe. He must hurry. A mere sliver of the current moon still hung in the sky; soon the Moon When Deer Shed Their Horns would be nipping at his heels. If the snows came early, they might strand him; and if they were heavy, as they had been the past winter, his Fox cousin or some other rival was sure to start sniffing around his unguarded den.

My conceited cousin has long wanted Small Doe, he thought. *He is a capable Good Young Man who might keep her among the women of our clan, but he does not follow I-Am-Savior. If she displeases him, he might toss her belongings outside his lodge, and who would provide for her then?*

As Pacing Wolf slung the frigid water from his hair, he shook off the distasteful possibility. One by one, he considered other clansmen; and one by one, his heart turned each away. All the Good Men he most admired had wives, returning Pacing Wolf to his second objection to Hunts-for-Death. Few men but those untried in battle remained unmarried, and how could he trust all he held closest to a man who might not protect them well?

I will speak with Bites-With-Dog about his eldest, he concluded. *Held-Back-the-Enemy walks closely behind I-Am-Savior, and though he possesses only one more summer than Small Doe, he displays much courage and sense.*

Last spring, Held-Back-the-Enemy had pinned down a stray party of Grass Lodges with his bow while his older companions circled around to attack them from the rear, earning him a new name and token of valor. Pacing Wolf had not been among them, but he had witnessed the young man's encounter with a great cat while the two of them were hunting last summer. Held-Back-the-Enemy had stood perfectly still, bow drawn, as the animal approached and had not let his arrow fly until the cat's crouching haunches confirmed its intentions. From that day forward, Pacing Wolf had watched him, growing so impressed with his skill and courage, he had acted as his sponsor when the Lumpwoods last initiated new warriors into their society.

I-Am-Savior, prayed Pacing Wolf, wringing rivulets of water from his long, sleek braids. *You know how it is between Small Doe and me. I have kept the promises I made the night she consented to become my woman, providing food for her belly and hides to keep her warm. I threw away my desire for vengeance, placing Wild Dog in Your hands.*

Do You want me to stand by as he shames more of my clanswomen? Often, I have asked You to protect my family, how can I do less for the Many Lodges? They have chosen me to lead them. Should I stay in my lodge and listen while they wail?

You are The-One-Who-Sees-All-Things. Keep my woman and son from hunger while I pursue her evil kinsman; and if I have finished what You set before me to do on earth, receive me to Yourself.¹ I am not afraid of Wild Dog or to make the journey home to You; but Small Doe is your daughter. To whom should I entrust her and our children?

COOL LITTLE HANDS, STILL padded with childhood, gently squeezed Kept-Us-Alive's smooth cheeks; and lips, just as cool and thickly padded, pressed a firm wet kiss squarely on her mouth.

"Do not wake her," scolded Among-the-Pines, scampering up next to her stepmother to grasp her brother's thin forearm. "The small-thing she carries inside makes her tired."

When his mother's eyes fluttered open, Wolf-Who-Lays-Down grinned and repeated his actions.

"I'm awake," she assured Among-the-Pines, reaching up to stroke the girl's loose hair, "and thankful He-Who-Sees-All-Things gave me the two most delightful children He ever made."

Half sitting up, she embraced them both, but as she glanced around the lodge for their father, the corners of her mouth fell downward. His war-shield sat near the lodge door beside the small rawhide bag he used for journeys. From the bulging look of it, he expected he might be away a long while.

"Let me up," she pleaded, squirming out from under the covers. "I need to dress."

Something in her tone made them instantly stop playing. Following her gaze to her father's bag, Among-the-Pines grasped the reason for her stepmother's sudden change and the concern that lay under her grave expression: The Shamer of Women.

When the little girl had lived only three summers, her father had found her mother lying in the grass, a deep slash across her belly exposing the nearly ripe small-thing she had been carrying. Among-the-Pines' memory of it was vague, filled with grief and a keen aversion toward the young enemy her father soon thrust into her dead mother's place.

Looking back, Among-the-Pines realized how unfair she had been. Her stepmother had not wanted him to steal her; Sparrow Hawk custom had demanded he do so. A few moons later, after Loping Coyote also found his woman shamed and murdered, the Good Men had rallied a war party. They had returned with several scalps and a captured bride for the grieving warrior, and all were glad that the murders had ceased. Last evening, however, three elderly clanswomen had stumbled across another victim.

Her father swung back their door flap, pulling her from her memories. One glance at Kept-Us-Alive told Pacing Wolf she had grasped his intentions. Her eyes looked clouded, though glistening with moisture, and streaks ran over the high bones of her angular cheeks. As he tenderly stroked a stray hair from her temple, her expression drew him back to an evening long ago when he had wondered what her eyes might hold should he die in battle. He did not wonder now. They held love, longing, and sorrow.

"I am giving you to Bites-With-Dog," he murmured, wiping away a fresh tear with his thumb. "He will care for you all until I return."

Kept-Us-Alive struggled to reply, her voice so soft and raspy he could barely hear her. "We...we do not know it is Wild Dog. We had all thought Loping Coyote killed him."

Pacing Wolf nodded. "But even you were unsure of the scalp hanging from Loping Coyote's lance. It lacked several of your clansman's trophies."

"What about the woman's husband? Why does he not go to avenge her?"

"Falling Bear goes with me," answered Pacing Wolf, "but I am the only one of us who has seen Wild Dog—on the morning I stole you from the meadow. The Many Lodges chose me to lead them—I must keep our clanswomen from further harm."

She knew this and admired her husband's courage, but she also knew Wild Dog. No one was so callous or void of conscience. Brushing her lips against Pacing Wolf's palm, she whispered, "I pray that He-Who-Sees-All-Things will keep you safe and bring you home."

Slipping his hand around the back of her neck, he caressed the soft skin beneath her gently waving hair. It filled him with yearning. He hated leaving all he loved, hated leaving them unprotected. *But they will be protected,* he assured himself, embracing his young daughter as she nestled against him. *He-Who-Sees-All-Things will keep His eye upon them, and Bites-With-Dog will care for them well.*

As Kept-Us-Alive laid her temple against the curve of his neck, she inhaled the fragrance of sweet tobacco clinging to his shirt. When would she smell it again or be able to let her fingers trace the veins that wandered over the hills and valleys of his arms? She did so now, only his shirt so quickly obstructed any contact that she slipped her hand down to its hem, under its fringe, and around to the small of his back. His skin felt warm and smooth beneath her palm, but the muscles beneath it felt taut like a bow prepared to spring into action.

Regretfully, he grasped her wrists to move her hands away. "If Falling Bear and I do not leave now, we will not cover enough ground before the sun lays down to rest." Lifting his tiny son, he firmly commanded, "Protect your mother and sister while I am gone." The boy puckered his lips and glanced up briefly but then returned to the elk-skin fringes he was fingering on his father's shoulder. "And you, my daughter, are to help move my lodge next to Bites-With-Dog's."

Setting Wolf-Who-Lays-Down on the robe-strewn floor, he gripped his shield and bag, opening the door-flap to the cool autumn sunrise. "I do not know where Wild Dog hides," he murmured, turning to gaze a last time at his woman, "but we will find him. If we are not back before the trees bud, Bites-With-Dog has promised to take you as his daughter. He is a Good Man. If I do not return, he will choose a fit husband for you after you have finished mourning."

Before Kept-Us-Alive could protest, Pacing Wolf ducked out of the lodge. She scrambled to her feet and hurried out to catch him, but before her eyes adjusted to the light, she heard the pounding of hooves moving swiftly away from the village. Staring gloomily at the two already shrinking figures silhouetted by the waking sun, her stomach felt as if it thudded against the ground.

She knew Pacing Wolf to be a valiant and skillful warrior, much like her father, Preying Eagle, and her grandfather, Running Deer. The bravery of all three was highly attested both by tribal lore and their many tokens, yet none of the three found delight in shedding blood. Wild Dog was quite different.

He-Who-Sees-All-Things will watch between you and me while we are hidden from each other's sight.
Genesis 31:49

Chapter 2

HEARING A CRUNCH of crisp fallen leaves, Kept-Us-Alive turned to find Last Woman, the tall Blackfoot captive who had become her closest friend, peering down at her.

"What is the trouble? You look as if you had swallowed a dish of burning embers."

"Pacing Wolf," Kept-Us-Alive replied. "He goes to help Falling Bear track down his woman's murderer."

Last Woman frowned. "Come. We will bathe and then fill our sacks with water."

"Among-the-Pines and I will fill them," chirped Little Blackfoot, Last Woman's young daughter, "and Wolf-Who-Lays-Down and my brother can help us carry them up."

Forcing herself to smile, Kept-Us-Alive picked her way along the path to the river while Last Woman's children raced her own two down the bank, shed their clothes, and began bathing with abandon in the frigid water. Last Son was already a head taller than Wolf-Who-Lays-Down, though he was scarcely two seasons older; and Little Blackfoot, several summers Among-the-Pines' senior, towered above all four. Her height and the faintest hint of a soon-to-be-budding figure drew such clear attention from a cluster of neighboring youths that her mother hurriedly waded into the knee-deep water.

Blocking their view, Last Woman motioned toward a clump of trees growing well into the river. "Over there—we will bathe behind those trees, and you will no longer get out of the water before you put on your blouse."

"But snakes live in the roots, protested Little Blackfoot, "and the water will pull at my hem when it becomes wet. It will feel all cold and clingy."

"Do as I say," scolded her mother. "Quickly!"

Little Blackfoot stifled another protest, moving past her brother to bathe behind the sparsely leaved clump of branches.

"Come back!" called Among-the-Pines. "The water is warmer here."

"Did you not hear Last Woman?" asked Kept-Us-Alive, wading out to join them. "Do not encourage your friend to disobey her mother!"

"Why can she not splash with me and our brothers? She did nothing naughty."

Her stepmother glanced over her shoulder toward the gawking youths. "You will understand as you grow older. We will go to her if you wish to play. Here—take my hand. The small-thing I carry makes me unsteady."

When she and Among-the-Pines reached their companions, the two little girls forgot the matter; but while Last Woman disrobed, she nodded toward the offenders. "They worry me. They think Little Blackfoot possesses more summers than she does."

Kept-Us-Alive pulled her blouse over her head. "They imitate their uncles and older cousins, casting eyes over any woman who crosses their paths, but they will not touch her. They own too much respect for Hunts-for-Death."

"For now," acknowledged the tall Blackfoot woman, sinking down into the river. "But fall will soon turn into winter and winter into spring. How many seasons will pass before some warrior conceals himself in a blanket to see which other suitors enter Hunts-For-Death's lodge?"

"For several more summers, she will be too young to draw their attentions. Four at least, perhaps five."

Deepening her frown, Last Woman briefly glanced toward the party of gathered bathers. "I do not want this life for her. Sparrow Hawk warriors treat their women as they treat buffalo ribs. Once they have eaten the best bits, they cast the bones away. My people's men-folk were not like this. They valued a woman for her ability to soften a hide or for her expert weaving. These warriors think only of sport—how they may display their prowess before their rivals or prove their hearts are calloused beyond feeling."

Kept-Us-Alive shuddered. She remembered well the horror she had felt during the first Moon When Everything Greens that she had lived here. After the Death-Staffs Ceremony, members of rival war-societies ducked into their opponents' lodges, pulling out their competitors' wives. Many women were willing, even hopeful. They had intentionally invited a particular warrior's attention—some because they belonged to cruel warriors and some because they were wanton. A few were taken against their wishes, but only their women-folk were allowed to intervene. Sparrow Hawk tradition forbade husbands to do anything, so warriors with status dared not protest.

If one did, the Good Men branded him a weak-hearted coward, incapable of leading.

"Allied men-folk are not like them either," she confided. "If a warrior pays too much attention to another man's wife, he may soon…"

Wolf-Who-Lays-Down flung himself against her, grasping her shoulders and pulling her further down in the water. "We go? I hungry!"

Hastily ducking her head beneath the surface, she finished bathing, emerged with Last Woman beside the branches that held their garments, and pulled her blouse firmly into place. The damp sheepskin clung uncomfortably to her torso, reminding her of Little Blackfoot's complaints, but she preferred this to immodestly parading past the others like The-Women-Who-Talk-Against-Each-Other-Without-Fear.

She did not wonder that warriors viewed lightly the trading back and forth of their wives, but before hearing Last Woman's comments, she had never considered this horrendous prospect for Among-the-Pines. Pacing Wolf would give consent only to a warrior who walked in I-Am-Savior's shadow, but she had noticed fewer and fewer men were joining their number. If none offered for his daughter, how would the girl live? A woman did not hunt buffalo as a man.

"I am hungry, too!" whined Among-the-Pines.

"Here. Fill as many water-sacks as you can carry, and then help me gather some firewood. After breakfast, we will take down your father's lodge."

AS THEY REACHED the top of the ridge, they found Bites-With-Dog waiting with his small round wife, Hopping Owl, and their son, Held-Back-the-Enemy. The eldest two greeted Kept-Us-Alive and her children reassuringly, inquiring about their health and at what time Pacing Wolf had left that morning; but the young Sparrow Hawk warrior remained as solemn-faced as he always did in her presence.

She had often wondered why he disliked her. He was a great favorite of her husband, and on the occasions she had observed him, he behaved to others with friendly ease. Toward her, he offered only token politeness to a point she had felt embarrassed. Once, while she was walking to her sister-in-law's home on the other side of the village, she noticed him approaching from the opposite direction. She knew he saw her also; but instead of returning the respectful nod she offered, he glanced away, as if intensely examining a passing dog. Though less pointed, meals shared in his father's home—or even in her own—were more awkward. He laughed and chatted with all present but treated her as if she were a spirit he could not see.

Shrugging off her unease, Kept-Us-Alive smiled at Hopping Owl, who insisted on helping her take down Pacing Wolf's lodge and tossing it up next to theirs.

"I will help also," Last Woman offered. "Lifting the heavier, longer lodge poles might make the small-thing she carries rush out too soon to greet his brother and sister."

Hopping Owl dropped her eyes to the mound beneath Kept-Us-Alive's elk-tooth covered blouse. "He is growing nicely. Does he often kick?"

"Yes," smiled Kept-Us-Alive, pressing her palms over her stomach. "He is like his father—always moving. I fear Pacing Wolf has made us a burden during a season that any extra load must feel unwelcome."

Hopping Owl pressed her lips into a straight hard line. "This killing of our women...your husband must stop it."

"He will not return until he has. I pray our Lord makes his arm mighty and his legs swift."

"We also pray this."

Once the three women arrived at Pacing Wolf's lodge, Kept-Us-Alive packed her family's belongings while Hopping Owl and Last Woman started the more arduous task: removing the buffalo hides from their frame and disassembling the long poles. Held-Back-the-Enemy arrived shortly before they were finished, pulling two of Pacing Wolf's horses into place. As he held the first still, his mother and her tall Blackfoot helper strapped one end of a lodge pole to its left side, lifting the other end to the same side of the second horse. While they repeated this on the right sides of both animals, the first horse began shimmying, bumping the pole out of Last Woman's grasp.

"Hold him still!" Hopping Owl scolded, forgetting her son's age and status as a warrior. "The pole barely missed Last Woman's foot. Do you want him to trample the children?"

Clenching his jaw, Held-Back-the-Enemy returned his attention to the lead horse, holding its bridle tightly while his mother and the Blackfoot woman stretched the lodge covers between the two poles, forming a soft platform, and helped Kept-Us-Alive load it with her household goods.

"Why was Hopping Owl fussing?" Kept-Us-Alive whispered to Last Woman as they led the conveyance down the central path.

"While Held-Back-the-Enemy was watching you, he let go of the horses."

"Me?" Kept-Us-Alive frowned. "Why?"

Last Woman shrugged. "He is probably concerned for your husband. All know he admires Pacing Wolf, and all also know the evil heart that dwells within your kinsman. What do you call him—Mad Dog?"

"Wild Dog. Each moment, I bundle up my fears and drop them before Him-Who-Sees-All-Things, but before I have finished asking Him to watch over Pacing Wolf, I have begun to gather them back up again."

"No Sparrow Hawk warrior is as clever or cunning as your husband. He will track down and rid us of this Shamer of Women."

"I am confident he will," Kept-Us-Alive nodded. "He is skilled at following trails, but among my father's people, Wild Dog is also renowned for cunning and courage."

"Ah, but Pacing Wolf is like the youth, Loved-By-the-Creator, who went out to meet that fierce, tall warrior.[2] He will return, and do not trouble yourself over Held-Back-the-Enemy. He is nothing like Goes-To-Battle. He walks closely in I-Am-Savior's shadow—too closely to covet another man's woman, especially a man he holds in such esteem."

"I do not fear him," answered Kept-Us-Alive. "I am afraid we are of putting him out of his own father's lodge—and he already does not like me."

Last Woman cocked her head. "Why? You have insulted him?"

"I do not know. As a youth, while he tended Pacing Wolf's horses, he used to grin when he saw me approaching. I think he grasped what lay in Pacing Wolf's heart toward me before I did. Now that he has become highly esteemed for his own deeds, he no longer offers me a greeting."

"Perhaps he is uneasy around young women."

Kept-Us-Alive considered the idea but dismissed it. Held-Back-the-Enemy was not tall, but his features were well shaped, and untouched women throughout the village whispered tales of his valor—tales she knew they did not exaggerate because she had first heard them from Pacing Wolf. Neither did she believe him to be arrogant, like some of the other Good Young Men, though he easily accepted admiration.

"You are also young," answered Kept-Us-Alive. "He is at ease with you."

"Why does he bother you?"

"I fear we will become like a sore—rubbed raw with each fresh bumping. I wish my family were like my friend Corn-Tassels'."

"Who?" asked Last Woman, crinkling her brow.

"The white woman with yellow hair," explained Kept-Us-Alive. "I brought her to meet you when she visited us with her father and husband—the long-knife with the hair growing above his lip."

"I remember," Last Woman laughed. "While Little Blackfoot Woman was recovering from small pox, she would watch him eat, guessing which bits of food his hairy lip would catch. Do you wish you were a white woman?"

"I am," smiled Kept-Us-Alive, realizing her friend could not know what she intended. "At least half. Corn-Tassels was born to my mother's closest cousin—not a real cousin, but since our mothers are both white, the people of our village considered them related. Her husband—"

"Hair-On-Lip?" asked Last Woman, unsure she was following the trail of Kept-Us-Alive's thoughts.

"No, her mother's husband—Corn-Tassels' father—Spotted Long-knife. He often took his family with him."

"To our village?"

"No—yes. He brought her here once, but I mean to his own. His tribe dwells far away in a land called Boss Town, near the place the sun awakens. When the leaves begin to turn yellow, they travel back there to live with his family during the hard moons—when the winds blow cold and animals hide in burrows. Then as the grass begins to appear again, they come home to my Allied village. My eldest brother, Straight Arrows," she chuckled, "would grow excited when we first spotted the tiny purple flowers sticking their tips out of the warming ground."

"Why? Was he fond of this white long-knife?"

"Yes, but that was not why. He planned to marry Corn Tassels."

"Then why did her father give her to the hairy-lipped man? You have told me often of this brother—any father would want such a warrior for his daughter."

"I do not know. I was here when they married. When Wild Dog murdered Among-the-Pines' mother, his tracks led Pacing Wolf to my father's village. They may lead that way again, which is what I meant about Corn Tassels. If my husband had taken us with him, we could see my family."

"But her father took them to safety; Pacing Wolf would be taking you to danger. You would not want this for your children and he would not allow it."

Kept-Us-Alive nodded. "Of course, you are right. My wish was foolish."

Last Woman did not answer, she could not—her friend's wish *was* foolish, but she was too polite to say so. For a while, the two women did not speak. Their thoughts were following different trails back to former homes, one Allied and the other Blackfoot, wondering how their loved ones fared. Kept-Us-Alive finally broke the silence. "You would like him."

"Who?"

"My eldest brother, Straight Arrows. I cannot guess why Spotted Long-knife turned him away. The old women say he is just like my father was when he was young: tall, handsome, fearless—but patient and gentle. My mother's cheeks still redden when she tells me how they met and of her first thoughts of him. By now, he is surely married."

Last Woman smiled sadly. "I also sometimes wish I could return to my family, but where can I find them? They are likely all dead, killed when these Sparrow Hawks attacked us in the ravine. How I hated your husband when he pulled me from the ditch where I was hiding. I was grateful he did not touch me but gave me to old Hair-Up-Top instead. I have you to thank."

"Me? Why? I did nothing."

"You held his heart and all his attention. He was interested only in catching my uncle's mare—the white one he gave to you."

"You never told me."

Last Woman shrugged. "I did not own the sounds to make your strange words, and by the summer I gained them, I did not want to ruin your joy in her. It is the way of war. She was Pacing Wolf's gift to you—enjoy her. And do not fret over Held-Back-the-Enemy. He will probably grow warmer now that Pacing Wolf has entrusted you to his father."

Much water cannot douse love's embers, nor will rivers flow over it. If a warrior traded all the possessions in his lodge for love, they would be utterly despised.

Song of Solomon 8:7

Chapter 3

PACING WOLF PULLED his sorrel to a halt beside a straggling chokecherry to examine a snapped purple-gray twig. It grew from a high branch, too far from the ground for a wolf or shorter creature to have damaged. "It is broken toward the wind coming off the lowlands."

Falling Bear narrowed his eyes. "This Shamer-of-Women is careless."

"No," murmured Pacing Wolf, squinting against the low-hanging sun. "He is leading us back over my trail of three summers past, when I snatched my woman from under his nose."

As he thought of her that day, her limbs smooth beneath his palms while he loosened the rope with which he had tied them, his insides grew warm. His prior summers had been like the prairie he and Falling Bear were traveling, offering only the barest shade. When he recalled her eyes— wide with terror as she gained her first clear glimpse of him—he wished he could have wooed her as he would have wooed a chosen Sparrow Hawk bride.

Wild Dog heads to the cavern where I took her, supposed Pacing Wolf, *but he is ignorant of its other mouth. I will steal up behind him while he rests secure.*

During the Moon of Changing Seasons, he and Held-Back-the-Enemy had scouted the far reaches of the Sparrow Hawk hunting grounds to look for signs of encroaching enemies. They had found some to the south, but when they had come to the cavern, he saw the vines he had spread across the lower entrance had intertwined around the brush he had piled behind them so thickly that he elected to skirt the cliff and enter from above.

"We will soon make camp," he told Falling Bear, twisting around toward the coral threads weaving softly into the dimming sky. "The sun grows weary and Wild Dog is no fool—he will not build an open fire. He will cover himself in darkness and wait for us to follow. I once tracked a buffalo to a still pool nearby. If it is not dry, we can refresh our horses and rest until the sun awakens."

← ← ←   → → →

KEPT-US-ALIVE KNELT in the center of Pacing Wolf's lodge, placing the tops of three sticks together over embers from the cook fire she had kept alive. The night would be cold without a husband's arms to warm her. Feeling two small hands, one pressing against her back and the other sliding down toward her elbow, she turned to smile into the quizzical black eyes peeking around from behind her shoulder.

"Father hunting?" Wolf--Who-Lays-Down's tiny lips looked like shiny ripe cherries on the verge of bursting as they wrapped around the words.

His mother breathed in deeply and slowly exhaled, calming herself before she answered. Her son did not understand shaming or murder, and she did not want to frighten him. "Yes," she nodded. He was hunting, though not for food.

The two little hands slipped up to her cheeks and held them gently as if he sensed the concern she was trying to conceal; and his eyes, searching hers, seemed to will her to receive the comfort he could not voice. The look was so like his father's that tears stung her sharply.

"No cry," he commanded, cocking his head as a tear threatened to overrun its bounds.

She smiled into his tender face. "I miss your Father. He went with Falling Bear to hunt down a dog."

"A dog?"

"Yes," Kept-Us-Alive answered. "You do not know this one; he is wild."

The boy's black eyes brightened as he scrambled from against his mother's knees.

"Where are you going?" she called, catching hold of his pudgy arm. "Look! The sun has gone to sleep and you must also. Last Son is probably curled up beneath his buffalo robes."

"I get rocks."

"Why?" asked his mother, pulling him back onto her lap.

Wolf-Who-Lays-Down drew his arm back, nearly hitting Kept-Us-Alive's face as he began to swing it forward. "Throw at the wild dog." Gently enclosing his raised hand in her own, she firmly shook her head "He is not here. Your father and Falling Bear have chased him away and will return to us soon. "

The little boy stared at her for a moment, as if he were considering what she told him. "I want Father," he mumbled. "Father come home now."

Kept-Us-Alive stroked his silky hair, hoping to provide him comfort, but though she found a measure of the same as he snuggled against her, she could evade her own sharp longing no better than her many unanswerable questions. "He will if he can," she whispered, as much to herself as to him, "but they are chasing the dog far, to make certain he will never again come near our village. They will likely be sleeping in the open. He-Who-Sees-All-Things is lovingly watching us and is also watching them. Shall we ask Him to remind your father how much we love…"

Ducking beneath the door-flap, Among-the-Pines did not need to ask what was utmost in their hearts. "Falling Bear has not returned either," the little girl reported. "Last Woman said they may be gone for several days." Slipping up close, she wrapped one arm around her stepmother's back and the other around her half-brother. "May I pray?" Kept-Us-Alive smiled and nodded.

"I-Am-Savior, You know where Father and Falling Bear are lying down for rest. You are with him, just as You are here in his lodge with us. Please protect him while he sleeps and tomorrow while he hunts the mad dog—and quickly bring him back to us."

←←← →→→

FALLING BEAR AWOKE with a start. Swiftly grabbing his knife, he peered through the starlight at the black shape bending over the pool. "Waugh!" he rasped, barely making out the tip of a feather poking up over the brush-line and three more tilting to the right. "Another breath and you would have felt a sharp pain between your ribs."

Pacing Wolf grinned. "You are like an old grandmother, sleeping until the sun has gotten out of bed. When you raise your lazy bones, follow the murderer's trail. I go another way."

Falling Bear wrinkled his forehead. "You found other tracks?"

"No—I follow my suspicions."

"Wait. I will fill my pouch and come also."

"No," replied Pacing Wolf, standing erect. *Falling Bear can only slow my pace; he does not know the cavern's twists and turns.* "If my instincts tell me the truth, we will both come upon him—better to beset him from two sides."

Falling Bear nodded. "While he gazes at the rising sun, he will not expect the moon. If we do not meet over his lifeless body, I will return to this place after my knife has scraped the scalp from the back of his head."

Pacing Wolf grunted in agreement while he swung onto the back of his sorrel.

As Falling Bear watched them disappear into the dark morning, he wondered where they were heading. He had long admired his Lumpwood brother's cunning, but lately, he had begun to question Pacing Wolf's judgment. Since the young Cuts-Off-Our-Heads woman had returned, she held too much sway over his heart, constantly reading to him from a bundle of leaves that she claimed had captured her spirit-guide's words.

He-Who-Made-All-Things does not live in markings on leaves, thought Falling Bear, spitting onto the ground beside him. *He is here, in the open, and up there, in the stars.*

LEAPING FROM HIS SORREL, Pacing Wolf scrambled up the short incline to the cavern's lower mouth. The vines looked untouched, except by a spider. He had crisscrossed them in an intricate design that encompassed a few dry and brittle leaves hanging from an encroaching sapling.

No one larger than a fox has slipped through them, deduced Pacing Wolf. *The spider's skill has kept the leaves in place. A passing man would have torn many supporting threads.* Several light-colored woven bundles, likely flies stored against the cold, lean days of the Moon When Wolves Run Together confirmed his conclusion: *the spider weaved his home after my last inspection.*

Turning his face toward the sun, drifting low behind the scrub that dotted the flatlands, he wondered what his woman and children might be doing. He missed the warmth and softness of Small Doe's voice, her gaze, and her skin. She was like a salve bringing healing and relief; and with every sun, his daughter grew more like her.

As he remembered Among-the-Pines' expression while they parted, he felt struck by another change. It had crept up so slowly he had not before noticed. He had always thought her a copy of her mother—like two crabapples pulled from the same limb, but Small Doe had somehow affected even her outward appearance. Among-the-Pines' neck had not grown longer nor her features sharper, but she had acquired her stepmother's grace of movement, her thoughtfulness of heart, and even her ineffable quality of peace. Perhaps the child intentionally imitated Small Doe or perhaps her outward appearance reflected a new peace in her heart.

He did not know. He hated to think what she would have become had he allowed her grandmother, Jackrabbit, to raise her.

Inevitably, his heart turned toward his little son, who often followed him so closely both had barely escaped several mishaps. He was training himself, while concentrating his attention on someone or something, to glance behind him whenever he felt inclined to step backward lest he topple over and crush the child.

Pulling himself from these pleasant recollections, Pacing Wolf weighed what he might next do. Should he cut through the vines immediately and sneak up the narrow tunnel that led to the spacious cavern or use dusk's cover to scout the upper regions of the cliff formation? He was inclined toward the former, convinced he could pounce before Wild Dog was aware he was present, and yet the caution that had often saved his skin held him back.

Once he had stolen up and around the cliff's face, he dropped to his haunches behind a small pine, observing three horses on the slope where he had once watched Small Doe plucking up a skirt-full of greens. They meandered leisurely, looking among the tufts of grass for the few remaining blades. One shook away a rope that hung down loosely, interposing itself between the horse's lips and his goal.

Three.

Two, he supposed, belonged to Wild Dog and his cousin. Pacing Wolf remembered the young man well. He had worn no tokens that attested to skill or valor and had soiled himself when he spotted his brother's bloody pate. *But,* he surmised, *three summers are long enough to have toughened his gut.*

Who rode the third mount, he had no way of guessing.

As dusk deepened, Pacing Wolf contemplated his plans. He had ridden all day, but the sight of the horses had sent blood pumping forcefully through his heart.

The darkness will be my ally. Wild Dog is arrogant and the night grows cold; he may build a fire, showing himself clearly. If not, it will not matter. I know every place I can safely step in these caverns. Before he knows I am watching, my ax will split his chest.

Creeping back down the cliff's side, he felt for the vines that covered the cave's mouth and with a few strokes of his knife sliced sufficient twining tendrils to allow him to pass through. The air smelled familiarly dank, offering him comfort even while his pulse quickened.

Silently, he ascended the winding passageway, higher and deeper into the cave, until a bend in the wall alerted him to step no further. The scent and faint crackle of embers warned of a hidden fire, and while he listened keenly to discern its direction, he soon heard voices that pricked his memory.

"Did you see her eyes widen? She thought we were ghost-warriors emerging from the forest!"

As responding snickers echoed off the stone walls, Pacing Wolf curled his upper lip. *That is not Wild Dog. Only cowards enjoy a woman's fear!* He had intended to wound any others, preventing them from helping their murderous clansman, but after hearing the callous laughter, he reconsidered. Tamping down the urge to spring forward, he tightly gripped his ax, avidly listening to confirm their number.

"Ugh—she smelled of sweat," groaned a deeper-voiced warrior. "Her fat trapped the stench inside its creases."

Another round of chortles left Pacing Wolf uncertain how many warriors were laughing, but before he could decide, someone—he guessed the coward—began to mock. "Better than that skinny Horned Enemy. She felt like a bag of stones covered with rough-bark! You are still angry you could not snare Light Bird."

As the hair on the back of his neck raised up, Pacing Wolf stopped breathing. Small Doe's grandfather had called her by that name, though Pacing Wolf had never known why. She was light-skinned but did not flit about. She possessed a young whitetail's slender, graceful limbs and large, liquid eyes.

"Wash her from your memory. You place us all in peril. You have your own woman; why crave that one?"

"I do not crave her," answered Wild Dog. "I crave her warrior's pain; and after I cut out his unborn potbelly, I will snatch the toddling son to raise as my own."

"For three summers we have tried to find her alone, but she keeps to his clanswomen. Let her be; she is our kin."

"I will get her," Wild Dog snarled, "and lie watching while he finds them."

Pacing Wolf could listen no longer. Springing from the darkness, he split the air with a shrill cry, bringing down his ax on the speaker's arm. Whirling swiftly, he pinned a second man struggling to rise from his heavy buffalo pelt and drove a knife between his collar and breastplate. He jumped up, hurled his ax at a moving shadow, and spun about to face Wild Dog, clutching a limp arm while he staggered to his feet. Leaping toward the faint embers, Pacing Wolf stomped them out to further his advantage but heard nothing except Wild Dog's muffled grunts and the trickling spring.

Let him bleed out, he thought, recalling the foul description of Falling Bear's pleasant woman. *A quick death is too merciful. Still, I cannot risk him surviving.*

Pressing himself against the rough wall, Pacing Wolf listened to rapid breathing, whether Wild Dog's or the shadow's, he was not certain. Concluding his ax had missed its mark, he picked up a few bits of loose gravel and rolled them around in his hand. They felt damp and cool, reminding him of the spring's dangerous run-off and a fitting end to these treacherous enemies.

Wild Dog would cut the small-thing from my woman's belly; let his clansmen try to cut him from the belly of this cliff.

Tossing the pebbles toward the slick trench, worn smooth by many summers of constantly running water, he listened to them splatter against rock and drop through a narrow opening. He also heard hasty footfalls darting toward the echo when the pebbles reached the watery depths below. Slowly, Pacing Wolf edged toward them, but he felt a searing pain so unexpected that he instinctively jumped back and reached for his side. He felt another in his leg, and warm, thick liquid oozing from the gash. Doubling over, he moved swiftly toward the spring, slipping behind a stone pillar thrusting up from the cave's floor, and began cutting the leather strips that bound his legging.

As he thrust his wounds beneath the frigid water, he bit his tongue to keep from crying out, but they soon grew so numb he was able to stand against the wall. He held himself perfectly still, reassessing his assault while he listened to an opponents' ragged breathing. He had allowed Wild Dog to provoke him, foolishly rushing out before he was sure of their number and hurling his ax without a certain target. He would not do so again.

While Pacing Wolf pressed his loosened legging against the gash to staunch the bleeding, a hard shoulder slammed against him, knocking him to the ground. Seizing the assailant's shirt, he levered his good leg to hurl him over his head and heard him yelping in panic as he slid helplessly down the slippery run-off. With a sharp crack and pop, the warrior plunged through the narrow opening. Shrieks of pain and terror reverberated down the tapering corridor while Pacing Wolf scrambled to his feet, bracing himself against the cool rock to catch his breath, and listened for a splash deep within the cavern's belly. He heard nothing.

The cave's jaws have caught him, he concluded, eliciting images of an excruciating death. Alone, in complete darkness, the man would slowly bleed to death or so shrivel from lack of water and food the jaws could no longer maintain their hold. He would plummet into the water he craved, gulping greedily to slake his thirst even as it pulled him downward. If this was Wild Dog, his arms would be useless. Pacing Wolf had severed one to the bone and the other sounded as if it had cracked or been wrenched from its socket.

Unable to hear above the piteous moans, Pacing Wolf toyed with edging back to silence the helpless enemy, but delivering a blow in the dark might only increase his opponent's pain. He would also make his own location obvious. Wincing as he gingerly placed weight on his wounded leg, he reached for the edge of the alcove in which he had once stashed Small Doe. The memories this place aroused selected his course. The risk was too great. He had underestimated this war party's cunning and strength; for his entire clan's sake, he must not do so again.

While he felt his way along the winding corridor, a gust of fresh air announced he was near the cave's upper entrance, and the feel of soft pine needles brushing across his cheeks flooded him with relief. He inhaled deeply. The steep climb had been arduous, sending a fresh supply of blood to trickle from his wound. As he leaned down to touch the tacky spot, an unnatural blackness so engulfed him that his hand flung out to grasp a bough nearby. He missed and toppled headlong into the starless sky.

A man grows weak and dies. He takes his last breath, and where is he?

Job 14:10

Chapter 4

During the

Moon When Deer Shed Their Horns

AS KEPT-US-ALIVE and Last Woman wound down to the river, they heard soft footsteps rapidly coming up behind them. They stepped into the brush to make way for the runner, but instead of hurrying past them down the narrow path, he stopped.

"Falling Bear has come back," Held-Back-the-Enemy told them.

Dropping her bundled washing, Kept-Us-Alive turned to bolt back up the way she had just come, but the young warrior took hold of her arm.

"No—stay. I wish to speak away from others' ears."

Last Woman gathered up Kept-Us-Alive's laundry, intending to continue to the river without her until she glanced at Held-Back-the-Enemy. His face looked grave, dousing the joyous sparks he had ignited in her friend's eyes.

"Wait," he advised Last Woman. "She may need you."

"Wh—where is Pacing Wolf?" asked Kept-Us-Alive. "Let me go to him!"

Only inches taller, the young Sparrow Hawk peered into her angular face, wondering how to soften what he must tell her. She had always reminded him of a gentle spring wind, warming all whose good fortune brought them near. As a youth, while tending her husband's herd, he would lay in the grass dreaming up ways to coax a smile to her lips or a joke that might make the corners of her eyes crinkle.

Once he had become a warrior, he began to avoid her. Pacing Wolf was not only a clansman but also the Many Lodges' leader, and once he learned Held-Back-the-Enemy wished to join the Lumpwoods—the Sparrow Hawk's most powerful warrior society—he had offered to become his sponsor. Pacing Wolf was also one of his father's closest friends and led all who walked in I-Am-Savior's shadow. He deserved loyalty, not envy over a woman, and all knew how firmly he held her heart.

I no longer need to avoid her, the young Lumpwood thought, but this idea offered him little pleasure. He could see hope and dread clearly wrestling in her expression and hated to be the one to decide their outcome. Still, he would rather that she hear it from him than from Hunts-For-Death.

Taking a deep breath, he hurriedly recounted, "Falling Bear followed The Shamer's tracks to the crag above the Muddy River. He found Pacing Wolf's sorrel wandering by a stream that runs out below it, just before the earth begins to rise."

"He found Wild Dog?"

Held-Back-the-Enemy did not ask who Wild Dog was—he did not need to—but he was not sure if the "he" she referred to was Pacing Wolf or Falling Bear. "Falling Bear spotted three strange horses near the cliff's top. Pacing Wolf knows the spot well. It holds a cavern that offered us shelter while we were…"

She understood why the young warrior abruptly dropped his gaze: he was recalling that she, too, would have memories of the place and what those memories likely were.

"I know this cave," she admitted. "Up high, within a cliff overlooking the river. Pacing Wolf found Wild Dog there?"

"Falling Bear believes so. Inside, he found several dead warriors. They were of the Enemy-Who-Cut-Off-Our-Heads."

Kept-Us-Alive was not surprised that he awkwardly glanced to the side. The dead warriors belonged to her former people. They might even be her brothers, though they would not have recognized the name he called them. Her people called themselves The Allies.

"Falling Bear suspects Pacing Wolf surprised them," he continued. "Their weapons were unused—except for a knife." He lifted his gaze as Last Woman slid a supporting arm around her friend. "It was dark with blood." Closing her eyes, Kept-Us-Alive pressed her hand to her stomach. "Wh-where is my husband? Is he wounded?"

"I do not know. A few suns after he left to follow his suspicions, Falling Bear found Pacing Wolf's sorrel—but though he searched long for Pacing Wolf, he did not find him."

Kept-Us-Alive felt her legs begin to wobble. Clutching onto her friend, she thought through his implication. Pacing Wolf knew each footfall of the caverns—she did not doubt he could take her tribesmen unawares—but surely Pacing Wolf himself was not…

The question was too horrid to consider. "My husband is mighty of arm and keen of wit. He has often cheated death. The old men say he will one day be their Batsetsi-kyashe—their Real Chief!"

Held-Back-the-Enemy said nothing, but his eyes so clearly betrayed his thoughts that Kept-Us-Alive had to look away. They were like dark cook pots, stewing with incredulity and sympathy.

"Why does Falling Bear think the blood is Pacing Wolf's?" asked Last Woman. "Bears wander into caves to take their winter sleep. One may have attacked if these warriors disturbed her."

"He may be lying wounded," Kept-Us-Alive fretted. "I will get my herbs and ointments. Will you take me to the cave?"

The young Lumpwood grimly shook his head. "The sorrel is Pacing Wolf's best war-horse. Only death could make your husband abandon him."

"But if he were dead," pleaded Kept-Us-Alive, "Falling Bear would have found his body."

"The warrior who owned the knife lay face-down in the spring's slick run-off, half swallowed by the mountain's open mouth. He had been fighting with an…"

Kept-Us-Alive shivered at the ghastly picture quickly forming in her imagination. Pacing Wolf had warned her to take care while stepping near it: if she slipped, it would swallow her whole. How differently she now felt about him than she had on that night. She had stood beneath the spring until its cold water numbed her senses, trying to bathe away all traces of the herbed oil he had rubbed through his long braids. It had so clung to her loosened hair and skin, she feared she might never rid herself of it. Now, she felt almost ill from yearning for the scent.

"The knife may have belonged to her husband," suggested Last Woman, but Held-Back-the-Enemy again shook his head.

"Falling Bear found it lying beneath the warrior's stiffened hand. All signs announce he was struggling with an assailant near the run-off before…" Held-Back-the-Enemy stopped as Kept-Us-Alive's hands flew up to cover her face.

"This warrior—what did he look like?" asked Last Woman, grasping for anything that might lead Kept-Us-Alive to a less gruesome image.

Yes, thought Kept-Us-Alive. *Perhaps the dead warriors belong to some other people, and Wild Dog—not my husband—attacked them. But what of Pacing Wolf's sorrel? He would not have…*

As her heart hurtled over question after question, the young warrior gently answered Last Woman, "We must go to Hunts-For-Death's lodge and ask Falling Bear. He brought back their weapons. Perhaps their arrows will tell her who they are. The knife can say nothing. It is one white traders sell."

"Thank you for telling me alone," murmured Kept-Us-Alive before turning to hurry up the path.

"I will do your washing," Last Woman called after her, "and feed Wolf-Who-Lays-Down."

Kept-Us-Alive tossed her friend a sad smile. The young Lumpwood's news had chased from her mind all other considerations. Stopping only once she reached Hunts-For-Death's lodge, she stood quietly for a moment to compose herself.

"I have brought Kept-Us-Alive," called Held-Back-the-Enemy, and gaining permission, he ducked through the door flap, pulling Kept-Us-Alive by the wrist toward a small group of warriors conversing intensely. The most prominent she knew well: Hunts-For-Death, the Sparrow Hawk's Real Chief. Long ago, he had acted as her husband's war-society sponsor. He also began providing for Last Woman and her children once old Hair-Up-Top had traveled to the Mystery Land.

Looking up at Kept-Us-Alive, he handed her a handful of arrows. "Do you know these? Do they belong to The Shamer?"

She recognized the characteristic colors painted on arrow shafts by all Allied warriors: yellow on one side and blue on the other. As she carefully turned them over, she felt as if she was gulping down a stone. "All five belong to…" She paused, aware the name her people called themselves would mean nothing to him. "They were crafted by Cuts-Off-Our-Heads warriors, but they bear three distinctly different markings. I cannot tell you with certainty that any of them belong to The Shamer. He came from a different band—a band living far from my father's village. He and his cousins visited only occasionally and were not my relations, so I never learned how they marked their arrows."

Grunting disdainfully, the Real Chief examined every line of her face. He had overheard all that Bites-With-Dog sent his son to tell her, yet though she seemed shaken and a little pale, she did not appear severely grieved.

"This lay beneath one warrior's hand," added Falling Bear, holding out the knife for Kept-Us-Alive to see. Dry, dark brown blood still coated its blade. "Do you know it?"

"No."

"And this?" asked Falling Bear, showing her a badly damaged, breastplate. "All can see it is like the one you weaved for our Lumpwood brother, the one we have often seen him wear."

Kept-Us-Alive gravely nodded. "It is a breastplate belonging to…my husband's enemies and looks like one I have seen The Shamer wear."

"And this?" He handed her a blood-stained collar of woven bones.

"I do not know. It may be The Shamer's or a cousin's. The cousin closely follows The Shamer's footsteps."

As the men murmured with relief, Hunts-For-Death turned to Falling Bear. "Recount for us how my Lumpwood son killed them. His woman will wish to sing his praises."

"I found one warrior trapped beneath his buffalo robe—too slow to draw a weapon. Her husband was cunning and swift; he must have surprised him. Blood soaked his robe and through this collar I have shown..."

Pausing while the Good Men murmured their admiration, Falling Bear lifted the collar for all to see clearly and then continued after they grew silent.

"Another enemy—tall and well-muscled—he flung into a gaping mouth formed in the mountain by a deep spring. I found him barely breathing, face down, his chest wedged in the mountain's throat and his legs limply dangling."

Kept-Us-Alive's head shot up when she heard this description, but as he propounded his gruesome observations, she suspected he embellished some of what he had seen. *How can he know anything of Wild Dog's legs if his chest and head lay exposed outside the mountain's throat?*

"A third warrior's blood spurted..."

As he droned on, interrupted only by their gasps or vocalizations, she tried to shut her mind to grisly details and had almost succeeded until White Belly voiced his own conclusion.

"I knew our clan leader well and always admired his stealth and cunning, but how can a warrior—even one who possessed his strength and great agility—shove such a man feet first through so narrow a mouth? Surely, he slipped in the run-off while they wrestled and pulled this enemy after him."

While several many-feathered heads began bobbing in agreement, Kept-Us-Alive grew as white as a scraped hide bleached by the summer sun. She felt bludgeoned by horrid images—too appalling to hold in her heart but too sensible to thrust away—until old Paints-His-Shirt-Yellow asked Falling Bear a question.

"And if this breathing warrior revives? He may return to his shame and his murder."

Falling Bear shook his head. "He cannot live. One arm was nearly severed by our brother's mighty blow and the other snapped in several places. Both hang loosely from his shoulders. He cannot pull himself from the cavern's jaws."

Still struggling to deny what she most feared, Kept-Us-Alive wanted to tightly push her fingers into her ears. Wild Dog and Walks-Behind-Them were nameless, faceless enemies to this gathering of Lumpwoods, but she had known them for much of her life. She had served them in her mother's dwelling and might also know the third warrior, though she could not guess who he might be. None of their arrows had told her anything.

Once the clan's Good Men grew quiet, she ventured, "Might Wild Dog or his companions have shamed another woman whose father and brothers tracked them to the cave? Wild Dog would have shamed me also if Pacing Wolf had not stopped him."

Several eyes that turned toward her were filling with contempt. "Pah!" spat Crazy Mountain Cat. Only a detestable warrior shames his clansman's daughter."

"And only an ungrateful woman," chided Crow Face, "casts doubt on coups her dead husband has counted.

A few, less prone to criticize, stared—incredulous—but Bites-With-Dog and Held-Back-the-Enemy wore only pity. They were well acquainted with the esteem in which she held their clan leader and suspected she was grasping for any hope that he might be alive.

Hunts-For-Death stared at her so long and hard that she pressed her lips tightly together and dropped her eyes. Although he took great pride in his ability to read hearts, he had never known what to make of his Lumpwood son's captive. Her appeal was not difficult to fathom. She was exactly as Pacing Wolf had once described her: possessing the long, slender neck and large, darkly fringed eyes of a graceful whitetail. Her countenance and demeanor furthered the impression. He had found her unfailingly deferential, gentle, and surprisingly faithful for a woman—so faithful his people had honored her with a new name. Despite all this, he could not bring himself to trust her, though, for her dead husband's sake, he remained polite. She possessed an unexplainable power that both troubled and repulsed him, a power he suspected had severely weakened several Good Men's hearts. Pacing Wolf never considered a woman's feelings before he snatched her, except perhaps his old grandmother's.

As the Real Chief continued to examine her features, he noted her increased pallor and revised his initial assessment. She was not indifferent towards Pacing Wolf's death; she was unable to face it. He also felt pleased that she had called her tribesmen enemies. Many captives cherished hope they might return to their own people, and though he would not object to her leaving, he did not like to tear a mother from her children.

He would give her one moon. She was young and could still bear the Sparrow Hawks many small-things. Little Wolf-Who-Lays-Down would soon forget his father and the small-thing she now carried would not remember him. Among-the-Pines, his Lumpwood son's little daughter, would not forget—but what did this matter? She would go back to live with her dead mother's family.

Under his penetrating scrutiny, Kept-Us-Alive wished she could evaporate like a morning mist. He appeared to blame her for something—whether for the loss of his Lumpwood son or for the distance that had recently grown between them, she could not tell. Perhaps she had not reacted as he had expected. Many women upon hearing a beloved husband had been killed wailed and cut themselves so deeply they bled to death.

Ending his examination as abruptly as he began it, Hunts-For-Death drew the Good Men's attention with his feathered fan. "Have you considered an answer for this woman's question? Could another warrior have killed The Shamer? Did you find other footprints?"

The sides of Falling Bear's mouth sloped downward. He, too, was grieving and understood her reluctance to face such loss. Though he had held his woman's ravaged body, part of him still grew eager to see her this morning while he was approaching their village. He searched for her face among the women before he thought to stop himself. Out of respect for his dead clan-leader, he wished to be kind, but she could not bring Pacing Wolf back by hiding her heart from the truth.

"Many moccasins led to or from the center of the cave and to or from the spring and the cave's mouth, but if our Lumpwood brother did not kill her tribesmen, where is he and how could he forget his favorite battle horse? Up our mountains, thick with trees, a clever warrior may prefer to travel by foot, but the flat lands offer little shelter when the winds blow cold and the way is slow. Only a foolish warrior would cross them this way."

Loved-By-the-Creator[3] served God's purposes during the summers he possessed and then fell asleep and decayed along with his ancestors.
Acts 13:36

Chapter 5

KEPT-US-ALIVE FELT relieved when the Real Chief released her to complete her chores. She had never been fond of attention, particularly from a gathering of hardened warriors, but her reprieve did not last. Everywhere she placed her foot she found fresh torment. Her husband's older clanswomen greeted her with pity, young wives' eyes trailed her every movement, and many untouched women did both along with something more—their eyes held an odd cross between doubt and impatience.

Worse than these were the stares of Pacing Wolf's Lumpwood brothers. While she was in Hunts-For-Death's lodge, most had shown her polite consideration; but as the sun began growing sleepy, they searched her face whenever they passed her on the path. At first, she tried not to notice. Those who liked her gazed at her with confidence. Those who did not looked at her with suspicion; but as the sun dropped below the tree line, the corners of every mouth began to sag.

After hurriedly gathering twigs for her family's embers, Kept-Us-Alive headed towards her husband's lodge. The first evening star was peeking through the darkening sky, promising blessed escape from their censure. As she stepped through her door, she felt Wolf-Who-Lays-Down squeezing past her and almost sighed with relief. She had dreaded venturing out to look for him and the curious eyes that might turn her way with each calling of his name.

Lowering her bundle of wood, she knelt down, pulled the tiny boy onto her lap, clasped him tightly to her chest, and buried her face in his soft hair. "Has anyone said anything to you about your father?"

He said nothing, but he clung to her so tightly that she did not press for an answer. She doubted he possessed adequate words to express what he was feeling. Besides, she was weary of both asking and answering questions—especially her own—and did not want to burden him with grief he could not understand.

White Belly's conclusion explains much, she admitted, *but I cannot imagine Pacing Wolf allowing Wild Dog to entice him near the run-off. He knows its dangers…*

As Wolf-Who-Lays-Down wound his chubby arms around her neck, she gently rocked him back and forth, and Among-the-Pines soon pulled back the door-flap.

"I am glad you are home," Kept-Us-Alive sighed, extending her arm in ready welcome.

The little girl responded immediately, but when she looked into her stepmother's puffy red eyes, her lower lip began to quiver.

"It is t-true? F-father is d-dead?"

Kept-Us-Alive shook her head.

"Where is he?"

"I do not know. Falling Bear found slain enemies, but not your father."

She could not bear to tell Among-the-Pines the details Falling Bear had recounted. The child might leap to White Belly's conclusions, and Kept-Us-Alive was far too weary to prop up the little girl's emotions. She could barely rein in her own.

"Then why are they saying he is? He has stayed away longer while hunting. He always comes back."

Kept-Us-Alive smiled, though she suspected Among-the-Pines' memory was inaccurate. The sun had drifted to sleep and awoken again nine times since Pacing Wolf had left. The girl's fewer summers likely made his former forays seem lengthier than they were. "Your father loves us very much. He will return if he is able."

"If?"

"Falling Bear found his war-horse. His reins hung loosely as if your father left him to pasture while he…."

"…Killed the Shamer?"

"Yes," Kept-Us-Alive responded, hoping she could at least allay the contagion of worry that had caught hold of The Women-Who-Talk-Against-Each-Other-Without-Fear. One only had to whisper the word for eyes to begin darting around or over shoulders. Feeling Among-the-Pines relax, she forced up the corners of her lips. "We no longer need to look behind every tree while we carry our washing to the river."

"It is time!" They heard a man calling outside their lodge.

"I am coming," Kept-Us-Alive responded, though she could think of nothing she would less like to do. Rising slowly to her feet, she opened the door to an older warrior she barely knew and glanced back at her children. Among-the-Pines' eyes were filling with questions. "The Good Men wish to recount to our clan your father's deeds of valor."

"I will go with you!"

"No. Stay here with your brother."

"But he is my father. I wish to hear Falling Bear's story."

"See there," her stepmother nodded toward Wolf-Who-Lays-Down. "Your brother is already sleeping. He may be frightened if he wakes up and finds himself alone."

Looking glum, the girl disrobed and slipped beneath the covers beside him while Kept-Us-Alive stepped into the night.

THE NEXT MORNING, as Kept-Us-Alive stirred her cook-pot, she heard several Women-Who-Talk-Against-Each-Other-Without-Fear approaching. Her marriage to their clan leader cast her as one of them, but she lacked both the quantity of summers and close relatives—mothers, sisters, sisters-in-law, aunts, and cousins—that would have allowed her to speak as frankly as their name implied. Still, most had been kind since the ravaging small pox, so when she spotted them walking up the central path, she offered them the most genuine smile she could muster.

Several looked beyond or around her as if they wanted to see who was watching or were looking for guidance from an elder clanswoman concerning how to act. One grimaced as if Kept-Us-Alive had spat, but the youngest, Otter Woman, bent down.

"We have brought you these," she murmured softly. "I hope they will help. He was a good man—always just and kind to the poorest among us. We had expected him to lead us many summers."

After handing Kept-Us-Alive a bag of root vegetables and then passing similar parcels to her from the others, Otter Woman straightened and stepped back onto the path. Her companions seemed eager to be away.

"She was smiling!" the shortest one whispered.

"Did you see her last evening? She danced in his honor but mumbled his praises—as if she did not care that he is dead."

"And her arms—look at them!" hissed another, prompting them all to glance backward. "She has not made a single cut!"

"Shush!" scolded Otter Woman, casting Kept-Us-Alive an apologetic twist of her lips. "She may hear you!"

"I do not care if she hears!" spat the eldest. "When my daughter's husband traveled to the Mystery Land, she cut herself deeply, as I will do."

"What do you expect?" asked a thin clanswoman. "She is only a captive."

"She has a son," contended Otter Woman. "If she cuts herself deeply, he will lose both father and mother together!"

"Captive or not, if I were such a warrior's woman, I would let my arms bleed until…"

As their chatter trailed away, Kept-Us-Alive felt as if they had kicked her in the stomach. She had hoped they might offer support, even sympathy, but the last had put into words what everyone expected—what they supposed any decent woman who mourned a brave, beloved husband would do.

But Pacing Wolf is not dead, she assured herself, *and I-Am-Savior, alone, has the right to decide if I live or die. Neither He nor my husband would want me to cut myself!* Shrugging her shoulders to slough off their scorn, a question she had not allowed herself to ask last evening began calling for an answer. *If he does not return, what will become of my children and me?*

Feeling tiny padded hands moving across her back, she turned to find Wolf-Who-Lays-Down peeking around her elbow. His grin was so like his father's—except for the size of his perfectly formed teeth—and the way he cocked his head as he looked into her eyes made her heart thud. *Pacing Wolf must have looked just like him at this age.*

As she recalled her husband recounting his pain-filled memories, first of losing his father and next of watching his mother cut herself as his gossiping clanswoman suggested she do, she grew even more resistant. Wolf-Who-Lays-Down was younger than Pacing Wolf had been and might forget, but she still could not consign him to so much sorrow.

Who would care for him? She wondered what Pacing Wolf would have done without Kills-Behind-Her-Dwelling, his old grandmother. *My mother would not know where to find him.* Palpable waves of homesickness, first for her family and then for her husband, seized her so strongly she momentarily forgot the task she was performing.

I would give anything to lay my head against him as we go to sleep, to feel his chest beneath my palm and his arm firmly around my back. Oh Lord, please bring him home! I do not think I can bear life here without him!

As Wolf-Who-Lays-Down ducked beneath her arm and climbed clumsily onto her knees, Kept-Us-Alive offered him the best of her cook pot's contents. He was growing swiftly, and she was not certain how long her foodstuffs—even with the clanswomen's additions—might last without a husband's frequent hunting.

"Give no thought for tomorrow," she quietly mumbled. "Tomorrow will have enough trouble of its own."[3] *No, I am certain Pacing Wolf would not want me to cut myself. He would tell me to stay strong so I can lead his children into I-Am-Savior's shadow.*

STRAIGHT ARROWS eluded several Raven Enemy sentries, creeping through a pine ridge overlooking a river near their village. As he examined them closely, he noticed unusual aspects of their hunting shirts and hair. They stiffened short thatches above their foreheads and divided the rest into a number of extraordinarily long braids. To his relief, each seemed more interested in the women dunking their clothing in the water than performing their duty.

Crouching down to watch, he suddenly felt weary. His brother, Pretty Face, and he had allowed themselves little rest since they picked up fresh tracks near the cavern. Until they discovered which enemy had slain their three tribesmen, how near their own village they camped, and what further attacks they might intend, the two brothers could not be certain their people were safe.

Perhaps Wild Dog's war party attacked them, thought Straight Arrows, remembering the repugnant tale his sister had once related. Enemies often raided each other to gain horses, train younger cousins to practice stealth, or gain bragging rights about secretly counted coups, but few drew blood unless provoked.

"She is Crazy Mountain Cat's woman," Straight Arrows overheard one sentry saying. "She gave me this in the summer, while he was chasing elk."

The other's mouth twisted wryly as he took the small, many-colored object from his hand. "I have heard him bragging about her. His heart may prove weak when you parade her before the Lumpwoods."

"And you?" the first sentry asked him. "After we hand out new death-staffs, whose woman will you snatch—a Big Dog's or a Muddy Hand's?"

"Also a Lumpwood's," the second replied.

"Who?"

"She is there—over there by the largest rock. Crow-Face's woman."

The first sentry shook his head. "She will not go with you; Crow Face is fierce. Twice, he has stood beside a Lumpwood death-staff, facing the enemy without shifting from the spot."

"She is not happy with him. She tosses me smiles when I catch her attention."

Hearing a familiar birdcall, Straight Arrows shot a glance at his brother, who had hung back toward the ridge's edge to alert him if more sentries were coming. Pretty Face had spotted another line of women winding down the path with their families' bundled garments.

When Straight Arrows' eyes landed on the first, he grew suddenly alert. She was striking, as tall as many warriors in their prime, and wore a solemn expression that tugged oddly at his heart. Some quality he could not define distinguished her from the women the guards had been discussing, though he could not decide if it lay in her features, her expression, or her clothing. Perhaps it was simply her regal bearing, so like his own silver-haired grandmother, Two Doves.

As he inspected her face, he found her eyes were less almond shaped than the eyes of the women he had been studying—and were clouded with trouble. Below them sat a straight, round-tipped nose that hung neatly above a full, wide mouth.

Her heart holds sorrow, he inferred, *but she bears up under it well. Perhaps she has lost a child or husband—or belongs to a warrior who beats her. She is surely married. She has too many summers to have remained untouched.*

A boy ran up and tugged on the fringes of her sleeve. "I am hungry!"

"You are always hungry," smiled the striking woman, shifting her bundle so she could reach into her pouch. "Here. This will keep the pain from your belly until our late meal."

Straight Arrows could not see the morsel his mother handed him, probably pemmican, but a grateful smile broke across the small face. When they drew several strides nearer the pine ridge, he realized the boy's height had led him to overestimate his age. His cheeks were smooth and fleshy, though like his mother's they were lightly pitted by a pox, and his fingers, toes, and the tops of his hands and feet looked soft and thickly padded.

He has been free from a cradleboard no more than two summers.

"Come with me!" the boy called to another, significantly shorter and much more padded than himself. "Over here."

This one is younger, Straight Arrows concluded, though by how many moons, he could not guess. At their ages, boys changed rapidly. While the tall boy pulled apart his treat and offered half to the younger, two girls scampered up to join them.

The smaller resembled the women by the river, her almond-shaped eyes pressed deeply in an apple-shaped face, but they captured and held sorrow surprising for one so young, returning his thoughts to the sad, tall woman.

He found this girl pretty for one so far from womanhood.

He thought her girlish companion might have already crossed that barrier. She was as long of limb as many of the women he had been observing. When she turned her head, however, he saw her height, too, had tricked him. Her face was a replica of the striking woman's, but in place of her mother's well-contained sorrow was the unmistakable exuberance of childhood.

Turning again toward the apple-faced girl, he wondered to whom she belonged. She looked nothing like the two children he guessed were siblings and nothing like the tiny boy. *Perhaps,* he considered, seeing another woman bringing up the rear of their party, *she belongs to…*

Straight Arrows stopped in mid-thought. The second woman looked so like his mother, he felt fleetingly startled; but as her black eyes glanced in his direction, a wide smile lifted the planes of his well-chiseled face. *Light Bird!*

Silently motioning to gain his brother's attention, he put a finger to his eye and then launched it toward their sister. He knew Pretty Face recognized her when his face broke into an answering grin. Now the only difficulty was making themselves known without rousing the sentries. Signaling for his brother to stay hidden, he eagerly watched the little party settle some distance from the others.

He felt sad when he noticed the first party of washers did not call out any greetings. Their white uncle, Spotted Long-knife, had said Light Bird seemed well-accepted when he had visited her last and that she had told him she was quite happy. By the look of concern that washed his brother's face, Straight Arrows knew that Pretty Face, too, wondered about the change, but this was not a moment for discovery. The sentries were standing up to peruse the pines.

Hunkering lower on his haunches, Straight Arrow barely breathed. The more alert of the two sentries was peering into the soft-needled branches as if the gentle breeze carried his enemy's scent. The other strode by so closely, Straight Arrows could touch have touched him. On another day, he would have, knowing Pretty Face would bear witness to his coup. Instead, he kept himself still, hoping he might find a chance to draw away their sister.

He will command His angels to take charge of you, to guard you in all your ways.

Psalm 91:11

Chapter 6

"COME BACK!" YELLED THE striking woman. "Stay with your sister and friends!"

Startled awake, Straight Arrows peered through the soft needles. The sun had settled on a mountaintop, richly drenching his pine ridge in shades of golden yellow. His legs felt cramped beneath him, complaining sharply as he stiffly began to rise and look over his shoulder to the place where his brother remained hidden.

He saw Pretty Face had also fallen asleep, leaning against a trunk for support, visible only because Straight Arrows knew where to find him. Sunlight dappled over his brother's green shirt and skin, like speckles on a fawn, blending him even further into the trees.

Let him sleep, thought Straight Arrows. *He will need the rest.*

Suddenly, Straight Arrows grasped why the striking woman had called out. Her son had darted up the bank, chasing a rabbit into the trees. Laughing as it hopped first one way and then the other, the little boy disappeared into the soft branches, almost colliding with Straight Arrows' brother.

Pretty Face slowly rose up, awakened by the tinkling laughter, and the boy abruptly stopped, backed away, and stood transfixed. The sun illuminated the young warrior's face and friendly smile.

Swiftly, Straight Arrows sought the sentries' location, but he need not have been concerned. They remained as they had been earlier, lazily watching the women or exchanging jokes. Still, he hoped his brother would shoo the boy away and back further into the pines.

Pretty Face did neither. He squatted down to the boy's level and showed him something or offered him a treat. Whatever it was, the boy took it and plopped it into his mouth. Next, Pretty Face spoke softly, so softly Straight Arrows only knew he was speaking by the movement of his lips, and then laid his fingertip against the boy's mouth. The little boy nodded, as if accepting what he had heard, and then turned quickly and ran back to his mother.

As he threw himself against her, happily prattling away, the strikingly tall woman peered over his head to scan the ridgeline. Pretty Face had drawn back further into the shadows, making himself impossible to see, but the boy began insistently tugging his mother's hand.

"Come!" Straight Arrows heard him pleading. "Come see!"

Shrugging to Light Bird, the striking woman laid aside the water sacks she had been filling and followed the taller boy toward the slope he had just descended.

Straight Arrows inwardly groaned. Even the dull and lazy sentries would notice if she began screaming. Hoping to offer his brother aid, he wound within the pine trees, placing down his feet so carefully they made no sound. The well-trodden path ran alongside his own, offering him frequent glimpses of the eager boy's face. It was filled with wonder, and he was beaming ear to ear.

"An angel!" Straight Arrows heard him whisper. "In the pines—watching over us, tall as the trees!" The boy stretched his hand up as high as he could reach in emphasis. "And his face shines like the sun—like the one in Kept-Us-Alive's book!"

Straight Arrows, pressed his hand to his mouth, afraid he might burst into laughter and ruin everything Pretty Face had accomplished. What his brother had told the boy, he could only guess, or the boy may have leaped to his own conclusions. He was certain, however, the mother could not so easily be fooled. Considering how they might keep her from crying out, he glanced at his sister and the other children. All four were still beside the stream, either squatting to fill water sacks or tossing rocks and watching the circles they created on the water.

As the striking woman began cautiously parting the pine boughs, she, too, glanced at her companions and then searched with her eyes for the sentries. Only Light Bird returned her gaze, her face displaying keen curiosity. She quickly returned her attention to the stream, however, filling water sacks for two households, handing them off to the girls to carry, and trying to prevent the tiniest boy from wandering too deeply into the river. When her striking companion slipped between the branches, Straight Arrows took one final look at the lounging warriors. They had not noticed anything amiss.

"See!" the little boy whispered. "Look at his face—it glows!"

The striking woman was too stunned to answer. Straight Arrows could not tell if this was due to the sunlight, which did indeed bathe Pretty Face with a golden glow, or because she was startled to find a strange warrior; but as she parted her lips, he silently stepped up behind her and clapped a firm hand over her mouth. Slipping his other arm tightly around her waist, he lifted her off her feet as she began virulently twisting.

Pretty Face did nearly the same with the boy, who began to struggle only when he noticed his mother's eyes widening in terror. Standing with his braced legs wide apart, Straight Arrows eluded her energetic kicking. The boy soon wearied; but after every pause to draw a few breaths, Straight Arrow's captive vigorously renewed her squirming. Not until the sun began to sink and his sister's tiny party started hauling both their laundry and water up the hill, did the striking woman finally tire.

When both, at last, became still, Pretty Face whispered, "We do not wish to hurt either of you."

Her only answer was a hard, fearful stare.

"We wish to talk with Light Bird."

The little boy shook his head beneath Pretty Face's hand and mumbled something impossible to understand. "No light birds," he repeated when his captor slightly loosened the pressure on his mouth. "Only red. The cold comes. They fly away."

Straight Arrows could not help smiling. "The woman you were with—by the river. She is our little sister. One of your warriors snatched her from our village more than three summers past."

Although Straight Arrows could not see his striking captive's expression, he felt her relax a bit beneath his grip. Then, as she intently studied Pretty Face, she appeared to reach a startling conclusion. She began to nod her head, not just once or twice but in rapid succession.

"You will not call out?" whispered Straight Arrows, glancing again toward the sentries. When she shook her head no, he, too, lightened his hand's pressure, but he held it ready to clamp down hard if she had deceived them.

"Not my warriors," Last Woman corrected, her voice holding an odd singsong quality. "They are Sparrow Hawk; I am Blackfoot. Captive—like sister." Once again, she nodded toward Pretty Face. "Kept-Us-Alive told me of her brothers—one owns a face like hers."

Pretty Face broke into a smile that lit his whole countenance. "My sister and I are like our mother. She was a white woman before she became one of our people. My older brother," he gestured toward Straight Arrows, "is like our father."

As Last Woman twisted around to look at the man she had been struggling against, she felt blood surging hotly up her neck. She had not been prepared to see such a handsome face or find eyes at once piercing and unexpectedly gentle. They seemed to gaze so deeply inside her that she could no longer think.

Straight Arrow's mind was no nimbler. From afar, he had found her striking; this close, she aroused in him a deep desire to wipe away the sadness he had earlier noticed and to shield her from further pain. Shaking off the irrational notions, he let her go and forced his thoughts down a more purposeful trail.

"After the sun goes to sleep, you will bring our sister to us?"

Last woman nodded, her tongue still unable to form sensible answers. At once, she understood why her cousins had often acted so silly, so incapable of discretion when appealing warriors were close by. When her father had accepted the horses of his clansman, she had felt nothing but dread; and when Pacing Wolf had handed her to old Hair-Up-Top, she had seethed with hatred.

Last Woman shook her head. Even if she could make her mouth form words, she did not know what to answer. She could not imagine how she might explain to the sentries why they were venturing out after dark. All knew of the dead enemies Falling Bear had found in the cavern, but no one could be certain they were the fearsome Shamers.

Without warning, the tall boy shot from Pretty Face's loosened grip and ran straight to the two trailing girls. "Angels!" he cried, first to his sister and then to Among-the-Pines. "Up there—angels!"

The two girls looked doubtfully at each other and then at Last Woman, who had hurriedly brushed through the branches to pull Last Son out of the sentries' earshot. Little Blackfoot Woman and Among-the-Pines followed closely behind them, eagerly asking questions the Blackfoot crossly shushed, but it was too late. The boy's chatter had roused the indolent guards. Each had drawn his weapon and was entering the woods.

Among-the-Pines outstripped Little Blackfoot Woman as they ran to catch up with her stepmother. Last Woman was not far behind, struggling to keep hold of Last Son, who was trying to break free to run back to *his* angels. Scooping him up with one arm and seating him securely on her hip, she glanced back toward the pines that hid her friend's brothers. The eldest's grip had combined the same odd mix of gentleness and strength she had seen captured in his eyes, as if he had intentionally restrained himself to prevent causing her pain.

If they do elude the sentries, she fretted, *my kicks may have bruised him badly.* Her stomach knotted up as she again peered over her shoulder, wishing his brother and he, like the angels Last Son thought them, could disappear into the golden-orange clouds.

"We saw two angels," spouted Last Son, as they reached Kept-Us-Alive and Wolf-Who-Lays-Down, but war whoops snatched away their attention. With a forceful wriggle, he broke free of his mother's arm and ran toward the commotion, his little face fraught with worry. Last Woman tore after him, afraid he might further endanger the brothers or discover in a most painful way that they were merely men.

As she caught and scooped him up again, Kept-Us-Alive, Wolf-Who-Lays-Down, their daughters, and an assortment of others from the village plunged through the pine ridge until they spotted the sentries. Several were in mid-mount, half hanging from their galloping horses, and a large party of their Fox brothers was rushing to their aid.

Tracking the direction of their progress, Last Woman could just make out their quarry: two warriors swiftly headed into the wind from the lowland, black hair streaming out behind them. She let out a deep breath, aware only afterward that she had held it. Whispering into Last Son's hair, his mother softly scolded. "Tell no one else about your angels! See the Fox soldiers?"

The little boy nodded, recalling his particular angel's smile and wondering why warriors were chasing them.

"Good. We will keep them a secret—just between you and me—until we have a chance alone to tell Kept-Us-Alive about them."

As he offered the merest hint of a smile, Last Woman pressed his head to hers, silently praying for the *angels'* safe escape.

Kept-Us-Alive found Last Woman and excitedly looked up at her. "He is alive!"

"Who?"

"Pacing Wolf! The dead warriors Falling Bear found were not The Shamers! They were here—on the ridge!"

Last Woman felt so many emotions at once, she did not know how to answer. She hated to wipe the joy from her friend's face by pointing out the sharp bend in her thinking and felt anxious for Kept-Us-Alive's brothers. Should she keep their presence hidden, shielding her friend from worry, or heap up her joy only to risk plunging her further into sorrow? *To learn they are in danger so closely on the heels of her husband's death might...*

"I saw angels!" broke in Last Son, nearly wresting the decision from his mother's hands, but as he began to launch into a description of the wondrous visitors, Last Woman glared at him in warning. "They were! I want to tell!"

"And I want you to go to your sister. She is with Among-the-Pines—over there." She angled her chin toward a vantage point the girls had found that offered them a better view of the racing war party. "Remind them to go back to our water sacks and carry them home."

Lost Son bounced on the balls of his feet, looking in his mother's face for a chance to argue, but he found none.

"Go!" commanded his mother. "Now!"

A COLD WIND blew against the outer layer of Pacing Wolf's lodge skins, intermittently moving the inner wall, but it could not reach the slowly burning embers.

"That will not hold," Kept-Us-Alive warned her stepdaughter, showing the girl a faulty knot in the chain of beads she was stringing. "Make it like this."

Among-the-Pines and Little Blackfoot leaned in closely to see how to tie it tighter. All the Women-Who-Talk-Against-Each-Other-Without-Fear admitted—some begrudgingly—that Pacing Wolf's captive woman surpassed most others of her age in skill with a needle. She and Last Woman exchanged techniques they had learned from their mothers, passing them on to their two girls, but Last Son and little Wolf-Who-Lays-Down could not imagine anything more boring. They were conspiring, as much as boys between two and three summers could conspire, to trail several of their favorite older cousins, when the door flap abruptly swung open.

"She," spat Jackrabbit, ducking in without invitation, "comes with me!" Although her mouth sagged down deeply at the corners, her round apple face bore a striking resemblance to the child to whom she motioned. "Her father is dead—I will raise her!"

As alarm darkened his sister's eyes, Wolf-Who-Lays-Down interposed himself between her and the old woman. "No! No take!"

"Hmph!" grunted Jackrabbit, fixing a flinty glare first on the tot and then on his mother. "I can see he is Pacing Wolf's son, but I have a right to my granddaughter. She is not your kin!"

"No, Grandmother," Among-the-Pines shook her head. "I want to stay with my mother and brother!"

"She is not your mother," insisted the older woman, her eyes daring Kept-Us-Alive to mount a challenge. "My daughter was your mother, and this Cuts-Off-Our-Heads captive can never take her place!"

Hearing the commotion, Hopping Owl called for admittance. "Why have you come?" she asked Jackrabbit, who thrust her round chin higher. "To claim what is mine. I have the right."

Looking into the little girl's eyes, which were earnestly pleading, Hopping Owl suggested, "The Moon When Wolves Run Together will soon be upon us. Let her have the rest of this one to grieve. You can see she wants to stay with her stepmother."

"When Pacing Wolf tore her from me, did he consider what she wanted? He has made Bites-With-Dog this captive woman's father, but your husband is no kin to my grandchild. I am taking her."

With that, Jackrabbit demanded the girl gather her things, and they left so quickly that Hopping Owl could think of no way to stop them.

He executes justice for the orphan and the widow and shows His love for the alien by giving him food and clothing.
Deuteronomy 10:18

Chapter 7

HOPPING OWL GLANCED from Wolf-Who-Lays-Down—who was glaring up at her as if she were an accomplice—to his mother. "All know Pacing Wolf would want her with you, but children belong to their mothers' clans."

"You were very kind to try," answered Kept-Us-Alive, pulling Wolf-Who-Lays-Down into her arms. "When Pacing Wolf returns, he will bring her home."

The older, rounder woman cast her a dubious but sympathetic look. "The child will not come back. Bites-With-Dog has forbidden Those-Who-Talk-Against-Each-Other-Without-Fear or their husbands to claim any of

Pacing Wolf's possessions, but he cannot keep them away for long. Many Lumpwoods and others among his clansmen will demand strands of your hair."

As Kept-Us-Alive took in what her new mother suggested, her eyes grew as wide as a warrior's earring. She had not thought of either. If Pacing Wolf's clansmen considered him dead, they would take all that she thought of as hers—the bed she shared with him, their buffalo robes, even the lodge in which she lived. They were the rightful property of his clan.

"Pacing Wolf is not dead," she murmured, stiffening her back. "They may take what they want—I do not care. I will keep only what he gave to me or his son."

Rising, she went straight to the mirror he had purchased from the white trader and took it from its peg, folded up the buffalo robe she had been wearing when he snatched her, grabbed the few items that belonged to Wolf-Who-Lays-Down, and placed them, along with her sewing, in her husband's large buffalo hide bag.

"They will take his bag, also," explained Hopping Owl.

"Then I give it to you. Perhaps, when they take my husband's home and you must make room for me, you will find it useful."

Hopping Owl nodded. She understood both her new daughter's intentions and her desperate desire to believe her husband was alive. She also knew nothing she could say would offer comfort. "I will come for it when his clanswomen divide his property. We are happy to offer you a place in our home."

As the older woman ducked out, a pall of sadness settled over the two families, smaller now by one. Kept-Us-Alive hated to lose Among-the-Pines. Their hearts had become so attached that she could no longer imagine a day spent without the girl by her side: working, learning, or laughing at Wolf-Who-Lays-Down's and Last Son's antics.

She would feel her loss more keenly at night. Since Pacing Wolf had gone, she went about her days much as she had when he was present, but nights brought a sharp reminder he was missing. Whether Among-the-Pines had sensed her stepmother's sadness or simply desired warmth, she had claimed her father's spot beneath their buffalo robes, keeping Kept-Us-Alive from feeling quite so lonely.

Last Woman's heart ached while watching her friend struggle to tamp down her emotions, and she hoped the tale she had been saving might offer some cheer. "I have kept a secret from you," she murmured, once the boys had slipped out.

Kept-Us-Alive looked up. She could not help noticing the corners of her friend's lips kept twitching upward and forced herself to return the smile. "Do you carry Hunts-For-Death's small-thing?"

Last Woman's eyes widened and shifted toward Little Blackfoot Woman, who had dropped hers to her sewing. "No. Hunts-For-Death does not come near me."

"I am sorry—if you want him to."

"No!" Last Woman shook her head wildly, chuckling as both her daughter and Small Doe peered up, identical looks of concern puckering their brows. "I am happy to sleep alone."

"Brother and I sleep with you, Mother," Little Blackfoot corrected.

"Yes, and you keep me very warm," smiled Last Woman, but she shrugged slightly as she glanced back toward her friend. "I would like to know what I am to Hunts-For-Death. During the past two summers we have dwelled in his lodge, he has not treated me as a wife, and his wives do not treat me as a daughter. I am nothing—just another dog sleeping near the fire. But this is not what I want to tell you." She glanced around, though she knew the lodge was empty, and whispered, "Did your children chatter about angels last evening?"

"Yes," replied Kept-Us-Alive, cocking her head to one side. "They wanted to take me to the pine ridge, hoping we might meet one."

Last Woman broke into a grin. "Did you go?"

"No. It was late. I had already fastened our lodge-door and blown our embers to flame." Pacing Wolf, who had enjoyed watching her perform this ritual, unexpectedly wafted through her memory, making it hard to pay attention.

"You remember last moon our boys complained because we made them stay inside while it was raining? You read to me from the book while they became engrossed in a game."

Kept-Us-Alive nodded. They had been reading of an angel visiting Daniel while he prayed.[4]

"Last Son did not show it, but he was listening carefully. While we were by the river, he chased a rabbit into the trees and almost ran right into one."

When Kept-Us-Alive's head shot up, Last Woman began to chuckle—she could imagine what her friend must be thinking—and the twinkle she spotted in her daughter's eyes announced her son had not kept their secret. "They were in the pines, watching us fill our water sacks."

"You—you saw them?"

"Yes," replied Last Woman, savoring the look on her friend's face. "But they were not angels; they were your brothers!"

Kept-Us-Alive's hand flew over her mouth. "My...my brothers?"

Gesturing wildly, Last Woman plunged into the entire story, describing how one angel grabbed her.

Kept-Us-Alive wanted to both laugh and cry. *To have them so close and yet not see them.* "You were not frightened?"

"I was until I peered closely at the younger angel's face." In the air, she drew a quick circle around her own. "It was yours, only man-like and mounted on a warrior's thicker neck."

"How did they find me?" wondered Kept-Us-Alive, stilling her hands upon her lap. "I have lived among the Sparrow Hawks three summers. Why did you not tell me, and why did they come?"

Last Woman laughed at her quiver full of questions. "I do not know. Last Son became too excited. He shot out of the trees to tell his sister and stirred up the guards."

"Were they the enemies the sentries were chasing? Oh—they may have been caught!"

"Do not worry; they are safe. I listened while Hunts-For-Death was talking to Falling Bear. They fled toward the wind from the lowlands."

"But the Fox soldiers..."

"They eluded them. The Creator brought them here and He will guide them home. Only He decides the day of death—that is what you tell me."

Kept-Us-Alive nodded. "What did they say?"

"Only that you were their sister and they hoped I would bring you to them."

"Where?"

"The pines—when the sun began to sleep."

"The sentries will now be watching—they cannot come back."

"No," Last Woman agreed, frowning a little sadly. "But if they have found you once, they will find you again."

ONCE THE SUN AWOKE, Kept-Us-Alive found every opportunity to walk past the spot on the pine-covered ridge, and the small-thing she carried provided ample excuse for her to walk very slowly.

"I hope all my family is well," she told Last Woman as she sewed Wolf-Who-Lays-Down a pair of larger moccasins.

"They did not appear to be grieving. When they told me who you were, their faces were bright with joy. But say nothing to the children, especially Last Son. I told him to keep his *angels* a secret, but he could not hold it in. Who knows who he has told?"

"They will think he has had a vision. Even if he spreads his secret throughout the entire village, my brothers will remain unknown."

Hearing a commotion, Kept-Us-Alive and Last Woman looked up as someone rudely yanked back the door-flap before requesting permission. Instantly, they each recognized the many-feathered black and silver pate of the Sparrow Hawks' Real Chief. Last Woman rose, assuming she was his quarry, but while he acknowledged her brief greeting, he strode directly to Kept-Us-Alive.

"Come," he demanded, brusquely signaling with his hand for her to get up. "A moon has passed and my Lumpwood son has not returned. The Good Men have decided it is time you honor your dead." Before she could protest, he drew out his knife and sliced off one and then the other of her thick braids. "His clansmen and Lumpwood brothers crave a portion of his strength."

Too stunned to react, Kept-Us-Alive stood quite still. She understood what he had done. Pacing Wolf's grandmother had explained their belief: hair contained the soul. By weaving strands of a fallen clansman's hair into his own, a warrior gained a portion of the dead man's courage. Pacing Wolf's hair was not available to take, so they required hers in its place. As she fingered the shorn off ends where her braids had just been hanging, Hunts-For-Death grasped hold of her wrist and thrust his knife into her hand.

"The blade is sharp. Go—honor your husband as a woman worthy of his name!"

Kept-Us-Alive stared up at him, unable to speak. Not only was she in awe of Hunts-For-Death—he was greatly respected by all the Sparrow Hawks, including her husband—but she also could not do as he expected. Backing away, she finally found her tongue.

"I will not grieve for my husband because he is not dead." Even she thought her words sounded feeble, devoid of conviction and hope.

"Then I will cast you out! You are nothing more to the Many Lodges than a dog or a wandering shadow!" Dragging her to the door, he pulled her through the opening and flung her onto the ground. "Come!" he called to his gathering clansmen and their women. "Take your clan leader's possessions. This captive refuses to honor him—she deserves none of the plunder his courage has gained."

Jackrabbit was among the first to enter, though she was not of Pacing Wolf's clan, pulling Among-the-Pines behind her. As Last Woman helped Kept-Us-Alive to her feet, the little girl tossed them a doleful glance; and Hopping Owl slipped past, she slid them a subtle smile.

"Come," Last Woman murmured. "We will wait in Bites-With-Dog's lodge."

"No," replied Kept-Us-Alive. "I must find Wolf-Who-Lays-Down. He may be frightened when he returns to find everything gone."

KEPT-US-ALIVE NEARLY collided with Held-Back-the-Enemy as she and her son entered his father's lodge, but instead of looking irritated, as many warriors would, his eyes were filled with compassion.

As he glanced from one freshly cut portion of her hair to the other, he was acutely aware of the waving strands that he, along with his father and many of their Lumpwood brothers, had already woven into his own black braids. She had lost none of her appeal, and her hair would grow back quickly; but as he wrestled with the urge to tell her so, a more potent desire made him ball up his fists. He longed to finger the newly curling ends, to feel their softness against his palms. They reminded him of freshly growing buffalo fur, curving and twisting in every direction.

"I am sorry," she murmured, tucking an escaping wisp behind her ear, "that my son and I are forcing you from your father's lodge."

Looking down at the large pile of necessities he carried, the Lumpwood warrior merely shrugged. "I go to my uncle's. He has much room."

Kept-Us-Alive smiled. She had always thought him generous of heart. "Soon, you will gain a woman who will be proud to toss up your lodge poles and cover them with hides she has carefully sewn."

Held-Back-the-Enemy's nod was so curt, she began to suspect he courted someone secretly, but when he averted his eyes, she began to question his confidence.

"She will be a fortunate woman," she assured him. "Many warriors are handsome or brave, but you are kind as well."

When he seemed determined to hurry away, she began to wonder if the girl were somewhere waiting or if he had found her comments embarrassingly personal, but she did not have time to fret. His mother was calling.

"Welcome! See—I was able to grab your bag before others Who-Talk-Against-Each-Other-Without-Fear noticed where you hid it. I also have your bed and several of Pacing Wolf's best buffalo robes. You and little Wolf-

Who-Lays-Down will not be cold."

As Kept-Us-Alive offered her plump new mother an appreciative smile, she set down her son and looked around at all the items. Hopping Owl had managed to collect a good many.

"Jackrabbit accused me of being greedy," Hopping Owl chuckled. "Otter Woman snatched the rest for you."

"Thank you…Mother. You make us feel very welcome."

AWAKING WITH A START, Kept-Us-Alive clasped her hand against her pounding chest. Oh—it was just a dream! As she slowed and deepened her breathing, her thoughts wended over the nightmare's frightening contents. Pacing Wolf had slipped in the spring's slick run-off and was plummeting down the darkness into the belly of the cave. His face twisted in agony as his hands helplessly grasped at the run-off's throat, desperately trying to stop his swift descent.

Shuddering, she peered into the tiny face nestled into her pillow, his rosebud lips all puffy from sleep, and admitted to herself what she denied before others. The sun had snatched from her something much dearer than possessions as it drifted to rest: her confidence that her husband would return. An entire moon had passed since he had left.

Oh, Pacing Wolf, she mouthed while treading back over happier memories. The sorrow that had been battering her heart broke it open, and even fear of disturbing Wolf-Who-Lays-Down could not stem her noiseless weeping.

Lord, surely, you have not brought me to this foreign place to leave me without husband or hope. I will do anything You ask—anything, only please bring him back to us! I long to feel his breath in my hair and lean back against his chest.

In the deep curling hair of his buffalo robes, she could still faintly smell the sweet tobacco that so clung to his clothing, and the turmoil she had been quashing spewed out with such force, it racked her chest with rhythmic jerking.

I know You are faithful, she acknowledged once she could calm her breathing. *And I will do anything You ask whether or not You… whether he is…is…*

She could not bring herself to put the fear into words.

You were not asleep when You allowed Pacing Wolf to snatch me, and You are not asleep now. I was so frightened that night and for many nights after, sure happiness and hope were forever stricken from my summers, and yet look at all You have brought me. I cannot fathom loving any warrior as I love Pacing Wolf—there is no one like him— and had he not stolen me that morning, I would never have known him at all or gained our precious son. You did me such an unexpected kindness, a kindness I could never have imagined—and I trust You still will. You are not like the moon—ever changing. You are like the sun—rising every morning to offer us life and warmth.

The steadfast loving kindness of the Lord will not run dry. His mercies will never end. They are new every morning.

Lamentations 3:23

Chapter 8

"STRAIGHT ARROWS AND Pretty Face are back!" cried Young Deer, sticking his head into Brought-Us-The-Book's dwelling.

As his mother smiled, the youth read plain relief in her water-colored eyes. "They have been gone for nearly half a moon."

"They are looking for Father and then heading this way. I go to help care for their horses."

As the youth backed his head out of his mother's door, she put down her Bible. "Lord, thank you for bringing them home and forgive me for worrying. I know you hold them in your hands, just as you have always held me."

Grabbing the fresh herbs she had gathered, she ducked out of her dwelling and into one they had erected next to it. By God's mercy, her patient's bone had broken cleanly and none of his wounds showed profuse swelling, but he had lost a great amount of blood.

"What might have happened," she murmured, "if my sons had not found you? You would surely have become some wild beast's meal!"

Half a moon ago, she had heard a lookout proclaiming a party of hunters was returning with a string of horses; but instead of hauling fresh game, each mount carried an Allied warrior slung across its back. When her husband, Preying Eagle, had asked after their two eldest, the hunters had told him Straight Arrows and Pretty Face had broken from their party to follow fresh tracks left by these kinsmen's killers.

"Who are they, Father?" she remembered Young Deer asking, twisting his head to get a better view of the dead men's faces.

"This one is Wild Dog, Red Fox's son—the warrior we chased from our village after the Raven Enemy snatched Light Bird. That other must be Walks-Behind-Them, his cousin."

Young Deer pulled up the second warrior's head from the horse's hindquarters to confirm Preying Eagle's suspicion. "I cannot tell. He is too badly damaged to identify."

"It is surely him," offered Running Deer, the youth's grandfather. "He is more a brother to Wild Dog than a cousin, and like Straight Arrows and Pretty Face, they are never apart. And the other?"

"A cousin," guessed Preying Eagle. "Come," he called Follows-His-Shadow, his youngest son. "Put your fingers beneath his nose. Do you feel it?"

The boy broke into a smile. Faint breaths, like a slowly beaten drum, were escaping the blood and grime-covered nostrils. "He is not dead!"

"Not yet," answered his father, shoving his hand up the last warrior's shirt. "But he grows cold. Help your mother and brother move the guest dwelling next to ours and then gather up extra buffalo robes. Your grandfather and I will take the dead to Red Fox and Swallow Woman so they may honor them."

"Will they not want to honor this other cousin?" asked Young Deer.

"Your mother will care for him. Once he is warm, the Creator may revive his spirit."

While Young Deer and Follow-His-Shadow carried out their father's instructions, Preying Eagle looked over the man's tokens. "Before we go to Red Fox," he told his father, "I will ask my brothers to guard him. Warriors who follow Wild Dog are all cut from the same rotting hide."

As voices outside pulled Brought-Us-the-Book from her memories, her two eldest sons stepped into the guest lodge.

"We found her!" exclaimed Straight Arrows.

"We followed tracks to the village of an enemy we did not recognize," explained Pretty Face, seeing her confusion. "And while we sheltered to watch within a thick span of pines, a young woman approached who possesses your features."

"Light Bird?" their mother whispered, a slow smile breaking across their mother's face. Hopping up from her patient, she began peppering them with questions."

Her sons grinned, pleased to have brought her happy tidings, while they nodded greetings to a string of other family members who were squeezing inside.

"Is she well? Did you speak with her? What of her husband—did you meet him?"

"She looks well," answered Straight Arrows, once she stopped leaping from question to question. "She has a son—healthy, about two summers—and a Blackfoot woman for a friend. We did not see her husband."

"I have a grandchild?"

"Yes, and in several moons you will have another." He paused to allow their relatives to offer congratulations, but as he and Pretty Face resumed telling their story, the corners of each mouth drooped increasingly downward.

"What of her husband?" asked Two Doves, the young warriors' silver-haired grandmother. "Does he treat her well?"

Straight Arrows shrugged. "We do not know. Before we could speak to her, the guards discovered our hiding place."

"We were glad," added Pretty Face, "to get away without arrows in our hides."

"How is this kinsman?" Straight Arrows asked his mother, nodding toward her patient. We thought all three were dead."

"For many nights, we expected him to quit breathing."

"Look." Follows-In-His-Shadow directed his brothers' attention to two lodge poles placed on either side of Wild Dog's cousin, extending above his head and below his feet. "After I helped Mother take off his breastplate, we tied him between these so we can flip him over."

"Very clever," smiled the oldest.

"We needed to bathe both sides of him and also restrain his thrashing. He is healing nicely, but I fear for his mind. It wanders to his woman and then leaps into frightening places."

"How do you know he is thinking of his woman?" asked Pretty Face.

"I guess I do not really, but once he awakened while I was changing his bandages. He looked at me tenderly and murmured a name. I suppose he might have thought I was his mother."

"What did you learn from Red Fox?" asked Straight Arrows, looking from his father to his grandfather.

"He belongs to one of Red Fox's sisters," answered Running Deer. "They married warriors from different bands, but their sons were known to raid with Wild Dog."

"What name did he call?" asked Preying Eagle. "Red Fox will know her and which cousin she married."

"I did not catch it. He mumbled very softly, and when I raised my eyes, he jerked backward. Had we not tied him down, he would have ripped apart his stitches."

Straight Arrows cocked his head, peering at what looked like ants traveling in a line. "They are holding well, and he is sleeping soundly now."

"Since then, I have been steeping crushed herbs in broth to dull the pain."

Sighing sadly, Two Doves shook her head. "I am glad this one does not also belong to Swallow Woman. To lose Wild Dog and Walks-Behind-Them in one day is hard—and Large Man not too many summers ago."

"Her wails rent the village," confirmed her husband, "and when Red Fox saw them, he turned black with rage. His heart is eager for vengeance, but he does not know whom to take it on. He will come here when this man recovers to question him and our grandsons. Then, he will return to his band to raise a war party."

"But if they attack Light Bird's village," fretted Young Deer, "they might hurt her and her children."

"This troubles me also," admitted Preying Eagle, slipping an affectionate hand around the back of the youth's neck. "The Creator claims vengeance as His,[5] but Red Fox refuses His path. Wild Dog likely provoked the Raven Enemy as he did the warrior who snatched your sister, but this will not matter. Red Fox will attack them, and the Raven Enemy will take vengeance in reprisal. Where does the killing end?"

"We must stop him," urged Straight Arrows.

"How?" asked Pretty Face, every warriors' expression echoing a similar question.

"We will pray," offered Old Many Feathers, Two Doves' ancient brother. "'The Creator will not scold us for our lack of wisdom but generously supply our need.'"[6]

"Father," asked little Follows-In-His-Shadow, "should my brothers ride back to warn her?"

"No," answered Preying Eagle. "They are weary, and you have heard your old uncle. We will fast and pray for the Creator's guidance."

"Red Fox will wait," the boy's grandfather added. "The sky grows white. As the sun awakens, our women will be trudging through an early snow for our families' firewood. Red Fox's people dwell close to wind off the great waters. For this night and many nights to follow, he will stay where he is. Besides, until he wakes up," Running Deer nodded toward the patient, "we cannot be sure the Raven Enemy killed them."

"We followed their tracks," offered Straight Arrows.

"You told us they were clear; they made no attempt to hide them. While we searched for your sister, we learned they sheltered often in those caverns. How can we know—until your mother's patient awakens—whether they killed our kinsmen or stumbled over them while hunting? When Red Fox comes, we will tell him nothing he does not need to know."

"YOUR FATHER IS CORRECT, as I have always found him," noted Brought-Us-The-Book, stooping to enter her dwelling. "I could barely push through the snow piled up against our door-flap. The lake may freeze; it is already hardening around the edges. I had to chip away a thin layer of ice to dip down my water-skins. Last evening, your mother and I gathered four times the firewood we will need today. If we conserve it carefully, we will all stay warm."

Brushing a large snowflake from his woman's hair, Preying Eagle thought how beautiful he still found her. The last time he had seen Swallow Woman, Red Fox's wife, he noticed she had begun strongly to resemble her mother, Talks-With-Bitterness. Both possessed mouths that sagged down sharply and eyes that looked as hard as his knife's flint blade. Not so with Brought-Us-The-Book. She possessed a loveliness of the heart that increased rather than diminished her beauty with every passing season.

"The snow still falls?" he asked, his fingertips traversing the smooth skin beneath her earlobe until they came to rest at the back of her neck. Cupping her jaw with his palm, he sent his thumb on the familiar journey over the scars an enemy had once carved into her cheeks. They were barely noticeable now, to the eye or to the touch, but in his mind, their presence had become inextricably linked with Light Bird. Like his daughter's absence, they reminded him of his inability to keep either safe.

Brought-Us-the-Book merely nodded, but a smile lit her eyes.

Resting his hands on her hips, he drew her closer and lowered his head until his cheek brushed her cool, damp hair. "You do not need many sticks for our embers; I will keep you warm."

Wending her palms up his chest and around his neck to caress the back of his well-shaped head, she sighed. "I must attend to Wild Dog's cousin. If his fire dies, he will not be able to light it. He will freeze to death."

Preying Eagle groaned. He knew she was right. The man could do nothing; she and his mother had trapped him between two lodge poles. Running his fingers tenderly across her furrowing brow and down to her smooth cheek, he tilted up her chin so he could peer into her darkly-fringed eyes. "Send our sons to stir his embers. You have already stirred mine."

"Which of these three acted as a neighbor to the man who had been attacked?" And he said, "The one who offered him care." And He said, "Go and do the same."

Luke 10:36-37

Chapter 9

KEPT-US-ALIVE SHIVERED as she brushed the newly falling snow from a dead log near the base of a white-bark tree. Pulling her warmest buffalo robe up over her head, she wrapped the lower half tightly around her legs and sat down while tucking the ends behind them.

"The Lord is my light and my salvation," she silently recited. *"Whom shall I fear? The Lord is the safe-place guarding my life, of whom shall I be afraid? What can man do to me?*[7] *Give no thought for tomorrow, for you do not know what a day may bring forth. Let the day's own trouble be sufficient for the day."*[8]

The waking sun had barely reached the lowest pine boughs, but she felt like she had repeated the last a hundred times. Puffing warm breath into her hands, she closed her eyes.

Father, I beg you to keep Pacing Wolf safe. Provide him with enough food and water for the day—and not only for him but for Bites-With-Dog's family. The snow has made game scarce; I do not want to be a burden to them.

I am also growing deeply concerned about our small family of Sparrow Hawk believers. Since Pacing Wolf has…gone, many are staying away when I read from your book. Others are acting oddly.

As she leaned back against the tree, she remembered the joyful day that Bites-With-Dog and his family, Twists-His-Hair and his first woman, and then old Paints-His-Shirt-Yellow had asked Pacing Wolf to guide them along the new path he had found. By the following autumn, the rest of Twist-His-Hair's wives and older children and all but Paints-His-Shirt-Yellow's middle son had asked Pacing Wolf to dunk them in the river, declaring before the village they believed I-Am-Savior and had decided to walk behind him. Even young Otter Woman had done so, though she feared her husband, Braids-His-Tail, might cast her away. He had not, and after several months of praying he too began ducking into Pacing Wolf's lodge most evenings.

When Kept-Us-Alive had moved in with Bites-With-Dog and Hopping Owl, they had asked her to continue the readings. Naturally, she had been happy to comply, but their decrease in numbers made her heart ache.

A twig snapped. Kept-Us-Alive opened her eyes to find Otter Woman, her small-thing bundled in the cradleboard on her back, squatting down beside her.

"Thank you for bringing many of Pacing Wolf's belongings to Bites-With-Dog's lodge!"

"I enjoyed planning with Hopping Owl what we would take. I am sorry I no longer come to hear the Creator's Book and for the hurtful tongues many of the younger women are wagging at you. Braids-His-Tail told me Hunts-For-Death is angry with him for defending Bites-With-Dog for taking you in. Now, though he still defends your new father, he has forbidden me to listen. He is my husband and I love him. What should I do?"

As a snowflake melted on Otter Woman's lashes, Kept-Us-Alive silently asked God for wisdom. "Here. Sit. There is plenty of room." She brushed more snow from the log. "Does your husband insist you abandon I-Am-Savior's path?"

The young Sparrow Hawk shook her head, carefully pulling her robe up over the infant behind her. "I could not if he did. I-Am-Savior has shown me kindness—kindness I do not deserve—and my heart has been so full since I began to follow Him. You did not know me well before you returned. I was full of bitter anger—even toward you. Pacing Wolf's dead woman had been my older sister's friend. I hated your clansman for what he did to her, and you for claiming her place."

"I felt you did not like me, but I understood. I am ashamed Wild Dog was of my people. Do not think of it. I forgave you long ago."

"I was also jealous. I could see that you have a quality I lack. Even when Pacing Wolf scowled, you did not appear to tremble. My heart feels like a leaf snatched up by every breeze. One moment it rests happily in the thick grass; the next moment a sudden scorching wind dashes it hard onto the well-trodden path. Braids-His-Tail says this sense of peace and your gentle ways were what drew your husband's heart."

Kept-Us-Alive half-smiled, half-frowned. "I was not peaceful but terrified—like a rabbit frozen by a sparrow hawk's sharp stare. But I-Am-Savior is faithful in all He does[9]--and now you also hold the heart of a fine warrior." Catching her lip between her teeth, Otter Woman did not reply.
"Is all well between you?"

"Lately, he is silent and often absent from our lodge. He is, as you said, a fine warrior. Many untouched women desired him and might still—and perhaps dissatisfied married women even more so. I am afraid he already tires of me."

Kept-Us-Alive tried to keep her eyes from widening. If this people were like her own, she could offer comforting assurances, but they were not. Here, if Braids-His-Tail were tired of her friend, he would simply seek another woman to pull from a rival's lodge after the death-staff ceremony. "Is he cruel or does he push you away when you care for his hair and clothing?"

"No."

"He may simply be taking refuge in his cave." As she watched Otter Woman furrow her brow, she realized she had never heard a Sparrow Hawk using the turn of phrase, so common among her Allied aunts and cousins.

"When my father or brothers became angry, my mother and grandmother warned me to leave them alone. They said every warrior goes into his own cave to grapple with his troubles and that I must not follow him. A bear who lives in that cave would hurt me if I did. I found this with Pacing Wolf also. Braids-His-Tail's desire to please his Real Chief may be wrestling with his desire for you—and perhaps not only for you but for I-Am-Savior."

The crease between Otter Woman's eyebrows relaxed slightly. "Do you believe this?"

"I do not know what your husband holds within his heart," answered Kept-Us-Alive. "We have not spoken two words apart from greetings, but he has been listening attentively to the Scripture and appeared to drink in my husband's counsel. Trust I-Am-Savior to work within him—to draw him by His Holy Spirit as He drew you. I cannot promise Braids-His-Tail will listen, but whether he listens or not, I-Am-Savior will take care of you."

Otter Woman let out a long, deep breath. "Lately, I have grown afraid he may cast me out, and since the pox took my father and uncles, I have nowhere to go. How would my daughter and I live or gain food? You no longer have a home to offer me, and Last Woman cannot welcome me into Hunts-For-Death's lodge."

"I have just been talking with I-Am-Savior about similar struggles. Still, 'the Lord is near to the broken-hearted and saves the crushed in spirit.'[10] 'He will never fail or forsake us.'[11] He is our father, our brother, and even our betrothed."

Both women sighed, one inwardly, the other outwardly, as they found comfort in the scriptures, but then Otter Woman asked, "Do you still believe Pacing Wolf is not…that he will soon…"

"Return?" Kept-Us-Alive answered softly. "Yes. He…he must."

Otter Woman glanced away, unable to bear the doubt and pain that had crept over Kept-Us-Alive's face or to think of anything to say. How could she encourage her friend to hope for what she, herself, did not believe? "How can you know?"

Tears began streaming down Kept-Us-Alive's cheeks. "I do not! My heart feels like a ball the youths hit with sticks. One moment, I agree with all the others. He has been gone well over a moon; he would not leave us so long to hunger. The next, I cannot make my heart believe this. I fear he is lying hurt somewhere without anyone to help him or that he has…."

She did not finish, too upset to describe her nightmare. When she had awakened to it a second time, she wondered if the Creator was telling her it was so. As she fought to regain her composure, Wolf-Who-Lays-Down trotted up, climbed onto her lap, and pressed his cold, padded hands against her cheeks. "I want Last Son," he announced.

"He is eating his morning meal," she rasped, hoping he would blame the falling snow for dampening her red cheeks. "In Hunts-For-Death's lodge."

The little boy stuck out his lower lip. "Good Men talking—loud!"

Otter Woman shot her a questioning look, but before either asked him anything further, Last Woman and her son found them. As Wolf-Who-Lays-Down happily scrambled down to join his friend, the tall Blackfoot seater herself on Kept-Us-Alive's other side.

"The Good Men are with Hunts-For-Death. Bites-With-Dog has been asking them to honor the dead by insisting their wives treat you more kindly. All know your husband loved you."

Kept-Us-Alive dropped her gaze. She could not help noticing that Last Woman, too, spoke as if Pacing Wolf was dead.

"What did they say?" asked Otter Woman.

The tall Blackfoot glanced away. "They chewed on Bites-With-Dog's words for a while before swallowing—at least they did not swiftly spit them out. They decided," she locked eyes with her freshly widowed friend, "since you do not grieve, Bites-With-Dog must announce an end to your period of mourning and give you to another Sparrow Hawk."

Kept-Us-Alive's eyes grew round. Looking sideways at her other friend, she found such sympathy that she struggled not to cry. "Would they want Pacing Wolf to return and find us given to another? The snows may have delayed him."

"The snows have only started," murmured Otter Woman.

"Here. We do not know where he is— how can we be sure the snow has not caught him?

Last Woman gazed down at her fur-lined moccasins. "Bites-With-Dog offered this thought to Hunts-For-Death, but he would not nibble off the smallest bite. He said if you refuse to marry, he will take Wolf-Who-Lays-Down and give him to one of Pacing Wolf's clanswomen—and also the small-thing you will bear. Then, he insists, Bites-With-Dog must cast you out."

"But…but he gave my husband his promise," sputtered Kept-Us-Alive, wrapping her arms tightly about her burgeoning waist.

Last Woman compressed her lips, but one glance told her Otter Woman had come to the same conclusion: supporting a false hope was crueler than urging their friend to face the obvious. "That promise put him at odds with his Real Chief. If Hunts-For-Death casts him and Hopping Owl from the people, who will take their side?"

"These cliffs let us see far across the prairie," Otter Woman gently added. "The sky there began to gray and thicken only after our clanswomen claimed your husband's belongings."

Frowning deeply, Kept-Us-Alive gazed through glistening branches.

"You have gained the respect of our Good Men. One of them is sure to want you."

"I want no other warrior."

Last Woman stared at the tree tops. "In four moons the grass will green. Have you considered what may happen once the war societies award their staffs and ropes?"

Kept-Us-Alive nodded. "We were just speaking of it." All too well, she remembered Goes-To-Battle barging into Pacing Wolf's lodge and demanding she leave with him.

"Then you know Bites-With-Dog will not be able to protect you. Hunts-For-Death is determined; he will make certain I am not there to help you. What can Hopping Owl do alone?"

"A good number of the Lumpwoods may be willing," offered Otter Woman, "You are still very young, and they held your husband in high esteem."

"And many will want you for your own qualities," added Last Woman. "But choose a warrior from the Many Lodges so he will not separate you from us."

"Out of respect for the small-thing growing in you," Otter Woman nodded toward her friend's mounding stomach, "a Lumpwood will not press you to warm his buffalo robes. A Fox or Muddy Hand might steal you to prove his daring, and if you resist him, he may become cruel."

Kept-Us-Alive began shaking her head as if she could to fling away their "I will not. I cannot. Few warriors—even among the Lumpwoods—follow I-Am-Savior, and the Creator forbids us to be joined to those who do not." Even while the words were leaping from her lips, she recognized the hurt they might cause her friend, but Otter Woman continued as if she had not noticed.

"When my dead clan-leader snatched you, you did not come willingly, nor did he walk I-Am-Savior's path. You grew to love him as you will grow to love another."

"Though the Lord causes grief, abundant compassion springs from His loving kindness."

Lamentations 3:32

Chapter 10

During the

Moon When Wolves Run Together

AS THE SKY TURNED the color of ashes, Kept-Us-Alive stole a moment to walk past the ridge of pines. Her common sense scolded her harshly, but besides the hope she might find her brothers waiting, she was desperate to be alone. Pushing between the thick branches, she dropped to her knees and pressed her head against the carpet of cold needles. She felt far too dispirited to hold it up.

If Pacing Wolf saw me hiding in here, she thought, *he would be furious.*

When he first brought her to The-Cliffs-that-Have-No-Name, she had often escaped to such places, a practice that provoked him to anger. Why, she had not understood at the time. She had only wanted to pray, but he later confided the reason. He knew what Wild Dog would do if he caught her.

Wild Dog—I need not fear him now!

A startling thought, like an unseen arrow, swiftly pierced her heart. While setting aside her husband's wishes, she was admitting to herself that he was dead, and anger spewed from her like mist from an earth-hole.

"Lord, You see and hear all things! Why did You let this happen—not only to Pacing Wolf but to me and to our children? You heard Last Woman. Hunts-For-Death will force me to marry or toss me out to beg. If You do not now intervene, they will raise him to think like their warriors."

As she spent her sobs, she imagined Pacing Wolf's death more vividly than in her nightmares. They came one after another, like an onslaught by a ravaging enemy, too quickly to fend off.

"I cannot bear the thought of him suffering alone—with no one to comfort him."

He is not alone. The words were clear, though whispered only in her heart, and fresh tears began overflowing their fringed boundaries. She still shivered from exhaustion and cold, but she also felt as if a perfectly sewn garment had slipped over and enveloped her heart.

"I am glad You were with him—are with him still—for he is with You and will never feel pain and heartache again."

She wished *she* felt less alone. People surrounded her so constantly, she had to hide to gain a few moments of privacy; yet, never since the first few moons in this place had she felt so lonely. With whom could she share her grief? Pacing Wolf's kinswomen had cast her away as unworthy of upholding his memory, and she did not want to trouble Wolf-Who-Lays-Down. His little legs still tottered and the few words he used were frequently unclear. Besides, he was too young to grasp the finality of death.

Last Woman loved her and had begun to feel confident of Otter Woman's friendship; but how could she confide to either of them the anger she felt toward the very Creator she was encouraging them to trust? Once she had spoken the words aloud, she would never be able to capture them again, and she did not want to cause either friend doubt or harm.

But I like my husband, I am not truly alone. The Creator said He will never fail or forsake me."[12] *I will take Him at His word.*

THE LODGE FELT tense when Kept-Us-Alive ducked inside. While she was dragging in her new family's water sacks, Bites-With-Dog had not looked up and remained so still he brought to mind the quiet before a thunderstorm. Hopping Owl appeared already to have unleashed a torrent. The corners of her mouth sagged and her cheeks were red and moist. She showed none of her husband's constraint, offering and then withdrawing such a quick succession of glances, Kept-Us-Alive could not tell if she was annoyed or apologetic. While she was deciding how to respond, Last Son trotted in with his sister.

"Who is Held-Back-the-Enemy hiding from?" he whispered.

Glancing from one child to the other, Kept-Us-Alive shook her head. She could not imagine what he meant and was in no mood to play. Hoping neither would point out her puffy eyes, she busied herself with the contents of Pacing Wolf's large buckskin bag.

When Kept-Us-Alive did not answer, Little Blackfoot Woman said, "He is not hiding. He is outside, between the lodges, standing like a tree trunk."

Tilting her head to one side, Kept-Us-Alive could not resist asking, "Why does your brother think he is hiding?"

"He is holding his robe across his face, like this." The girl demonstrated. "Peeking out of a slit."

As Kept-Us-Alive began to understand, she could not help smiling. She had suspected as much from his recent behavior. "He is watching the lodge of one of our neighbors. Their untouched daughter must have attracted his attention. He is waiting to see if any other warriors come to court her."

"This lodge," Last Son corrected, pointing to the opening from which they had just entered.

Kept-Us-Alive ruffled the little boy's hair, chuckling affectionately. "If he is wrapped up, how can you tell where he is looking? Maybe the warrior is not Held-Back-the-Enemy—it would be hard to tell if he is hiding within a robe. Look," she made a wide sweep with her arm. "Can any of you find any untouched women in this lodge?"

The children shook their heads and giggled as they craned their necks in all directions pretending to search the dwelling, but after a few moments, Little Blackfoot Woman grew thoughtful. "It *was* him," she announced. He was wearing the moccasins I helped Hopping Owl bead. Her fingers are fat; she has trouble with the shorter quills."

"Well," concluded Kept-Us-Alive, lowering her tone as others began to enter. "One of our neighbors will have a happy daughter. Held-Back-the-Enemy is handsome and very courageous. All the untouched women blush when they see him drawing near."

Hopping Owl smiled. She felt proud of the man her son was becoming, but so many people were now squeezing into the lodge, she scurried to her place behind Bites-With-Dog and whispered in his ear. Kneeling, she made room for Otter Woman and elbowed her arm as Braids-His-Tail ducked inside. Held-Back-the-Enemy came in last; but instead of sitting next to his father, as usual, he kept himself a little apart, just inside the door.

Kept-Us-Alive had little time to wonder about his strange behavior or why the moods of both her adopted parents seemed significantly brighter. Hopping Owl was chatting animatedly with Otter Woman and Bites-With-Dog looked as if he was hiding a pleasant secret. Only Held-Back-the-Enemy acted oddly, often casting his eyes to the ground and avoiding Kept-Us-Alive's altogether. As his father signaled for her to begin, she read the first verses of the letter from Grasping Man.[13]

Be joyful, my brothers, when you face trials and testing. You know the testing of your faith produces strength to endure; so let this strength to endure affect you wholly, so you may become perfect, complete, and lack nothing. If any of you lacks wisdom, he should ask God, who is generous and gives without reproach. He will give it to you when you ask, but you must firmly trust Him without doubt. A man who doubts God is like water tossed about by the wind. The two minds he possesses make him unstable. He cannot expect to receive anything from the Creator.

As Kept-Us-Alive finished reading, she reflected on her earlier spurt of anger and her decision, long ago, to return to The-Cliffs-That-Have-No-Name. She had wanted to show Last Woman and her children, who had decided to follow Jesus, where to find His moccasin prints. Without the Word to guide them, she feared they might go astray.

"No," Bites-With-Dog was saying, pulling Kept-Us-Alive from her private thoughts. Braids-His-Tail had asked if he needed to be certain of I-Am-Savior's path before he placed his feet on it. "These verses are about a man who already knows I-Am-Savior, but when I-Am-Savior leads him through a dismal place, he begins to doubt He is a trustworthy leader. This sort of man becomes unsure of where to put his feet. He sees I-Am-Savior's moccasin prints, but fear of what lays ahead urges him toward a different path—a path that appears secure but will crumble into a snake's den. The warrior who trusts I-Am-Savior accepts His counsel. Though a path looks too narrow and the ground unable to hold his weight, he crosses it anyway, confident I-Am-Savior knows where He is heading and cares what becomes of him."

Kept-Us-Alive smiled. Although Bites-With-Dog was speaking to Otter Woman's husband, God had been speaking to her.

"What you are saying reminds me of a verse your new daughter read to me this morning," added old Paints-His-Shirt-Yellow. 'Though You lead me through a ravine overshadowed by death, I will not fear evil. You are with me.'[14] Not even a youth will lead his herd through a dark or dangerous place unless he knows it is the best of all choices, but a horse who has not yet learned to trust him will balk and pull away. The way is good, but if a horse sees only his own fear, what guidance can even the most skilled warrior offer?"

All began to nod their heads, except Braids-His-Tail, who grew eager to ask a question. "But horses know the warrior who keeps them. When a rock becomes stuck in a horse's hoof, the warrior pries it out with his knife. When another's coat is full of burrs, the warrior takes care when he cuts them away. When they thirst, the warrior leads them to good, clean water. These horses have reason to trust this warrior. How can I trust I-Am-Savior when I do not know him?"

Kept-Us-Alive glanced from her friend's husband to her adopted father to see if he intended to answer. He did. "That speckled pony you took from the Grass Lodges—how will he discover whether you will neglect or care for him well?"

"My other horses assure him. They nicker with pleasure when they smell me approaching. If I were stingy with my care, they would pound the earth or shy away."

Bites-With-Dog smiled. "Just so—but what if that pony proves very wary? What if his last owner hit him with a stick or left him to suffer from thirst?"

"He will learn. I will treat him well, and he will soon see that my hand holds good things—that my touch soothes. As the sun rises and sleeps, he too will begin to offer me welcome."

"You have answered your own question," replied Bites-With-Dog. "Talk to I-Am-Savior. Listen to His voice as my new daughter reads the words written on these leaves. Ask Him to show you if He is good. Then you will know for yourself and no longer need to trust these horses' nickers." He gestured toward the others. "Does the passage announce He will not guide you until you trust Him? No. It says until you trust Him, His guidance will not help you. You will disregard His counsel and walk in a path that appears more pleasing."

Another warrior told Braids-His-Tail of his own experience, and then Held-Back-the-Enemy asked him a question, but Kept-Us-Alive's thoughts were like dandy-lion puffs carried on a breeze. They landed for a while on the hidden doubts their discussion had uncovered then glided into thanking I-Am-Savior who—like an attentive herdsman—had proven Himself faithful summer after summer. From there, they drifted back to Pacing Wolf who was ever mindful of the people in his care, plunging her once more into grief and yearning.

Oh Lord, help my unbelief! I like that balky pony, pulling back from Your lead because the way looks bleak. You are worthy of my...

"Give me your wrist." Kept-Us-Alive looked up to see Bull-Will-Not-Fall, one of Pacing Wolf's clansmen, stretching down his hand toward her. "When my sister carried a small-thing, she had difficulty rising."

Kept-Us-Alive felt unsure of what she should do. She barely knew the man, and the little she knew, she did not like. He belonged to the Foxes, the keenest rivals of the Lumpwoods' war-society. During her first spring among the Sparrow Hawks, after the New Death-Staffs Ceremony, Pacing Wolf had pulled her from his lodge. The warrior standing before her was riding down the central path with a neighbor's youngest wife perched proudly on the rear of his mount. His Fox companions' taunts and whoops so deafened the village she had wanted to cover her ears and duck back inside.

Glancing around quickly, Kept-Us-Alive saw that everyone but Hopping Owl had left, but she assured herself she need not fear him. The war-societies did not award new death staffs until the Moon When Everything Greens. He had come to Bites-With-Dog's lodge for the reason others did: to hear the Word of God, and she did not want to cause him offense.

Offering her wrist, she soon grew grateful for his aid—her legs had fallen asleep—but once he had helped her to her feet, he would not allow her to pull away.

Tugging her closer, his eyes slowly wandered over her hair, her cheeks, her lips. "Hunts-For-Death has given me your dead husband's lodge," he murmured. "It feels empty without a…" He abruptly dropped her wrist and stepped backward as Held-Back-the-Enemy ducked inside.

What he stopped short of saying, Kept-Us-Alive could only guess, but as she read Held-Back-the-Enemy's eyes, she felt warmth rushing up her neck. He had been assessing what had passed between them, and what he concluded, she did not try to discover. She was far too tired from grief and strain. Still, she did not want him to think she had sought Bull-Will-Not-Fall's attention or that she was growing eager to warm a warrior's buffalo robes.

Shivering, she began to place aside their guests' backrests and straighten the small portion of the lodge in which she kept her belongings, but instead of allowing her to finish her tasks, Held-Back-the-Enemy closed the distance between them.

"Hunts-For-Death is not right to say you cared little for my Lumpwood father. Before I was a warrior, while I tended his horses, my eyes told me what lay in your heart."

As the corners of her lips tilted upward, he began to back out the door. He knew she was not smiling at him but at the tender memories he had evoked. Glancing at his mother, he acknowledged her briefly, but she did not notice. Her eyes had followed Kept-Us-Alive to the pile of robes on which Wolf-Who-Lays-Down lay sleeping, and she was watching her brush the shining black tresses from his brow. Hopping Owl guessed easily of whom she was thinking. The tiny boy was so like his father.

While Held-Back-the-Enemy slipped silently away, Kept-Us-Alive slipped between her covers, curving herself around the boy as if he were still a small-thing. Soon, her shuddering shoulders confirmed Hopping Owl's suspicions. She was dampening the boy's hair with silent weeping, as she had each night since the dog of doubt had slunk stealthily past her defenses. It had begun howling to Fear and Pain, alerting them where they, too, might find lodging, and before she was aware, they slipped in also, gnawing at her insides. Hopping Owl watched each night, praying for a way to offer comfort while feeling an intruder on so private a grief.

When Kept-Us-Alive heard her new mother blowing on the dozing embers, she wished she would let the fire sleep. The night had grown cold, but darkness brought relief from the soft-hued surroundings. She knew every handbreadth of Pacing Wolf's lodge as well as she knew her own body: his death-staffs, thrust above his door flap or hanging near his pipe; his shields, leaning against the lodge wall until they were needed; his sharp ax, close to their bed; and several half-finished bows, lain toward the back.

Bull-Will-Not-Fall now owned the hides she had scraped with such care and lain in such a tight pattern they would not permit the strongest wind entry. She longed for these beloved surroundings as if it were a living thing, part of Pacing Wolf and of their life together, a covering for intimacies and a refuge from cold and pain—pain that had lately become so excruciating she thought it might never end.

All night long I flood my bed with weeping and drench my buffalo robes with tears.

Psalm 6:6

Chapter 11

"GET UP!" STRAIGHT ARROWS lightly cuffed Pretty Face on the hip. "Hurry!"

"What?" complained his brother, raising his head in Straight Arrows' direction.

"The sky no longer snows. If we leave now, we can make it to Light Bird's village before the sun returns too often to its rest."

"I want to go!" cried Young Deer. He sat up, eagerly throwing off his covers.

His eldest brother quickly put his fingers against his lips, warning the youth not to wake their parents, but he shook his head. "Father and Mother would not allow it. You are still a youth and the Raven Enemy are fierce—we barely returned with our hides."

The youth looked dejected but did not argue. He hated the number of summers and accomplishments that separated him from his two older brothers. He wanted to come and go at will, as they did. Before he had lain back down and pulled his buffalo robe tightly over his shoulder, his brother, Pretty Face, had dressed and was dipping into the family's supply of pemmican. Straight Arrows and he would be traveling swiftly and neither wanted the delay of a hunt.

Walking quietly past the hill that sloped beneath the ancient crabapple, they swung onto their horses' backs and headed from the waking sun. They had gained the cavern before it slept and were approaching the far mountains when it grew weary from its fresh journey across the sky. Once it rose the third morning, they would travel the path that had led them to the pinewood, but they planned to tether their horses farther away—before they reached the last turn.

KEPT-US-ALIVE DROWSILY rolled over beneath her husband's buffalo robe, hoping she might find him lying on his back. She wished to snuggle against his side, nestling her head in the warm, pliant flesh between his chest and shoulder; but as she opened her eyes, she felt as if a cold wind had blown open the door flap.

Why, she questioned, *did her memory fall asleep each night along with her exhausted limbs? Every morning was the same: she felt happy and at peace upon rousing from sleep only to have the stark awareness of his absence slap her awake.*

Putting on her skirt and blouse beneath the covers, she pulled her sleeping son onto her hip, flung her robe around their shoulders, and then stepped out into a dense mist rising from the river. It so enshrouded the village, she could catch nothing but an occasional glimpse of the black topmost branches of the trees reaching like disembodied arms toward the barely dawning light.

← ← ← → → →

STRAIGHT ARROWS AND PRETTY FACE strained to see the rocks peeking above the river that lay close to the Raven Enemy village. Stepping carefully from one to the next, they reached the bank opposite the path and lay in low shrubs, listening for arriving women. The heavy fog drenched their hunting shirts, making their bellies so cold that each was tempted to risk standing until they heard clear childish voices moving toward them from the distance.

As silent as a spirit, their sister's tall companion emerged out of the wafting haze, but the girl and little boy bounding through the snow at her heels hastily dispelled the eerie impression. Straight Arrows, staring hard through the mist beyond them, spotted a sliver of cheekbone and chin, delicate replicas of the masculine jawline hidden within the brush beside him. Once their owner stepped through a foggy patch, Straight Arrows gaped at her unexpected changes. Wisps, like downy tufts belonging to the under-feathers of a waterfowl curved in all directions around her well-shaped neck.

As his eyes traveled from them to her face, he saw she looked no happier than she had when they last waited for her, though something like peace had settled about her features. He watched the tall Blackfoot glance back at her with the same protective gaze he had previously noticed, but one difference stood out distinctly: he could not locate the little apple-faced girl.

Lying motionless, the brothers peered through the thinning mist, barely making out the forms of other gathering women who settled as they had before, far enough away to make their meaning clear; but soon a pleasant-faced young woman with a cradleboard strapped to her back parted from their company and headed directly for their sister and her tall companion. Straight Arrows was glad his sister had gained an additional friend, but if this stranger remained, she would surely add trouble to their plan. All he and Pretty Face could do at present was wait.

As voices from both groups carried across the water, the brothers found answers to several of their questions. Their tiny nephew asked why his father had stayed away so long; and though their sister offered a calm reply, they suspected he was tugging loose her tightly clutched composure.

The Blackfoot proved less willing than Light Bird to endure the other women's insults. "Come," she commanded her small boy and daughter, pinning Light Bird with a look that insisted she follow; and the forlorn little party, having found sufficient kindling for their bundles, trod out of their earshot.

As Pretty Face cautiously began backing from the bank, Straight Arrows motioned for him to stay down and nodded toward the other side of the river. Sauntering lazily through the haze were four sentries—two more than previously posted. They perused the women dipping their sacks in the water, making clear gestures to indicate a preference for one's bent over hindquarters or dislike for another's, or whistling tunelessly to catch their desired prey's attention.

Some women responded, some ignored them, but few besides the well-guarded untouched daughters acted according to the brothers' expectations. Several possessing as many summers as their mother cast sidelong glances at the sentries of their choice or walked with an exaggerated rolling of their hips that even the drifting fog could not hide.

Straight Arrows and Pretty Face felt as baffled as they were put-off. Why, they wondered, would any married woman intentionally risk arousing another warrior's notice? She invited sharp division between her kinsmen and begged her husband to slit her nostrils, ensuring she could never again attract anyone. As each separately tried to make sense of the women's actions, Pretty Face's lips broke into a wide grin.

The Blackfoot's son had returned to the river with their sister's tiny boy toddling through the snow behind him. Keeping low, both brothers crept toward the place farther upriver where the little boys were taking turns throwing rocks onto a slim bit of ice. Their nephew threw haphazardly, having yet to learn to coordinate the movement of his arm with the distance of the target. He hit the patch once, though only by chance, but the Blackfoot's son possessed more skill. Of his seven aims, he hit it four times, nearly dispersing the ice beneath the cold water.

Straight Arrows glanced toward the sentries, who were meandering after the women retreating to the village, and determined this was the best chance for him and Pretty Face to act. Signaling his intention, he reached for a stone the size of his nephew's fist and threw it across the slender river. It found its mark, crashing down on the patch with such force it splintered the ice.

"Waugh!" cried Last Son. "Who threw that?" Looking from the shattered shards across to the bank opposite, the little boy's mouth dropped open and refused to shut. The tall angel he had seen last moon was standing amidst the brush and tree limbs, his copper visage gleaming in the increasing morning light. Grabbing Wolf-Who-Lays-Down's tiny arm, he thrust his chin in Pretty Face's direction. "See? There! It is the angel—*my* angel! He is watching over me!"

The tinier boy just stared, looking as puzzled as he was astounded, but his older companion picked his way down the bank as if he intended to walk across the river. Pretty Face's palm shot forward, signaling for him to halt, and then he gestured toward the rocks where he and Straight Arrows had crossed downstream.

Noiselessly, the two brothers slipped through the forest, but just as they were about to step out of the brush and down the bank, they heard their sister's alarmed cry. She was rushing toward her toddling son as fast as her encumbered midsection allowed and grabbed his arm so suddenly, he spun around and fell to his knees.

"What are you two doing?" she scolded, her face blanched the color of a newly bleached doeskin. "The river is cold. If you fall in you may freeze! Go—play with the other children up in the field."

"B-but," sputtered Wolf-Who-Lays-Down. "The angel."

"There!" added Last Son, casting his gaze across the river where Pretty Face had stepped, smiling happily, into the open.

Kept-Us-Alive stared as if he were an angel indeed, and then out stepped another warrior. The second had so matured, she at first thought he was her father, but when she heard footsteps, she whipped her head around toward the village path. Too late. Last Woman had also seen them, but rather than raising an alarm, she stopped as if suddenly frozen.

"They are my brothers!" Kept-Us-Alive whispered, lest coming to her senses her friend should stir the guards. Then she remembered Last Woman's story. She would not have thought it possible, but not only was the tall Blackfoot unable to move or speak, red splotches were also spreading up her neck and cheeks.

Angling his head toward the rocks, her brothers beckoned for them all to cross, nodding to assure them they were not slick. Kept-Us-Alive—or Light Bird to her brothers—smiled from ear to ear. Scooping up Wolf-Who-Lays-Down, she crossed with alacrity, falling into Pretty Face's arms on the other side while Last Woman still stood frozen on the opposite bank.

"Come," mouthed Straight Arrows, holding out his hand to welcome her and Last Son.

It was all she needed. Letting Last Son go first, in case he wobbled and she needed to catch him, she crossed the rocks without any help; and though she did not need the warrior's hand, she allowed him to guide her lest he deem her rude.

Once each son and mother stood safely on the other side, both warriors warmly embraced their sister, but when she began to introduce her son, Straight Arrows shook his head. "Let him believe as he does. If he recounts our visit, no one will listen."

Kept-Us-Alive smiled. "That is what Last Woman said the afternoon you fled, and she was correct. They all think her son sees spirits."

Gently, Pretty Face touched the waving wisps around her face and his eyes grew as dark as a sudden storm. "Who did this to you?"

As his sister dropped her gaze, he almost wished he had not asked. "My husband's Real Chief. They believe a man's soul lies in his hair. If they take his hair, they capture his strength."

"You are not a man," stated Straight Arrows. "Have you become a renowned warrior since you last slept in our mother's dwelling?"

Kept-Us-Alive could not help but laugh. "No. My husband has not returned to us for over a moon, and his kinsmen are convinced he is dead. They took my hair in place of his."

Straight Arrows thought it a strange custom but he did not want to discuss such things on the outskirts of an enemy encampment. "We came to warn you. Wild Dog is dead and the prints we tracked led us here. When the snows thaw, his father will raise a war party to avenge his death. If your husband is dead, come with us. We will return you and your son to our mother and father."

"I cannot," she answered, though Pretty Face read so strong a yearning in his sister's eyes, he had to look away. "From the length of his absence, I fear they are right, but what might he think if he returned and found me missing? And what of the reasons I returned to this place? This is the friend," she indicated Last Woman, "I told all of you about in our people's village, and now there are more. Pacing Wolf—my husband—has been leading them in The Savior's path, but they need me to read from The Book."

"You have no family here," answered Pretty Face. "Who will provide food for you and your children if your warrior does not return?"

"His friend, Bites-With-Dog, the warrior who guided Spotted Long-knife and me home, has adopted me as his daughter."

Straight Arrows frowned. He did not like to trust them to someone he did not know, especially if this warrior's heart resembled the hearts of the lewd sentries. "He cannot be a good hunter if he has eaten his own dog."

"Not Eats-His-Dog!" Last Son laughed. "Bites-*With*-Dog!"

Watching him draw his brows together, Kept-Us-Alive explained. "Sparrow Hawks do not name their children as our Allies do. They believe by calling them foolish names they can trick evil spirits. If a name announces the child is of no consequence, they believe evil spirits will leave them alone."

"Is this why they call you Last Woman?" he addressed the Blackfoot.

She shook her head, embarrassed to admit how she received her name.

"My family called me Sings-Her-Songs."

Kept-Us-Alive turned her head sharply. "I did not know this."

"Where is your family?" asked Straight Arrows.

"We lived toward the cold wind," replied the Blackfoot, nodding north. "But all are dead. When the Sparrow Hawks attacked my people, Pacing Wolf pulled me from the gully where I was hiding."

"He gave you to our sister?" asked Pretty Face, surmising this might explain the Blackfoot's loyalty.

"No." Her neck turned crimson. "To their ancient Real Chief."

"Did you find the enemy warrior who killed Wild Dog?" their sister interrupted, hoping beyond hope they could deny her night terrors.

"No," replied Straight Arrows. "Only Allies."

As Kept-Us-Alive closed her eyes, deeply drawing in the cold morning air, he suspected what she was thinking; but this was not the idea she brought forward when she flung them open.

"I cannot go with you," she repeated, "but my friend and her children could go."

"What of her husband—this 'ancient Real Chief'?" asked Pretty Face.

"He is dead," his sister answered.

Noticing that the Blackfoot had said nothing, Straight Arrows addressed her directly. "You wish this?"

Last Woman nodded, turning red once more under his intense scrutiny; but when she found her tongue, she mumbled, "I cannot. Your sister came back to this village for me, not knowing how she might be treated. She kept my children and me alive. I cannot leave her."

"Do not stay for me! Perhaps this is the Creator's answer to our prayers for Little Blackfoot. You can get her away from the Sparrow Hawks before one makes her his woman! In my father's village, she can marry a warrior who walks as we walk, who will not treat her like a…"

Her brothers understood little of their sister's reasoning, but they saw plainly she had hit her mark. Though Last Woman resolutely shook her head at first, while she listened, her eyes began to brighten. "Yes—no. Not me. I will not leave you now, but Little Blackfoot Woman…."
"Your daughter?"

"Yes," she answered, though she had trouble meeting Straight Arrows' questioning gaze. "I want better for her than to marry a Sparrow Hawk. They swap women as if they were trinkets. You will take her?"

Neither brother desired such a hindrance, much less to rob a mother of her daughter, but almost against his will—and certainly against Pretty Face's—Straight Arrows heard himself consenting. The Blackfoot obviously hated to part with her daughter as ardently as she wanted the child to go. Her eyes were as full of sorrow as they were pleading; and though he did not fully comprehend what lay behind her request, how could he refuse this small favor for one willing to bear his sister's pain?

Allow the little children to come to Me, and do not hinder them; for the realm of God belongs to ones like these.

Luke 18:16

Chapter 12

ONCE PRETTY FACE NODDED in agreement, the two women ran to the village. "Little Blackfoot," her mother called when she spotted her daughter playing in the snow. "Come! Quickly! Go to Hunts-For-Death's lodge and slip the new dress I sewed for you on top of the one you are wearing and trade this buffalo robe for the larger one laying on our bed—and bring your doll."

"Why, mother?" asked the little girl, frowning up into Last Woman's agitated face.

"No time for questions. Do as I say—and tell no one!"

Little Blackfoot complied, returning shortly after Kept-Us-Alive retrieved a small pouch of pemmican.

"For your journey, little one," she said, tying the pouch to the little girl's belt, but when she saw the child's puzzled face, she realized Last Woman had not yet told her.

"We are going?"

"Sh-sh!" shushed her mother. "Not now. I will tell you all once we cross the river."

The little girl complied readily, but after they had crossed to the other side, she tugged on her mother's skirt.

"Where are your things, and where is my brother?"

Squatting down, Last Woman cupped her little daughter's face in her hands, glancing from her to Kept-Us-Alive. "Do you remember the stories our friend has told us of her family?" Little Blackfoot nodded.

"You are going to visit them."

"But…but…who…" stammered the little girl, growing silent when Straight Arrows and Pretty Face stepped out from behind a large trunk.

"These are her brothers," said her mother, pulling the girl into her arms. She could not bear to watch the doubt and fear rising in her daughter's eyes.

"Last Son thought they were angels, and like angels, they will care for you."

"But…what about you?"

Last Woman felt the child trembling. "You love Kept-Us-Alive. You will love her mother. She will care for you as I do."

"When will I come home?"

"Their village will be your new home, just as this one became ours when…"

"But…but…I do not want a new home. I want you!"

"I know, my daughter," she murmured, pressing the small head more firmly against her chest. "And I want you, but I do not want this life for you. Do you remember how we had to rescue Kept-Us-Alive from her husband's cousin?"

She felt the little girl nod.

"Do you remember how terror-stricken she felt?" Again, the child nodded.

"I wish to keep this terror from touching you. Few summers will pass before you become a woman. Our friend's father will adopt you as his own and see that you marry a different kind of warrior, a warrior like these sons of his, who run after I-Am-Savior's shadow. Now stop crying; do you want them to think you are afraid?" Tightly tucking her warmest robe around her daughter's slim shoulders, Last Woman led her the few steps to Straight Arrows. "How can I deny you such a happy prospect? Perhaps the Creator will make a way for us to come to you."

Even as she said the words, she knew they were hollow. She would gladly go with Last Son's angels were it not for her friend. Three times Kept-Us-Alive had saved her. First, she told Pacing Wolf of Little Blackfoot, restoring her daughter and mending both their breaking hearts. Second, she introduced her to I-Am-Savior, who saved her soul from sin and death. Lastly, after the pox, she nursed her and Last Son back to health. How could she leave now—when Kept-Us-Alive needed her most?

Straight Arrows lifted Little Blackfoot, dusting the snow from her high moccasins while he promised to convey her and his sister's love to his family, and then he and Pretty Face said their farewells. Leaving behind their water-sacks, the women followed closely, but when the party mounted their ponies and began the descent from The-Cliffs-That-Have-No-Name, neither dared to go further. Someone—particularly their tiny sons—might notice they were missing and prematurely raise an alarm. In longing silence, they watched Little Blackfoot gazing back at them, a look of sad resignation clouding her small features; but not until a bend in the road concealed each from the other's view did Last Woman freely pour out her agony.

Kept-Us-Alive exhaled deeply, not only feeling the loss of Little Blackfoot but also remembering the horrid moment she helplessly watched her men-folk disappear across the Muddy River. "Why must life be so full of parting? I am weary of saying good-bye. I look forward to heaven, where we will never need to part with a loved one again."

When at last they retrieved their water-sacks, their hearts felt far heavier than the loads they were carrying. They agreed to go about their other chores as they did between any other sun's waking and sleeping. Last Woman soaked pieces of dried meat in heated fat, and Kept-Us-Alive returned to her mending. Only when the sun began to drift behind the pines did they become a flurry of activity. They began trotting from cook-fire to cook-fire, asking clanswomen if they had seen Last Woman's daughter. Many shook their heads, some shrugged; but not until they had combed nearly every foot-length of the Many Lodges' side of the village, did a few clanswomen or their husbands begin asking questions.

"Where did you see the child last?"

"She was with us while we were by the river and then went up the far path."

"Why did you not call for her to come back?"

"She often wanders, looking for cones that have fallen," her mother answered truthfully. "Now that The Shamer is dead, we possessed little cause to worry."

THE NEXT MORNING, BEFORE word Little Blackfoot was missing had spread like a contagion to the other side of the village, Kept-Us-Alive left her son with Hopping Owl and set out to discover where Never-Sits, her sister-in-law, had erected Mountainside's lodge. She was sure to find Jackrabbit's home beside it. She did.

"I wish to come in," she called, looking up as a frosty droplet landed on her nose.

Among-the-Pines response was immediate. Thrusting back the door-flap, she sputtered, "Mother! Is Father...is Father home?"

"No," confessed Kept-Us-Alive, trying hard to stomp down her emotions as she stomped off the snow. Stepping through the opening, she squatted to look directly into the girl's almond-shaped eyes. "He left when the leaves had just fallen; now the branches that held them are popping with breaking ice. I fear....I fear Falling Bear was..."

Among-the-Pines cast her eyes to the floor. "Grandmother told me I was foolish to hope.'"

"Hoping is *not* foolish," her stepmother corrected, warmly cradling the crumpling little face in her hands. "But God does not...does not always... *grant*...us our hopes."

Hearing the catch in her voice, Among-the-Pines lifted her gaze and each—possessed by the same thought—began gently wiping an escaping tear from the other. "I have missed you, Mother," the little girl whispered. "Where is Grandmother? She will be angry to find you here."

"I have missed you, too, my little one," rasped Kept-Us-Alive, pulling the girl against her. "But do not worry about Jackrabbit. She is by the river with your aunt. They will be a while. They were talking far more than scooping up clean snow and water."

Among-the-Pines nodded against her stepmother's chest, content to remain within the comfort of her arms.

"I have come for a few other reasons and know the first will tear at your heart. Little Blackfoot has gone away."

Among-the-Pines raised her head. "Gone? Where?"

All the while Kept-Us-Alive had weaved through the lodges she had been anticipating these very questions and debating how to answer. She did not want to cause her stepdaughter unnecessary pain, but if she divulged the truth, the child might let it slip and endanger her brothers—or worse. Who knew how Hunts-For-Death might react? Though he cared nothing for Little Blackfoot, he cared deeply for his honor; and if her brothers' stealthy incursion wounded their Fox soldiers' pride, as Real Chief he might feel bound to raise a large war party against her whole village.

"Do you remember the angels Last Son saw—the ones he said were watching over him from the stand of pines?" Among-the-Pines nodded. "They took her to a new home where she will be safe and very happy."

The girl snuggled even closer, laying her head back against her stepmother's chest, and Kept-Us-Alive did not budge her. The child had endured continual losses.

"Where? Can I go too?"

"Perhaps one day," her stepmother whispered. "But for now, I need you to stay here with your grandmother. Look! I was going through my mending and found this."

As curiosity compelled the little girl to lift her head, Kept-Us-Alive held out a bundle she had earlier set aside and unrolled a small blouse adorned with elk-teeth along the collar and hem.

Among-the-Pines' eyes glistened. "It is beautiful. I thought I would have nothing that fit to wear this summer. Grandmother no longer possesses good eyes. See—my shirt is coming apart."

"I am surprised you have not mended that," answered Kept-Us-Alive, examining the splitting seam. "Your stitches hold well."

"It is too tight," replied her stepdaughter. "I am afraid I will make it tighter."

"Get me a needle."

Immediately, Among-the-Pines began rummaging through Jackrabbit's mending bag, but once she armed her stepmother with the desired tool, both began to frown: the sheepskin was tearing along the edges. Asking for a scrap, Kept-Us-Alive began shaping it to look like a tiny pocket and guided the little girl in both the placement and sturdiness of stitches.

Just as they finished it off, the lodge flap opened. "What are you doing?" demanded Jackrabbit, seeing the child cuddled against the captive she hated. "Mending a seam," replied her granddaughter, pointing to the patch. "Now the wind will not whistle through the hole and make my ribs cold."

Jackrabbit looked like she could not decide how to react: pleased that her granddaughter's clothing would no longer cause her shame or angry to find an intruder. "Why are you here? Have you not harmed my family enough?"

"I brought your granddaughter a blouse left with my clothing," answered Kept-Us-Alive. She did not mention she had made it, afraid if she did, Jackrabbit might toss it away. "But for one so young, she forms excellent stitches. She wanted to surprise you by mending her blouse herself."

"Pshaw!" sneered the older woman, pulling Among-the-Pines by the arm to shove her behind her back. "I do not need you to tell me about my own granddaughter. You would not be here if your people were not evil!"

"I am truly sorry for all The Shamer of Our Women did," Kept-Us-Alive admitted. "But he was not of my men-folk."

"Not your kinsman, perhaps, but the warrior you desired!"

Kept-Us-Alive shook her head. "He was not. His mother grew up in my grandfather's village, so I knew his family, but I wanted none of his attention. I feared and avoided him."

Ignoring what the younger woman said, Jackrabbit examined the neat, regular stitches of the pocket-patch. "She is just like her mother. My daughter was the choicest of any of the untouched women in the village when Pacing Wolf begged my husband to have her. All of our warriors, from the most valiant Good Men to the lowliest youths, coveted her notice—and with Among-the-Pines, it will be the same."

Kept-Us-Alive listened politely, surprised Jackrabbit spoke so freely of her dead, but she did not answer. Long ago, she had surmised Among-the-Pines looked like her mother—she certainly did not look like Pacing Wolf— but she was sure Jackrabbit exaggerated. She could not imagine Pacing Wolf begging for anything, let alone a woman. Still, she would accomplish nothing by disputing what the older woman said.

"Were it not for Pacing Wolf," Kept-Us-Alive ventured, "Wild Dog would have done the same to me as he did to…to your eldest. He related these intentions to his cousins. Can you not separate me from his misdeed?"

"You did not do *his* deeds, but you have done other things."

"Then I ask you to forgive me. I never intended to hurt you or even to replace the daughter your heart longs after."

"You *stole* the heart of her husband away! It should have belonged to my daughter forever, just as my heart belongs to her dead father! And even with this, you were not satisfied—you have snatched the heart of my grandchild!"

"I did not steal them; the Creator gave them to me as gifts. Who can argue with what He does?"

"Your tongue babbles foolishness."

Assuming her grandmother thought the words foolish simply because she had not understood them, Among-the-Pines enunciated more clearly and louder, "She means my father and I are gifts to her from the Creator—and she was His gift to us."

"Stop shouting—I am not deaf! Your dead father, not the Creator, thrust her upon you!"

"The Creator brought her to us so we could understand what He is like. Since she places her feet where He places His, He is shaping her heart to look like His own. Father told me!"

"Your father was very foolish!"

"My father was right! My stepmother has treated me kindly though I was cruel and heaped much sorrow into her lap. And she did not snatch my father's heart—he gave it to her willingly." The little girl cupped her hands together as if they surrounded something precious that her grandmother could not see. "He knew she would hold it safe."

"Pshaw! These are senseless notions from her white man's book."

Among-the-Pines shook her head. "I did not hear this from her book, Grandmother. I found it here." She patted her chest. "Inside me."

Unable to argue, Jackrabbit fell silent, a deep frown furrowing the creases around her mouth.

"The Creator wrote the book for *us!*" her granddaughter continued. "Do you not remember, Grandmother, the old stories you have told me? The white man stole the Creator's book and left us a bow. Her mother brought His Book back."

As Kept-Us-Alive listened, she was grateful neither required her to speak. The lump that had formed in her throat would not allow it; but when her stepdaughter grew quiet, she became freshly aware that Jackrabbit was eying her. She lifted her gaze, steeling herself for another harsh lash of the woman's tongue, but instead of a glare, she found only confusion.

"Before summer arrives, may I help you with your sewing and mending?" she offered. "Your granddaughter is growing."

Jackrabbit only grunted, but eyeing her granddaughter's worn skirt and blouse, she begrudgingly nodded. "And I will ask Pretty Crow Woman to help when she arrives. No woman possesses greater skill."

Kept-Us-Alive doubted both this and Pretty Crow Woman's willingness to help, but instead of voicing her thoughts, she smiled. "I would like to know her better."

Among-the-Pines crinkled her forehead. "She tried to hurt you! Father told you to stay far from her."

"She is your close family," answered her stepmother, running her fingers affectionately down one of the little girl's braids. Afraid if she stayed longer, Jackrabbit might change her mind, she offered both a friendly farewell and slipped out to search for Last Woman.

"Has Hunts-For-Death noticed Little Blackfoot is missing?" she asked once she had found her.

"Not until he heard me wailing," smiled her tall friend.

"Was that hard—pretending?"

Last Woman's smile fell flat. "I was not pretending. My heart feels like a vacant cave. I do not know if I can do this. I long to go after her."

Kept-Us-Alive did not know what to say. Although she admired Last Woman's decision and knew the child would find much love, she doubted she could let Wolf-Who-Lays-Down go for any reason. "Has Hunts-For-Death raised a search party?"

The Blackfoot shrugged. "He cares nothing for my daughter, though his older wife whined about the fewer number of sticks gathered for her fire. To them, Little Blackfoot was another dog, chasing away mice and waiting for a spare morsel."

"And the others?"

"What is a Blackfoot girl to them? Besides, they are afraid."

"Of what?"

The tall Blackfoot's eyes began to twinkle. "Last Son's warrior-angels."

"You told them this?"

"No, but I told Last Son, knowing they would ask him. She *did* leave with his *angels*."

Kept-Us-Alive chuckled. "That was what I told Among-the-Pines. Did they believe him?"

"These Sparrow Hawks are no different from any other People," Last Woman shrugged. "They place a high value on visions, but Last Son could not tell them which direction the angels traveled. Only Bites-With-Dog and Held-Back-the-Enemy took the trouble to search for her; but we alerted them too late last night to follow the *angels'* trail, and—as you see—the Lord made the sky drop fresh snow while we slept. It covered every track."

If your enemy is hungry, offer him something to eat. If he is thirsty, offer him a drink.

Proverbs 25:21

Chapter 13

AS THE MOON began to wax larger, Kept-Us-Alive once again wound through the many lodges that lay between Mountainside's home and the lodge she now shared with Hopping Owl and Bites-With-Dog. Her heart was full of wonder. Among-the-Pines and she had spent the afternoon repairing poorly stitched seams in Jackrabbit's clothing, talking of everything from the break in the unusually heavy snows to special stitches, weaving knots, and the wondrous Creator.

She could barely believe the door flap He-Who-Knows-All-Things had opened between her and the older woman, an opening for which she had prayed for several years but without much faith. She had feared Jackrabbit would be like Talks-With-Bitterness and her daughter, Swallow Woman, both of whom her mother had once hoped to lead toward I-Am-Savior.

Smiling to herself, she thought, *Isaiah described the Creator well: He has His own ways.*[15] *At least one thing good may have come from her taking Among-the-Pines, which Pacing Wolf would never have allowed. Lord, please forgive me for being so slow of heart and faith. I know You hear and see all things and arrange them together for our good.*[16]

I miss my husband so much, but I see that I had again begun doing what my old Aunt Quiet Woman warned me against: placing my confidence in him instead of You for our food and shelter, safety and security—even happiness. As I look inside my heart, I feel so disappointed. Will my heart never be faithful? It crept from You with the smallest of steps, like the slow, silent creeping of an enemy.

"Mama, Mama! Where were you?" asked a bouncing, black-haired pouch-full of life.

"With your sister." Kept-Us-Alive bent down so Wolf-Who-Lays-Down could reach around her neck and scooped him up with one arm. "We were mending some old clothes, and I took her a skirt I have been sewing for her to wear with the blouse I had made."

The tiny boy grinned "Why?"

"So she can wear them as the red grasses begin to sprout."

"Why?"

"Because I love her."

"Why?"

"For the same reason I love you. You are Pacing Wolf's son—and mine!"

At once, his bright, teasing eyes filled with clouds. "When will Father come home?"

"I do not know."

The tiny boy drew his lips and brows down sharply. "Falling Bear says Father dead. He not come back, I never see him."

Kept-Us-Alive's heart dropped. Although each rising sun further convinced her he would not, she did not know how to explain death to one so young. "We will see him—he will live forever—but the Creator may have taken him to the Mystery Land."

"Where?"

"To the place I-Am-Savior dwells."

"Why?"

"I do not know," Kept-Us-Alive murmured, caressing the boy's smooth, shining hair. "The Creator knows what will happen tomorrow, and this summer, and all the summers of your life. He planned them before you were born, while He was weaving you together inside of me.[17] I do not know where your father is now, but I know one thing."

"What?"

"The Creator loves him—and us."

"How can you know this?" asked an aged voice behind her shoulder. She immediately recognized it as White Moccasins', one of Pacing Wolf's eldest and kindest clanswomen and, without question, her favorite.

"Because I know Him," answered Kept-Us-Alive. "I know His nature just as I...knew...my husband's. The Creator's heart is good. He would never do anything to harm my...my dead's children or me. We are His."

"What do you mean, you 'are His'?" asked the old woman.

"He adopted me into His family, just as Bites-With-Dog adopted me as a daughter, though I used to be His enemy."

"Whose enemy?" asked White Moccasins. "Bites-With-Dog's?"

"At one time: before I came to the Cliffs-That-Have-No-Name, but I meant He-Who-Sees-All-Things. I did not want Him; I wanted my own path."

The aged brow wrinkled deeply. "The Creator expects no different."

"No, because He knows all. But if I had been carrying Wolf-Who-Lays-Down on my back when I came to the Many Lodges, would he have been your dead clan-leader's son or the son of your enemy?"

"The son of my enemy, but my dead clan-leader would have soon made him his own."

"How?"

"He was a good and patient warrior. He would have taken Wolf-Who-Lays-Down with him as he tended his herd and shown him how to string a bow or ride a pony. He would have allowed the boy to become familiar with his ways."

"And if Wolf-Who-Lays-Down only ran from him?"

"If you wore him on your back, as you said, he would have been a small-thing—still in his cradleboard."

"But if Wolf-Who-Lays-Down refused to obey him as he grew into a boy and then became a youth—if he walked the other way when he saw your dead clan-leader approaching or threw rocks at his head?"

"No warrior could desire such a son. Our clan would take up sticks and drive him out."

Kept-Us-Alive smiled and nodded. "This is how I once was to the Creator, but instead of driving me away, His own Son, I-Am-Savior, took my punishment."

The old woman peered hard at Kept-Us-Alive. She knew her well, had thought highly of her from the first moment they met, and had been happy to welcome her into her sewing guild. No one could find a kinder, more loyal or considerate woman among all the Many Lodges, nor among the Kicked-in-the-Bellies or the Whistle-Water clans, but this talk she was making seemed like nonsense or mad ravings. As she shook her head, concluding grief had driven her young friend's mind away, she began thinking of Kills-Behind-Her-Dwelling, Pacing Wolf's dead grandmother. The old woman, who had loved Kept-Us-Alive dearly, had also spoken of this I-Am-Savior. She had held Him in great respect.

Watching the crease between White Moccasins' brows grow even deeper, Kept-Us-Alive sought a way to make herself clearer. "You asked me how I knew what I told Wolf-Who-Lays-Down is true. When you described how my...how your dead clan leader would have treated him, you described what the Creator has done for me. He has shown me His nature, shown me that I can trust Him with my troubles—even those I think are beneath His notice—and taught me how much better His path is than the path that led to the village of His enemy."

"What enemy?"

"A trickster spirit who pretends he possesses the sun's light and beauty. He pretends his path leads to plentiful game and water, but he is the Real Chief of a poor, dark village."

The ancient shoulders lifted slightly as White Moccasins shook her head. "I do not understand your talk," she admitted, "but you have always been my favorite of all my clansmen's wives and were very good to the dead."

Kept-Us-Alive smiled, as much at her memories of Kills-Behind-Her-Dwelling as White Moccasins' kind words; but in that instant, the old clanswoman yanked her arm, pulling her and her son off the path.

As Kept-Us-Alive turned, she saw the village crier hastily riding toward them.

"Go!" he shouted. "Go to your lodges. Pull them down. We break camp!"

Both women understood they must respond immediately. Trotting back to Bites-With-Dog's lodge, Kept-Us-Alive packed her few belongings and helped Hopping Owl unpin the lodge skins and pull them from their tall, conical frame. She noticed her new brother left as soon as he saw her, but before she finished pondering the suddenness of his departure, he returned with three snow-dusted horses. One was the white mare Pacing Wolf had given her, the wooden saddle he had carved tossed across its back; the two others were for his mother's use.

What became of him afterward, she could not say. She grew absorbed in both maneuvering and keeping his mother's mount in place while Hopping Owl hung their lodge-poles between this first horse and the one that would follow. Craning her neck all about to locate Wolf-Who-Lays-Down, she finally spotted him astride her new brother's shoulders.

"Has Bites-With-Dog told you why we are moving?" she asked her adopted mother.

Hopping Owl motioned toward the river with her chin. "It is too narrow and shallow. Already it is almost frozen and the ice will soon be too thick to break through. We will travel toward its mother. Like all older women, the years have made her deeper and wider. She will be less likely to harden over as she eats the bitter cold."

As Kept-Us-Alive considered the comparison, she was not sure she thought it accurate. She knew women who were forgiving in youth who grew even more so as they aged, but the bitter ones had grown harder, not more yielding. She had read something like this in The Book, something about reaping the sort of seed you sowed: tobacco seeds producing tobacco and cherry pits producing cherry trees.[18] Before she could recall the verse exactly, however, Last Woman drew up beside her.

"He squirms often?" she asked, gazing down at the large mound Kept-Us-Alive was caressing.

"No. I have been so busy, my constant moving has lulled him to sleep."

"You must be careful. Travel slowly, and if your pains begin before we reach our new camp, drift toward the back and drop behind. Hopping Owl can take Wolf-Who-Lays-Down."

"I dare not. The soldiers will beat me or maim my mare."

"When do you expect him to come out?"

On her fingertips, Kept-Us-Alive counted off the moons since her last stay inside the Women's Lodge. "The Moon When Buffalo Drop Their Calves."

Last Woman raised her brows and slowly shook her head. "We will meet him sooner than that, I am guessing he will come during The Moon When Buds Begin to Form; and by the Moon When Water Fowl Return, that warrior will ask you to be his woman."

Kept-Us-Alive's head shot up. "Who?"

Last Woman nodded toward a young Sparrow Hawk walking in their direction.

"Held-Back-the-Enemy?" Kept-Us-Alive quickly glanced around, afraid his mother might have overheard and felt relieved to spot her talking with her cousin. "He regards me as a sister—nothing more."

Her tall friend cast her a dubious look while helping her climb into the beautifully carved saddle, but since the young Sparrow Hawk had sauntered up within earshot, both dropped the matter. He lifted his tiny charge off his shoulders, silently set him down in front of his mother, and then disappeared into the amassing Many Lodges.

"He has been as attentive to you and your son," reasoned Kept-Us-Alive, "as he is to me and mine."

"When?"

"Did you not see him holding the reins of Last Son's pony and making sure his load is secure?"

"Yes," answered Last Woman, once she had swung her leg over her own mount. "But where was I?"

Kept-Us-Alive narrowed her eyes. "Here—with me—a moment ago."

"Um-hm."

Kept-Us-Alive took the hint and looked as if she might argue, but instead, she fell silent and urged her mare toward the line of waiting women. "I was afraid you meant Bull-Will-Not-Fall," she confided once her friend had drawn up beside her. "Since Hunts-For-Death declared Pacing Wolf dead, he has paid me an uncomfortable amount of attention. Held-Back-the-Enemy is polite, nothing more. See—he has taken his place with the Lumpwoods' Good Young Men."

"You are the one who will soon see. If the path becomes slick or a pass narrow, he will be by your side, making sure you do not plummet into a valley."

"There is much sadness about you today," observed Kept-Us-Alive, wishing to change the subject. "Are you concerned for Little Blackfoot?"

Her tall friend nodded. "How can she find us if she returns? She will go to The-Cliffs-That-Have-No-Name, but we will not be there."

Kept-Us-Alive breathed slowly, praying for words that might offer any comfort. "She will not return. You told her what you want from her, and she will obey you. My mother and father will welcome her into their home as a replacement for the daughter they lost, and my brothers will watch over her as if she were me—turning away all unsuitable warriors."

As she saw the corners of Last Woman's mouth lift slightly, she introduced more pleasant musings. "Straight Arrows startled me—I thought he was my father."

"You were relieved or disappointed?"

"Both. I love my brother, but I also love my father. Straight Arrows always resembled him, but he has grown to look like my father's reflection."

"How many summers does he own?"

"Shortly I will possess eighteen, so he must own twenty-four—older than my father was when he took my mother. I wonder if he has married. I did not think to ask."

"In my village, many mothers would push their daughters into such a warrior's path."

Kept-Us-Alive shot her friend a grin. "You think he is handsome!"

Last Woman shrugged. "A warrior's looks and trophies matter little to me. Most handsome faces hide proud hearts."

"Then why has your neck become the color of a woodpecker's topknot?"

The Blackfoot's lips began twitching upward, waging a battle with her will. "He had kind eyes," she finally confessed. "Even when they held pain—I kicked him hard—they also held patience. I have often imagined this look in the eyes of I-Am-Savior."

While Kept-Us-Alive broke into a pleased smile, Last Woman's expression grew so like one belonging to the wooly herd animals that roamed the mountains, she pressed her no further. "You have understood him well. I spent more time following Pretty Face—he possesses fewer summers—but even as a little girl, Straight Arrows was the brother I ran to when I was hurt. Pretty Face only pointed out what I had done to invite the trouble."

BROUGHT-US-THE-BOOK scolded herself as she ran to meet her sons. *I have lived among The People for decades. Will I ever learn to tamp down my impulses?*

Forcing herself to slow her pace, she conformed to the pattern of her mother-in-law's restrained, regal strides until the sight of Straight Arrows brought her to a sudden halt. Either her first-born had gained a great amount of weight during the scant half-moon since she had seen him or something lay bundled within the folds of his buffalo robe. Drawing nearer, she saw the head of a little girl dozing against his hunting shirt, her chapped, drooling lips creating a damp spot.

"Who is this?" she whispered, unwilling to scare the child by waking her from so deep a slumber.

"Your new daughter," smiled her eldest, glancing beyond his mother to include his approaching father.

Preying Eagle swiftly crossed the distance between them, his strong warm arms gently receiving the sleepy little bundle Straight Arrows lowered down. While she groggily began opening her lids, he wondered if this was how Wooden Legs had felt when he had first gazed at Hides-In-Shadows' white, freckled cheeks.

Alarm quickly flitted over the child's small features, but as he tilted her up to see his woman, she grew calm. Shyly smiling, she reached slender fingertips toward Brought-Us-The-Book's blue-green eyes.

"Where did you find her?"

"Beyond the Muddy River," answered Straight Arrows, pinning Pretty Face with a warning glance. "She is Blackfoot. An enemy attacked her people."

When sadness darkened the child's eyes, Brought-Us-The-Book offered her a reassuring stroke. "You are welcome here, little one," she cooed, thinking no further of the child's origins. The event was far too common to arouse any notice. "What do they call you?"

"Little Blackfoot Woman."

"Come. We will make you a pallet in my dwelling and find some salve for your dry lips."

Preying Eagle sat the girl upright in his arms, but instead of attempting to place her down, he carried her behind his woman and indicated with his head that his sons should follow.

The Lord said, "Surely, just as I have intended so it has happened, and just as I have planned so it will stand."

Isaiah 14:24

Chapter 14

AS THE SUN BEGAN WANING, the Many Lodges pulled to a halt, scrambled off their mounts, and began lining up in single file. The snows had lasted nearly a moon, freezing the ground beneath the tall drifts, and Hunts-For-Death proposed a trail fraught with risk: across iced-over water to a less difficult way through the forest.

Just as Last Woman had predicted, Held-Back-the-Enemy seemed to spring from the earth when the two friends most needed him. He guided each of their horses, one after the other, across the solid river, steadily soothing both mount and rider whenever either became nervous.

Once they gained the other side, Kept-Us-Alive felt truly grateful as he lifted her son, set him on a sturdy branch of a leafless tree, and then slipped his hands firmly under her arms. She had grown frightened during the crossing and felt unsure she could have relaxed her grip on her mare's rope without his help. While she leaned into his grasp, she peered into gleaming black eyes and noticed, for the first time, their surrounding creases.

Held-Back-the-Enemy stood barely taller than Last Woman, allowing Kept-Us-Alive to continue the perusal of his face even when he set her on her feet; and what she found there took her by surprise. His expression held the unmistakable confidence of a warrior. While Pacing Wolf had considered becoming his Lumpwood sponsor, he had regaled her with stories of the young man's prowess; but until that very moment, she had not paid enough attention to recognize his changes in appearance. She was glad when Wolf-Who-Lays-Down's chattering drew away his eyes.

"You see?" asked Last Woman, interrupting her thoughts. "Already, he takes charge—not only of you but of your son. He is a Good Young Man, well respected among his clansmen and able to support a wife."

Kept-Us-Alive slid her friend an uncertain glance, but her forehead wrinkled as she watched her son toddling after Held-Back-the-Enemy's retreating form. Wolf-Who-Lays-Down had begun following him around as he used to follow his father.

"Why do you refuse to consider what is so plain to all the Many Lodges?

Betrothal to him would protect you from war-society rivals who might pull you from Bites-With-Dog's lodge when everything greens."

Kept-Us-Alive chewed on the possibility for a while before answering. "I cannot promise myself to anyone until I am certain Pacing Wolf is...is gone."

Last Woman's eyebrow darted up. "Women do little choosing. Do you think I wished to warm Old Hair-Up-Top's robes?"

"No, but that is not the same. When Pacing Wolf gave you to him, you knew your Blackfoot husband was dead. His hair hung from Short Neck's lance."

"What of the quiet old aunt you described to me—the one who your old uncle found hiding after a battle—did she learn what happened to her husband?"

Kept-Us-Alive shook her head, pressing her lips closed tightly.

"And now she is safe and happy—even glad he took her."

"That too is different. My uncle found her after our warriors had defeated her people. She could not have imagined her husband was alive."

"And you have reasons to think yours is? What could keep him away for two moons from all he loves?"

Kept-Us-Alive looked away, unable to reply. *Last Woman is correct,* she decided, *and I fear the way Bull-Will-Not-Fall watches me.*

As the two mothers and their sons approached the spot Bites-With-Dog had chosen for his lodge, Hopping Owl smiled broadly.

"You will soon have joy: he is almost here!"

Kept-Us-Alive's heart nearly leaped through her chest. *Pacing Wolf!* she thought. *A scout has spotted him?* Glancing beyond Hopping Owl's shoulder, she saw no one but Held-Back-the-Enemy, grinning down at her laughing son. Many Lumpwood and Muddy Hand warriors were milling near the center of their hastily tossed up camp, but she could not pick out a recently arrived scout or messenger.

While Held-Back-the-Enemy grasped her mount's loosely hanging rope, his mother spread her fingers across Kept-Us-Alive's growing belly. "See!" She laid the edge of her hand against her adopted daughter's lowest rib. "He was up here when you came to us. He has dropped down, in front of your hips. If he delays long, he will be larger than his brother was. When do you expect him to greet us?"

Kept-Us-Alive felt as if her mount had fallen out from under her. *My small-thing—she was speaking of him.* When she did not immediately answer, Hopping Owl looked at her Blackfoot friend.

"The Moon When Buffalo Drop Their Calves," replied Last Woman, "but I do not think he will wait that long. He sleeps much and, as you say, has already begun to drop low—and see how she reaches around to rub the small of her back?"

"The journey has made me ache."

Hopping Owl cast her a doubtful look. "When we are finished, go inside and rest. I will haul our water-sacks and gather our evening wood."

AS KEPT-US-ALIVE lay upon her pallet, her thoughts drifted from her earlier disappointment to her conversation with Last Woman. Held-Back-the-Enemy was more considerate than most Good Young Men and less harsh by nature than Pacing Wolf. No one questioned his desirability as a husband; at least no one who had ever given him thought. Just last evening, she had watched a group of untouched women posturing or blushing as he walked by, but they were as young as her cousin, Smiling Girl, back home.

Smiling Girl is no younger than I am! she realized. Of course, she had always known her cousin's age, they grew up beside each other, but she felt as though she had outstripped her cousin by many seasons.

Perhaps because I have been married nearly three summers, have one small-thing and carry another—or perhaps Pacing Wolf makes Held-Back-the-Enemy seem young. He possesses nearly ten more summers than I do; surely, Held-Back-the-Enemy possesses no more than two.

As she considered the Sparrow Hawk's New Staff Ceremonies, she admitted a betrothal might offer safety. *But Held-Back-the-Enemy could marry any untouched woman among the Sparrow Hawk clans,* she reasoned. *Why should he choose the daughter of an enemy—a woman who has already belonged to a man and brings additional mouths to feed?*

"I am hunter!" cried Wolf-Who-Lays-Down, bursting into the lodge with Last Son. "I shoot a rabbit!"

The boy proudly held up his bloody prey, but Among-the-Pines, who had followed them inside, rolled her eyes toward the smoke hole. "Held-Back-the-Enemy held him as he aimed," she explained.

"I shoot!"

"With his fingers covering yours!"

"It is a first step," smiled Kept-Us-Alive. "Now who is going to clean it?"

Wolf-Who-Lays-Down began bouncing on his toes. "Among-the-Pines! She cleans—I am brother!"

Groaning deeply, Among-the-Pines looked at her stepmother, hoping she might contradict him.

"Alright," Kept-Us-Alive answered. "Your sister and I will skin him together, but let us all go outside or we may spoil Hopping Owl's best buffalo robes." Taking the limp animal out of her son's tiny, warm hand, she slipped into the chilly sunshine.

"I wish Held-Back-the-Enemy was my father," confided Last Son. "Hunts-For-Death never sees me. He walks past."

Kept-Us-Alive began sharpening her knife. "Does your mother wish this?"

Last Son shrugged his thin shoulders. "Hunts-For-Death passes her also."

"They are not married," explained Kept-Us-Alive. "He cares for her as Bites-With-Dog cares for me—like a father, not a husband, and he has much to consider. He leads our whole band."

"I wish Held-Back-the-Enemy wanted my mother."

"He possesses one less summer than she does."

"So?" Last Son tilted his head. "I will marry Among-the-Pines. She is older."

"You will?" smiled the girl's stepmother, glancing up to see her daughter's reaction. "Then you must improve your manners. It is not polite to use someone's name while they are present."

"Ugh!" groaned Wolf-Who-Lays-Down. "Why her?"

"Many warriors will want her when she is old enough," answered his mother. "She is kind, skilled, and very lovely to look upon."

"She pushes me," Wolf-Who-Lays-Down retorted. "I take woman like you. Cook, wash clothes, smile, dress me."

Kept-Us-Alive chuckled, thinking his description came close to one many warriors held. "Then you must distinguish yourself. No woman will marry a man until he proves he can protect and provide for her."

"I hunter now!" he answered, shooting with an imaginary bow and arrow.

"Me too!" added Last Son. "I am a hunter."

Kept-Us-Alive smiled broadly, remembering she had yet to clean her son's rabbit. She had little doubt both would distinguish themselves one day. *His father will teach...*

Too late, she realized Pacing Wolf would never again teach him anything, turning her thoughts back to Held-Back-the-Enemy. Though she thought highly of him, she would much rather he granted Last Son's wish. Even in death, Pacing Wolf firmly held her heart.

HUNTS-FOR-DEATH sat among his Lumpwood brothers in his newly erected lodge, exclaiming. "Make her stop! This book poisons our people!"

As stiffened thatches, some shiny and black, others dulled by gray, nodded in agreement, Bites-With-Dog shook his head. "Come to my lodge. Allow your heart to listen. See if the Creator does not call to you."

A wrinkled old man drew up his top lip. "I do not need this captive's *book*. It is like smallpox, taking one Good Man and touching another until the whole tribe bears its scars. The Creator calls to me when the sun rises with the wind from the lowland."

"I-Am-Savior brings healing," argued Braids-His-Tail, Otter Woman's husband. "Since I was a boy, my heart was torn by hatred and jealousy. Last moon, he made it whole again."

"No!" declared another. "This spirit-guide is a trickster. He tears our people in two. He is not content with leading some; He insists all must follow. We have worshipped He-Who-Sees-All-Things long before this captive began reading the markings on these leaves."

"We follow the ways of our fathers," exclaimed another.

"No more!" agreed Hunts-For-Death. "We will not stand by while an enemy weakens our people."

Bites-With-Dog rose from his place. "Kept-Us-Alive is not our enemy, and I-Am-Savior does not lie. I know Him just as I know you. He has created a clean heart within me—I will not cast Him aside or demand the others do so."

"Then take the Blackfoot and her children," commanded Hunts-For-Death, gesturing toward the woman offering him food from a wooden trencher. "I will keep her no longer."

THOUGH THE SUN shone brightly, Held-Back-the-Enemy shivered. The snow had added several days to his journey, and his hands felt stiff with cold. Climbing down from his black and white pony, he examined several frozen twigs that had snapped as a creature had brushed against them and then scanned the surrounding vegetation for signs of man.

Frost, sparkling in the sunshine, covered strands of a torn spider-web hanging from a sapling. The disrepair proclaimed it abandoned but did not account for the rupture. Following the web to a family of vines growing down the steep mountain, something struck him odd about their pattern. Instead of intertwining, they hung loosely like a warrior's wet scalp lock. When he laid a hand on them, he drew it back in surprise. He expected sloping earth, but there was nothing.

Tentatively stepping forward, he passed unhindered between the trailing stems. They dropped into place behind him, obliterating the sun so thoroughly he could no longer distinguish the nails on his calloused fingers. Backing out to look for something he could light: a long, thick twig or fallen branch—anything sturdy and dry—he hastily reconsidered his course. Ice had painted everything. He might enter the cave more easily from a high path above the Muddy River.

During the Moon of Changing Seasons, Pacing Wolf and he had entered there while scouting the area for signs of an enemy. Still, he hoped this way might reveal traces of his Lumpwood father that Falling Bear had missed. Sweeping the vines aside so the afternoon light could penetrate the emptiness behind them, he discovered what he half-expected: branches laid carefully inside, obscuring the way for unexpected intruders.

As his heart grew encouraged, Kept-Us-Alive sprang to mind, whispering sweetly to her white mare. He had been nearby when Pacing Wolf had given her the horse, but though he had withdrawn to the far side of the herd to allow them privacy, he still remembered the pleasant surprise in her voice. It had ridden on the breeze, offering him his first sharp taste of jealously.

As he wondered what she was doing, another image stepped from his memory: Last Woman calling to him in her musical foreign tongue. Her forehead was deeply furrowed, as it had been when she asked him to search for Little Blackfoot Woman, but instead of mentioning her daughter, she spoke frankly about Kept-Us-Alive.

"She cannot fully face what all of us see plainly," the Blackfoot had confided. "If you want to keep her from your Fox rivals, you must find a way to convince her he is dead."

While Held-Back-the-Enemy listened, he had noted the fine shape of her eyes and the lovely full lips that seemed, as she expressed her concerns, to be separate living things moving and curving so pliably beneath her rounded nose that he had to look away. He had never given her much thought. She was simply a Blackfoot Pacing Wolf had captured to warm old Hair-Up-Top on the evenings he awoke shaking; but during these past moons, he had been noticing her many valuable qualities. She was Kept-Us-Alive's constant companion, a faithful comforter when others turned away.

Grabbing branches from the pile of brush, he lit the longest and probed further inside the black entrance. Then, as the bough burned too near his hand, he lit another and another as he proceeded up the incline. The last, tossed into the darkness ahead of him, reflected warmly off stippled brown walls and landed on packed earth, assuring him he would not immediately fall down a precipice or stumble into a sleeping bear. It burned only briefly before leaving him immersed in utter blackness.

Shaking off panic, he felt along the rock ahead of him for unexpected gaps or turns; but though the way was steep and he had slowed his pace, he soon spied sunlight streaming down through a small crack in the high ceiling. He recognized it immediately, increasing his footfalls until he stood in the cave in which he and Pacing Wolf had camped.

As he glanced around, he saw signs of their last visit: a bundle of firewood, old buffalo robes laying to one side, and a bow Pacing Wolf had spent the evening shaping. Several other items had been left more recently: a collapsed tripod of half-burnt twigs, a hastily cast aside blanket similar to the one the hairy-lipped long-knife had kept rolled behind his saddle, and his Lumpwood father's decorated war-ax lodged deeply into a crevice. While pulling the weapon free, he dropped his eyes and saw the brown blotch on the blanket was not the woven pattern he expected but the dry remains of a wide pool of blood.

The sound of water trickling coaxed him to the spring, where he lifted cold handfuls to his mouth to slake his thirst. Though the light was dim, he noticed the area around him had been recklessly disturbed. Someone had wildly scattered pebbles as they hurriedly scuttled by, and a dark stain he had not noticed on his previous visit had dyed the run-off's narrow, moist throat. Swiping a finger across it, he touched it to his lips but tasted nothing. He did not need to; he already knew it was blood, but where were the Shamers' corpses?

Supposing an animal might have dragged them off, he searched for and spotted a confirming pattern in the softer earth and followed it up a corridor he recognized. The marks climbed sharply toward the cave's upper entrance, but as he reached the top, he lost them beneath the freshly melting snow.

Stepping into the bright light, Held-Back-the-Enemy laid aside the ax and allowed his eyes to adjust. Pines grew halfway over the entrance and out onto the cliff face, casting such shadows that he needed to sweep aside several branches to better view a tiny dark circle he spied. It had dropped onto the edge of a descent so severe that he knelt on all fours to approach it. No man could balance where it lay and maintain his footing. An old dropping from a bird, he suspected, rubbing his thumb across the small spot, but it felt perfectly flat.

Blood.

Backing up before standing, he noted something had stripped the nearest pine of many needles. He accounted for this easily—his Lumpwood father had likely shoved the enemy through them before tossing him over the cliff—but as Held-Back-the-Enemy peered over the ledge, he pinched his brows together sharply. Many needles farther out had been bent or haphazardly broken, damaged no doubt while the dead enemy hurtled toward the ground.

Rubbing his hairline with his fingers, he stared absently through the snow-sprinkled boughs, deciding where he might next look for his Lumpwood father until something unexpected caught his eye. Pierced through by a jagged, snapped branch a good distance below him was a piece of a well-cured hide, dyed an unmistakably familiar shade of green. He would not have seen it had the pine grown on the cliff's northern, less sun-washed side; and how it lodged there, he was hesitant to fathom.

His stomach lurched as he lowered his eyes toward the ground below and spotted the remains of a buckskin legging hanging a good leap above the snow. Though it appeared stained and stiff, he instantly recognized its red-painted stripes, each recording an enemy's stolen life, and the black strands of hair fluttering down one side. Kept-Us-Alive, who had cared well for her husband's clothing, would have her undeniable proof.

Grasping hold of a few icy pine boughs, he swung himself away from the cliff face and managed to land on the thickest limb within reach. He carefully positioned his moccasins on one branch after another, cautiously descending toward the pierced green hide; but the boughs closer to his goal had been so badly bent or broken that the several he gripped for balance gave way, nearly causing him to fall. Lowering himself beneath them, he braced the balls of his feet between two limbs closer to the trunk and, stretching up as far as he could reach, snatched the swath of hunting shirt and tucked it into his belt.

Glancing down at Pacing Wolf's legging, he considered how he might safely retrieve it. The twig that had caught it extended a precarious distance from the trunk or any other branches sufficient to support his weight. Pondering the possibility of reaching it from below, he gazed through the boughs above him. He could not climb back up. The tallest branches had held as he swung downward, but they were neither stiff nor strong enough for him to push off from them to reach the ledge.

The drop below was much too far to leap, and the boughs, though pliable, would chew him up on his descent. Worse yet, a sturdier limb might snag his clothing—as the broken one had snagged Pacing Wolf's—and helplessly suspend him until it or his garment gave way. Deciding to stay close to the trunk, he picked his way from branch to branch with such care that the sun threatened to hurry off to bed before he was low enough to drop to the ground.

He located the darkened legging once he had done so, leaped up to grip the branch from which it hung, and shimmied hand over hand until he could grab it. Once he dropped back to the ground, he examined the dark stain and saw it was exactly what he suspected; and the buckskin's stiffened shape announced its purpose. His Lumpwood father had used it to staunch a wound's flow.

Surveying the patchy snow below the trees, he looked for a spot where his sponsor might have fallen or a trail that announced a direction he had ventured. He knew in his gut that he would find nothing. Besides his own marks in the snow, he spotted only fox prints atop an icy rise and tiny squirrel paws racing up a trunk of a hickory.

The legging was more forthcoming: it proclaimed Pacing Wolf's wound had been deep. If he had survived the fall, he would have been easy prey for a passing animal; and if the noise of his plummet had not announced his location, the smell of his blood surely had. The thought made Held-Back-the-Enemy ill, let alone the prospect of informing Kept-Us-Alive how her husband had died.

Finding no other trail to his clan leader, he wended up the path to the cave and picked up the ax. The sun had been rapidly dropping behind the cliff, so Held-Back-the-Enemy retreated to the lodge-place, made a meager fire, and took the scrap of hunting shirt from his belt. As he carefully studied each marking, the color stole away all remaining doubt. It was a particular shade his Lumpwood father favored, and now that Kept-Us-Alive helped with his family's mending, he easily recognized her meticulous stitches. They were neat and clean, tiny and secure, and had earned her a reputation for this skill.

Pulling out the legging, he began turning it over until he again feared he might heave up the remains of his last meal. The buckskin had soaked up so much blood while it dried, it had conformed to the contours of its owner's leg.

At least, thought Held-Back-the-Enemy, he is now safely home with I-Am-Savior, forever enjoying the Mystery Land.

Create in me a clean heart, O Creator, and renew an upright spirit within me.

Psalm 51:10

Chapter 15

During the

Moon When Buds Begin to Open

"WOLF-WHO-LAYS-DOWN grasped Kept-Us-Alive's hand as they doused themselves with clean water in the shallow portion of the icy river. "Where is Held-Back-the-Enemy?"

"I do not know. Ask Hopping Owl. See—she is there, coming toward us."

As the tiny boy hid behind her leg, Kept-Us-Alive greeted her new mother; but she did not ask Wolf-Who-Lays-Down's question. He needed to learn to speak up for himself, and she was afraid of conveying too much interest in the woman's son. After they chatted cordially for a few moments, Hopping Owl went her way and Last Woman waded in to join them.

"Why did you not ask her?" Kept-Us-Alive whispered.

The tiny boy only rubbed his head against his mother's thigh and then tottered up the bank after Last Son, who had begun chasing a red bird flitting in the branches.

"Ask who?" replied Last Woman.

"Hopping Owl. Wolf-Who-Lays-Down wanted to know where Held-Back-the-Enemy is. The sun has risen and slept several times since we have seen him."

"Is this why your chin has been drooping toward the ground?"

Kept-Us-Alive shook her head. "No, but I am afraid you tire of the reason: I have been missing my husband—especially at night. When they were cold, he always welcomed my head against his shoulder and I quickly drifted into the deepest most enjoyable sleep."

Last Woman's lips dipped slightly downward. "I envy you this memory. My first husband was gruff. He did not welcome my affections unless he wanted to…to please himself. Old Hair-Up-Top wanted nothing from me but warmth, but he was bony and felt cold to touch."

Kept-Us-Alive's dark eyes softened, sad her friend had not known the sort of tenderness that she had so taken for granted.

"What?" asked Last Woman when Kept-Us-Alive sighed.

"Nothing. You have made me realize how ungrateful I have been. Each winter was as I said, but each summer I have struggled with the fear he no longer wanted me. He would shrug me off when I tried to lay against him, saying he was too warm. My father always wanted my mother near. Through summers and winters, he slept with one arm and leg atop her or she curled up against him."

"Perhaps that is why they have five children."

"Six. My mother was carrying my little sister on her back when Spotted Long-knife took me home."

Last Woman's brows shot toward her hairline. "In my people's village and even here, most have one or two children, three at most."

"It is the same with most Allies, though my grandmother bore four—all sons."

"Your...your dead showed he loved you in other ways."

"Yes." Kept-Us-Alive smiled, though it did not reach her eyes. "While he was still here, I-Am-Savior began to show me that I, not my husband, was causing my hurt—assuming any man who cared for his woman would want her to sleep against him."

"I have learned to expect nothing and be grateful for what the Creator provides."

"You make me ashamed."

"Ashamed? Why? Because you want him back?"

"I am always wishing that, but I was also wishing our whole families could have returned with my brothers to my parents' village. You would no longer be bereft of Little Blackfoot and you could marry a trustworthy warrior—perhaps my eldest brother if he has not taken a wife."

Tugging her clothes back into place, Last Woman frowned. "He is both skilled and handsome. Why would he want a foreigner? Besides, I have belonged already to two men—both older than your father—and been tossed out by a third."

Kept-Us-Alive's fingers grew still on the braid she was weaving, surprised her friend's estimation of herself differed so vastly from her own. "Hunts-For-Death is not angry with you but I-Am-Savior and seeks to wound you because of Him. Any warrior should be thankful to gain you. No woman is more loving or loyal—or so pleasant to look upon. Do you remember how jealous I felt when I saw you riding behind Pacing Wolf?"

Although Last Woman's lips turned up at the memory, her eyes announced she had shrugged off the compliment. "Your brother has his choice from any of your people's untouched women. He will choose one who is like you—who has obediently followed I-Am-Savior from childhood."

"You did not choose Old Hair-Up-Top's bed—and even if you had, when you placed your feet on I-Am-Savior's path, He gave you a new heart and made you alive again."

"No, I did not choose him, but you did not know me before your husband brought me to this village. I was like the sweet flag warriors chew, growing bitterer with every passing moon. Even now that He has given me a new heart, I have thoughts I know are not pleasing, unkind thoughts about my neighbors or jealousy over the closeness they enjoy with their kin."

"I doubt anyone's thoughts are constantly pure, apart from I-Am-Savior's. Before I began following Him, I was as dead in my sin as you were and no amount of obedience could make either of us alive again. Dead is dead—just like Lazarus and Jairus' little daughter.[19] Was she less dead than him because they had not yet wrapped her in a burial cloth?"[20]

"But if our goodness does not matter, why does the Creator's book tell us to be holy, just as He is holy?"

As Kept-Us-Alive was about to answer, she felt a small arm slip beneath hers and curve about her back. Among-the-Pines had sidled up to them so silently that neither had noticed her presence.

Smiling down at her little daughter, Kept-Us-Alive asked, "Why do I teach my little daughter to make good stitches?"

"All know your skill. You wish her to learn to dress her husband and children well."

"Are mine bad?" asked the little girl, tilting her head up to clearly read her stepmother's face.

"No, I asked this to make something clear I find difficult to weave into words. Do you like for me to teach you?" Among-the-Pines nodded happily.

"Why?"

"I want to be like you when I become a woman—and I want to be near you."

"I want to be near you also" Kept-Us-Alive admitted, affectionately squeezing her stepdaughter's shoulder. "And you have answered my friend's question."

"How?" The child turned toward Last Woman. "Are you learning new stitches?"

"No," laughed Last Woman, "but I-Am-Savior is teaching me other things, and your mother is correct. You have helped me understand."

The little girl just cocked her head, a puzzled frown wrinkling her tiny brow.

"Your efforts reveal what lies in your heart," Last Woman explained, "just as my efforts reveal what lies in mine. And if I own confidence in I-Am-Savior, I not only listen to what He says, I do it."

Among-the-Pines smiled. "When I have learned, I will teach my little sister." Pressing her cheek against her mother's growing midsection, she waited until she felt a good sharp kick and then scampered off to play with her brother.

"I am afraid she may be disappointed. White Moccasins insists I carry a son."

While the two friends crested the ridge, covered lodges seemed to rise like small, bright mountains. "You have begun sighing again."

"The village guided my heart back to my wishes."

"Little Blackfoot sits on the outskirts of all my thoughts, though I cannot regret sending her to your mother."

"I am glad—and I know my endless wishing is foolish. 'Godliness joined with contentment is great gain.'[21] I am glad I do not need to earn a place in I-Am-Savior's lodge. We were just talking about trusting I-Am-Savior, and yet here I am, wishing He would change His mind about where He has placed me."

"If He granted your wish, Jackrabbit would not allow you to take your stepdaughter. Wolf-Who-Lays-Down also—he is a Sparrow Hawk. His clansmen would not let you take him—or the small-thing you carry—any more than they would let you take their sister."

Kept-Us-Alive halted. She knew she had no rights to Among-the-Pines, but she had never considered whether someone besides Pacing Wolf might demand her children.

Oh Lord, please forgive me for complaining! If Pacing Wolf is dead, as I fear, please help me content myself with staying here—and provide Wolf-Who-Lays-Down a godly example...

All at once, she realized that I-Am-Savior already may have begun answering her petition; and once she had admitted this thought into her heart another quickly ducked in behind it.

I, too, miss Held-Back-the-Enemy.

She had been so busy shoving away all Last Woman's notions, she had not been aware she had begun to depend on him. Not only had he helped and protected her, but he had also alleviated concerns for Wolf-Who-Lays-Down—and no one could doubt either's attachment to the other.

Where has he gone? she asked herself. *The snow is deep and the ice is thick—a treacherous moon in which to climb mountain passes in search of game.*

The hair on her arms began to prickle as she remembered an angry ram she once encountered. *I have seen Hopping Owl's stores of pemmican; if we are careful, we have plenty to last until the sun hauls warmth across the prairie. And our clan has just moved camp; Hunts-For-Death would not have sent him to find a new one.*

"You have grown very quiet," observed Last Woman.

"I was chewing on what you said and…and thinking of…other things."

Last Woman knew her too well to pursue of which other things she was thinking; if she had wanted to name them, she would have named them. She could not help noticing, though, that the same bright color she felt creeping up her own neck each time she heard Straight Arrows' name had sprung up in full array between her friend's collar and chin.

AS KEPT-US-ALIVE knelt beside her new mother's cook-pot, she noticed several Lumpwood warriors ambling down the central path and felt disappointed she did not find Held-Back-the-Enemy among them. She had spent the past six afternoons on Never Sits' side of the village, had gathered wood at dusk and dawn below a stand of trees, and had often trod to the river to bathe or fetch water, but not once had she caught a glimpse of him.

My disappointment means nothing, she told herself. I only miss his kindness and welcoming expression—and who would blame me? Since Hunts-For-Death declared my husband dead, many whom I counted friends have withdrawn from me, and even those who remain grow impatient for me to stop grieving. How can I? Part of me has not yet started. Pacing Wolf has been gone little less than three moons and though I know what they insist, I cannot bring myself to quit hoping…

Once her heart began picturing her husband walking toward her, she forced it to leap from that treacherous trail and run swiftly to the safety of the other. *It is natural I notice Held-Back-the-Enemy's absence; Wolf-Who-Lays-Down whines and pines for him almost as much as he does for his own…*

"He is back!" yelled Last Son, tearing toward her so hurriedly he knocked her backward.

Her heart nearly hurtled through her chest as she scrambled to her feet and whirled around; but just as quickly, she turned again and dropped glumly to the ground.

As Last Woman perused the curious clansmen aroused by her son's announcement, she at once grasped the reason for her friend's disappointment.

"Now he can teach me to care for his horses!"

"Go," his mother ordered. "Find Wolf-Who-Lays-Down. I saw him with his sister near Hopping Owl's lodge."

"I went there," the little boy answered. "But he and Bites-With-Dog were talking."

Last Woman's lips tilted upward. "Good. You are learning not to interrupt. A grandfather and grandson have much to talk about."

Kept-Us-Alive was glad Last Son absorbed his mother's attention. His announcement had felt like an unexpected gust that blew open her door-flap and exposed her half-naked, and she was determined to pull it tightly shut again. Attempting to sound cheerful, she looked up from her work and added, "Wolf-Who-Lays-Down, also, will be happy Held-Back-the-Enemy has returned."

She continued slicing white roots over the steaming water, but when she became aware that her friend had grown unusually still, she twisted around to see if something was wrong. Her knife dropped from her fingers: level with her eyes hung her husband's war-ax, tucked into a belt above Held-Back-the-Enemy's leggings.

As the young Sparrow Hawk squatted down beside her, the expression he wore grew so grim that she involuntarily shuddered, and as she lowered her gaze to his outstretched hand, her whole body began to tremble. He was carefully unfolding a familiarly dyed scrap of hide, spreading it across his calloused palm for her to see.

Too stunned to offer the slightest greeting, she picked up the torn piece of hunting shirt and repeatedly turned it over. It told her nothing of her husband's death, sparking a fragile hope that lifted her eyes to Held-Back-the-Enemy's, but what she found renewed her quaking. Following them to his pouch, she watched him pull out the bloodstained legging.

Her mind felt like a muskrat she had seen last moon, caught in the frozen river. As she slid her fingertips across the stiffened buckskin and down the matted strands dangling from its seams, the blood drained from her face. Her husband's trophies were unmistakable. Her own hands had formed each knot, a type her mother had taught her and that she had been teaching to Among-the-Pines. As she remembered him assuring her none was her men-folk, she started to both laugh and cry.

Burying her face in the beloved tatters, she rocked back and forth, shrieking with unrestrained grief. She felt a pungent urge to slash her arms, hoping severe pain might deaden the anguish ripping apart her heart. She had thought she had surrendered Pacing Wolf to the Creator, thought she was coming to accept what all his clansmen had insisted, but his bloody legging had stolen her last sinew of hope.

As her wailing reached the outskirts of the village, Women-Who-Talk-Against-Each-Other-Without-Fear left their chores and rushed toward Hopping Owl's cook fire. Their Good Men gathered also, asking Held-Back-the-Enemy where he had gone and demanding he show them his proof. He could not. Kept-Us-Alive had doubled over it in a quivering heap, half burying herself in the snow.

From very far away, she could hear Last Woman enlisting Hopping Owl's aid, fearing the snow might blacken their friend's fingers or cause her to catch a chill. Next, she felt them yanking her to her feet; but once they had set her upright, a deep darkness swallowed her whole.

I am the Creator; there is no other. I am God; there is no one like Me. I make the end known from the beginning; during your Grandfathers' summers, I revealed what is to come. 'My purpose will stand and I will bring to fruition what pleases Me.'

Isaiah 46 9-10

Chapter 16

WHEN KEPT-US-ALIVE awakened on her bed, she felt dazed by her surroundings. She remembered neither how she had come there nor why her new mother was smoothing her hair from her brow until she became aware of the soft scrap of hunting shirt she still clasped in her hand. As her memory launched an assault, she began searching for the other scrap also, a last— though bloodied—memento.

"My husband's legging—where is it?" she asked Hopping Owl, raising up on her elbow to look all around her.

"Hunts-For-Death has taken it as proof of...of his Lumpwood son's valor."

"How did I come here? The last I...I..."

"You dropped to the ground—as if your spirit had suddenly departed for the Mystery Land. My son pushed through our clanswomen and hoisted you over his shoulder."

Only when Hopping Owl nodded proudly toward Held-Back-the-Enemy did Kept-Us-Alive notice they were not alone. Last Woman and her son stayed in the shadows, comforting or tending to Among-the-Pines and Wolf-Who-Lays-Down, and both her adopted father and brother sat in their places by the embers.

"Go," Bites-With-Dog told Held-Back-the-Enemy, who briefly locked eyes with Kept-Us-Alive as his father rose to move near her. "My son has brought you proof of what we feared. I will grant you time to grieve the dead, but I cannot give you long. Last Woman has told you of the choice Hunts-For-Death has offered me: to give you to one of my Lumpwood brothers or stand by while a rival claims you. When your husband asked me to care for you, he also asked me—if he did not return—to give you to a certain warrior. That warrior is willing, even eager, but I wish for you to go to him of your own will."

"My husband is dead. Give me to whomever you wish or cast me out," muttered Kept-Us-Alive. "I do not care."

"You may not care," her father gently reasoned, "but my Lumpwood brother did, and I do also—and not only for you. You must consider his son and the small-thing you carry. Do you also want them to hunger?"

Kept-Us-Alive shook her head and mumbled, "I-Am-Savior will care for us."

"Yes, but I-Am-Savior most often uses natural means. The Book tells of bread coming down each day from heaven[22] and the widow's oil that kept refilling,[23] but these are only a fistful of mentions. He did not promise his mother this bread from heaven; He handed her into the care of LovedMan.[24] Hunts-For-Death is the Real Chief and has the power to take your children away. Do you want him to give them to one of your dead husband's clanswomen?"

"No. Give me to the warrior my husband chose."

Bites-With-Dog's eyes faintly twinkled. "Your grief speaks loudly, but I also wish you to consider this warrior. He is a fine man, worthy not only of your respect but also of your loyalty and love. Though he is willing, he does not want to force you. My woman tells me the small-thing inside you will soon come out to greet the sun. You have until after he arrives to decide."

"Who is the warrior you have chosen?"

"He will tell you in good time. He wishes to woo, not oblige you."

AS PRETTY FACE leaned over his mother's patient, he thought the man looked fit enough. He was not tall like his vicious cousin, but he looked every bit as capable. The veins on his arms stood out sharply over well-honed muscles, each sinew made more evident by a lack of fitting food.

Perusing the man's features, Pretty Face noticed a scar running across his chin and another near his jawbone. Both were straight and likely created while dodging swipes of an enemy's knife. His nose began higher towards his brow than Pretty Face's own, but that told him nothing. He could say the same of Straight Arrows', their father's, and most noses belonging to their many cousins.

His hunting shirt looked like Pretty Face's own, though short curling fur peeked out from between the stitches of a patch. While he curiously slipped his fingers beneath the hem to feel the lining, the patient's eyes fluttered open and the edges of his lips softly curved.

Pretty Face returned the smile, welcoming a chance to discover the warrior's name and people; but the stranger recoiled backward, straining his against his restraints.

"Sh-sh-sh," murmured Pretty Face, holding up his hands to show he had no weapon.

Unable to pull free, the patient closed his eyes, trying to shut out the frightening figure looming over him. It had appeared to him repeatedly, though whether while asleep or awake, he could not say. At first, he had mistaken it for his woman, drawing comfort as she glided cool fingers across his forehead or softly thanked the Creator for the healing He brought.

Which parts of him needed healing was no clearer than his state of wakefulness or dreaming. He felt as if an enemy had replaced his skin with a robe of sharp stones, scraping or bruising him with every twisting. His muscles cried out to move, but though he could wriggle his torso and arms, he had lost the ability to make his legs obey. They lay rigid and straight, as heavy as a buffalo carcass.

For what had felt like moons, he had been lying on his back, his woman's soft voice either swirling above him or through his memory; but when he looked into her face, terror swallowed his heart. In place of her loving black eyes, he found mirrors reflecting the sky, or when they were the right color, the head they were lodged in looked wrong. It was larger of bone with thicker brows, and from its lips poured deep, rich tones.

Supposing the patient wanted to sleep, Pretty Face slid a hand beneath his pallet to lift him up high enough to pour steeped herbs between his lips; but when the man's eyes flew open, he laid the broth aside. "We are Allies," he explained, tapping his fingers on his chest and then the patient's. "You are in our guest-dwelling—safe. My mother has been caring for you."

As the man glanced from him toward the entrance, Straight Arrows slipped in and caught his first glimpse of their patient's open eyes. "Has he told you where his band lives?"

"No," answered Pretty Face. "His mind is as Mother said: consumed by fever. He shuts his eyes or glares at me like I am an ugly, evil spirit."

Straight Arrows chuckled. "Then his sight is good."

"You stay with him. Though his eyes follow you, he does not look at you this way."

"I cannot. Old Uncle Many Feathers is gathering a council. He also wants you. Mother will send our brother, Young Deer, to take your place. They want us to travel with Grandfather to Red Fox's village."

Pretty Face shook his head. "He will give them few answers. The fever has snatched away his senses—if he had any. 'A man is known by his companions.' Who but a renegade or fool would prowl about after Wild Dog?"

As the stranger's eyes flitted from brother to brother, much that passed between them seemed muddled; but before the swirling pool of his herb soaked mind succeeded in sucking him downward, one name stuck like a death stake in his memory's broken soil.

KEPT-US-ALIVE GASPED. The small-thing she carried seemed to have decided to burrow a path straight through her lower back. When a sharper, deeper, spasm had momentarily usurped her attention from the dull constant ache, she had barely mustered the will to leave the women's lodge. Now her new mother and Last Woman were insisting she mount her mare.

"You must," urged Hopping Owl, combing back a stray wisp that clung to her new daughter's sweat-soaked face. "The herald proclaimed we are moving from this place."

"Go. I will come when I am able."

"We cannot leave you behind; you know what the Fox soldiers do to stragglers! If they were Lumpwood, they would respect their dead brother and might treat you kindly, but they are Fox."

"Let them beat me!" panted Kept-Us-Alive, glancing fretfully at the mare and its beautifully carved saddle. "But...take her...with you—and Wolf-Who-Lays-Down."

"What will you do—bear the small-thing by yourself? Who will cut his tether?"

Kept-Us-Alive motioned toward her knife, grimacing as a fresh wave of pain ripped through her lower abdomen.

As Last Woman eyed both Hopping Owl, who had painted her face with worry, and the horses Held-Back-the-Enemy was pulling into their tandem places, she suggested, "You go. Take her son and mine on her mare. I will stay here to help her."

Hopping Owl quickly shook her head from side to side. "They will treat you worse than her! You have no father for them to fear, and now that Hunts-For-Death has tossed you out..."

The older woman could not finish her sentence. She felt ashamed of her Real Chief. By breaking his promise to Old Hair-Up-Top, he had consigned

Last Woman to a horrid fate. No warrior would want a woman his leader deemed unfit.

As Hopping Owl trailed off, the Blackfoot set her jaw and pressed her lips into a tight straight line. "Ask your son or husband to lend me his lance. All know I can use it. I will stay with my sister-friend until she spills her small-thing onto the snow—and give me another buffalo robe. She will need plenty. After she exhausts herself, she will grow too cold."

"I will stay with them," declared Held-Back-the-Enemy. "The Fox are rivals, but they know my skill with an ax."

"I would stay also," added Bites-With-Dog, "but Hunts-For-Death requires me with the Good Men. I dare not refuse him."

"Come," Held-Back-the-Enemy directed Last Woman. "Help me get her into that stand of pines; they will shelter her from the wind. Mother, say nothing to The-Women-Who-Talk-Against-Each-Other-Without-Fear. If they see and hear nothing, they can say nothing to alert Fox husbands or sons."

Hopping Owl nodded. Once she saw they had reached the pines, she removed a bundle from her household goods, looked around surreptitiously to make sure no one was watching, and scurried up the hill to slip between the branches. "Here. Two robes and a soft deerskin for the small-thing, and you have the robes the three of you are wearing. Your father and I will be praying for a quick birth, a painless birth." Even as she offered these hopes, she did not believe they were possible. Kept-Us-Alive's labor was hard, so hard she suspected Pacing Wolf's small-thing had grown too large. While rushing toward the line of other travelers, she apprehensively glanced backward, hoping Held-Back-the-Enemy would think to disguise her prints in the snow and that the move occupied her clanswomen too fully for them to miss the stragglers.

Last Woman gathered handfuls of shed needles and spread them over the most protected spot within the pines. "For him to slip out into," she smiled. "They are not as thick as straw, but they will be warmer than snow."

"Where are…Wolf-Who-Lays-Down…and Last Son?" panted Kept-Us-Alive. "If Held-Back-the-Enemy stays…they will…stay."

Her Blackfoot friend shook her head. "Held-Back-the-Enemy put them atop your mare and has entrusted them to Otter Woman. He warned them sharply what he would do if they do not go with her."

Once Kept-Us-Alive knew they were safe, her whole body relaxed— but not for long. She clutched hold of the lance her protector had driven into the ground, pulling against it as she knelt, legs spread wide apart, upon the dried needles.

Held-Back-the-Enemy did not know what to do with himself. The stand of pines was narrow and short, too short for him to move a good distance away. He heard her teeth as they clattered together and her sharp stunted breaths—though whether to attribute them to pain or hard efforts, he could not decide. It set his memory running down a path to a summer long ago, the first summer his father had allowed him to help with a mare's whelping. The horse had whimpered and moaned as her foal tried repeatedly to emerge until both lay depleted, joined in death as they had been in life. Unable to rid himself of the memory, he began reciting a Psalm he had recently stored in his heart.

"You are He-Who-Sees-All-Things. You have searched me and know me. You know when I sit and when I rise. You listen to my thoughts from afar. You search my path and my lying down and are acquainted with all my ways. Before my tongue forms words, O Creator, You know all I will say. You surround me on all sides. You place your hand upon me. Such knowledge is too vast for me. It is too high for me to grasp. Where can I run from Your Spirit or flee from Your presence? If I climb as high as the clouds, You are there, or lie down in a grave—there You are also!"

As images sprung to mind of Pacing Wolf fending off a bear, he glanced briefly at Kept-Us-Alive, wondering if she also fought them. He could not tell. She pinched her face together with an effort that twisted her pleasingly shaped mouth. He thought her the most entrancing woman he had ever known. Her courage only added to her beauty. "More!" she spurted. "Please."

"If I could rise on the wings of the waking sun or dwell in the deepest part of the great water, Your hand would still lead me; Your right hand would seize hold of me. If I say, 'Surely the darkness will overwhelm me' and the light closes like night, even the darkness does not hide from You. Night is as bright as the sun. Dark and light are the same to You."

"Do not stop," suggested the tall Blackfoot when he paused. "It helps her."

"For You created my inward parts. You wove me in my mother's belly. I will praise You for I am fearfully and wonderfully made. Your works are astonishing; my soul knows this well. My bones were not hidden from You when I was created in secret, skillfully woven in the deepest part of the earth. Your eyes saw me as an unformed thing. You recounted all the summers You fashioned for me before there was one."

As the last portion brought to mind his dead Lumpwood father's bloodied legging and the changes this proof might bring, wonder overcame him. *I-Am-Savior was not surprised when my Lumpwood father…*

Three sudden, coinciding cries yanked Held-Back-the-Enemy from his reverie: one of indignation, one of joy, and one of relief. Forgetting his reserve, he took the angry small-thing from Last Woman's arms and continued reciting the remaining verses.

"How precious are your plans, You-Who-Are-All-Mighty. My thoughts cannot reach their heights! If I recount them, they are more in number than grains of earth. When I awake, I am still beside You."

At the sound of his voice, the small-thing quieted, breathing in jerks that quickly settled. The Lumpwood warrior stared into its tiny face, marveling over the perfection of each feature: its mounded, tightly shut eyes, a nose no larger than the shield-garbed insects that lived beneath rocks, and a mouth that reminded him of a wildflower's soft petal.

When his eyes traveled over the small-thing's torso, his head shot up in surprise. The tiny mouth was too pretty for a man-child. Startled by the sudden movement, the babe screwed up his whole face until it was the color of a ripened cherry.

Held-Back-the-Enemy frowned, stretching out his arms to hand the babe to Last Woman, and admired her calm while the little one regaled her with war cries. As his gaze collided with Kept-Us-Alive's, he read something there that shooed away other thoughts: gratitude and admiration. They softened with love also, not for him but her small-thing, followed by a sadness that announced of whom she was thinking.

STRAIGHT ARROWS BEGAN TO wonder if the snow would ever stop falling. Not since he was a boy could he remember such cold and relentless winters as these past two. He hoped the present one would not last as long. His legs ached to run and his senses longed for stirring. Sitting beside his mother's patient, he heard nothing but the stranger's even breathing and smelled little more than the dwindling embers. His eyes longed for color—any color—but a white blanket covered both forest and field. Besides, he could not brush from his mind his sister's solemn face and was anxious to return to the enemy village where they had found her.

"No." The stirring warrior held up his hand to ward off the dish Straight Arrows was bringing to his lips. "I go."

Straight Arrows solemnly shook his head. "You have broken a bone."

"My woman…my children.…"

"If you break it again, of what use will you be to them? You will be unable to hunt for food or protect them from our enemies."

"How...?"

As the patient's question trailed off, Straight Arrows guessed what he was after. "An enemy attacked you in a cavern, high on a cliff in the dark hills."

"Is he..."

"Dead?" Straight Arrows nodded. "We thought you were also when we found you. You do not remember?"

The warrior shook his head so slightly, Straight Arrows was uncertain whether he gave an answer or felt grief too private to express.

"We returned your cousins to Red Fox and planned to return you to your people, but..."

"Ah—he is awake," interrupted Brought-Us-The-Book, hauling in fresh supplies. "Your father and brothers are gathering in our dwelling to hear The Book. Go call them and your uncles and ask them to come here. This dwelling is not as large as ours, but as the falling snow is keeping many away, it is large enough. The Word will be good for our guest."

Creator, lead me In Your righteousness. Because of my enemies, make Your path straight before me.

Psalm 5:8

Chapter 17

AWAKENED BY THE SOUND of thrashing, Kept-Us-Alive sat bolt upright to find a figure pushing through the sheltering pines. Her breath caught sharply as its hair—stiffened and rising from its pate—was silhouetted clearly in the bright sunshine.

"You have lagged behind," stated Bull-Will-Not-Fall, grasping hold of her wrist. "You know what our people require!"

Looking all about, Kept-Us-Alive tried to locate either of her two companions, but found neither; nor could she pull away, so she folded back a corner of her buffalo robe to reveal her tiny son.

Bull-Will-Not-Fall smiled. "He is a fine boy—looks strong. Get up. Gather your belongings. I will lead you to the others."

Before the Fox could carry through his intentions, Last Woman silently hauled a bundle of twigs through the other end of the pine grove. "She cannot ride. The small-thing's journey was hard; she has lost much blood."

Bull-Will-Not-Fall released Kept-Us-Alive and rose up to his full height. "Go. Fetch your horses."

When Last Woman did not comply, he stepped toward her, striking her so hard that he knocked her to the ground.

"Stop!" barked Held-Back-the-Enemy, as he slipped between the branches holding a dead rabbit. Glancing from the broad-shouldered back of the seasoned Fox to the woman at his feet, he saw a red welt rising beneath the skin above her jawline.

Bull-Will-Not-Fall abruptly swung toward him, lowering himself far enough into a crouching position that Kept-Us-Alive grew alarmed.

"My father has entrusted them to me," Held-Back-the-Enemy stated levelly. "We will join the others when the small-thing and his mother are able."

As the Fox soldier glared in return, his top lip curled so faintly that Kept-Us-Alive absently wondered if this was its natural shape. "I will allow this," he snapped, "but do not delay long! We camp beside the Echata.

Arrive before we cross!" Nodding abruptly, he strode back to the boughs he had bent and exited as suddenly as he had entered.

Kept-Us-Alive scrambled up and rushed to Last Woman, creasing her brow as she examined the distinct red mark. "He has hurt you—it is my fault!"

"It is nothing," murmured the Blackfoot, watching Held-Back-the-Enemy a bit warily when he squatted down to probe her jaw.

Nothing felt amiss besides an unwelcome urge to run his thumb across her full mouth. "What did he want?" he asked Kept-Us-Alive, though he already knew the answer. He was stalling, shaking off his own errant impulse while trying to detect if she cherished any preference for his rival.

"He is Fox," she murmured, surprised he asked. "They are charged with finding stragglers and hurrying them along."

"Bull-Will-Not-Fall did not find you by chance," scoffed Last Woman. "He was watching for you, waiting to offer you aid."

Held-Back-the-Enemy agreed but said nothing. He admired the Blackfoot's good sense, which sent him back over a trail he had just trodden. He knew none so loyal, even among his own clanswomen. This was not the first time she had risked her hide for her friend, and he commended her for the calm with which she had guided Kept-Us-Alive through a difficult whelping.

Hunts-For-Death was a fool to cast her aside.

AS THE SUN REACHED the crest of a clear blue sky, Held-Back-the-Enemy fetched several horses. Last Woman had already skinned and roasted the rabbit, stretching out its fur over a hastily fashioned frame to dry in the sun as everyone ate. New Son ate heartily also, laying one hand atop the other afterward while he drifted off to nap.

Held-Back-the-Enemy led them without mishap to the banks of the Echata. As they approached the hodge-podge of cook-fires and hastily tossed up shelters, no one gave any indication they had noticed their absence. Even Bull-Will-Not-Fall, though he stared hard in their direction, acted as if he saw nothing out of the ordinary when the three—now four—pulled up beside the place Bites-With-Dog had selected to make camp.

Kept-Us-Alive was relieved when she felt the snow-covered ground beneath her feet. She had slept the better part of the morning, but she still felt exhausted. Smiling a warm greeting, Hopping Owl inspected her new *grandson,* unfolding the blanket wrapped around his limbs, hands, and feet to examine his fingers and toes. She cooed ecstatically when he began to wriggle, but as he started to whimper, she handed him back to his mother. Bites-With-Dog, though not as demonstrative, looked well pleased with both child and mother, but he walked away with his son as soon as his wife settled Kept-Us-Alive on a place to rest.

While Last Woman accompanied Hopping Owl to the riverbank, she learned the women were not gathering fallen limbs and twigs for rafts but cook fires. Hunts-For-Death had decided the Many Lodges should set up their village in the customary pattern, with the most essential lodges flanking the central path and those of less importance extending out beside them. Everywhere, women tossed up the poles of their round, peaked homes, relieved they need not cross the mighty Echata until more of the ice had melted.

AS HELD-BACK-THE-ENEMY ducked into his father's lodge, Kept-Us-Alive met his eyes. She had seen him often since they had returned to the Many Lodges, and they had developed a new ease of conversation. During many mornings, he took charge of Wolf-Who-Lays-Down and Last Son, freeing Last Woman and her to attend to other responsibilities; and during evenings, he often took the baby when he fussed, soothing him with soft songs or amusing him by gently blowing on his tiny face.

She appreciated all this deeply, considering the untouched woman who would one day gain his interest as very fortunate; but her own feelings were like a stewpot of sadness seasoned with a few small bits of joy and tenderness. Wolf-Who-Lays-Down adored his tiny brother, though he sometimes resented the attention the babe stole from him, and Among-the-Pines turned into a little mother. She often found chores or excuses that brought her to Hopping Owl's home and gathered the small-thing up in her arms if her stepmother happened to lay him down. Once, she had asked to wear his cradleboard and gladly would have fed him had she been able.

As old Paints-His-Shirt-Yellow, two of his sons, and several others of the clan filed into Bites-With-Dog's lodge, Kept-Us-Alive flipped through The Book to find a passage they had last read together. Between foul weather, several moves, and her new small-thing's disturbances, they had proceeded slowly of late. She hoped since she had just fed him and he was soundly sleeping, she could finish reading the next part of Grasping Man's letter.[25]

[14] How is it useful for one among us to claim he possesses faith though he possesses no proof? Can this kind of faith save him? [15] If he tells a man who owns no clothing or food, "Go. Be at peace; get warm and full," without

offering what the body lacks, what use are his words? ¹⁷Just so, a faith that does not show itself by deeds does not possess life. ¹⁸But some might say, "You possess faith and I possess deeds." Show me your faith apart from deeds, and I by my deeds will prove I possess faith. ¹⁹ You believe that God is one. You do well; evil spirits also believe and shudder.

Feeling her baby squirm against her back, she paused, raised her head, and noticed Bull-Will-Not-Fall had come in and seated himself opposite her.

"I have never stolen," he proclaimed, looking at her directly, "and when we gain much spoil from an enemy, I give food or horses to the poor. My deeds already prove—as you have just read—that I already walk the right path."

While she paused to allow Bites-With-Dog to answer, his son began to speak. "The passage does not speak of people who have not yet met I-Am-Savior, but those who claim to follow Him while refusing to walk as He walked."

"I have also considered these questions while I listened," remarked Braids-His-Tail, Otter Woman's husband, "and have come to this conclusion: this proof is like the coups we count. A warrior shows the Good Men a weapon he has taken before he expects them to award him a token of valor; or if he has nothing to show, he asks his brother to recount his brave deed. What youth does not imagine himself a warrior? Yet none are awarded tokens for their courage until they show by deeds they possess it."

Bites-With-Dog could not help noticing Last Woman, who was sitting with Otter Woman behind Braids-His-Tail. "You have something you wish to say?"

The Blackfoot nodded but looked down. She felt hesitant to speak beyond her small group of friendly women, but if she kept quiet, she feared her insides might burst.

"Speak, Daughter."

"I was thinking of the cherries we dry to make pemmican. We know which trees to climb because we see the dark red fruit hanging from the branches. If a bare-branched tree sprouts up near them, we do not bother to climb it. We can all see it possesses no cherries."

Bites-With-Dog nodded with approval. "And if my woman takes the cherries she has gathered and hangs them to dry from this bare tree, no one among us—not even the youngest—would mistake it for one bearing cherries. The fruit must bud from deep within. When I-Am-Savior gave me a new spirit, I began to feel, speak, and act differently than I once did; but I did not *win* this new spirit by these changes—the new spirit produced these changes in *me*."

While she watched Bull-Will-Not-Fall set his jaw, Kept-Us-Alive admired her new father's understanding and ability to explain something she had found difficult. She also could not help noticing his son. They had seated themselves next to each other and were gesturing or making expressions that were very much alike. She never considered whether Bites-With-Dog had been a handsome young man; he was merely her husband's clansman, close friend, and now her father. Yet, as she saw his similarity to his son, she understood how he had won Hopping Owl, whom her clanswomen in her youth had considered an accomplished beauty.

Looking past his shoulder, she found her new mother smiling pleasantly—a smile that reminded her of the sweet blue flowers dotting the forest edge. They were not profuse like the blossoms of the ancient crabapple that grew in the meadow near her village, but they held a gentle beauty that brightened the deepest shadows. As she glanced from Hopping Owl back to her new father and then to their son, she felt warm gratitude for her dead husband. Pacing Wolf had planned as well for her care in death as he had in life. She could not imagine any home, outside of her own mother's, where she would have received such love and welcome, and now that Last Woman and Last Son also lived with them, she had something she had always wanted: an older sister.

Catching her glance, Held-Back-the-Enemy offered her a quick smile, though he kept it corralled within his eyes more than allowing it to spread across his lips. *Perhaps Last Woman is right,* she thought, feeling her neck begin to warm. *He has become a fine warrior, obedient to his father and gentle with his mother, and though he does not often seek me out, he is attentive to my sons and always kind and helpful. Even my tiny small-thing shows him marked favor, and my eldest constantly dogs his heels. Who—now that we know Pacing Wolf is dead—could Wolf-Who-Lays-Down prefer for a father?*

As the gathering began to pray, her newborn again began squirming in his cradleboard, so she glanced up to discover the least obtrusive path to slip outside to feed him. Bites-With-Dog, his son, and those who had gathered fervently bowed or closed their eyes to worship, but a single head remained erect and was watching her boldly.

Kept-Us-Alive felt caught. She wished to duck out before her small-thing began to fuss, but she dare not now. If she sought a private place to feed him, Bull-Will-Not-Fall might follow and the very privacy she needed might become a trap. Hoping her son would drift back to sleep, she closed her eyes and rocked back and forth, but though he settled for a moment, her reprieve from his fussing was short.

She rose up and headed for the door flap, heedless of who followed, but as she turned to look behind her, she found exactly what she expected.

Bull-Will-Not-Fall had not waited for the gathering to conclude but was slipping out, looking down the path to discover her direction.

Hastily, Kept-Us-Alive wound through several lodges. Her natural inclinations were to find a lonely place, but with Bull-Will-Not-Fall about, she headed instead for the one home she knew held occupants in which she might find welcome: Jackrabbit's.

"May I enter?" she called, waiting only for the briefest hint of an answer before she did so.

Jackrabbit's eyes were wide with questions, but her granddaughter squealed with pleasure. Scrambling away from her grandmother's hairbrush, she threw herself against her stepmother and then skirted her side to peer up on tip-toes at her fully awake brother.

"Ah, let me hold him," purred Jackrabbit, helping to lift him down. "He is light—much lighter than Among-the-Pines was."

Kept-Us-Alive bristled. The woman grasped every chance to paint her dead daughter as superior—but managed to smile. After all, Jackrabbit was not only correct but she was also—although unwittingly—providing a hiding place from her predator. She was certain Bull-Will-Not-Fall and Jackrabbit were related, but she could not imagine him visiting the old woman, especially since she had gained renown for her sharp tongue.

"My son came earlier than we…than I…expected," admitted the younger woman.

When she heard this, Jackrabbit's eyes grew large again, quickly narrowed, and unexpectedly dampened.

"What is it, Grandmother?" asked Among-the-Pines. "What is wrong?"

The older woman at first could not answer. "It is my fault," she choked out eventually. "I cursed your stepmother's womb the afternoon I met her."

"No—look, he is fine. He-Who-Hears-and-Sees-All-Things does not let undeserved curses alight."[26]

Jackrabbit looked as if she wanted badly to argue, but instead, she began to weep. "I have been unkind to you, forcing you to taste the bitterness of my heart, but you…you have been good to the dead—and to me."

Aware she had done nothing more than a little mending, Kept-Us-Alive eased her small-thing beneath her sheepskin blouse, where she felt him root briefly and latch on. "There is nothing amiss with his appetite," she smiled.

"My granddaughter has told me of your grief," Jackrabbit continued, "not only for the dead but from missing her. She has told me also of your care—that you have been as generous with her as you are with your boy. Where is he?"

"He is asleep in Bites-With-Dog's lodge."

"And why have you come to see me?"

Kept-Us-Alive felt caught for the second time that evening. She had not come to this dwelling to visit its inhabitants, but she genuinely cared for them, did not want to hurt either of their feelings and continually hoped to foster the new ease between her and her stepdaughter's grandmother. Neither did she want to lie.

"I came to escape," she admitted. "A Fox has been sniffing my heels, hoping I will turn and tempt him with something to nibble."

"Will you? You cannot bring the dead back to life by ignoring your own desires. You are young. How many summers?"

"When the grass greens, I will possess nineteen."

"Ah...when the grass greens. Do not let this Fox cause you to fear. Cast your eyes toward the warrior of your choice—Fox, Muddy Hand, or Lumpwood. By the Moon of Green Grass, the warrior you choose will carry you off on the back of his pony. Better to be a young widow than an untouched woman! An untouched woman marries her father's choice. Once married, a woman chooses for herself! This is what I tell Pretty Crow Woman when she grows jealous over her handsome husband. Let him sniff after other women. When the grass greens she can take her revenge."

As Kept-Us-Alive drew her small-thing out from under her blouse, she could not think of a reply. She certainly wanted none of the attention Jackrabbit was so eager for her to gain. Neither could she condone the old woman's advice for her daughter. This was the accepted way with this people, and she had no idea how to make Jackrabbit aware of one better.

Worse yet, she did not know how to keep her stepdaughter, whom Jackrabbit constantly fed this poisonous snake meat, from traveling down this adulterous path. Their young women went from warrior to warrior, gaining one and leaving another until they grew too old to rouse anyone's desire.

The lucky ones had daughters of their own or sons who would provide for them, but some begged or gathered food wherever they might.

As she held out her small-thing, Jackrabbit accepted him eagerly. "He looks like you," she told his mother. "His mouth is too pretty for a boy-child."

Tamping down the desire to retort, Kept-Us-Alive smiled and reached for her stepdaughter's brush. "Your grandmother is occupied. May I finish your hair?"

Among-the-Pines nodded, eager for a reminder of their former closeness. While her grandmother cooed over her tiny brother, Kept-Us-Alive took the porcupine tail and drew it carefully, gently, through each long silky strand of hair. Afterward, she drew a part down the middle and wove each side into a long, tight braid. "Soon they will be..."

"Will be what?"

Kept-Us-Alive smiled. "I was about to say they would be as long as mine, but now I cannot. I can barely tie mine behind each ear."

"Waugh, do not worry over that," replied Jackrabbit. "Your eyes look all the larger—even more like the doe-spirit you possess that so fascinated… the dead."

Kept-Us-Alive quickly looked up, as surprised by the announcement of Pacing Wolf's feelings as she was by Jackrabbit's compliment. She longed for her to continue; Pacing Wolf had never easily expressed his thoughts with words.

"Do you not own a mirror?" asked Jackrabbit. "Look into the lake when the sky is clear. You will see."

This was not what the younger woman hoped to hear, though she was not surprised that Jackrabbit said nothing further. She knew their customs well. They felt it disrespectful to speak of the dead. Smiling appreciatively, she reached for her small-thing's cradleboard and then bent down to take him. "I must go. Hopping Owl and Bites-With-Dog may grow concerned if I am gone too long."

Jackrabbit looked disappointed, but she helped the newborn into the cradleboard and lifted onto her visitor's back. Once Kept-Us-Alive tightened him into place, she bent down to hug and kiss Among-the-Pines and then impulsively did the same to the older woman. Jackrabbit stiffened and stepped back, but offered a tenuous smile.

"Do not go," whispered the little girl, putting her arms tightly around her stepmother.

"I must, little one, but tomorrow—if your grandmother agrees—you can help me gather sticks for both our lodges." When Jackrabbit briefly nodded, she ducked out, glad to be safe from her pursuer, but her relief soon turned to panic.

The wicked conceive evil and brings forth lies.

Psalm 7:14

Chapter 18

A HAND CLOSED OVER Kept-Us-Alive's upper arm, swinging her around until she nearly collided with its owner's broad chest.

"Where have you been?" growled Bull-Will-Not-Fall. "Your father and mother—and many others from…your father's lodge…have been looking for you."

As she looked up at his eyes, she wondered if they flared with worry or frustration. Whatever he felt, she did not intend to stand nearly embracing on the path. Attentive passersby might assume they were courting, and the face this thought tossed into her mind did nothing to put her more at ease. She had not known until then that she cared what he thought, or at least she had not been ready to admit it.

"I have been visiting my stepdaughter," she told him. "And her grandmother, Jackrabbit."

Bull-Will-Not-Fall neither replied nor released her, though his grip on her arm lessened to a firm caress. Seizing the opportunity, she began to pull away, but he slipped his other around and up to cradle her head. Only then did she notice the dark outline of a warrior that he—she was certain—had already spotted trotting toward them. The warrior abruptly halted, refusing to close the gap as Bull-Will-Not-Fall entwined his fingers in her untidily sprouting waves.

Kept-Us-Alive stood frozen, caught between the urge to kick his shin and fear she might disgrace her new parents until the warrior from the shadows sprang forward. Grabbing Bull-Will-Not-Fall's shoulder, he had wrenched him backward, pulled out his knife, and lowered himself into a crouching position before she was certain who he was. Just as swiftly, the Fox responded, sending her heart into her throat. Bull-Will-Not-Fall was not only taller and broader, but greater summers of raiding and warfare had made him harder. When they heard others approaching, they came to their senses, rising so subtly the searchers who brushed past them toward Kept-Us-Alive might have mistaken them for friends.

"I am sorry," she murmured to the bevy of relieved faces. "I never meant to cause concern. My small-thing was about to disrupt our praying, so I sought a place I could privately tend his needs."

Last Woman, watching Bull-Will-Not-Fall as he turned and trotted away, jerked her head in his direction. "That Fox stirs my fear. He did not wait until we had finished praying before he followed you."

As Hopping Owl noticed her new daughter glance from his retreating form to Mountainside's part of the village, she said aloud what she was thinking. "Jackrabbit—we should have known you would go to Among-the-Pines."

"But Jackrabbit despises you," stated Otter Woman.

"She hated what my tribesman did to her daughter. I have lately visited her several times, and she has begun to *appreciate* my stitches."

As the four chuckled, the baby began fussing again, so they started down the path toward their lodges. Where Bull-Will-Not-Fall went, no one knew, but as Held-Back-the-Enemy watched him retreating, he decided he would move back into his father's home.

"THROW DOWN YOUR LODGES!" cried the herald.

Held-Back-the-Enemy glanced over to Kept-Us-Alive's pallet to see if she had awakened and found her gazing down at her new son as if he were the most beautiful creature He-Who-Created-All-Things had ever formed. He agreed. From birth, the small-thing had possessed his mother's thickness of hair and his features were already recovering from his difficult journey to greet his clansmen. His rosebud mouth was very like hers also, only puffier, leading Held-Back-the-Enemy to conclude he had just finished his morning meal.

As his eyes darted from son to mother, he concluded her loveliness reached far beyond a mere balance of well-formed features. She possessed an inner radiance that even the darkness of grief had not dimmed. He was glad to see some of her sadness diminishing, perhaps because her new son lately garnered most of her attention.

After seeing her with Bull-Will-Not-Fall last evening, Held-Back-the-Enemy had decided he would no longer hold himself back. He had never observed her seeking or encouraging the man, but only a sightless person could have missed Bull-Will-Not-Fall's attentions. The sooner he secured her for himself, the sooner he could insist they cease.

Kept-Us-Alive wished she could will away the herald's loud command. She would much rather spend her waking moments as she was, enjoying the delicious closeness of her two precious sons. While she stroked a thatch of hair from Wolf-Who-Lays-Down's brow, a faint nearby noise propelled her glance to the other side of the lodge.

Held-Back-the-Enemy had already arisen, his strong, lean frame darkly outlined by the dim early light; and although she could not distinguish his features, she sensed he was also looking at her. She did not mind. In fact, she was growing used to his attention, more marked since the birth of her youngest.

As Wolf-Who-Lays-Down yawned and stretched, she noticed Hopping Owl and Last Woman had risen and were beginning the arduous task of packing their household belongings.

"Why another move?" asked Hopping Owl as Bites-With-Dog lifted the door flap and ducked in.

"The Old Ones tell He-Who-Leads-The-Moving-Band that a great wind is coming, carrying much snow. He and Hunts-For-Death have decided we need to go now if we are to move to better shelter across the mighty Echata."

"I will gather our water and wood," offered Kept-Us-Alive, hastily dressing Wolf-Who-Lays-Down and encasing her small-thing in his cradleboard. "And make our early meal."

Hoisting the cradleboard onto her back, she shifted its weight between her shoulders and set about her morning tasks. The camp resembled the bare carcass of a mighty buffalo, and each waking woman added to the illusion, stripping their lodges' hides to uncover the beast's tall ribs.

Once her new family had eaten, Hopping Owl, Last Woman, and she cut low hanging limbs from trees along the river and helped their men-folk construct a raft for their household goods. Held-Back-the-Enemy led his mother's horse into the shallows, but the animal began to falter and dance, hastily backing up the bank. With admirable skill, he eased both his mother and her mount into the frigid water and then turned to locate the tall Blackfoot.

She had already removed her clothing unessential for modesty and was wading into the river. Gripping the bobbing bed of sticks behind Last Son, she swam behind their belongings, helping Bites-With-Dog float them into the river. Lastly, Held-Back-the-Enemy attended to Kept-Us-Alive. She stood transfixed, recalling the swirling raft that had trapped her beneath its irregular form, pressing her down to a watery grave. Every summer since, she had crossed the Echata without incident, but always under Pacing Wolf's guiding hand.

Without pause, Held-Back-the-Enemy swept her up and onto the back of her white mare and then settled Wolf-Who-Lays-Down in front of her. Then, after mounting his black and white pony, he tightly grasped her white mare's reins and pulled them beside him into the rushing water. The two horses slowly swam against the current, jostled now and again by a stray branch or bumped by a neighbor's raft, until they reached the other side.

The entire throng of clansmen and mounts emerged as a shivering mass, but all agreed that He-Who-Leads-The-Moving-Band had been correct. The river, though frigid, was still navigable. The Old Ones had also been correct. The sky had begun dropping its promised bounty, obscuring the divide between river and bank. By morning, high white drifts would bury their lodges.

As chilly gusts froze rivulets into tiny icicles, it sent painful tremors over their uncovered limbs and stiffened their wet clothing. Moving became difficult and slow until so many cook-fires began springing up, they appeared to be connected in a snaking river of flames.

AS THE DAWN painted swaths of darkest blue behind the trees' black branches, Pretty Face led Little Blackfoot the few steps to the guest lodge. "Sh-sh," he murmured as he reached for the door flap. "Mother's patient may be sleeping. His body is healing, but she wants you to crush these herbs into his mush. They will help him to feel less restless. She no longer puts them in broth. He draws up his lip and turns his head away."

"He will not taste them in this?" She rubbed the tiny leaves between her thumb and the side of her forefinger, sprinkling them into the bowl she carried.

"No. Mother added buffalo fat to mask the flavor. Do not tell him. It is our secret."

"What if he will not eat it?"

Pretty Face grinned. "What warrior can resist offerings from such a pleasant care-taker? Unless he still sleeps, he will be eating from your fingers before the sun peeks through the smoke-hole. You must stay with him until our mother calls you to help her with her chores."

"I want to go with you and Straight Arrows."

"Your tall Blackfoot mother told you to do as your new parents and brothers asked. Will you not obey her?"

As disappointment washed her face, he almost regretted his answer. He had grown attached to the child, though her frequent presence at his or Straight Arrows' side occasionally tried his patience. He supposed they formed a knot that tied her present to her past. Whatever the reason, she must learn to content herself with his mother and grandmother's company or the company of his aunts and many cousins. Red Fawn, his mother's close friend, had a daughter just Little Blackfoot's age. Hoping a worthwhile task might draw the child's mind from her losses, he had suggested she begin to help care for their patient.

"What happened to him?"

"We do not know. We are guessing the Raven Enemy attacked his raiding-party, but he either does not remember or is ashamed to recount his part. We were surprised to learn he was alive."

"Who are the 'Raven Enemy'?"

The young Ally cocked his head, setting a feather woven into the hair behind his ear to swaying. "The people who captured you and your mother."

The girl's eyes grew as round as a skittish mare's. "Where?"

"A cave across the great river."

Little Blackfoot tucked a lip between her teeth and began tugging it nervously.

"You are afraid?"

The girl quickly nodded and clutched the bowl she was carrying closer to her stomach.

"Why?"

"He is a shamer! They wait for women who are alone to…to…" She was unable to put what they had done to Falling Bear's woman into words. No one had explained beyond saying she was dead, but The-Women-Who-Talk-Against-Each-Other-Without-Fear grew silent whenever she or other girls drew near.

Pretty Face frowned. During the past moon, he often had sat with the patient, answering questions regarding the weather, the village, his family, and I-Am-Savior. Although he easily believed Wild Dog guilty of the vile deeds Little Blackfoot feared, he could not imagine this pensive cousin posing such dangers.

Putting a hand on his new sister's shoulder, he gave her a reassuring squeeze. "Come. I will tell my father and the elders all you have told me, but now we must do as our mother asked."

A bit tremulously, Little Blackfoot followed Pretty Face into the guest lodge; but when her eyes met the patient's, she almost dropped his breakfast. Setting the bowl down, she threw her arms around his neck. "We thought you were dead!"

The warrior held her tightly, pressing her head against his hunting shirt head. "What are you…why…how is Small Doe?"

"They brought me here," the girl beamed, "to replace…"

Swiftly snatching her up and dumping her to the side, Pretty Face grabbed the stranger by the shirt. "Get up!" he growled, hauling him to his feet and outside into the open. "I will not soil my mother's buffalo robes with your stinking blood!"

"No!" pleaded Little Blackfoot Woman, who had scrambled out behind them. "He is *not* a shamer. He is my friend!"

Pretty Face cast her a quick glance as he shoved the heel of his hand into the man's shoulder. "My mother tended you like a son! For two moons she has fed you—an enemy who snatched her only daughter, who wet her robes with tears and creased her face with sorrow!"

Pacing Wolf accepted every blow, teetering backward until he fell into a drift.

"Stop!" cried Brought-Us-The-Book, slipping out of her dwelling to interpose herself between the two. "His leg will snap!"

"Let it snap!" barked Pretty Face, brushing his mother aside. "I will kill him as I longed to when he shamed her!"

As Pacing Wolf watched Brought-Us-the-Book silently mouth her daughter's name, he vehemently shook his head. "I did not shame her. She offered me her pledge."

"She had no choice!"

"No," rasped Pacing Wolf. "But she was sensible."

"Get up!" barked the younger warrior, crouching to attack.

"I will not fight you."

"Stop!" commanded Preying Eagle over the gathering crowd. "Come." Jerking his head toward a wooded slope, he turned and strode away, not once glancing back to see if his son was following.

"He is The Enemy!" thundered Pretty Face. "The man who stole Light Bird!"

Preying Eagle halted, too stunned to reply. He had seen that his son was ready to attack the unknown Ally and read his woman's clear distress, but he had not heard what went before either.

"If not for him," Pretty Face seethed, "she would be *here*—where she belongs—married to Standing Elk." Only after he had caught up could he clearly read his father's eyes. They were dark with rage.

"She did not *want* Standing Elk," declared Running Deer, who had leaped up the hill on his grandson's heels. "She *wanted* this enemy."

"Light Bird?" asked Straight Arrows, glancing down at the little girl clinging to his wrist. When Pretty Face had refused to listen to her, Little Blackfoot had run up the precipice to enlist their oldest brother's aid, but she had been too short of breath from the steep ascent to do more than tug pleadingly. "She returned to him long ago. You heard her—he is dead. Why argue about him now?"

"He is *not* dead!" bit out Pretty Face, nodding toward Little Blackfoot. "She knew him."

Straight Arrows narrowed his eyes and drew his brows down sharply.

"Our Unnamed Cousin?"

"No cousin—a Raven Enemy!"

Straight Arrows tightly clenched his jaw, a glowering mirror of his father. As he remembered the shattered ghost of the carefree, loving girl Spotted Long-knife had returned to them, anger and disbelief began wrestling in his chest. "He has become like our brother."

"You are certain of this?" asked Running Deer, many summers of practice keeping his face impassive.

Pretty Face fixed his gaze on Little Blackfoot, then on his brother and grandfather. "When she saw him, she squealed with glee."

"He deceived us!" snapped Straight Arrows. "Come. Let us…"

"Where are you going?" asked Running Deer, grasping both grandsons' arms.

Pretty Face jerked his head toward the guest lodge. "To free our sister from obligation!"

"Have you listened to yourselves? Of *course* he deceived us. This warrior is deserving of the reputation Spotted Long-knife recounted, but can he fight off our whole village? What man among us would not wish to tear him to pieces?"

"No!" cried Little Blackfoot, grabbing Straight Arrows' wrist again as he reached for his knife.

Tightening his grip, Running Deer asked, "Would you murder a man who can barely walk!"

"We will do as you and our old uncles did when your old aunt's husband beat her—we will lay him in a shallow grave!"

Hearing this, the little girl intensified her pleading, but no one paid her any heed.

"We did not know the Creator."

"Would He have looked away while her husband beat her?"

"The stranger did not beat your sister."

"I too crave vengeance," fumed Preying Eagle, "but I will not let cravings twist my will. Come. We will consult I-Am-Savior on the matter."

Running Deer motioned for his grandsons to draw closer, but though Pretty Face complied, he kept his arms firmly by his sides. Little Blackfoot, afraid what I-Am-Savior might answer, squished into the middle; and before long, Two Bears, Little Turtle, Elk-Dog Man, and a host of other elders had joined them.

"Father, You see all—You know all. You knew this warrior would snatch my beloved granddaughter before You placed her in Brought-Us-The-Book's belly. You knew her heart would long to return to the Raven Enemy though he cast her aside, and that my grandsons would bring him here. Did you deliver him into our hands so we might carry out Your justice? Our hearts cry out to restore what this enemy has stolen, to return Light Bird's laughter to her grandmother and mother. Yet, You declared that vengeance is Yours, that You would repay.[27] Is this the retribution You planned?"

As Little Blackfoot's pleadings reached hysteria, Straight Arrows scooped her into his arms and added, "You hear all things. Even before a word leaped from our lips, You knew the anger and dismay stirring in our hearts. They cry out for…"

"Justice!" interjected Pretty Face. "You watched this enemy rob us and heard our mother and grandmother wailing with grief. You have watched him pretend to be our brother, as one who owns a double heart! Would You leave our sister to waste away from misery while the Raven Enemy raise her sons? They will teach them to hate their own kin!"

Even Little Blackfoot grew quiet while each listened, hoping God would speak; but after a while, Preying Eagle broke the silence. "All that my father and sons have said is so. We know You are a just God, a God who makes all people tremble. Your book declares it is fearful to fall into Your hands. Our enemy has fallen into ours and our hands are Yours. What would You have us do?"

He-Who-Sees-All-Things always watches those who fear Him; His eyes remain on all who hope in His unfailing love.

Psalm 33:18

Chapter 19

AS BROUGHT-US-THE-BOOK helped Pacing Wolf to his feet, she could not look him in the eyes. She was afraid of what he might read in hers if she did. At first, her mind felt as dull as stone, unable to grasp that this warrior—whom she had tended diligently, with whom her husband and father had discussed God's Word, and whom her sons had begun considering a friend—was the enemy who had shattered her daughter's innocence. As her brain began to work again, her sundry emotions began thundering like a spooked herd, so shaking her legs she feared they might buckle beneath his weight.

Part of her wished they would, dropping him to the ground where she could release her frustration in frenzied kicking. She yearned to shake him by the shirt, asking what right he had to ruin such loveliness and demand he restore Light Bird to her whole. A more sensible part recalled Wild Dog's crime. Within the newly united American states, many a man would have taken vengeance for such a heinous act. Even more did so in the territories, where courts were slow, and her adopted people required vengeance to honor the dead.

She also felt irrationally angry with her new daughter. The child had done nothing but reveal her patient's identity, spoiling the joy they had all felt with his good progress. Indeed, Brought-Us-The-Book regretted this for the girl's sake more than for her own.

Little Blackfoot had lately begun settling in, crying less and laughing more with her new brothers—particularly Straight Arrows. Whenever he was near, she either dogged his steps or sat so close to him she leaned partly over his lap. He, in return, offered her infinite patience, plentiful hair-tussles, and constant welcoming grins.

The child held her new father in far too much awe to behave so familiarly, but occasionally during meals—when Preying Eagle intentionally disappeared from view behind one of her new brothers and suddenly reappeared again—he so engrossed her that she forgot much of her fear and offered him a diffident smile.

She had taken to her new mother straight away, very likely because Brought-Us-The-Book and Kept-Us-Alive shared not only looks and gestures but also tones of voice and occasional slightly anglicized turns of phrase. The child eagerly helped her with chores, listened attentively when Brought-Us-The-Book instructed her or read from The Book, and had recently begun to recognize some of the words depicted by its markings.

Brought-Us-The-Book had loved her from the start, but her youngest son was less enthralled. Exactly Little Blackfoot's age, Follows-His-Shadow did not appreciate the attention his *new sister* stole from Young Deer, their next oldest brother, or from either of their two eldest. Her tiny toddling daughter had not yet revealed what she thought. She stared at Little Blackfoot through huge black eyes or tugged at the hem of her skirt when she wanted something. Otherwise, the girl might have lived in their dwelling all along.

Aware the current upset placed Little Blackfoot at odds with her family, Brought-Us-the-Book prayed it would not strain their recently formed bonds. The child might begin to feel alone again and without comfort, making her desperate for the Blackfoot mother she had lost.

As she settled the warrior back onto his bed, she recalled the name Light Bird had called him: Pacing Wolf. It no longer fit. He could do little more than limp a short distance, gingerly favoring his healing limb. She had been praying for him for nearly four summers, asking the Creator to stir love in his heart toward her precious daughter and spur him and his clansmen to follow I-Am-Savior's path. Apparently, the Lord had answered, softening her present ire. From the first syllables he had uttered, she had been convinced that he deeply loved his woman; and he had listened eagerly whenever anyone recited or read the Scriptures, asking them many well-founded questions.

They were too complex for a new listener. I should have realized…

Glancing surreptitiously in his direction, she saw that he possessed the same difficulty she did: he could not look her in the eyes. Why, she could only guess: perhaps shame, perhaps fear. She thought the latter unlikely but became distracted as Little Blackfoot, struggling to squelch her tears, crept quietly into the dwelling.

"He is right," Pacing Wolf stated.

Brought-Us-The-Book glanced back from the door-flap she was about to duck through but said nothing. She felt unsure *what* to say and did not trust herself—given a clear opening—to refrain from expressing much she might regret. A word, once spoken, was impossible to retrieve.

"Your son," he continued. "The one who possesses my woman's features—your features. The vengeance he desires is just."

Hearing this, Little Blackfoot again began to weep. "I do not want them to kill you. You must leave—quickly! Kept-Us-Alive needs you!"

"What did you call her?" asked her new mother, wondering if she had made a mistake.

The child shrank up, aware her new mother had stiffened and afraid it was her fault. "Kept-Us-Alive. Everyone calls her this but him. He calls her Small Doe."

As Brought-Us-The-Book relaxed, she looked at Pacing Wolf, who nodded his head.

"She owns doe-like looks and ways."

Her mother thought for a moment. She had been told so frequently that her daughter was the exact replica of herself, apart from their coloring, that she had never given thought to Light Bird's resemblance to a doe; yet as she did, she felt struck by the similarity. Her daughter possessed grace of both form and feature that she, herself, lacked: a longer neck, more willowy limbs, and her grandmother Two Doves' elegance of movement. Sitting down beside Little Blackfoot, she asked how Light Bird had come by the other name.

When the girl finished telling of the spotted fever and how helpless she had felt until Small Doe's return, all three had so calmed their emotions that Brought-Us-The-Book dared ask Pacing Wolf why he had sent her daughter away. She listened quietly, remembering all the heartache his decision had caused.

As he finished, she sighed deeply, a new respect for him growing alongside the love she already cherished. His decision had cost him dearly—far more dearly considering the little he had grasped at the time than it had cost Light Bird. As she studied his face, rife with regret and sorrow, she remembered what he had said earlier.

"The revenge Pretty Face desires may be just, but it is not right. He is eaten up with anger, and before the Creator visited this village, all of our menfolk would have felt the same, but vengeance belongs to God alone."[28]

"I know this passage, but I also have a little daughter..."

"Among-the-Pines," Little Blackfoot interjected. "My sister-friend."

"I-Am-Savior has forgiven me, but how can you—or your clansmen?"

"How can we not, when Jesus paid so dear a price to remove *our* sins?"

"Your sins are small. I have watched you."

"Most sins are not seen, even by the keenest eye. They lay deep in the heart."

A slight smile began tilting Pacing Wolf's lips. "You are like your daughter. You welcome the undeserving and eagerly thrust aside your own desires."

"The Creator has granted me frequent opportunities to repent and offered me grace after grace. No one, not even—what do you call her?"

"Small Doe."

"Not even Small Doe is able to earn the Creator's approval. Has she read you from the words of Small Man?"[29]

Pacing Wolf nodded. He suspected this Sent One[30] had been a member of his tribe. Who but a Sparrow Hawk would call their child by such an unflattering name?

"In a message he sent the Philippi People, he recounted many great accomplishments. He was as renowned as any warrior among the people of his birth and a fierce enemy of all who walked in I-Am-Savior's shadow; but he regarded his accomplishments as uneatable scraps we toss outside or fruit that became a dwelling for flies."[31]

"Ew!" groaned Little Blackfoot. "I picked up a cherry last summer that was filled with their tiny white small-things."

Brought-Us-the-Book chuckled. "My white cousin—the one who wrote the Creator's Word in our people's tongue—told me this expression was not correct. The one Small Man used was even worse!"

Pacing Wolf pursed his lips. "Why did your cousin make false markings?"

"He felt embarrassed. My white fathers consider speaking freely of their bodies impolite."

"What should he have written?"

"Dung! So if Small Man's great deeds are dung, what are any of mine? I have nothing to offer I-Am-Savior."

Little Blackfoot looked like she might burst. "But you brought the book to this people!"

"They honor me with this name, my little one, but I did not bring it; the Creator did. He just used my pocket to hide it in."

"But you…"

"Happened to have it with me when I came. Sin is sin. When I make stew for us, I fill my cookpot with good meat our men-folk have hunted and vegetables I have dug from the generous earth. If you watched your little sister pick up a fistful of dung left by Young Deer's dog and toss it into our stew, would you still eat it?"

Little Blackfoot scrunched up her nose. "No."

"What if she pinched off only a tiny piece and then dipped her fingers in the cooling stew to rid them of the smell?"

Both the girl and Pacing Wolf shook their heads from side to side.

"I could add more good meat and fresh clean water and many vegetables."

"It would still be fouled," answered Pacing Wolf, wondering where she headed.

"My heart is like my cookpot. As the stew it holds is heated, it may give off an aroma that causes cravings in an empty belly, but I could never add enough good food to rid it of even the smallest touch of filth. I must toss the contents away, just as I would a cookpot stuffed with dung, and burn the cook-pot in the fire. Just so, I-Am-Savior does not favor one fouled cookpot over another. He rids us of filth and makes us new cookpots, clean and ready for His use."

AS BROUGHT-US-THE-BOOK slipped beneath her buffalo robes, she slid her sleeping potbellied daughter toward the edge, made certain the toddler's chubby torso was fully covered, and took her place next to Preying Eagle. He was awake, tensely staring at their smoke hole.

"I am a warrior," he murmured, topping the hand she had smoothed leisurely up his arm and across his chest. "I have been raised from childhood to protect our people and have taught this to our sons. Can I forbid them to grasp the justice my own heart craves? We did nothing to draw this enemy's vengeance, and yet he snatched our child. Should I lay idle when I can set her free?"

Brought-Us-The-Book did not answer. She could think of nothing to add that either their sons or their grandfather had not already voiced.

"I too crave justice," added Straight Arrows, who also had been lying awake. "But what of I-Am-Savior—and Light Bird? What would she wish?"

"Waugh!" scoffed Pretty Face, listening while his eldest brother ventured into their parents' conversation. "How can we know what she would wish?"

"You heard what Little Blackfoot said your sister," whispered his mother. "Does she sound like she is eager to be free of him?"

Preying Eagle grunted, raking his fingers stiffly through his loosened hair.

"How can we know what she feels?" snapped Pretty Face, glaring angrily through the darkness.

"Sleep," his father commanded, raising up on one elbow. He would not scold him for answering his mother this way while all their feelings were so raw.

Pretty Face turned over, glaring instead at the lodge cover.

Laying back, Preying Eagle returned his gaze to the smoke hole and his hand to the one atop his chest. "Since I discovered her hair on his robe, I have wrestled hard with hatred. Waugh—I cannot think of what transpired there. If I do, I will leap up to kill him! For these past four summers, I have imagined his face whenever I have asked Our Father to forgive my debts as I forgive those indebted to me."[32]

"While you were praying with your father and our sons, he explained much to me that I had not understood—not about his vengeance quest but about sending her home with Spotted Long-knife."

"Who knows what evil they practice in such a place?"

"Will you continue to tend his wounds?" asked their eldest.

"Yes," Brought-Us-The-Book answered softly. "I-Am-Savior told us to love our enemies[33]—how much more should we love His children?" Little Blackfoot confirmed all he told me. He met I-Am-Savior long before you brought him here, while Standing Elk was courting Ligh…Small Doe."

"You would call her this?"

"He is her husband. He has the right to call her what he wishes. And it suits her."

Leaping through his memory, Preying Eagle tried to recall when the man had said he had encountered I-Am-Savior, but he could not. He—and probably each of them—had assumed it was while he lay near death in their guest lodge, though the man had never said so. He also could not avoid admitting his father had been right. This warrior was clever—clever enough to hide who he was when he found himself surrounded by an enemy.

As he trod back over the last two moons, he came to an unexpected realization: not once had he heard the Raven Enemy speak falsely. He had allowed them to leap to their own conclusions.

"What of Red Fox?" asked Straight Arrows.

Brought-Us-The-Book waited for her husband, but he was too lost in thought to answer. "He cannot be ignorant of his son's behavior. All Allies know we cast Wild Dog from our village. Can they doubt we had just cause?"

"That will not matter." Preying Eagle rejoined the conversation. "I know Red Fox—have known him from boyhood. He will seek vengeance, and we cannot stop him. Should we—for an enemy—tear the bond between our bands?"

"Wild Dog tore that bond the morning he plotted to ruin our daughter."

"Why does God say that?"

All their heads swiveled toward Young Deer, whom they had thought was asleep.

"What?" asked his father.

"About vengeance. If my little brother takes my bow, you do not shrug and tell me to be silent. You make him give it back. I would have hunted him down!"

"We tried! The Raven Enemy and she had become like the white wisps you see disappearing through our smoke hole..."

As his voice began to constrict, Straight Arrows picked up his trail. "Grandfather and I scoured the ground around the cave's mouth. I climbed the cliff, examining every hint of damaged grass, but no trail became wide enough to let a man pass. Even our uncles, who are well-known trackers, found only prints that led back to the..."

"To the place he forced her!" spat Pretty Face.

Preying Eagle's hand tightened around Brought-Us-The-Book's until his grip became uncomfortable, but she could not tell if he tensed from his own frustration or Pretty Face's mutinous temper. "He did not force her," she countered, hoping this might calm both son and husband. "She told me so when Spotted Long-knife brought her home, and he confirmed this today. She offered him her marriage-pledge."

"She had no choice!" answered Young Deer.

"Neither does any captured woman, but she offered it and has grown to love him. Perhaps this answers your question about vengeance. The Creator alone knows all men's hearts. He knew before He fashioned either of them that the stranger would snatch her."

"She did no wrong," argued the youth. "Why would the Creator make him steal *her*?"

"He did not *make* him, but He knew what this man would do, just as He knew Joseph's brothers would sell him to slavers.[34] You remember the story; we have often read it. Joseph's dreams revealed what was in the Creator's heart. Though He does not cause anyone to sin, He gives us the freedom to do as we will, then uses even those choices to accomplish His purpose. If slavers had not carried Joseph off to Egypt, his family would have starved in the famine and I-Am-Savior would not have been born to them. Perhaps He used the man's vengeance quest to bring his people news of I-Am-Savior."

She felt as much as heard her husband's groan, but he loosened his grip and began absently stroking her small hand. He knew she was right, but his heart could not yet loosen its grip on his war-club.

For how many summers she wondered, *have I lived as Preying Eagle's wife? Twenty-four? Seven more than I lived with my father. Still, though I love him, he often seems as foreign as he did that day we first met.*

Long ago, she attributed this foreignness to their different origins, which she admittedly found fascinating, but she did not feel this with either his mother or his aunts.

Perhaps, she thought, *he is so different because he is male. He seems woven from an altogether different fabric.*

As his fingers grew still and slipped over his stomach, she nearly chuckled over her choice of words. She had not seen fabric since her white *cousins* departed permanently to Boston. Returning to her former occupation, she smoothed her palm over the mounds atop his chest. They were as firm as the evening she first shyly touched them.

Spotted Long-knife had once wondered if she would miss the finery of home. Although she had always loved her grandmother's blue and white dishes and her dark, highly polished furnishings, she had realized even while living there that they could never satisfy her deeper longings. In fact, not until that very moment had she recognized something she felt constantly during girlhood and did not miss at all: loneliness.

As her husband rolled over and laid his arm across her waist, she felt such relief, she exhaled deeply, waking him again. He peered into her face, setting her to wonder if he could read what she had been thinking, even in the dark. From the first, he had possessed an uncanny ability to do so, and if he ever felt her as foreign as she felt him, he never offered the least indication. Stretching to press her lips against the scar near his shoulder, she knew she would make the same decision to marry him again.

When his fingers grew still on her hip, she realized he had drifted to sleep and did likewise; but two other pairs of eyes were wide-awake. One, round like his mother's and sister's, hardened with determination. The other, almond-shaped and large below her child-sized forehead, clouded darkly with foreboding.

He does act toward us as our sins deserve or trade us the just measure for our iniquities. For as high as the heavens are above the earth, so great is His loving kindness toward those who fear him.
                                                                Psalm 103:10

Chapter 20

PACING WOLF SAT WITH his leg extended, rubbing a hand over the tidy row of scars Small Doe's mother had created when she mended his wound. He was now certain who inflicted it; Straight Arrows told him they pulled Wild Dog from the mountain's jaws.

The stitches could easily have been Small Doe's, he mused, lifting the leg and moving it sideways, as he had done often each sun since Brought-Us-the-Book had released him from the lodge-poles and bandages. Although it now held his weight, he despaired of it ever regaining its former vigor. It reminded him of a shriveled stalk, as if it had been unable to find a path to the food she heartily supplied him.

Recognizing the voices beyond the lodge covers, he stilled his limb and tried to make out what they were saying. Young Deer's timbre was easy to pick out; but Preying Eagle and Straight Arrows sounded so alike, Pacing Wolf needed to hear their words to tell them apart.

Although his Sparrow Hawk breeding cast Small Doe's family as his enemies, the gratitude he felt toward her light-eyed mother and poor-sighted grandmother had ripened into genuine affection. These two were as different as their looks and color, but each bore plain similarities to his woman. Clearly, the qualities he so prized in her had sprung from roots planted deeply in the rich, well-tended soil of both their generous hearts.

Greater yet was his swiftly increasing reverence for her father, grandfather, and eldest brother. The words that flowed from them tasted like clean, sparkling rivers, slaking the thirsty cravings of his soul. Along with several uncles—most notably Old Many Feathers and Wooden Legs—they brought to mind the Old Ones described in the Creator's book: Many Sons, Drawn-Out-Man, The-Creator-Hears, Loved-By-the Creator,[35] and even I-Am-Savior. He had been growing more and more eager for each of their visits this past moon and had looked forward to gaining answers to his plentiful questions.

For too long, he had lacked a father or grandfather, though Kills-Behind-Her-Dwelling, his old grandmother, had done her best to raise him.

Hunts-For-Death had once inspired him with awe, but even before the chasm grew between them, Pacing Wolf had begun finding his counsel lacking. Only old Hair-Up-Top occasionally had allowed his heart's proud covering to slip to the ground, exposing tender and often regretful recesses underneath.

For several summers, he had begun to weary of his clansmen's boasting and their demand he hide behind an equally proud war shield to retain their confidence and esteem. The handful of Good Men who walked in I-Am-Savior's shadow were slowly changing, but they were brothers looking to him for guidance, not the seasoned fathers he craved.

Once he had picked out Preying Eagle and Straight Arrows' voices, he felt ashamed of the envy he felt. Straight Arrows surely owned six or seven summers fewer than he did, but the young warrior possessed not only his father's and grandfather's trust but their confidence in his counsel. The three were as likeminded as any warriors he had ever encountered, reminding him of something the Israelites Real Chief[36] had once said: "A three-fold rope is not easily broken."[37]

What will her father's eyes say when I next see him? I need not guess what Pretty Face feels.

Pacing Wolf grieved deeply over his disavowal. Besides Small Doe's mother, Pretty Face had held first place in his affection. He had been Pacing Wolf's most constant companion, regaling him with stories of the village, stories of the family—including the capture of his sister—and stories of his clansmen's feats of valor. Pacing Wolf had longed to prod him to speak more of Small Doe, but he dared not show too much interest. After all, Pretty Face had not until yesterday realized Pacing Wolf knew her, and doing so would have stirred the young warrior's already avid curiosity.

His reflections carried him back to a path he had been treading all morning: how he might leave. The discussion he was now overhearing added urgency to this desire, for he longed not only to see Small Doe and his children but also to get away before he caused her family trouble. If these very men-folk he so admired decided not to kill him, they would still regard him as an enemy: he had read as much in her mother's face. Though she spoke of her own equal debt to I-Am-Savior, her water-colored eyes held wariness and pain.

If this Red Fox they were discussing were anything like his son, Pacing Wolf could guess what to expect. The man would raise a war party that might threaten this entire village. For their sakes as well as his family's, he needed to leave, whether his leg had fully mended or not. A smile curved his lips as he imagined Small Doe's joy-filled welcome and relief, but as he envisioned her ripening belly, a furrow creased his brow.

The trees are setting buds. The buffalo will soon drop their calves, and she will drop our new small-thing along with them.

Praying her pain would be brief, his mind wandered to Hopping Owl, with whom she was surely now living, and smacked straight into her son. His gut twisted sharply as he recalled their conversation: he had urged Held-Back-the-Enemy to take her quickly, and the young Lumpwood had readily agreed. What might Pacing Wolf find when he reached them?

He knew Small Doe loved him and that the small-thing she carried might prevent a swift physical union, but he also remembered how steadfastly she kept her word. A faithless woman would have betrayed him to her clansmen while they hid in the cave or called out when she spotted them by the river. Glancing down at his leg, he groaned.

She is better off with Held-Back-the-Enemy. What good can I do for her or my children? If they depend on me to provide food, they may starve.

"MAY I COME IN?" called a hesitant young voice from outside the guest lodge.

"Enter," invited Pacing Wolf, but when Little Blackfoot slipped in, she did not feel very welcome. Though she saw him glance up briefly, he was pressing his lips tightly together.

"I have warm stew for you," the little girl offered. "Without dung."

As the reminder tugged him from his thoughts, his eyes slightly crinkled. The child had courage. Though she risked much that was desirable, she had returned to him as often as her chores allowed and remained staunchly by his side, a small dog determined to interpose herself between her master and any new assailants.

"Straight Arrows gave me a pony from his herd," she told him, pausing until he engaged her eyes. "He is gentle and not too tall. I will bring him to you."

Pacing Wolf's brow arched upward, but as he waited for her to continue, her little face began to crumple.

"Pr-Pretty F-Face rides to The Sh-Shamer's v-village," she stammered, though her bottom lip so quivered he strained to catch the words. "H-He will come. He will ki-kill you! I give you my p-pony. Ride away—n-now!"

Pacing Wolf touched the girl's braid as he peered into her eyes. "You cannot. They will be angry with you—Straight Arrows and your new family."

The little girl somberly shook her head. "You make Old White Hair buy me from the tall angry woman. You make him return me to my mother."

As Pacing Wolf watched a tear spill over her lightly pitted cheek, he lifted up her chin. "Why did your mother send you away?"

Little Blackfoot raised her eyes only to quickly drop them again. "She wants a better life for me. She did not want my heart to own sorrow each spring when the grass turns green."

Understanding perfectly, Pacing Wolf nodded. "She is wise and her love for you is deep. She chooses the best path for her daughter and leaves only sorrow for herself to eat."

As the girl again glanced upward, her eyes showed a mix of gratitude and grief. "Tell her I am happy with Kept-Us-Alive's family," she whispered, wiping away several tears that had dribbled down to her chin.

Pacing Wolf nodded, holding out his arms to draw her close. At first, she did not know what to do. For several summers, she had held him in too much awe to behave so familiarly. "Come," he urged her. "I will take your embrace and carry it to your mother, and give me one for Among-the-Pines and another for my woman."

At once, the child forgot her hesitation, and though she did not throw her arms around him as his daughter would have done, she allowed him to hold her in his.

"Has she married?" he asked.

"Mother?"

"Small Doe. Has she married Held-Back-the-Enemy?"

"No," replied the girl, raising her head sharply. "Mother says she must, but she refuses. She cries for you and waits. Hunts-For-Death took away your lodge and handed it to Bull-Will-Not-Fall, but Hopping Owl made a place for her and Wolf-Who-Lays-Down in Bites-With-Dog's lodge."

Pacing Wolf breathed in deeply and then slowly out again. "And my children and the others who walk behind I-Am-Savior?"

"They are well. They read His Book in Bites-With-Dog's lodge. Many come. Many listen."

Pacing Wolf gave her a gentle squeeze. Although he had more questions, he would not ask them. She was very young and had a limited understanding of tribal workings or rivalries between the war-societies. Besides, her own troubles already overflowed her heart; he could not ask her to carry his. "Leave the stew; I will eat it. Wait until the sun sleeps to bring your pony—and not into the village. After all the untouched women have finished gathering their firewood, leave him by the old crabapple."

PRETTY FACE GAZED UP at the sky in front of him, above him, and then back over his shoulder toward the way he had come. The brilliant blue beyond his roan's nose gave way overhead to the color of a lake beginning to set with ice. Behind him, the sky looked pale and dismal, declaring it would soon smother his mother's dwelling with a dreary blanket. He could not turn back.

The air was no warmer than the cold foreboding that gripped his heart. Since boyhood, he could not remember placing himself at odds with his father, and—even worse—he was beginning to suspect he had been wrong. His anger had felt like a ravaging fire, impossible to quench until it burned itself out. It had, leaving him charred misgivings that were impossible to will away—no matter how often he recounted the justice of his reasons.

Like a wolf pup he had once found, his mother's counsel persistently pressed its nose into the yielding flesh of his midsection, nudging around for a way to wriggle beneath his hunting shirt and lodge between the mounds of his warm chest. He had laughed while that pup's cold nose tickled his ribcage, but he was not laughing now.

His plan had been impulsive, as poorly thought out as the position in which he now found himself. His grandfather's eyes would have filled with disappointment had he made such a blunder during one of their youthful war-games, and his father would have harshly scolded had he acted with such little thought against an enemy. Indeed, whether in sport or in battle, such a headlong rush was bound to cost him much. Had they both not taught him to avoid plunging into anger as he would a swiftly running stream? Such a foolish warrior would find himself scraped and battered.

Although he now yearned to turn back, the sky robbed him of the choice. If he did, he too would soon be smothered beneath a heavy white blanket—only without the comforts afforded by his mother's lodge covers.

What was it she said? he asked himself, trying to recall the answer she gave his little brother. *"Perhaps the Creator, Who alone knows all men's hearts, allowed this enemy to snatch her so that she might bring his people news of I-Am-Savior."*

"You see my heart also, I-Am-Savior," he whispered. "You are a just God; I also crave justice, but You are The One who plans the end from the beginning. Please show me a path of escape from my own foolishness.[38] Your spirit constrains me so that I cannot go forward, but the snow will not permit me to go back. Show me what to do!"

As he envisioned the nameless enemy that he had so often imagined beating Light Bird, the harsh lines of that man's face melted into the tender lines of the strange warrior who had so often called her name. *Small Doe.* He agreed with her enemy-husband: it fitted his sister well.

If my heart cherishes evil, The Almighty One will not listen, but surely He has heard and heeded the voice of my prayer. I revere The Creator, who has not spurned my prayer or turned His love from me!
Psalm 66:18-20

Chapter 21

ONCE THE VILLAGE GREW quiet, Pacing Wolf crept out of the guest lodge to find Little Blackfoot's pony tethered, as he had instructed, to the ancient crabapple. Memories of pleasant laughter that had drawn his eyes across the meadow engulfed him as he reached around its gnarly trunk. As he remembered Small Doe's first horrified glimpse of him, he wished he could have spared her such pain, and yet he still could not regret snatching her. She had crowded his lodge with love and, more importantly, had brought him to The One that filled his empty heart to overflowing.

As he untied Little Blackfoot's pony, she shimmied to the side, nearly throwing him off balance. He had already begun to tire from the effort of crossing the meadow, and his normally agile legs felt as if Brought-Us-the-Book still kept them bound between her lodge-poles. Grasping a fistful of the animal's hair, he swung himself up as he had countless times during his thirty summers, holding on tightly to balance himself and then resting for a moment atop her neck.

"I am sorry, small one," he whispered, "for parting you from the warmth of your herd. We will not travel far—just far enough for the falling snow to cover your hoof prints—and then together we will find shelter."

Twitching her ears, the well-formed brown and white pony responded to the pressure of Pacing Wolf's legs, turning away from the crabapple to trudge up the hill and then cover the long familiar route he had traveled on his sorrel three summers past. When they, at last, reached the trail that bent toward Apsaroke, she did not respond. She wandered to the left and then slightly to the right until he eventually feared she might circle back in the direction they had come.

He understood her problem. His newly mended leg could not apply enough pressure to indicate the way he wanted her to head; so though he guessed she had already carried him halfway to the Muddy River, when the snow began to thicken she trotted toward a clump of grey rough-barked trees. Pulling her rope, he managed to slow her and then leaned, hoping his weight might make up for his leg's loss of strength; but instead of making his will clear, he tossed himself so off balance that his heavy buffalo robe dragged him to one side. He squeezed his legs together, using his taut torso to vault his seat back onto the center of her back. Since his boyhood, he had learned to shift on his mount from one side to the other, a skill he had often used to evade an enemy's arrow or lance; but his stiffened leg refused to grip and he thumped with an "Ouff!" onto the frozen, snow-covered ground.

For some moments, he lay on his back, gripped with intense pain that turned rapidly into panic. The fall had so forced the air from his lungs, he could not will them to expand, but just as he feared he might suffocate, they began to open. Relieved, he sucked in great gulps of air until all his limbs began cramping. Staring up through the trees' leafless canopy, he silently began to pray.

I-Am-Savior, help me! If I do not reach the Cliffs-That-Have-No-Name, Held-Back-the-Enemy may take Small Doe as…

When a flake floated onto his forehead, followed by another and another, he grew aware of a much more urgent threat. If he could not get himself up, the storm might soon bury him. He tried with all his strength to rise, but the most he could gain was a sitting position. His legs had mounted a rebellion, refusing to do more than jut out stiffly. Twisting his torso, he turned onto his stomach, hoping he might push himself up with his arms; but as he dropped his head forward, gasping from his efforts, he sucked in a mouthful of thick, chilling wetness.

Sputtering, he lifted his head and pushed his chest off the ground, dragging himself and his heavy buffalo robe forward until he had no more strength. His face fell into the snow again, now deeper, freezing his nostrils as he breathed it in. With a snort, he blew it out, laboring to twist onto his back, only to look up through the same stark branches. He had moved a few handbreadths.

While blinking away the flakes, hot tears he had not allowed to escape since boyhood stung his eyes. *How*, he wondered, *could such tiny enemies launch so fierce an onslaught, attacking and attacking, as many as the stars.* As they crusted his lashes, he began to laugh. *I have stood by the death-staff as warrior after warrior met my ax or lance, and now I meet defeat by this most fragile war party!*

Breathing in the cold air, he thought of Small Doe and their children, one he now knew he would never meet. He almost felt relieved. *I-Am-Savior, You are my Real Chief and friend. Your hand is not too short to save, but what can I offer them—a warrior too weak-legged to stay astride a small and gentle pony? But Held-Back-the-Enemy—he has much courage and is not arrogant like our Sparrow Hawk clansmen. He will be to them as You have been to me, bringing joy without adding sorrow…*

"YOU ARE VERY QUIET," observed Preying Eagle as he watched his woman blowing new life into their embers. Throughout the day, she had seemed as silent as the village after the sky had emptied its contents, keeping both her limbs and face unusually still. He always knew by the latter that something troubled her spirit. Even after many summers living apart from her people, she still struggled to keep thoughts from altering her features or from shining clearly through her water-colored eyes.

"I am grieved," Brought-Us-The-Book murmured, slipping under their covers. "I keep asking myself why he would betray our trust."

Preying Eagle did not ask whom she meant; he had suspected Pretty Face had caused her stillness. "To stay here, he would have to face what I-Am-Savior requires. By going, he is free to chase his own desires."

"But why? Have we not taught or shown him well enough how to walk behind I-Am-Savior?"

Preying Eagle pressed his lips so tightly together their corners sloped downward. He loved his woman deeply, but sometimes he thought she expected too much—not only of her sons but of herself. Each man possessed his own sin nature and no amount of good training or teaching could rid him of it.

Brought-Us-The-Book once more fell silent, sensing her answer had not pleased him. Slipping between their buffalo robes, she turned on her back instead of laying her head against his chest. He was so still that she suspected he had already fallen asleep, and her heart felt too raw to risk further hurt by stirring up his irritation. Closing her eyes, she expected to hear his normal light snoring, but instead, he drew in a deep breath and let it loudly out again.

"Pretty Face is not like our eldest, who has learned to hold the reigns of his anger firmly. His temper flares like fat tossed into the fire, but it dies away just as quickly. Offer him a wide path so the Creator can speak to his heart. Pretty Face cannot outrun Him."

Turning over, she lay her cheek against his arm; but when he did not lift it up to slip behind her shoulders, she realized he had already drifted away.

How can he let the matter go so easily? she fumed. *He would not allow our children to run from his wishes; how much less should Pretty Face run from God's!*

As she listened to her husband's even breathing, she glanced over to their new daughter. The child seemed restless or unable to find a comfortable position, and when she turned toward the embers, light glinted off black open eyes.

"What troubles you?" Brought-Us-The-Book whispered.

The little girl merely shook her head and shrugged her small shoulders, but with the slightest sound outside, her eyes darted toward the door-flap.

"What have you heard, little one? An owl? Perhaps a wolf howling from hunger? Do not be afraid; we will not let them harm you."

Again, the child said nothing, but when the light reflected in her eyes began to dance, Brought-Us-The-Book knew she was trying not to cry. Assuming she understood the problem, she slipped over to stroke the child's hair, softly murmuring words of comfort and assurance until Little Blackfoot's eyelids grew so heavy she could no longer keep them open.

Brought-Us-the-Book began to close hers also and was just entering a dream when Straight Arrows startled her awake by jerking bolt upright.

"Sh-sh-sh," she murmured drowsily. "I have just gotten this little one to sleep. What is it?"

"I do not know," answered Straight Arrows. Something disturbed my spirit." Strapping on his warmest leggings, he pulled on his moccasins, a hunting shirt, and wrapped himself in his heavy buffalo robe.

"Where are you going?" his mother whispered, but her question fell unheeded as he ducked into the frosty night. Unsure if he had heard her, she thought of calling after him, but did not. She wanted to awaken neither her new daughter, who had squirmed half into her lap before she had fallen asleep, nor the rest of her tired family.

Let them rest; the day has been difficult. He likely needs to empty himself of water. Gently lifting Little Blackfoot's head and shoulders back onto a pillow, she scooted underneath the child's covering and slipped into exhaustion.

WHOOPS VOLLEYED through the biting air while young Allied warriors Pretty Face had not seen for several summers rode out to greet him. His heart felt full as they ushered him toward the village center: full of pleasure as the moon illumined their welcoming faces, full of gratitude that he had outraced the whirling blizzard, and full of a niggling unease he wanted to neither think about nor name.

The journey had been hard, his limbs felt stiff, and his eyebrows crusted with ice where they peeked from beneath his buffalo robe. Masking his aches, he slid from his mount, searching the surging crowd of faces for his father's old ally; but before he found him, a particular set of eyes caught and held his attention. They were startlingly familiar and yet, as they dropped toward the ground, he did not recognize any other portion of their owner. Only when he spotted a scar across her right earlobe did his memory give him a sudden, sharp slap.

She is little Plays-With-Her-Earrings!

He had given her that scar. As if wanting to confirm his conclusion, her hand wandered toward her ear and began fingering a polished circular bone hanging from its lobe. He followed its halting descent along the curve of her neck as she dropped it down to disappear beneath the thick fur wrapped around her shoulders. A glimpse of white teeth peeking through lovely curving lips had replaced the hollow gap he last remembered, and the scraped up limbs that formerly stuck out below her doeskin now looked shapely and smooth. He had never witnessed such a remarkable transformation.

An older warrior, a hand or so taller than Plays-With-Her-Earrings, pushed through the melee to take the place beside her. "You remember my daughter?"

Pretty Face nodded. Red Fox's nose was more prominent than Wild Dog's had been, and his form was not tall but stocky. In fact, now that Pretty Face studied him squarely, he concluded Wild Dog had taken after Swallow Woman.

"If your people had joined us for The Dance last summer, you could have watched her dancing among our untouched women."

Although Pretty Face understood Red Fox's scolding, he could not tell whether he merely upbraided his band for missing the Allies' gathering or was inviting him to gaze longer at his daughter. Before he came to a decision, several young warriors began pressing in around him.

"We are glad to see you," said one, gripping his shoulder. "The snows have kept us by this lake with only these few ugly faces for company."

As several companions joined in the young man's laughter, Pretty Face returned their greetings. An older one did indeed look ugly, glowering at him as if he were not an ally but an enemy. Turning back toward Red Fox,

Pretty Face discovered why: though Plays-With-Her-Earrings remained quite still by her father, her eyes flitted over each of Pretty Face's features. They plummeted to the ground as he caught her.

Warmed by her shy admiration, he drew himself up to full height. He was not as tall as Straight Arrows or the girl's dead brother, but compared to her father and the surly warrior, he felt like an oak standing between elms.

"You will sleep in my woman's dwelling," offered Red Fox. "And tell me all you have learned from the wounded stranger. He is not either of my sisters' sons as we believed. The eldest arrived here this morning. When the ice thaws, we will raise a party to avenge ourselves on our dead's enemy."

The hint of relish in the older warrior's tone sharply jabbed at Pretty Face's conscience. He could imagine, too well, what they would do when they found his sister's husband had been the assailant; and though he might not be ready yet to let go of his anger, he saw a clear distinction between Pacing Wolf and Red Fox's quests.

With a little trepidation, Pretty Face accepted the invitation. Not only did it promise a warm fire and a full stomach, but it also offered a further chance to assess the changes the past summers had brought the man's daughter. He was disappointed, however, when the churlish man followed.

Plays-With-Her-Earrings' feelings for this man quickly became apparent. Although she shyly engaged Pretty Face's eyes while offering what was left of her family's late meal, she refused to look at any part of Angry Man above his knees. Only once did her eyes flicker upward, causing Pretty Face to wonder if the aptly named man had taken some unseen liberty. If so, she either did not welcome it or wished to keep it hidden. She continued onward to the next guest as if she had felt nothing.

"Your eyes are often on my daughter," observed Red Fox, leaning close so Pretty Face might hear him. "Angry Man wants her, but I have not decided. He has earned many trophies for the coups he has counted—more trophies than you wear—but she does not like him."
"He is old; he must possess thirty-five summers."
"Thirty-six."
"She is still very young. She cannot possess more than sixteen."

Red Fox nodded. "She will not remain untouched for long. Angry Man is her boldest suitor, but there are several others. She looks much like her mother, does she not?"

Pretty Face agreed, understanding her father's intent, but this likeness offered little allure. Though he had heard Swallow Woman had been a great beauty in her youth, her features were now etched into a decidedly sour scowl. "Are they alike in temperament?" he wondered and was half-startled to realize he had muttered this aloud.

"As alike as any mother and daughter I have known. You know I snatched my woman right out from under the nose of your father?"

Again, Pretty Face nodded, unwilling to insult his host by recounting his parents' or uncles' versions of the story.

"Does your father still keep that woman with the oddly colored eyes?"

"My mother?"

Red Fox pulled sharply backward as if he felt surprised to learn of the relationship, though Pretty Face could not credit the notion. All knew his father had only one woman, and apart from her coloring, he was her very image in man-form.

"Yes. Both are well."

"And how is my son's companion?"

"Both legs recover," the young warrior answered carefully, "but we are less certain he will regain full use of his mind."

"Then why have you come to us, and where is your older brother? We assumed your father had sent you."

"Straight Arrows stayed in our village," replied Pretty Face, grasping for a plausible explanation until he noticed his host's lovely daughter kneeling before an old, toothless warrior. "A young woman draws his attention."

As Red Fox's lips tilted upward, Pretty Face wondered what he would say if he learned she was eight.

"So—though you and Straight Arrows sleep in different villages tonight, you are on the same hunt."

Pretty Face remained impassive. He felt trapped, wanting to neither betray the discord between him and his family nor encourage the older warrior's conclusion. Plays-With-Her-Earrings had attracted his attention, but he did not intend to pursue the girl. Her mother had caused his own much grief, vying openly and bitterly for his father, and her brother had caused his sister's ruin. In addition, he remembered why her grandparents had left his family's band. They opposed the elders who had begun following I-Am-Savior.

Could Plays-With-Her-Earrings be any different? Red Fox would not allow him to find out unless he declared his intentions, and he would not declare any intentions unless he found out. The Creator's Word was clear and sensible: two cannot walk together while they are traveling separate paths.

Light arises in the darkness: full of grace, mercy, and justice.
Psalm 112:4

Chapter 22

During the

Moon When Buffalo Drop Their Calves

LEAPING FROM HIS mount, Straight Arrows gripped the dark lump lying beneath the rough-barked trees, shaking it so hard that he parted its snow-covered buffalo robe. "Wake up!" Thrusting a hand into the gap, he felt a sudden shudder and then lighter, quicker shivers. "Do you hear me? Wake up! Do you wish to freeze?" As the lump began to stir, he tightly tucked its robe back about it and tromped towards a taller shadow.

Little Blackfoot's pony—the lump is Light Bird's captor!

At once, Straight Arrows' mind tied several odd strands together: the looks the child kept casting him that evening—like a dog expecting to be kicked—her absence after their late meal, and the trouble she had falling to sleep. He had supposed that she missed her mother, but looking back, he recalled that her eyes had incessantly traveled to the dwelling's door.

Staring intently at the dark heap, he grew keenly aware that he could—without lifting a finger—end Pretty Face's vengeance quest; but an old, often recounted story, offered him a sharp rebuke.

Can I do less for him than my mother did for our father?

Feeling for the pony's woven rope, he brushed the snow from her back, led her closer to the lump, and bent down to roll his sister's enemy-husband out of the heavy, sodden robe. He intended only to make the man lighter so he might more easily hoist him onto the pony, but the unexpected cold roused the lump to waking.

Squatting closer, Straight Arrows asked, "Are you hurt?" The total silence of the snow-laden night magnified his voice so that even to himself it sounded harsh and strained.

The man moaned and muttered indecipherably.

Bracing a shoulder against the Raven Enemy's torso, the young Ally hefted him off the ground and heaved him onto the pony's blanket, retrieved the sodden buffalo robe, and tossed the drier side over the pony's limp load. He had noticed a thick stand of firs in the distance, looking black against the stark fresh snow.

They are farther away than they appear, he calculated, *but they will offer us more shelter than these leafless gray-barked trees.*

ONCE STRAIGHT ARROWS had comfortably situated his sister's captor, he started a small fire from a handful of twigs he had cut from the firs' underbellies. They would burn slowly, providing a little extra heat. Besides, he needed to be careful. Though the falling snow would keep most enemies inside their warm lodges, smoke from a fast-burning fire might invite trouble.

He rubbed a hand over his tired eyes, removed the buffalo robe slung over his shoulder, and laid it atop the one he had tucked around the Raven Enemy. Screwing up his nose, he also slipped beneath them. He would need to provide all the warmth he could muster if he did not wish to find himself sleeping with a corpse by morning. Shuddering as he came into contact with the man's cold flesh, he feared he might already be too late.

As he lay looking up at the fragrant fir branches, he was unable to force his thoughts to make peace. One moment, he asked the Creator for mercy; in the next, he imagined the horrors Light Bird endured, sending his thoughts galloping down a dark trail he had often traveled since discovering the man's identity. Then, just as his anger began to burn hotter, snatches of their friendly conversations began extinguishing the flaring flames.

What had she called him—Pacing Wolf?

As he reflected on the name, he remembered a time when he had sharply disappointed his father. How, he could not recall, but he vividly remembered the remorse he felt and the fear his father might no longer want him.

"Your father does not love you for what you do or do not do," his mother assured him, "but because you are his. And when he looks at you, he sees not only the youth you are now; he sees the man you are becoming—a man who is beginning to think and act like your father and even I-Am-Savior."

"But how can he?" Straight Arrows had pressed his mother.

"Do you remember the branch Grandfather cut for your first bow? Your confidence in him was all that assured you he had chosen wisely. A bird singing overhead had stained it badly, but little by little, Grandfather stripped from it all he did not deem useful. He considered its natural bent and where best to form a handhold and then carefully shaved the unyielding spots from its belly. He gave it gifts: a perfect arc so your arrows would fly swiftly and embellishments that looked appealing but promised to stay out of your way. Now it is clean and strong, wrapped with sinew and ready to do your bidding."

My sister's captor, Straight Arrows concluded, *is also like that bow, and I-Am-Savior has been stripping him as He is stripping me—shaping us both into....*

Too weary to stay awake, he sunk into a deep sleep, recoiling neither from the cold flesh against his back nor the man who inhabited it.

← ← ←   → → →

"I WILL CARE for your small-thing," offered Last Woman as Kept-Us-Alive stooped to lift her new son's cradleboard. "You will have difficulty enough tromping through the snow."

The young widow glanced at Hopping Owl to see her reaction. If her small-thing began fussing, he was sure to wear on everyone's nerves, and she did not want to impose further on her new family's kindness. To her surprise, not only Hopping Owl but also Bites-With-Dog nodded, each tossing the other inscrutable looks. Last Woman seemed to share in their secret, offering her a faint but knowing smile.

Although she wondered why her sister-friend had decided not to join her, Kept-Us-Alive did not dawdle. She needed to gather more firewood if they were to warm their early meal. The slim limbs they had woven into rafts were too water-soaked to burn, and she wanted to return before her youngest woke. Trotting quickly toward some tall pines, she bent to cut their dry branches, all the while asking herself what secret her friends might share. She soon found out. Spying two warmly clad calves approaching, she glanced up to discover a warrior had followed.

"I wish to speak with you," said Held-Back-the-Enemy, holding out his open palm. "Over here."

When she offered him her wrist, he led her deeper into a lonely place between the pines, but his tongue appeared to be frozen harder than the ice crusting his moccasins. He stared at the top of her head, inanely noting how a golden ray of yawning sun sparkled off the small bits of white fluff clinging to her curving strands.

"You are cold," he stated, hearing her teeth began to chatter. "My robe is large. Come inside."

Kept-Us-Alive acquiesced, feeling oddly as if she were an onlooker, not the recipient of his attentions. He *was* very handsome, though she could not remember if she always thought so, and he smelled of fresh herbed oil she suspected he had selected for this occasion.

"When your…dead…asked my father to care for you, he asked something of me also, proving the keenness of his eye and wit. I did not hesitate to offer him my answer. For several summers, I have thrust away the stirrings of my heart and looked at something else if I noticed you approaching."

Perfectly still, Kept-Us-Alive willed herself to keep breathing. Every fiber in her body cried out for Pacing Wolf, who had understood his Lumpwood son as she had not, and who had—rather than feeling threatened by his observations—stored them away to use later for her benefit.

"I would not speak so soon if I trusted Bull-Will-Not-Fall. He is a Fox— your dead's rival and my own—and you know well what he may do when our war-societies hand out their new staffs.[39] I desire to keep you safe."

Although she did not want to hear these words, they held sense that she could neither avoid nor deny, and she knew what she must answer. Held-Back-the-Enemy was kind and honorable, chosen for her by the very man for whom she longed. Already, he had proven constant in his care, and she knew her alternative: to continue imposing on his family while fearing Bull-Will-Not-Fall, goaded by his Fox brothers until he became drunk with rivalry, forcibly snatched her from them.

Mistaking her silence for objection, the young Sparrow Hawk placed his cheek gently against her soft hair and whispered. "I have watched you grieving for my Lumpwood father as I once watched you grieve for the people of your birth. Both are gone to you now, but as your regard for him increased, so may your regard for me. I will expect nothing of you until then."

His breath on her ear filled her with unexpected responses that tore her between shame and panic. She had grown used to receiving Pacing Wolf's affections and supposed he, alone, was able to stir her desires. As she began instinctively to withdraw, Held-Back-the-Enemy pulled her closer, pressing her with an offer that would require her to answer.

"My lodge is warm.
I will hunt when you hunger
and provide skins to clothe you.
I will care for your sons
as if they were my own,
and the small-things you bear me
will heal your sorrow."

The words sounded horridly like those Pacing Wolf had uttered stiffly in the cave; yet Held-Back-the-Enemy's offered protection, not terror, and encouragement, not dread. She answered as she had then, with the traditional reply handed down from each Allied mother to her daughters.

"I am yours altogether."

He tightened his embrace, emboldened by her ready acceptance, and she did not pull away. Instead, she tentatively leaned her cheek against his shoulder and relaxed as his arms warmly encircled her waist.

"YOU HAVE MADE our hearts full!" cooed Hopping Owl, clasping her hands together. "When the snows have melted, my husband and son will follow the herds with the other Good Men and bring us hides for my son's lodge."

Bites-With-Dog nodded with approval. "Our son possesses much courage and skill with a bow. Your dead chose him for you, and my woman and I desire you for him."

Returning their smiles, Kept-Us-Alive once again felt like an onlooker. Wolf-Who-Lays-Down appeared the happiest of all, bouncing up and down while swinging his arms as if they, too, were wild with joy.

While she watched Held-Back-the-Enemy and him talking, she could not decide which she felt greater: gratitude for her betrothed's obvious affection for her son or sadness for Pacing Wolf, whom Wolf-Who-Lays-Down would soon forget. She felt this less on behalf of the babe in the cradleboard hanging on her back.

He has not met his father and will not feel any loss. I have never been betrothed, she mused. She had always thought the word sweet, but as she silently rolled it over her tongue, she tasted little more than relief.

Last Woman congratulated her warmly, but Last Son looked glum. Remembering the wish he had confided, Kept-Us-Alive squatted down so they could talk face to face. "You will live here with your mother and we will dwell beside you. Held-Back-the-Enemy will be an uncle: he will take you with him everywhere he takes Wolf-Who-Lays-Down and show you how to hunt and track."

"I want him for father."

Pulling him into her arms, she ran a hand over his silky black hair. "He is already like a father to you and will continue to be. There will be little difference."

"I want him to love *my* mother. Have husband to give her soft looks."

"I wish the same for her," Kept-Us-Alive admitted, "but she does not want Held-Back-the-Enemy. If she did—and he wanted her—I would step aside."

The little boy shot from her lap. "Momma!" he cried. "Sister-friend says she give him to you!"

Last Woman cocked her head, raising her eyebrows, and Held-Back-the-Enemy sat up, alert.

"Held-Back-the-Enemy take you—make *you* his woman!"

Kept-Us-Alive felt her neck growing hot as Held-Back-the-Enemy rose to his feet, but Last Woman just laughed. "He wants my sister-friend and will take her once she has stopped grieving."

The boy's head drooped, embarrassed he had misunderstood until Held-Back-the-Enemy stepped forward. "Come," he nodded toward the door, stretching his hand out to Wolf-Who-Lays-Down also. "We will see if we can find some good, thin branches to make small bows."

Both boys scrambled toward the door-flap as the young Lumpwood nodded toward Last Woman. As he tossed Kept-Us-Alive an amused grin, he nearly collided with an unannounced guest. The boys halted, staring at their imposing Real Chief and looked sorely crestfallen when their hero turned back to resume his seat.

"So," Hunts-For-Death nodded toward Last Woman, who had receded into the background. "You have welcomed my cast-off Blackfoot."

Bites-With-Dog nodded as he took in his Real Chief's impassive expression. Catching Hopping Owl's eye, he motioned toward his pipe, which she brought immediately along with several backrests. The two younger women aided her efforts and then left with their sons to give the three men privacy.

"Cast her out," insisted Hunts-For-Death, once Last Woman had slipped through the doorway. "And that Cuts-Off-Our-Heads captive."

Slowly lighting his pipe, Bites-With-Dog lifted it toward the four winds, and once he had exhaled the sweet-smelling smoke, he nodded toward Held-Back-the-Enemy. "She belongs to my son. He will take her and raise our dead clan leader's children as his own."

The older man's eyes widened almost imperceptibly, but he kept his facial muscles placid as he turned toward the young warrior. "Wolf-Who-Lays-Down closely follows your trail. Keep him and your dead clan leader's new small-thing. Keep the Blackfoot's son also. Raise them well to hate their mothers' tribesmen, but also take one of our untouched women and give them to her. If no daughter from Mountainside's clan appeals to you, take one from the Whistle Waters or Those-Who-Live-Along-the-Outer-

Rim, but this captive must go. We bore with her while my Lumpwood son was alive, but the Good Men and I will tolerate her no longer."

"Why?" asked Bites-With-Dog. "What has this woman done? She proved faithful to our dead clan leader and has proved a friend to our people. Do you not remember how she earned her name?"

"I remember. But she has brought us a disease more dangerous than the one she helped us endure. It has infected the souls of many Good Men, young and old. I watched as her spirit-guide weakened the heart of my Lumpwood son, and now Braids-His-Tail has accepted its bridle. We must rid our people of both it and her."

"And what of my woman?" asked Bites-With-Dog. "She walks in the path of I-Am-Savior. Do you wish me to cast her out? And what of my son and I? We walk His path also. Will the Many Lodges chase us away?"

"You have long been my Lumpwood brother and owned my trust. When my Lumpwood son left us for the Mystery Land, I hoped that you and this Good Young Man would clear your minds of this Divider-Spirit and drive it from your lodges. Your son has shown much courage." He looked from the feathers woven into Held-Back-the-Enemy's hair to Pacing Wolf's ax hanging from his side. "Our Good Men and untouched women speak admiringly of him. He may one day become a leader of our people. Do you want a daughter of our enemy to bend him to her will? Join me—both of you—in mending what her spirit-guide has torn."

As Bites-With-Dog began to offer Hunts-For-Death the pipe, the older man rose to his feet. "I will mingle my breath with yours once our hearts become united."

"I have offered her my promise," declared Held-Back-the-Enemy, "and given my word to my dead Lumpwood father. Would you have me break my pledges?"

The corners of the older man's mouth turned down. "Keep your pledge. Take her. You own a good heart, a strong heart—strong enough to withstand for a while the weakening of such a woman. But when you tire of her, pass her off to a Fox or Muddy Hand rival. As one rival passes her to another, she will lose her ability to make men weak, and all will see this foreign spirit-guide possesses little power. In the end, only an old man will want her—as our dead Real Chief wanted the Blackfoot—to warm his robes on nights that are cold."

Bites-With-Dog discreetly placed his hand over his son's nearest knee, preventing him from jumping to his feet. "This is not the time for anger," he warned, once their Real Chief had slipped out into the bright sunlight, "but for considering and planning. Hunts-For-Death is a seasoned warrior. He is poking a stick into the embers in your belly, trying to stir them up.

Do not allow him this advantage. Go. Find her and our Blackfoot sister. He-Who-Hears-All-Things has listened to the man's insults, and He will tell us how to answer."

If the world possessed you, the world would love you as its own. I have chosen you out of the world; that is why the world hates you.
John 15:9

Chapter 23

PRETTY FACE'S MIND BEGAN to wander from his host to leaping the chasm he had created within his family, and for the first time since he had shoved his sister's captor, he felt a sense of peace. *When the snows abate, I will find Light Bird and bring her home.*

Catching a scant movement with the corner of his eye, he realized Red Fox's churlish kinsman was watching him. Pretty Face instinctively wished to protect Plays-With-Her-Earrings, to keep her from a sorrow-filled life, but how could he? Her father already granted Angry Man consent to court her.

The warrior is a sister's son, he reasoned. *Red Fox must know how he earned his name.*

As if sensing Pretty Face's thoughts, the young woman knelt before him. Anyone watching could tell his hunger had been sated. She was making her desire for his attention obvious, so obvious it stirred his fear. If her father did not chasten her, Angry Man might make her pay. Pretty Face was acquainted with many warriors like him—warriors who cared more about their damaged pride than a young woman's tender feelings.

Trying to draw away Angry Man's ire, Pretty Face returned her smile. He was safe. His uncles were not present to argue for his suit, and though Red Fox must own a reason for encouraging him to consider her, he suspected if his uncles were there, her father would rebuff them. Red Fox had been among those who often voiced suspicion concerning the changes I-Am-Savior had brought their tribe.

His plan worked. Angry Man barely noticed when Plays-With-Her-Earrings sauntered out of her father's dwelling. He was too busy boring a hot hole through Pretty Face's back and trying to listen to his conversation with her father.

"When the south wind drives back the snow," Red Fox continued, "I will accompany you to my old Allies' village. As our wounded kinsman heals his mind may grow stronger, or perhaps you have not asked the right questions."

Searching for a way to put him off, his eyes again fell on Plays-With-Her-Earrings. "So soon? I wish to stay for a while in your village."

Red Fox, following his gaze, acquiesced, though Pretty Face again wondered why. Perhaps, he—like any good father—sought a tactful means to spare the girl from her repellent suitor. Whatever were his motives, Pretty Face would need to be very careful. He had not outright declared any intentions, but the girl was obviously willing and her father was no fool.

← ← ←   → → →

"BITES-WITH-DOG refused my counsel," sneered Hunts-For-Death, surveying the Many Lodges' village atop his mount on a nearby cliff. "He has eaten the words of this foreign spirit-guide and will not spit them out."

"This is your dead Lumpwood son's doing," muttered Falling Bear. "From his youth, Bites-With-Dog has made good choices. Twice, you have offered him a death staff, and twice he has taken it—and fought courageously for our people. I trust him as I trust myself—and his son is like him."

"I also have noticed changes in those who place their feet on this spirit's path," replied White Belly, old Paints-His-Shirt-Yellow's second son. "All good. Since my youngest wife began praying to him, she has become more welcoming and carps much less. I am no longer hoping a Fox rival will catch her eye. And you remember what Hopping Owl was—a spewing steam hole. For many summers, I could not understand why our Lumpwood brother refused to put her out. Jackrabbit also."

"Pah!" spat Hunts-For-Death. "Jackrabbit would sooner take up a hatchet against the dead's widow than follow the words in her book."

"Lately I have seen them together and have been watching to see if she, too, changes."

Hunts-For-Death arched one brow, waiting for White Belly to finish.

"Her eyes are not so full of bitterness, and her tongue—which bites like a horsefly—hungers less for blood."

"Hmph," responded the Real Chief. Although he would not say so, he almost regretted casting Last Woman out. She had worked hard and expected little, and the quiet gratitude she showed for her family's food and shelter had offered him a good measure of reward. Still, he was glad he need never again listen to her conversation. She scarcely spoke, except to her children, but when she did—whether to them or his wives—she often mentioned this spirit's odd teachings. His wives hated her.

"Why act in haste?" continued White Belly. "This spirit-guide possesses great power. His tribesmen killed Him, but when they looked in His gravelog, they found it empty."

"Waugh! This is a woman's tale!" snarled Bull-Will-Not-Fall. "The warriors who walked his path crept out late at night and snatched his body."

"No," countered White Belly. "He appeared to these followers, talking and eating fish. Over five hundred men saw him.[40]"

"Ugh—a fish eater!" Hunts-His-Death drew up his lip. "No dead man comes to life. He lives again only in the Mystery Land. This book owns a lying spirit."

"I too thought this until my father told me a peculiar thing. When these followers refused to deny their claims, their tribesmen murdered many of them also. What trickster risks his skin to prove a tale he fashioned is true?

Hunts-For-Death narrowed his eyes. "Do you also walk in this I-Am-Savior's footsteps? A soft woman may be of use to a warrior, but a soft-hearted warrior is of use to no one."

"If your dead Lumpwood son was weak, why did we and our other Good Men covet his widow's hair for our braids?"

"Dead men do not eat fish," Bull-Will-Not-Fall interrupted. "Have you spoken with the warriors who claimed to see him?"

"I have told you they too were murdered, but our dead clan leader told me an amazing tale. This spirit-guide spoke to him."

"Hmph. He told me this also," scoffed Hunts-For-Death. "Many warriors have visions. Call the clan leaders and other Good Men to my lodge. All who have woven his widow's waving strands into their hair must tear them out to toss in the fire lest they, too, fall prey to weakness. Then let each pledge to shut their ears when they hear this spirit-guide's teachings. We will return to our old ways—the ways of our fathers, the ways that have kept our hearts and arms strong."

"Leave the widow to me," offered Bull-Will-Not-Fall. "When the grass greens, I will snatch her from Bites-With-Dog's lodge so that all the Fox will shout in triumph."

The Real Chief pinned him with a sidelong glare. "Do you forget that I am also Lumpwood? Why do you want her?"

When Bull-Will-Not-Fall did not answer, White Belly snickered. "You have waited too late. She belongs to Held-Back-the-Enemy. She will not want you."

"That pup!" the Fox soldier sneered. "He would not know how to satisfy a woman."

"And you do? That is not what I heard from my youngest woman. If you snatched this widow, you would not know how to keep her!"

As the three Lumpwoods laughed, the vein that coursed up Bull-Will-Not-Fall's face began to pulse. "Your youngest woman smells like a half-eaten skunk. I did not want her."

"I have not found her so," taunted White Belly. "Perhaps she drenched her braids in skunk fat each night when she saw you coming."

"Enough! Save your gibes for the new death-staff celebrations," snapped Hunts-For-Death, turning from the White Belly to their Fox rival. "You have not answered my question."

"I will teach her proper respect for a Sparrow Hawk warrior."

"We will see," goaded Falling Bear. "She possesses a tongue like a rippling stream, singing softly as it cuts channels through rock."

"We Fox do not fear a woman's words. She will keep her tongue still or learn to cower when she sees me."

Hunts-For-Death stiffened. "And if she does not?"

"I will wait until a black night swallows the moon and cast her into the darkness."

"Good. Coyotes have keen noses. As she wanders, she may fall and gash herself, and they will smell her blood on the wind."

"Is this how we Lumpwoods honor our dead leaders?" White Belly asked Hunts-For-Death.

"When the sun awakes, the Blackfoot who dogs her steps will find what is left of her, and our women will become like prairie grass whipped in a circle by a strong wind. They will turn quickly from this spirit and embrace their old ways."

White Belly wheeled his mount to face their Real Chief squarely. "What of the Good Men who follow this spirit-guide? Most are Lumpwood, my father and brother among them."

Hunts-For-Death shook his head. "Paints-His-Shirt-Yellow is my oldest clansman. The stripes on his leggings attest to his valor, but this pox shows no preference. We must lay a red-hot knife blade to every eruption."

As Bull-Will-Not-Fall smirked, he reminded Hunts-For-Death of a rabid wolf he had once watched on the prairie: Staring into the distance above the bustling village, he watched the huge orange sun sinking down beyond the mountains.

"You will gather your Fox brothers," he decided. "All but those who lap up this spirit-guide's whisperings. Command them to refuse all death staffs. I will instruct the Lumpwoods to do likewise and tell Mountainside to warn the Big Dogs and Muddy Hands not to accept their societies' ropes. This will leave only warriors who follow this spirit-guide to thrust our emblems into the earth. When the enemy comes, I will forbid their brothers to yank their emblems up; so these followers will soon weary, and the enemy will cut them down. This way," he looked at White Belly, "none of us need to lift our hands against our own or be guilty of spilling their blood."

"Their spirit-guide may offer them aide," cautioned Falling Bear. "Then our Young Men will award them the greatest honors and crave this power for themselves!"

"Here—look through my long-eye." The Real Chief handed him a Long-knives' spyglass and tilted his chin toward the doe-like woman weaving between clansmen on the central path. While she had passed a tall, prominent lodge, his lips had curved up smugly. Her face had looked stricken when she glanced away as if she were willing herself not to see it. "If this spirit-guide possesses such power, why is my Lumpwood son dead, and why does his woman make herself ugly with grief?"

Once Falling Bear lowered the long-eye, Bull-Will-Not-Fall grabbed it from him. He agreed with all his Real Chief's assessments except those about his dead rival's widow. Though he would cut out his own tongue before confessing to his rivals, he wanted her for more personal reasons than he had admitted. He admired her ability to accept staggering circumstances and had liked the feel of her when she struggled in his arms. Watching her scurry past her husband's former lodge last evening, he had felt a potent urge to pull her in.

"I will again choose the Fox to act as our soldiers," Hunts-For-Death confided. "As the Many Lodges make the journey to meet our other Sparrow Hawk bands, I will encourage the Lumpwoods to guard our rear. Tell your Fox brothers to search among them for clansmen this spirit-guide has infected and cut them off so they begin to straggle. Then your Fox soldiers must do their duty—beat all who lag behind and show no mercy to their horses. Forced to walk, their sore-footed women will gladly accept any Fox soldier who pulls them up atop their mounts. Then their Good Men will become disheartened and may turn from this sickness."

Watching Bull-Will-Not-Fall's eyes flare brighter, the Real Chief nearly regretted his decision, but he quickly swatted all remorse away. The spirits had entrusted him with a great burden in leading the Sparrow Hawk People. He was determined not to fail them.

AS THE SUN rose high into the branches, Straight Arrows arched to stretch his back. His limbs felt frozen, but not from the snow covering the sloping branches overhead. It had acted as a thick blanket trapping the two enemies' warmth, but his muscles, unused to remaining so long in one position, threatened to revolt.

Touching the limp arm of the lump beside him, he drew his brows down towards the high bridge of his nose. The arm felt cool, much cooler than his own, but not cold. Unsure if his or the Raven Enemy's own heat had warmed it, he slid a hand up under the firm jaw jutting out from the man's neck and pressed the pliable skin. He found a strong, rhythmic beat pulsing against his calloused fingers.

Exhaling deeply, he lay back down against mother earth. She felt almost as cool as the flesh he had just touched, but he knew she was much warmer than the bright white covering that he spied from beneath the boughs. *I must awaken him,* he determined. The position of the sun peeking through a bare spot announced it had spent too much of its light.

Straight Arrows pushed himself up to standing. He would let the Raven Enemy sleep a little longer. His own need for privacy was urgent and the man would be too weak to help him prepare their horses. As he brushed between the yielding branches, he felt glad he had not removed his high moccasins. The storm had piled the snow layer upon layer beyond the firs, so that he had to lift his knees half level with his hips with every step.

Calculating the time they had ridden last night, he supposed they would not reach his village until well after the stars appeared, perhaps longer considering the height of the small pony's legs. A line of trees, looking smaller than a row of tiny insects, snaked toward the wind ridge, stretching in vast numbers until they disappeared behind a distant rise. Beyond them, he suspected, lay the great river he had crossed only six times, all either in search of an enemy or because his heart yearned for his sister.

The time before last, he had made some excuse to Pretty Face, something about exploring the cliff for game, but once he had recognized a distinct outcropping, he longed to touch the cavern walls that she had touched or see the robes that had borne witness to her shame—anything that might connect him to her presence. He had not expected to find Wild Dog, much less the very enemy who had stolen her.

His gut churned while recalling his father's face crumpling as he lifted his sister's long, black spirals, and he could almost hear his father's wails echoing off the thick rock walls. His grandfather and he had barely been able to convince Pretty Face to leave the place, or rather convince him not to set off wildly in any direction that took his fancy. There had been nothing to follow, as if an eagle had swooped down and lifted them into the clouds.

Turning back toward the clump of firs, Straight Arrows tamped down the urge to beat his sleeping charge senseless or simply go home, taking Little Blackfoot's pony. The man could not walk far, if at all—he might have shattered his freshly healed leg during last night's fall—and without food or coverings, he could not last.

Why should I not take them? One robe is mine; the other is my mother's. He could not bring himself to do it. He knew his mother well; she would count the robe a gift, expecting nothing in return.

"Get up!" he barked at the still-lying lump, unsure the man could even do as he demanded. When he saw no response, Straight Arrows nudged him with his foot.

The Raven Enemy did not groan. He barely moved, but this slight indication he was sentient was sufficient.

"Get up!" Straight Arrows repeated. "If we do not delay, we can sleep in warm dwellings tonight."

As if pulling his mind through a lengthy, dark tunnel, Pacing Wolf began to make sense of what the young Ally was saying. He did not understand where they were, how he came to be with his woman's brother, or why the warrior was angry. Then, all at once, recollections of the past few suns began pummeling his memory.

Rolling halfway over, Pacing Wolf tossed back the two heavy buffalo robes and attempted to stand up, but his leg gave out beneath him.

Immediately, Straight Arrows came to his aid. "You injured it when you fell. Here, lie still. Let me see if it is broken." Removing one legging with care, Straight Arrows examined the area of skin where he had once seen a bone sticking out. It had held and seemed firm beneath the shriveled muscles. "It feels sound."

Pacing Wolf nodded, hearing Straight Arrows' inner struggle in his tone; but as the younger warrior raised his eyes, they held more questions than anger. "I could not stay," Pacing Wolf explained. "This Red Fox, Wild Dog's father, would force your family to choose between two knife blades."

Straight Arrows understood but merely nodded. Even while much of him cried out for vengeance, he knew if Red Fox came what he or any of them would do—and Red Fox would come. Grasping Pacing Wolf's forearm, Straight Arrows pulled him to his feet, winding an arm behind his back to support him as they walked.

Pacing Wolf submitted, gripping a snowy branch for balance as they walked outside, and then watched while Straight Arrows both tended and readied their mounts. "Here," he grinned, reaching inside a pouch and bringing out pulverized buffalo held together with boiled fat and dried berries. "Little Blackfoot Woman gave it to me."

Straight Arrows smiled. "That little one is resourceful—and loyal. I am glad. I did not expect to track you far and brought nothing but what you see." Shoving the pemmican into his mouth, he helped Pacing Wolf hobble to the pony and hoisted him up; but when he began to take hold of her reins, Pacing Wolf caught him by the wrist.

"No—I go that way." Pacing Wolf jerked his head toward the line of trees dotting the horizon. "To your sister. Red Fox is not my sole reason. A young clansman promised to make her his woman if I did not soon return and act as a father to our children. Like a wiggling thing inside its woven blanket, this pledge threatens to burst open with every passing of the sun, beyond my ability to keep it from flying."

"I go with you," declared Straight Arrows, gravely considering his point. "The river is wide. You will fall in and drown, and then what will become of my sister?"

O Creator, rebuke my opponents. Do battle with those who battle me. Take up Your war-shield and lance. Stand and give me aid!
Psalm 35: 1-2

Chapter 24

OLD PAINTS-HIS-Shirt-Yellow drew in slowly from the pipe Bites-With-Dog offered and breathed out several poorly formed circles. Passing it to his eldest, he closed his milk-white eyes, savoring the sweet aroma wafting above and all around him. His eldest son drew from it deeply and then tilted the long stem toward Braids-His-Tail who, in turn with Twists-With-His-Hair and Held-Back-the-Enemy, sucked the fragrant smoke into his chest and swirled it out again, mingling his breath with the others until no one could discern where his stopped and his Lumpwood brothers' began.

Once the warm pipe had traveled back to their host, he handed it to Hopping Owl, who silently carried it outside to return its revered contents to the earth. Where she went afterward, the warriors neither knew nor considered; but after a while, the old man opened his mouth to speak. All turned toward him, their ears ready to taste his words, but he instead closed both his eyes and lips. He breathed deeply, evenly, as if he might have fallen asleep, but just as the younger warriors began exchanging questioning glances, he flung his milky eyes open.

"My son—not my eldest, here, but the one born from my second woman—has brought me a tale I cannot keep hidden. Astride his speckled pony, he surveyed our land with our Real Chief, Falling Bear, and another—the restless Fox born to Cries-While-Laughing."

"Bull-Will-Not-Fall," his eldest suggested.

"Yes. This is what the people call him, though he owns the heart of a cunning rabbit.

Several warriors nodded.

"He plans evil for this daughter you have recently adopted," he told Bites-With-Dog. "The one who reads from the leaves of I-Am-Savior's book."

Held-Back-the-Enemy kept quite still, waiting to catch and hold each word the old man uttered.

"He plans to steal her when the grass greens so that he might treat her cruelly, and Hunts-For-Death did not dissuade him. We can no longer follow our Real Chief. He lays out a plan to bring us all to harm—all who follow I-Am-Savior. You," he turned his half-seeing eyes toward Held-Back-the-Enemy, "must take this woman you desire and her children and flee our village—and take the Blackfoot with you. All of you must go who do as I-Am-Savior has taught you,[41] caring for your wives as you would your own body."

Each warrior looked at his neighbor, trying to decide if they could credit the tale. All had known Hunts-For-Death since their childhood and had been among those who chose him to lead; but when Bites-With-Dog repeated all the Real Chief had told him and Held-Back-the-Enemy, the others all began talking at once.

The old man held up his hand, unwilling to answer their flurry of questions. "If they planned only to beat you, I would not speak. What are a few broken bones compared to a break with our clan? But they will not stop until we step off I-Am-Savior's path and begin treading the ways our fathers, the ways that did not bring us peace. I will not guide my sons' decisions and will not guide yours. The cost is heavy. Each of you must decide."

← ← ←   → → →

PLAYS-WITH-HER-EARRINGS laughed up at the tall warrior enclosing her within a borrowed courting blanket. Though his features were not as strong as her dead brother's, she considered him the most handsome man standing at this moment in her village. She wished the snow had not abated. He had told her father he would leave when it did. Still, though the sun had dispatched the deepest drifts, here he was, smiling down at her with eyes at once firm and tender.

"Your father and I leave as soon as he is ready," Pretty Face confided. "The journey to my village is long. I wish to arrive there before the sun hides beyond the prairie."

As sadness sprung into her eyes, his gut began to tighten. He had known not to court a woman he did not intend to marry, but he could form no other plan for a delay. Her father was growing restless to begin his vengeance quest. When remnants of the blizzard had become a thin excuse, her obvious attraction seemed the one plausible reason for him to stay.

Even so, he felt something was amiss. Her father too eagerly pushed her forward, and she asked too often about his mother's patient. She sprinkled the man throughout their conversations, asking questions he had already answered several times in other forms.

Does she or her father suspect I withhold the truth? he wondered. *I can think of no other reason the man should hold such interest.*

"You will return?" she asked coyly. She hoped he might speak of fine horses he intended to bring Red Fox, but when he did not, her eyes began to sting.

"I wish I could," he admitted. "You have always made me laugh."

Even while she was a mere child, he had liked her, though only recently had she set his blood to pumping. Perhaps it was the way she stood—so near that he smelled the sweet fragrance of her hair—or the way her soft, warm fingers brushed the edge of his breastplate while she played with her braid. Just as he mustered up the will to force her away, he noticed a tear over-flowing its bounds and slowly wandering down her high cheekbone. "What is this?"

Plays-With-Her-Earrings merely shook her head, ashamed her poise had faltered and afraid—if she spoke—it might slip away altogether. After a time, she whispered, "Angry Man grows eager for me to warm his buffalo robes."

"He cannot take you without your father's permission."

She dropped her eyes and did not raise them again. Her father knew what Angry Man had done and how she felt, and yet he still insisted she let him court her. With Pretty Face gone and her brother dead…

"You are cold," he observed as she shuddered. "We should walk back to your mother's dwelling."

"No," she pleaded, grasping hold of his breastplate.

Pretty Face gazed down at her, unable to fathom why she seemed so desperate. Surely, she did not believe Angry Man and he were her only choices. She was a lovely girl with a well-renowned father.

As he gently pried open her grip, she whispered, "When you leave, I will have no one to talk with me about the Creator." Glancing up swiftly, she read in his eyes that she had hit her mark. "No one here speaks of him as you do—as if he is a friend, present at your side."

Pretty Face breathed in slowly and then out again. *How do I answer this? I-Am-Savior, have you sent me here on purpose? I thought when I spoke of you that my words barely grazed her ears. I wish my mother were here—or Straight Arrows. His words so often echo Yours that I understand how Your brothers must have felt.*

Looking down as she gazed up at him, he blurted out what he was thinking. "When snow no longer blinds, come to my village with your father—during the Moon When Water Fowl Return. My mother will welcome you into her dwelling and answer all your questions. She understands a woman's heart and knows also the heart of I-Am-Savior."

"Ask my father," replied Plays-With-Her-Earrings. "Look—he is coming."

←　←　←　　→　→　→

OTTER WOMAN LOOKED BACK over her shoulder past Held-Back-the-Enemy, tracing in the melting snow the long line of horse tracks stretching from the Sparrow Hawk village. Although she could no longer distinguish her mother or grandmother's features, she knew from the way they held each other that they were sobbing.

"I do not want to go," she whined to Last Woman. "We are leaving all we love."

"All?" asked the Blackfoot. "I see your husband up ahead and you carry his daughter on your back. How can we stay? You heard what Hunts-For-Death has demanded."

"Three moons back," added Kept-Us-Alive, "we were praying for Braids-His-Tail to walk I-Am-Savior's path—do you wish him to desert it now?"

Otter Woman dropped her head, slowly shaking it back and forth. "But my mother and aunts," she pleaded, "...my sisters. Why is the Creator allowing this?"

As Kept-Us-Alive watched her friend's soft eyes fill with tears, she considered how she might answer. Had she not asked the same questions when Pacing Wolf had died? She still asked them, but before she could think what to say, Otter Woman continued fretting.

"What will become of us without the Many Lodges? We are too few to face the weakest enemy."

"When my mother found herself in my father's power," began Kept-Us-Alive, "before she knew he was worthy of her trust, she searched The Book for words I-Am-Savior confided in Friend-of-Horses[42] and discovered she had turned it upside down."

"What did He say?"

"'If a man serves Me, he must follow Me; and wherever I am, my slave is also.'"[43]

"Of course," replied Last Woman. "Where else would a slave be?"

"In her heart, my mother had flipped it over. She thought He had said He would be with *her* wherever *she* went."

"But is that wrong?" asked Otter Woman. "The Creator's angel sets a camp around all who fear Him."[43]

"Yes, but *He* does not follow *us; we* follow *Him*."

Last Woman shrugged. "Where was I-Am-Savior going?"

"To be hung from the tree—and He refused to ask His Father to save Him. He was born as a man for this purpose."[44]

"I remember hearing these verses," acknowledged Otter Woman, "but I do not understand how they answer my question."

"She means," Last Woman cut in, "that we are much like that war-horse your husband is riding. Though the horse does not know the path we travel, he knows your husband and understands where to turn by the pressure of his legs. Where Braids-His-Tail wishes to go, the horse also goes."

Kept-Us-Alive nodded. "Once, you told me Braids-His-Tail risked his life to protect him from a prowling bear."

"He cares for this horse deeply and considers him a friend."

"I have watched your husband talking to him and feeding him handfuls of sweet grass, but Braids-His-Tail has raised him for more than companionship. He raised him to do as he does—to risk all against the enemy."

"Why does Hunts-For-Death hate us?" asked Last Son, riding closely behind his mother. "We ate in his lodge and slept by his fire."

"He does not hate us, son," Last Woman answered. "He hates our master—much like the horse we were discussing. The Grass Lodges did not shoot at him because he made them angry. They were trying to kill Braids-His-Tail. If they could have captured his horse, they would have kept him and cared for him as their own."

As Last Son tried to ask a second question, his soft voice became lost among pounding hooves. Tiny Wolf-Who-Lays-Down began squealing and squirming, lifting his face from Kept-Us-Alive's chest while excitedly reaching his chubby arm behind her.

Craning their necks back over their shoulders, all three friends saw a party of warriors racing toward them, the lead rider holding high his feathered lance. They tightened their grips on their reins, fearing Hunts-For-Death had sent Fox soldiers, and then breathed in great sighs of relief when they recognized White Belly. His war shield still hung from his mount and his bow was slung across his back. Galloping past them, he reined in beside Bites-With-Dog, who was leading their small band of wanderers, while the others with him blended into the line.

What the two Good Men discussed, the women could only guess, but after a few moments, White Belly dropped back to greet his father and brothers. Old Paints-His-Shirt-Yellow leaned out so far and so quickly to embrace this son, they feared he might fall from his brown stallion. Not far behind them trailed White Belly's two grown sons, followed by their women and several of White Belly's youthful sons and grandsons. Last of all was his newest wife, Speaks Softly. She looked relieved, even happy, but two of the youths' faces showed mixed emotions. They clearly welcomed a new adventure, but their excitement seemed lessened by some other, less obvious trouble.

Perhaps, thought Kept-Us-Alive, *they are sad because their mother does not follow.*

As two other riders galloped up behind Held-Back-the-Enemy, Kept-Us-Alive and Last Woman broke into irrepressible smiles. He began motioning with his lance in the three friends' direction, nodding his head encouragingly as he answered several questions. When the smaller of the two riders spotted Kept-Us-Alive, a grin broke across her face, and in an instant, she was pressing her heels against her pony. Wolf-Who-Lays-Down began bouncing up and down so wildly that his mother worried he might fall from her wooden saddle. He did—directly into his sister's arms. The two squeezed each other as if many moons, not one morning, had passed since they had seen each other last.

Laughing all the while, the little girl announced she was coming with them, but the joy bubbling up in her stepmother and *Aunt* dampened as Jackrabbit twitched a quirt against her horse's rump. Her expression looked far from happy. Kept-Us-Alive grabbed Among-the-Pines' bridle, pulling the child's pony to her further side. When Jackrabbit had last charged at her, she had pulled her to the ground so swiftly that only Pacing Wolf's intervention had prevented her death. Surely now, though, the older woman felt differently. Glancing at Held-Back-the-Enemy, she saw that he looked relaxed, even pleased.

Sympathy replaced all fear as Jackrabbit drew closer. Tears streaked the weathered apple-round cheeks and the lips that once cursed her so twisted and quivered they could not form words.

"Take her with you," choked out Jackrabbit, once she gained her voice. "She will be happier. Who does she have here but me and Never-Sits, and Never-Sits has her own woes."

"Come with us, Grandmother," Among-the-Pines pleaded.

Jackrabbit shook her head. "I have handed your new mother much reason for hatred. She would not want an old woman to add to her burden."

"Of course we want you!" cried Kept-Us-Alive. "And you are not old! You will be of great help wherever the Creator leads us."

"No." Jackrabbit firmly set her mouth. "I have no one besides my granddaughter among those who are leaving, but I am grateful that you want me. I go back to Mountainside, my brother, and when our band meets up with the Whistle-Water Clan, I will stay with Pretty Crow Woman. She was rounding with her husband's small-thing when I last saw her, and she may need my help."

"Are you certain?" asked Kept-Us-Alive. Pretty Crow Woman's tongue had grown as sharp as her mother's. "What of I-Am-Savior? I do not think I have answered all your questions."

The older woman glanced at Among-the-Pines. "My granddaughter has been telling me many things you have taught her, but I am too old to learn. Maybe one day, when I badly miss her, I will ask this foreign spirit if He can see her and how she fares—and also about you and your sons. My place is here, with The-Women-Who-Talk-Against-Each-Other-Without-Fear. She tells me I-Am-Savior forbids all gossip. Dwelling in such a lodge would be very boring."

"We will both miss you," Kept-Us-Alive replied. "I will care for her as if she came from my own belly."

"I know—and I remove my curse! When you marry that handsome warrior guarding the rear, I hope you will have many sons. He is not like other warriors—so proud and high-handed. You will find much happiness with him."

As Jackrabbit caressed her granddaughter's cheek and wheeled her horse, Kept-Us-Alive wondered if the older woman had been hinting at Pacing Wolf. The woman had never liked him, but neither had he been fond of her.

Watching her ride past Held-Back-the-Enemy, Kept-Us-Alive took a moment to study the young Lumpwood. He held himself with an air of confidence; and yet, as Jackrabbit had observed, he was more likely to offer service than commands.

For a moment, she did not realize Among-the-Pines had been telling her something—her eldest son also was chattering away—but as she turned her attention on the girl, she found a bright smile softly fading. "What is the matter, Daughter? Jackrabbit—in returning you—has made my heart leap with joy."

Instantly, the child's smile returned, only to fade again. "I am glad, Mother, but I miss Little Blackfoot Woman. I am here with you and her mother but she is not. Why did the angels take her away?"

Taken by surprise, Kept-Us-Alive nearly blurted out the truth, but the secret was not truly hers to tell. She would ask Last Woman whether she could share it now that all threat that Hunts-For-Death might attack her own parents' village was past. As she thought of her family, a fresh hope began bubbling up in her chest. She did not know where Bites-With-Dog intended to lead them, but she knew where she wanted to go.

Why not? she asked herself. *Is not kinship between children born of God even stronger than the bond produced by common ancestors?*

Pay heed to the kind of love The Father has given us: We are called His children—and we are!

I John 3:1

Chapter 25

"NO," STRAIGHT ARROWS answered firmly. If you fall into the river, the current will carry you away more swiftly than I can follow. What would I tell my sister?"

Pacing Wolf groaned. He saw the sense in her brother's answer, but as he allowed him to strap his wrists to his ankles beneath his tall black horse, he felt as useless as dead prey. "An elk would fill hungry bellies and a skillful woman would find a use for his hide. Even his teeth would be of value."

"What?" barked Straight Arrows, checking to make certain he had securely tied Little Blackfoot's pony to his own mount. She was old, but he was fond of her. His first memory was the back of her head bobbing forward as she carried his mother and him to their old summer place. He had liked to trace the irregular edges of her white splotches with his tiny hands or lean forward to stroke her long, brown mane. Guessing the Raven Enemy had only moaned, he swung up on his mount just behind him.

As Pacing Wolf felt the tall horse picking his way down the riverbank, he could not help remembering Small Doe tied across his sorrel in the same manner. He had considered ending her life and realized he could do nothing to defend himself if this same impulse rose within her brother. *If he meant to kill me,* he reasoned, *he would have allowed me to risk the river alone. It would easily pull me beneath its surface or deposit me among the tangled roots downstream.* Still, since Pacing Wolf had first awakened, he had been unable to discern her brother's thoughts. Besides smiling over Little Blackfoot, he had said little and most of it terse.

The icy water parted around the horse's girth, carrying his braids along with the current as it swirled through his hair. His heart carried him in divided directions also, urging him toward the joy of seeing Small Doe and his children and then casting him into despair. His head was no stiller. It bobbed against the stallion's glossy black coat and then into his owner's water-soaked moccasin. Occasionally it slipped between the two.

Once they climbed the other bank, he felt Straight Arrows untying his bindings and pulling him down onto the very rock on which Small Doe had caught her first glimpse of him. The thatch that stood erect above his head that evening lay plastered over his wide brow while her brother rubbed his wrists and ankles to restore their proper blood-flow.

Returning to their mounts, they ascended to the cavern's mouth, each entangled in pungent memories that marked the place. Neither uttered a sound, but Straight Arrows set his lips so grimly that Pacing Wolf felt relieved when they dismounted, passed the treacherous ledge, and pushed through boughs into blackness. As he was limping down the long, sloping corridor, however, the back of his neck began to prickle. No spot on earth could be better suited for executing vengeance.

Shaking off the notion, he turned toward the dwelling room, dropped onto the pile of buffalo robes, and brushed the shorn locks from his forehead; but as he followed Straight Arrows' eyes, all his muscles tightened. A curling, dusty strand had caught between his fingers, illumined by the sunlight filtering through the cavern's smoke hole. It fluttered like an otter tail hanging from a death-staff, begging Straight Arrows to vent his pent-up fury; but though the young warrior gripped the handle of his war-club, he abruptly turned and fled.

Thrusting his head beneath the cold spring, Straight Arrows asked the Creator of all mercy to help him offer his sister's captor good instead of evil. *I do not have it in me—it is impossible!* he groaned, but the very word came to his aid. *"With men this is impossible,* he mumbled, *but with God ALL things are possible!"*[45] *Oh, create a clean heart within me, O Creator-of-All, and set aright the spirit within me.*[46]

HELD-BACK-THE-ENEMY kept watch as, one by one, the small band of Sparrow Hawk wanderers spread out pallets and lay down. He could not help smiling at Last Son. He half-sat, half-lay within earshot, urging his tall Blackfoot mother to allow him to stay up.

"Held-Back-the-Enemy needs me," the boy pleaded. "I can keep him awake!"

"I am sure you can," replied Last Woman, leaning down to stroke her son's hair. "But I also need you—to provide me with warmth."

The young Lumpwood admired her answer: rather than demanding the boy submit, she appealed to a generosity with his resources he would one day need if he wished to grow into an admirable warrior. As he nodded goodnight to his own mother, he stretched out one leg; squatting after a day of riding was making it cramp. He would, as Last Son understood, find staying awake difficult.

Perusing the women settling down to sleep, he located the graceful form for which he searched. She had given him her pledge, accepted his attentions, and even occasionally sought him with her eyes, but he still did not quite think of her as his own. After she tucked her son and his stepsister into a robe, she slipped over to Last Woman's pallet and bent down to tell her something.

What do I consider Among-the-Pines? Held-Back-the-Enemy wondered when he overheard the Blackfoot saying her name. Sparrow Hawk children belonged to their mother's clan, but he did not know any among their newly formed band who claimed kinship to Jackrabbit, her brother, or either of her remaining children. *I will welcome her as a daughter,* he decided. *Kept-Us-Alive loves her, and all know a daughter lightens a mother's load.* He also hoped by adopting her, he might further woo her stepmother.

As he listened to the two friends whispering, he could not decide who had the lovelier features. He had always admired Kept-Us-Alive's, but the Blackfoot's, though bolder in form, were also balanced and attractive.

Some quality about her touched him, though he could not decide if it was something that she possessed or lacked. Many young women seemed like small brown ducks, quacking at minor provocations or flapping about to gain the brightly feathered males' attention. Last Woman was a swan cutting a smooth path through the water, neither squawking nor taking sudden flight.

Of course, he could say the same of Kept-Us-Alive. If he was describing either to a warrior from the Whistle Water band, the stranger might assume he described the same woman. The essential differences in their characters were harder to put into thought. Both were graceful. Both prone to silence; but whereas the swan owned an aloof but admirable strength that signaled anyone with sense to approach with caution, the doe possessed a vulnerability that inspired his protection and invited his touch. The less fearsome of the two put an end to his musings, approaching to kneel by his side.

"I have a favor to ask of you," she murmured.

Pleased she had come to him, Held-Back-the-Enemy tilted up the corners of his mouth. He enjoyed listening to her voice and the look of burgeoning trust in her eyes.

"What would you like?"

"I...I thought...if you...and the other Good Men..."

When she cast her gaze downward, he gently touched lifted her chin, but her eyes held so many mixed emotions he was not sure what lay behind any of them.

"My father's band, though not all of my people, are much like the band we have now become. All—or most—have placed their feet on I-Am-Savior's path and many from our other bands avoid them."

He was not surprised. He had learned as much from his dead Lumpwood father; but what about this turned her hesitant, he could not fathom. Suspecting that she, like the young creature whose qualities she possessed, might bolt if he made too sudden a movement, he tamped down his impatience and waited silently for her to continue.

"They would…would…welcome us."

Held-Back-the-Enemy pressed his lips together. He had not expected this and was not sure what to answer. "We are their enemies."

"Not enemies—brothers. They are born from above as we are, sons of the very same Father."

As he looked into her eyes, soft and uncertain as she pleaded, he understood his Real Chief's misgivings. They inspired impulses he could not easily name, and her few words flew straight to their mark. Once he found his voice, it sounded low and oddly husky. "My father and I will ask our Good Men."

"Thank you," she whispered, her eyes holding such grateful relief, he had to look away.

He had guaranteed her nothing, yet she made him feel like the wisest and most generous of warriors.

"For twenty-four summers, my father and many of our elders have walked in I-Am-Savior's moccasin prints. The Good Men could learn much from them, and our womenfolk could gain answers from my mother that I am not able to offer. She has been walking the Creator's path since childhood."

As he rested his hand reassuringly on the curve between her neck and shoulder, he watched another question forming in her eyes.

"Yes?" he asked, one eyebrow raising. "I know you wish to ask me something more."

Following her gaze to her lap, he saw her picking at her nails; and when he raised his eyes to her face again, he found her faintly shaking her head.

"What?" he asked, unsure if she was telling him, "No," or was counseling herself to press no further.

Once she garnered the courage to engage his eyes, she found them both warm and obliging, but she could not bring herself to answer. *Pacing Wolf,* she mused, *selected my new husband very well. Not only will he provide for and protect us, but he will also hold my heart gently. Still, I cannot ask him.*

"Ask what you wish."

"I have no right. You have been patient and kind, not only to me but to my sons and even my sister-friend and her family."

"This is no hardship; you belong to me. Your sons bring me joy, and your friend has proved loyal. I give you the right—what do you wish?"

Taking a deep breath, she plunged ahead. "All the journey, a longing has been calling to my heart for admittance. I have tried to ignore or shoo it away, but it only calls more insistently."

Held-Back-the-Enemy wrinkled his brow. When the women he knew talked of longings, they spoke of a desire they felt for a warrior or their hope to bear a small-thing. He could not imagine her speaking of either. From her own lips he had learned she both esteemed him highly and thought him attractive; but though he had observed her regard increasing, he was keenly aware she still grieved.

"I long to return to the cave to…to pay my respects in the…the place where he died."

The young Lumpwood's eyebrows jerked up sharply. "Why? Why do you wish to feed your heart sorrow?"

"I do not know," Kept-Us-Alive admitted. "Perhaps because we had no one to lay in a carved out log, no body to cherish for the last time and bid farewell."

Gazing down at her, he felt a tugging so strong that he again thought of Hunts-For-Death's warnings. Her face was full of earnestness and confusion, yearnings to hold on and the need to let go. As she dropped her eyes, he nodded. "I will need to ask my father and my Lumpwood brothers. Our band is small; they may wish to keep each one of us with them until we are established in some place."

"Thank you. I…I…"

What she would have said, he did not know, but he pressed his fingertips to her lips. "Wait until the sun awakes. I do not know what they may say." He cast a look toward Among-the-Pines, who was staring eagerly in their direction. "Your stepdaughter is waiting. I am sure she has much to tell you, and you both need to sleep. The sky is clear. We will mount our horses early."

Kept-Us-Alive arose and made her way carefully around several sleeping friends and clansmen, but before she scooted between her buffalo robes, she tossed him a smile that turned his heart to the most malleable clay. If he nursed any doubt about her feelings, she was rapidly clearing them away.

Three things are too high to grasp. Four things I do not understand: the soaring of an eagle in the sky, the course of a snake on a rock, the path of canoes atop the waters, and the way of a warrior and a young woman.

Proverbs 30:18-19

Chapter 26

WHILE HELPING Pacing Wolf hobble to the spring, Straight Arrows abruptly halted. He could see with one glance that Pacing Wolf also felt the faint quivering. Standing perfectly still, they assessed the increasing rumble beneath their moccasins and recognized its cause: pounding hoof beats. The horses were not moving rapidly, but judging from the repeated thudding they were numerous enough to carry a vengeance party, and both warriors were certain of their destination.

Pacing Wolf nodded toward the cavity in which he had once stashed Small Doe and limped past a shielding pillar while Straight Arrows spryly trotted to the dwelling room to retrieve their weapons. Though neither of them hungered to draw blood and the recess would hide them well, it owned no way to escape.

As Pacing Wolf took the bow and quiver Straight Arrows thrust toward him, he pondered the tenuous trust renewing between them. He hated his own dependence. It stirred fears to the surface of his heart that he wished to keep trapped on the bottom, not only about Small Doe but also about his ability to lead the Many Lodges. Once he returned to the Cliffs-With-No-Name, the Lumpwoods would laud him for courage and award him tokens; but few Good Men would risk their skins by following a maimed warrior into battle. They would respect his counsel but set him aside, expecting him to remain with the Old Ones atop a safe rise, watching from a distance while they defeated their enemies.

If I reach Apsaroke before my Lumpwood son has taken Small Doe, what will her eyes say when she thinks I am not looking? Little Blackfoot said she grieves for me, but this will pass. No woman prefers a broken man to a thriving warrior.

While Straight Arrows was helping him squeeze into the shadowy recess, Pacing Wolf noted several unguarded expressions trot across his handsome face and inwardly commended him for his keen intelligence. He knew, though neither uttered a sound, the younger warrior had assessed the cavity's attributes and pieced together the events that had puzzled him during the past four summers. Later, when they had rid themselves of the present threat, he would show him how he and his sister had vanished.

A startled cry announced a bat or pine bough had brushed against a warrior entering the long, sloping passageway. As silent as the wall that hid them, Pacing Wolf and Straight Arrows listened while barely perceptible footsteps padded toward the dwelling room. What the younger warrior was thinking, Pacing Wolf could not tell—the darkness hid his well-formed features—but the pattern of the padding feet struck him as odd. They should naturally have turned toward the right and become fainter, but they instead headed toward the spring.

Pacing Wolf drew an arrow from the quiver slung across his back, but the height of the cavity's opening was too restrictive to raise his bow. He slid down to his knees, bracing his arms against the stone gap, and interposed himself between Straight Arrows and the intruders. Without knowledge of the alcove, Red Fox might assume Pacing Wolf was alone and, satisfied by drawing his blood, might probe no further.

Motioning for Straight Arrows to stay inside, Pacing Wolf dragged his damaged legs out through opening, managing noiselessly to stand and limp to the pillar that had once hidden him from Small Doe's father. He fit an arrow against the bowstring and then pulled the strong sinew back until it could stretch no further. Though his arm cramped from lack of use, he held it tightly, aiming it straight down the path from the dwelling room. If an enemy entered the corridor, he would soon feel a sharp arrow piercing his gut.

It was a warrior. Pacing Wolf could not see his features, but sunlight streaming through the crack high in the dwelling-room's ceiling silhouetted feathers attesting to his valor. As Pacing Wolf waited, peering through the dimness for identifying clothes or markings, the man turned his face sharply to warn someone over his shoulder, and Pacing Wolf instantly stepped from behind the pillar.

The warrior whipped his head toward the movement, sinking low as he drew his ax, but a joyful squeal tore past him. Hurling herself against Pacing Wolf, Kept-Us-Alive knocked him off balance and sent his bow clattering to the ground. Had he not heard her voice, he might have flung her into the run-off; but instead, he grasped her to his chest, pressing her to him so tightly she could hardly breathe.

"What...why are you here?" he sputtered, tasting a torrent of salty tears streaming from her eyes.

She pressed her lips against his cheeks, his temple, his ear, his neck—any unclothed surface she could find—as she had watched her white mother do to her father. Only after she regained her decorum did he realize their embrace was without impediment and, setting her back from him a little, gazed at her belly. "Our small-thing? Where is it—and Wolf-Who-Lays-Down?"

"Last Woman has them," she laughed, turning an irrepressible smile toward the clump of Sparrow Hawks that were gathering as close as they could to see who was causing the commotion. Then, without warning, she scrunched her face together and spurted, "Why did you not return? We thought you were dead! Where…"

At once, a thought she had hastily brushed aside began calling to her loudly: s*he* had knocked him backward. Searching his hunting shirt, she saw the patch and knew exactly where to find its twin—hidden in the large hide bag on the back of her mare.

"You are hurt!" Lifting the hem, she felt for a scar and began exploring his thighs for the place he had wrapped with his legging. "It was stiff with blood. How did you…"

Her questions trailed off as a shadowy, tall figure unfolded from within the hidden cavity, and with another squeal, she scrambled toward her brother. "How…why…"

Straight Arrows grinned, though she noticed he was glancing over her head with a wary eye. Several unfamiliar warriors were now pressing about them, all assessing his tokens and mode of dress. One looked as old as Many Feathers, his grandmother's brother.

"Who are they?"

"Pacing Wolf's kinsmen and ours," she answered, glancing back at the gathering Sparrow Hawks. "They have become our brothers." Locking eyes with Held-Back-the-Enemy, she held them briefly before he turned abruptly and slipped behind the others.

As Pacing Wolf watched the exchange, his earlier qualms found relieving answers. Her eyes, when they met his Lumpwood sons', held compassion, even guilt, but he detected no regret or concealed longing. When they turned back in his direction, they danced with happiness, leaping over every feature of his face.

Held-Back-the-Enemy squeezed past his father, Braids-His-Tail, and Old Paints-His-Shirt-Yellow's three sons as they descended the long stone corridor that led from outside. He craved fresher air. Peering down from the ledge, he recalled how close he came to plummeting to the ground and wondered how his wounded Lumpwood father could have survived. Pacing Wolf either possessed the power his clansmen so coveted or the Almighty had a quest He wished him to complete.

He believed the latter. Apart from his own father, Pacing Wolf was the warrior he most admired, but though his clansmen's regard for Kept-Us-

Alive conflicted as sharply as the battle now raging in his heart, the tales they told of her husband had begun to sound more like fables. He knew he should be happy—his Lumpwood father was alive!—yet he could not quell the disappointment spewing up bitterly within him.

I should have taken her, he decided. *Then her decision might not have been so simple,* but even as he thought it, he knew he was lying to himself. *A blind man could have seen her reaction—or heard it. And how do I blame him for wanting to keep her!*

Inhaling deeply, he realized there was one person alone with whom he could justifiably be angry: The Creator he claimed to follow. Loved-By-The-Creator wrote that He-Who-Sees-All-Things had already recorded his suns—and hers—before either of them left their mothers' bellies.[47] He had recited these very words as she bore Pacing Wolf's small-thing! Now, all his desire for her amounted to nothing more than coveting his clan leader's woman.

As frustration pawed at his heart, a tiny hand grasped hold of his fingers. "Where is Mother?" asked Wolf-Who-Lays-Down.

Gazing down at the tiny boy, he tried to tilt up the edges of his mouth, but he was not certain he succeeded. He had begun to regard the boy as his, not only taking him into his heart but also planning the good things he wished to teach him.

"In the cave," he muttered, glancing at Last Woman and Hopping Owl, who were approaching with Last Son and Among-the-Pines. He knew he should tell them Pacing Wolf was alive, that the strange mounts they spotted grazing on the ascent belonged to him and Wolf-Who-Lays-Down's uncle, but he could not bring himself to form the grievous joyful words.

"Can we go in?" asked Last Son.

"Go," he told him, returning his attention to the smaller boy. "You too. They are waiting for you." As he noticed one of the tall Blackfoot's brows begin to rise, he knew he could not so easily put off her questions. "Pacing Wolf," he murmured flatly. "He lives."

Her expression, at first full of joyful disbelief, changed quickly to concern and then sympathy. She stood still, unable to find a way to offer him comfort or even ask how he was feeling. She did not need to; the vexation he felt showed clearly in the eyes he returned often and sadly to the cradleboard she carried. Grasping the two little boys by the wrist, she signaled with her head for Among-the-Pines to follow. If she could not offer him what he needed, she could at least give him privacy with his mother.

"We are going in."

He did not try to stop them and wished his mother had followed. He did not want to talk with anyone.

KEPT-US-ALIVE stepped aside while her husband's Lumpwood brothers as they helped him into the dwelling room. While he watched her remove the cradleboard from Last Woman's shoulders, he guessed what she was going to do and longed to follow. He wanted to gaze at the tiny face he had so often imagined.

He could not. He was unwilling to insult the Good Men who crowded about him, asking him for further details about his incursion with the Shamers. Once he had recounted all that transpired, they awarded him two new feathers to honor his courage and two fresh red stripes to paint on the new leggings he would ask Small Doe to make for him. The old ones were beyond saving.

As Small Doe patiently listened, she was tempted to slip outside. She had discovered, more often than not, few things were as bad as her imagination painted them, but Wild Dog's death was far worse. While she tried to will away the vivid depictions that came to mind, she noticed Among-the-Pines leaning against Pacing Wolf, far too enraptured with his presence to feel disgusted by his grisly story. Wolf-Who-Lays-Down was sitting in the hollow of his father's crossed legs, wrapped in arms that deepened Kept-Us-Alive's distress. They looked thin and were less prone to ripple into hills and valleys as they moved.

Glancing over to Straight Arrows, she wondered how he might be reacting to Pacing Wolf's tale. He and Wild Dog knew each other well, but when she noticed where he was sitting, her heart lightened. Her husband had offered him the place of honor, and his clansmen were casting him looks she would scarcely have believed had she not witnessed them with her own eyes. They held approval, even admiration, for the aid he had given their clan leader, twice saving his life. More significantly, they seemed to sense a shared bond much deeper than common tribal ancestry or custom.

How good and pleasant it is, she thought with the Psalmist, *for brothers to dwell as one.*[48]

When Bites-With-Dog brought out his pipe, not one Sparrow Hawk objected to mixing his own exhalations with her brother's, not even White Belly. Why he had joined their new band was still a mystery, but along the journey, she often had noticed him talking late into the evening with her new father.

Once they had finished smoking, the Good Men recounted their reasons for leaving the Many Lodges and came to a pleasant agreement: they would follow Straight Arrows to his village and learn from his esteemed elders the ways of I-Am-Savior.

Since she had seen Pacing Wolf, Kept-Us-Alive's heart had felt like feathers fastened to a lance, swinging from joy to concern and then back to joy again. *How,* she asked herself, *could any of this have happened? Who would have ever supposed she might return to her people with the very person who took her from them? Surely, only heaven could hold more wondrous prospects.* As she considered how much more the Creator had done than she ever thought or imagined,[49] she looked at Last Woman.

Tears streamed unchecked down the tall Blackfoot's lovely face, reminding Kept-Us-Alive what this decision meant for her: soon, she would see her daughter! Soon also, a warrior might begin to court her, a warrior who would love her, and to whom she could go without dread—a warrior like Straight Arrows. Kept-Us-Alive had not missed the direction of her friend's gaze whenever she glanced up to discover or confirm who was speaking.

As Kept-Us-Alive turned her attention toward Held-Back-the-Enemy, she wondered what he might be thinking. While she was praying the Lord would heal any hurt he was feeling, her ears suddenly perked up. White Belly was saying something about her, something that had prompted him to break with Hunts-For-Death. She could not recapture all of it, but she noticed Pacing Wolf looked dark with rage, as did Straight Arrows, Bites-With-Dog, and even Held-Back-the-Enemy.

It was the first time all evening she had caught any expression on the young Lumpwood's face. Other than a tender glance now and then at Last Son, who was sitting in his lap, he had kept it an impassive mask, hiding the warmth that she had grown to expect in his eyes and smile.

What Hunts-For-Death had said that so angered them, she did not care to know; but as those gathered turned toward her, she found a mix of regard, protective loyalty, and sympathy of which she had been unaware during these past moons of grief.

She closed her eyes, thinking after this nothing could ever dim her happiness, and when she opened them again, she smiled at her brother. He was sitting directly across the circle, absorbed, so she thought, by watching her; but she could not understand why he refused to return her affection. Perhaps he thought her improper to show it freely with so many strange warriors present. Perhaps the shadows hid her face; but as she peered at him intently, she discovered he was not studying her at all. He had fixed his gaze on someone seated to her right, and he looked as if his thoughts were very pleasing.

From the beginning, no ears have heard and no eyes have seen a mighty Creator apart from You, who makes preparations for those who long for Him. You show Yourself for the one who rejoices in doing right, who remembers Your ways.
Isaiah 64:4

Chapter 27

During the

Moon When Water Fowl Return

PRETTY FACE HOPED Red Fox and he might arrive in his family's village before the dark clouds overhead let loose their torrents. Though the air was moist and chilly, he had found the journey home far easier than the journey north. Not a trace of ice clung to his eyebrows, his forehead did not ache from cold, and a party of pleasant memories were tossing up lodgepoles in his heart. Best of all, his conscience was no longer full of accusations.

He grew eager to tell his father he had not betrayed Light Bird's husband—though Red Fox's presence might make this difficult—and to alert his mother she might soon receive a lovely young woman-guest. The thought of leaving her to Angry-Man felt like a pebble that had worked its way into his moccasin.

Why her father allowed the man near her, he could not fathom, but before he had considered the matter for long, Red Fox was directing his attention far into the distance. Two riders were approaching at as high a gallop as their own, their hair soaring behind them on the wind. Straining in the dusky light, he recognized their horses and, as they neared, the way each sat his mount.

"Father! Grandfather!" he shouted. As they whooped in welcome, all doubt about his reception floated off like puffballs on a breeze. Each pulled his horse to a halt and leaped off, swiftly engulfing him in a double embrace. "I have told Red Fox nothing," Pretty Face whispered before letting them go. "Where is Straight Arrows?"

"Gone," replied Running Deer. He smoothed the frown from his forehead as he turned to greet Red Fox. "Come. You are welcome! My grandson looks as if you have fed him well."

Red Fox's expression was as controlled as Preying Eagle's as each grasped each other, hands to arms, and exchanged inquiries about their families. "Has the strange Ally you found with my dead son recovered?"

"Yes," answered Preying Eagle, "but you will find no answers for your questions. He left when the darkness consumed the past moon."

"With which band do his people dwell? I will go to them."

"You will not be welcomed," replied Running Deer. "He is not an Ally but an enemy. A Blackfoot child my son adopted recognized him."

As Red Fox glanced from him to Preying Eagle and Pretty Face, he barely disguised the disgust that flashed across his face. "Blackfoot—why did you let him go?"

"He fled in the night," replied Preying Eagle, turning toward his son. "The little Blackfoot's pony is gone also."

Pretty Face narrowed his eyes. "The one Straight Arrows gave her?"

His father nodded.

"And my brother—where is he?"

Preying Eagle swung onto his horse. "Your mother said he heard something that sent him into the night."

"Which night?" asked Pretty Face, mounting his horse along with Red Fox.

"The night after you left," answered his grandfather, mounting also. "Your mother will be glad to see you. She has felt uneasy with the two of you away."

"Straight Arrows chased him?" asked Red Fox, his voice thawing a bit.

Preying Eagle shook his head. "I cannot say." He suspected he had and guessed the place they headed, but he did not intend to divulge it. Let Red Fox conclude what he may. For now, he would offer his suspicious Ally hospitality, and when the visit concluded, he hoped Red Fox might set out for Blackfoot country.

AS THEY BEDDED DOWN for the night, Kept-Us-Alive could not take her eyes off her husband. She did not want to close them for fear she might awaken from this wondrous dream. She had thought she would never feel the warmth of his skin against her own or feel his tender caresses. Yet, she could not help noticing his arms had grown less taut and that his legs obeyed him poorly.

While she silently prayed The-Creator-of-All would restore them to their former health, Pacing Wolf began murmuring in her ear, not of tender remembrances but of the fear that he might be unable to provide for and protect her.

"My white grandfather often told my mother something that she, in turn, often told my father, my brothers, and me: 'You are borrowing trouble.' Life is more than food and our bodies greater than clothing.'[50] Our Father, who kept you from death, knows what we need—and look! We are all together, even Among-the-Pines!"

Pacing Wolf smiled but did not answer. *I am grateful,* he thought, *and stunned by all that has happened in Apsaroke, but Wild Dog...*

Before he carried the thought farther, the Holy Spirit brought to mind the remainder of the passages his woman had quoted, and he knew she was right. He was convinced from his depths that the Creator, who had twice sent Straight Arrows to rescue him, did indeed see and know all things and must have further use for him.

He is worthy of my trust.

As he stroked the small-thing nestled between them, he felt Wolf-Who-Lays-Down's hand wending around his waist from his other side. Among-the-Pines also seemed unable to sleep. She raised her head above Small Doe's arm to peer at him.

"I missed you, Father," she whispered.

"Me too," chirped Wolf-Who-Lays-Down

Looking down at her newest brother, his little girl asked. "What do you think of him?"

"I think my eyes have never seen anything so pleasing—not him alone, but you and your mother and brother. I have missed you also."

Smiling broadly, the girl lay back down and snuggled close to her stepmother. She could hardly believe what the Creator had done. As she remembered how desperate she had felt the day Jackrabbit claimed her, she asked I-Am-Savior to look down on the old woman with favor, and then she drifted off to sleep.

"YOU HAVE ALL betrayed me!" spat Red Fox, hearing Follows-in-His-Shadow's disclosure. "Where is he?" He grabbed Little Blackfoot's arms and shook her, doubling the chagrin her new brother felt. The boy had wished to toss the girl into trouble—that is until he had succeeded.

"Stop!" demanded Preying Eagle, pulling the little girl away and putting her behind him.

"Until the day he left," explained Old Many Feathers, "we thought he was your sister's son. His recovery was slow."

"He raved about many things and often acted like he saw evil spirits," added Little Turtle. "Ask my brother's son; he will tell you."

Pretty Face nodded. He had told Red Fox as much while he stayed with him.

"Once he regained his right mind," added Preying Eagle, "he asked only after your dead."

"I would not have thought you, my old companion, would be so easily taken in. A trickster's spirit must possess him."

"No, he follows I-Am-Savior as we do." chimed in Young Deer, though the look his father shot him quelled the desire to say more.

"Pah!" spat Red Fox, looking as if the boy had offered him a bowl full of dung to eat. Leaping to his feet, he glared at Preying Eagle. "You are all possessed by a trickster spirit. This light-eyed woman beguiled you with her tales, but you would not heed our Allies' warnings. Now, all see what comes of following this deceiver. He has turned you against your own kinsmen and made you protect a man who brought your daughter shame."

"What woman, Grandfather?" asked Follows-in-His-Shadow. "No one owns light eyes but Mother."

While Running Eagle answered, Red Fox gathered his belongings, thrust aside their door, and strode straight to the horses.

"Wait!" called Pretty Face, trotting behind him.

"Let him go," advised Preying Eagle, catching up with his son and gripping his shoulder. "He will not give you his daughter. He toys with you for some evil purpose."

"Plays-With-Her-Earrings is not like him."

"Whether she is or is not does not matter. He intends to hurt you, and she is his weapon."

"Why? What have I done?"

"You are my son. His woman wanted me, and he wanted your mother. Both hold bitterness in a tight grasp, and you know the scriptures: Men who love darkness hate light, lest it expose their deeds.[51]

While they walked to Brought-Us-the-Book's dwelling, Pretty Face told him of the Holy Spirit's whisperings to his heart. "I have heard the Word since I was a little potbelly and you and Grandfather insisted often I hide it in my heart, but until I walked alone, I did not grasp how widely our path differs from our Allies. They were like deer wandering from one clump of grass to another, never understanding where they are going or to what danger their appetites might lead."

"I was as they are," replied his father. "Though your grandfather and grandmother raised us to do what we knew was right, to respect all living creatures and the earth from which they spring, I felt something was missing deep inside of me. Not until I found your mother did I gain an idea of what it was."

"You needed a woman?" laughed Pretty Face. "I also feel that need."

His father smiled. "Not a woman, though I am very glad to have her. The Creator has made a place in all of our hearts that only He can fill. Nothing satisfies longer than it takes those clumps of grass to pass through a buck's stomach. Straight Arrows has long understood this."

"I have often wrestled with jealousy toward him and am ashamed. He is my brother and closest friend, but he has been of one heart with you and Grandfather in a way I was not. I am sorry for the grief I have caused."

"You are forgiven," Preying Eagle declared, stopping to grasp him by the shoulders. "I have also felt this difference. I cared for you as I care for him, but our hearts were as you say. Each man comes to I-Am-Savior by himself. No one can ride long on his father or mother's shoulders."

As he wound his arm around his son and pulled him close, his heart felt full to bursting. This had long been his deepest desire, and the Creator, ever faithful, had granted it.

←←← →→→

AS HELD-BACK-the-Enemy tugged his mother's mount beside the cave's upper entrance, he glanced furtively at Kept-Us-Alive. Relinquishing the care of her felt strange, but stranger still was Pacing Wolf's neglect. He left her to fend for herself, relieved only by occasional assistance from her brother. She did not seem to notice. She looked wholly content, contrasting sharply with her long moons of sorrow and stirring up the jealousy Held-Back-the-Enemy had barely quieted yesterday. Gripping onto Small Man's advice, he began thanking the Creator,[52] though at first, he could think of little to say. He felt like a hungry man who had snared a rabbit only to watch an eagle swoop down to snatch it away.

Would I trade away her joy to gain my own, or wish my Lumpwood father dead to gain what is rightly his? No, this is not the way of I-Am-Savior.

Looping a bridle over Last Woman's mount, he considered all that took place during the past moons and wondered if Hunts-For-Death would have challenged Pacing Wolf so openly. The Many Lodges held his Lumpwood father in too high esteem for both wisdom and valor.

Perhaps I-Am-Savior allowed us to think he was dead for this reason.

He was certain—offered a choice—Pacing Wolf would not have led the Many Lodges away from the Cliffs-With-No-Name. He was much less sure of the way Kept-Us-Alive's people might receive them. Her older brother, at least, seemed welcoming.

Once he settled Hopping Owl on her horse, Last Son begged to sit in front of him instead of riding with Last Woman. He relished the thought. The boy was full of affectionate admiration and constant questions that led his mind down many interesting paths; but when the lad told him Straight Arrows was an angel, he did not know what to reply.

Dropping from his place in line, he urged his mount down the cliff path toward Kept-Us-Alive's brother, but Pacing Wolf and he were traveling so closely together, Held-Back-the-Enemy did not have room to ride abreast until they all reached wider ground. Pulling his paint's reigns toward Straight Arrows' other side, he patiently waited for Last Son and Wolf-Who-Lays-Down to exchange somewhat noisy greetings, but before he could ask any questions, the company began dismounting beside the vast Muddy River. Only then, did he notice why his Lumpwood father had not offered his woman help: he could not get down. Her brother had tied him to his mount.

As one man, the wandering band did as they had so many times before: they looked for or cut down branches to weave together into rafts to port their belongings. Straight Arrows watched in amazement. After he had followed Pacing Wolf's instructions, helping his sister and her sons onto the raft and out onto the water, he looked for Last Woman, but she did not need him. The young Sparrow Hawk warrior called Held-Back-the-Enemy urged his painted horse into the river beside them, ensuring both she and her son were safe.

Once every Sparrow Hawk reached the other side, Bites-With-Dog sidled up to Straight Arrows. "You are certain your people will welcome us? I remember well how they last received me."

Pacing Wolf's head shot up, unaware of what he meant.

Glancing uncomfortably at the older Sparrow Hawk, Straight Arrows explained, "We all felt much pain over the loss of my sister. We eat no sorrow now, and Grandfather will restrain them as he did then—and I will also."

While Bites-With-Dog recounted the full story to Pacing Wolf, Held-Back-the-Enemy waited to ask his question. He had thought Little Blackfoot's abduction odd, or rather her mother's reactions had not felt right; but he had not wanted to cause further grief by asking many questions. When he finally had a chance to ask Straight Arrows if he were indeed an angel, the young Ally broke into a wide smile. He explained to both him and BitesWith-Dog all that had transpired and how Little Blackfoot's arrival had sent Pacing Wolf fleeing to the cave.

At first, Bites-With-Dog felt angry. He had searched long and hard for the child and had felt much sadness over her disappearance; but as he considered the Creator's hand in it, his anger softened and eventually changed to joy. During the entire moon that their believing Good Men were asking Him how they might respond to their Real Chief's threats, He already was preparing a place for them.

"Before I was afflicted, I went astray, but now I keep Your Word."
Psalm 119:67

Chapter 28

STANDING ELK NUDGED LITTLE Turtle with his elbow. "Look—a war party!"

As Little Turtle followed his gaze to the open grasses beyond the forest, he signaled to Pretty Face, who cast his eyes in the direction he nodded. About thirty riders, replete with war-shields and lances, proceeded toward the village below the promontory. The cropped hair above their heads stood up stiffly, and they wore hunting shirts that were so long they pooled about their hips.

As the other sentries clambered up the rise to lie beside them, Pretty Face called softly to a younger cousin. "Run! Tell Old Many Feathers and our other elders an enemy is approaching."

"Wait!" corrected Little Turtle, the youthful messenger's father. "Look." He directed Pretty Face's attention to the oddly configured center of the party, where they spotted a good number of horses traveling in tandem, lodge poles and covers slung between them. "What war-party hauls household goods? Half the riders are too small to be warriors. They look like women and children."

Peering down, Two Bears nodded. "You are right, little brother. None of their mounts wear war-paint."

"That is Straight Arrows!" cried Pretty Face, jutting his chin toward the lead rider. "See. The black horse wears one white legging."

Little Turtle nodded, peering intently at the man riding beside his eldest nephew. "And your mother's patient."

"Are you sure?" asked Elk-Dog Man, Pretty Face's youngest uncle. "His hair stands up as stiffly as the others."

"He is one of them," their nephew answered.

"Why have they come?"

"I do not know, but look who rides behind him." Smiling broadly, Pretty Face tilted his head toward a young woman sitting atop an intricately carved saddle.

"Light Bird!" murmured Elk-Dog Man, one side of his face deeply dimpling.

"Little Blackfoot will be happy. That is her mother. The tall woman. Riding beside my sister."

Catching Light Bird's name, some of the sentries scrambled to their feet. A few stayed or moved to better vantage points to watch the Raven Enemy approach, but Pretty Face and his uncles rushed down to find her father, mother, grandparents, and other siblings. By the time the small contingent reached the outskirts of the village, a throng of relatives and friends were trotting out to greet them. Many stopped, noticing the number of warriors, but as Straight Arrows signaled a greeting, all but Pretty Face continued cautiously to seek the one other person they knew well.

"Mother!" Little Blackfoot yelled, running at top speed when she spotted Last Woman.

The Blackfoot leaped down so hastily, she nearly knocked her son to the ground. Grasping him beneath the arms, she righted him just in time for her daughter to fling herself upon them.

Kept-Us-Alive searched among the taller heads for her father's and the shorter for her mother's. She spotted him first and saw so much satisfaction corralled in his eyes, she thought he could light a dwelling. Behind him was the grey-haired grandfather she so loved and respected, leading her silver-streaked grandmother by the wrist. A shower of pebbles scattered as she heard a woman squeal; and her mother, abandoning all the decorum the past twenty-four summers had taught her, rushed toward her with a smile as wide as her face.

Once they had held each other for what seemed a half moon, Brought-Us-the-Book spun her around so she could take a first look at her grandson. "He is beautiful," she purred, "but I thought he was older from what your brothers said."

Just then, Pacing Wolf approached, holding a tiny boy. "This is Wolf-Who-Lays-Down. Your older grandson."

As she took him from his father's arms, she thought her heart might burst. "Why have you…"

"Come," called Preying Eagle, indicating all should follow. "We will all talk in my woman's dwelling."

"Father," replied Kept-Us-Alive, turning two men's heads. "Do you remember the man who last guided me home to you?" She wanted to remind Preying Eagle of Bites-With-Dog, but to say his name while he was present was very rude. "While my husband was gone, he became my father and cared for me and for your grandchildren. I owe him much."

"Spotted Long-knife's guide," answered Preying Eagle, turning to greet the middle-aged Raven Enemy. "His voice holds admiration when he speaks of you."

"He is here?" asked Bites-With-Dog, brightening at the prospect of seeing the Major. As they last journeyed together, Spotted Long-knife had introduced him to I-Am-Savior.

"No. He and my red-haired cousin live with their children in the Village of Much Washing." Catching Brought-Us-the-Book's eye, he signaled for her to supply the name.

"Washington," she answered. "Spotted Long-knife was chosen to be one of their fifty-two-elder council. He speaks as often as he can on our behalf."

"What of Hair-On-Lip and his yellow-haired woman?"

"They live among his parents' people not far from Spotted Long-knife," answered Brought-Us-the-Book. "Toward the rising sun. They are farmers."

Bites-With-Dog looked puzzled.

"They plant seeds in the earth and wait for them to grow," she explained.

"As Sparrow Hawks do," added her daughter. "With your sacred tobacco."

While her two fathers discussed the practice, Kept-Us-Alive ducked into her mother's dwelling, kneeling out of habit in the place she had taken during most of her summers. As she watched her families, both Allied and Sparrow Hawk fill up the places around her, she became lost in the wonder of God's plan. Here she was, in her own parents' home, surrounded not only by her best-loved relatives but also by enemies she had grown to love. When she glanced at Straight Arrows, she found further cause for joy. He was openly watching Last Woman, though the tall Blackfoot had not noticed. She had yet to take her eyes off her little daughter.

Only one thing dimmed her happiness. She had hoped to see Pretty Face but had not spotted him since a first brief glimpse. As she searched for him among the faces filing into her mother's dwelling, she spotted Held-Back-the-Enemy; but though she wanted to acknowledge him, he cast his eyes on anything that presented itself or on nothing at all. To her relief, they soon landed on a place to his liking, crinkling up as Last Son scrambled over to sit down beside him.

"Come. We will walk."

When Kept-Us-Alive turned to see who was speaking, she found Running Deer, summoning her with his hand.

"Yes, Grandfather."

Once outside, they walked slowly, deliberately, as they always did when her grandfather had something he was working out in his mind, until they reached the promontory that overlooked the vast forest. Neither spoke for a while, each deeply satisfied in the other's presence and caught up in wonder as the yawning sun painted the sky. The lovely shades reminded her of the prairie flowers springing up in swaths of bright, soft colors.

Glancing at the village below them, her grandfather gestured toward a stiff-haired warrior talking with Pretty Face next to her mother's cone-shaped dwelling. She could not clearly read either of their faces, but their postures announced she was witnessing something important. After exchanging a few words, they embraced, and Pretty Face's shoulders began shaking.

"He has treated you well—this Raven Enemy?"

"Yes," she smiled, wondering what he might be thinking. When she was a child, she had felt amazed by her grandfather's ability to pick out the slightest knot in the threads she sewed across her heart. "They call themselves Sparrow Hawks for the handsome hook-beaked birds that hover high above their prey. He *was* our enemy, but once you learn what lies in his heart, you will find…"

She paused when she noticed a smile overflowing his eyes to tickle the drooping corners of his mouth.

"You already know this. I had forgotten."

"You do not prefer the young Sparrow Hawk who follows you with his eyes?"

"No, Grandfather," she answered, surprised again by how little he missed. "He has been kind, but Pacing Wolf possesses my heart. Though the past summers have offered me much that has been difficult, I am thankful Wild Dog led him to me."

"I am glad. When the Creator handed him to us, we felt torn. We did not wish to return you to a wolf's sharp jaws. Red Fox is angry that we did not hold him captive."

"Had Pacing Wolf not killed Wild Dog, he might have continued to…"

Running Deer held up his hand, letting her know he would not presently address the concerns hurtling through her eyes. "We know and sent his father on his way. The little potbelly on your back looks like Pretty Face at that age. Your small boy is the water-image of your husband, though, like your father, he possesses my nose."

"Then he is sure to be handsome," she replied, folding away her fretful questions as she examined the bold feature. She loved both him and her father dearly and hoped to pass on something of their looks to her children.

Pulling her against him, he rested his chin lightly atop her head, as had been his habit of old. "We no longer know what to call you. I remember what I named you long ago, but I have heard these Raven Enemies calling you Kept-Us-Alive."

"It is not for me to decide," she answered frankly, drawing back to look into his loving, black eyes. "But I do not deserve the name they call me. The Creator kept them alive; I only brought them food and water."

"Let them decide what they wish to call you. I will call you the name that suits you best, the name your mother heard your husband calling: Small Doe."

Earnestly, I tell you, if a man leaves his dwelling or his tribe, his woman or his children for the sake of the kingdom of God, he will receive many more in this life and eternal life in the world to come.

Luke 18:29

Chapter 29

FOR THE SECOND TIME since the new moon, the sentries watched a small party approaching, but though the horses were adorned with war shields and lances, no one felt alarmed. Their garb announced they were Allies, each protecting vital areas with chokers and breastplates and draping buffalo robes across one shoulder for warmth. The lone woman in their party wore a traditional doeskin dress.

When they spotted Red Fox, an eddy of tension began swirling from sentry to sentry and then down through the village, carried on a current of rapidly spread warnings. Straight Arrows sent Young Deer to tell Pacing Wolf and his Sparrow Hawk brothers to remain inside lodges and sent Follows-His-Shadow with similar tidings for his sister and her tall friend.

As Old Many Feathers and the other elders, all of their sons, and most of their grandsons went out to greet Red Fox, he dismounted, waived the young woman's mount forward, and then roughly pulled her to the ground.

"Take her!" he spat at Pretty Face, and then he turned his eyes on the young warrior's father. "Since we were youths, we have been like brothers. I would not have expected such disrespect and callousness from your son."

"What do you say he has done?" asked Preying Eagle, carefully ridding his face of emotion.

"See for yourself!" Red Fox grabbed his daughter by the arm, grasped the back of her dress, and balled up the excess within his fist.

Pretty Face's mouth fell open. He had wrapped Plays-With-Her-Earrings within his courting blanket but had done nothing that might cause her belly to round. Quickly counting off the moons since he had last seen her, he was about to protest, but the eyes she raised to his were so full of pleading he closed it again.

The surly cousin Pretty Face had met in Red Fox's village leaped also from his mount. "He does not speak," he snarled, casting a meaningful glance at Plays-With-Her-Earrings. "Where are all the words that dropped like water from his mouth—words he claimed were spoken by their book-god?"

"The little potbelly she carries *cannot* be his," asserted Running Deer. "The deed was performed a moon, perhaps two, before my grandson set foot in your village."

"He has dishonored her," insisted Red Fox, "and will pay me the bride-price."

While they were speaking, Brought-Us-the-Book had been studying Pretty Face's expression. He had pressed his mouth into a straight, hard line and his eyes smoldered with anger; but each time he glanced at the young girl, they softened. Stepping forward, he grasped her by the wrist and pulled her to a place behind him. "I claim her—and the potbelly!"

Two Doves nudged her daughter-in-law as she heard the onlookers gasp. "What are they playing at? Their talk is clear, but my ears do not believe the words, and my eyes are too weak to offer help."

"I am not sure," answered Brought-Us-the-Book, "but I feel as you do. Red Fox is staring smugly at Preying Eagle—not like a man who is satisfied that a wrong has been righted, but like an opponent who has gained some sort of victory. And the disagreeable man...I do not understand who he is to her. He is not her brother. Perhaps an uncle?"

"What is he like?"

"His manner is as peculiar as their talk, though I am not sure I can tell you how. It just sets oddly. He ought to have been mollified when Pretty Face accepted the girl, but for the swiftest of heartbeats his eyes widened in surprise, and he now glares at Pretty Face as if he would kill him."

"He should be surprised! All know her potbelly cannot be my grandson's! No mare rounds so soon with her first foal. If Pretty Face had dishonored her the morning he left us, the moons would not be enough. Why did he claim her?"

Brought-Us-the-Book grimaced. "I do not know, though he has spoken of this girl to me."

"And her?"

"She begs with her eyes for mercy, but her father and his angry friend seem uninclined to give it."

"Pah! This is not about the girl. That Red Fox and his woman have been simmering like a cook-pot full of fat ever since you brought us the book. I have believed for many summers that he has been casting about for an opportunity to bring us shame."

"But she is his daughter!" exclaimed Red Fawn, Two Doves' niece, who had slipped through the crowd to join them. "From the bruising on her face, I am guessing Red Fox beat her. Before Pretty Face pulled her from his reach, she cowered each time he moved his hand."

"Does my grandson care for her?" asked Two Doves.

"It would seem so," answered his mother.

"Five horses—not one less!" demanded Red Fox. "Each one healthy."

Pretty Face nodded. Guiding Plays-With-Her-Earrings to his mother and grandmother, he trotted up the rise toward his herd. Preying Eagle wished to go with him, but he knew he must stay to corral Red Fox and the raging buffalo bull of a man he had brought with him. Straight Arrows felt no such constraints. Quickly closing the space between them, he clamped a hand on his brother's shoulder. "What is this Red Fox says?"

Pretty Face felt tempted to shake the hand off. He was reeling from his hasty decision and the shame it caused and in no mood for his brother's questions. "I do not know," he answered honestly.

"Do you wish us to send them all way?"

Yes! thought Pretty Face, until he envisioned the expression on the young girl's face. "No. I do not know what she has done, but I know I did nothing."

"What she has done is plain for all to see."

"Is it? If not with me, who? She showed no preference for any other warrior while I was visiting their village—only a great fear of that churlish cousin."

"Then why should you…"

"Red Fox will hand her to *him*."

Straight Arrows looked back toward the village for a moment. "Is that why he is angry? He wants her for himself?"

Pretty Face nodded, holding the lead rope to a string of three good horses out to Young Deer, who had run after his older brothers. "Take these. I go to gather more rope I have been weaving."

As Pretty Face trotted toward the village, Straight Arrows watched their mother and grandmother walking with the girl toward his family's dwelling, inclining their heads as if they were asking or answering questions. What his brother was thinking, he could not imagine, though his wish to protect the girl was clear. Inwardly counting off all the members of Red Fox's family, Straight Arrows finally realized who she was: the scrawny little goose that always trailed after Wild Dog.

"But why?" he muttered, though no one was close enough to answer. "She can possess no more than fourteen summers—perhaps fifteen counting the approaching moons."

Thinking over the bits his brother had mentioned, he suspected what had happened and returned to his father's side, remaining silent while his grandfather extended Red Fox an invitation to stay in Two Doves' dwelling. Before anyone could do the same for the surly man, Straight Arrows stepped forward. "You will leave us. You are not welcome in our village."

Preying Eagle and Running Deer nodded so slightly to each other that only the most attentive observer would have noticed. Flanking each of Straight Arrows' sides, they tightened the space between them, prompting uncles and cousins to do the same until Angry Man faced a long wall of warriors.

No one could mistake their meaning, but Red Fox, turning to see Angry Man's response, sharply raised one eyebrow. The man looked offended—as Red Fox had expected—but he did not look the least surprised. While Red Fox regained control of his features, Pretty Face strode up, wordlessly placed the lead rope of two more horses into his hand, and set off toward his mother's dwelling with a white-faced ginger-colored pony.

Plays-With-Her-Earrings recognized his voice and answered his summons, but the shame she felt overshadowed any shreds of joy. When he tilted up her chin to better see her features, she could not bring herself to look at him; and though she thought the white-faced pony beautiful, she did not smile as he held out the rope.

"One?" she asked, looking into the pony's large eyes. They were well-formed and as dark as its mane. "I do not blame you for valuing me so little."

As she turned to lead the bride-price to her father, Pretty Face grasped her arm. "He has his horses," he murmured softly. "This one is for you." Taking the rope from her hand, he let it drop and drew her within his buffalo robe. "Dwell with me. I will care for you and raise the little potbelly within you as my own."

While waiting for her answer, he wondered if he had mistaken her wordless pleas or should have more pleasingly worded his offer. Tears ran across her quivering lips, wetting his hand as he wiped them away, but she offered no indication of acceptance and did not return his pledge. As his insides churned, he began to feel trapped with no way to extricate himself; but his qualms melted away as she pressed her cheek into his palm, telling him with this simple action what her lips could not say.

"WHAT CAN YOUR parents think of me?" murmured Plays-With-Her-Earrings. Small Doe had taken her to the farther side of the village, asking her to help dig up roots with which she planned to dye a doeskin.

"They think as I do: that you have been treated harshly. They cannot help seeing the purple marks you try to hide with your hair." As the girl instinctively touched the tender swelling, her expression wrenched Small Doe's heart. She had seen it worn by dogs with cruel masters. "I have a cousin who used to receive frequent beatings. You may know her: Black Swan. She owned five summers more than I do."

"I remember," mumbled Plays-With-Her-Earrings.

"She did nothing to deserve her beatings. Her husband possesses an angry heart."

The girl cringed. "My...my father says I...I did. That I must have...have done...something or he would not have... have...dared."

Kept-Us-Alive wanted to ask who the man was and why Red Fox blamed Pretty Face, but when she glance up, she saw Among-the-Pines and Little Blackfoot were running toward them.

"That churlish man is gone," they cried in unison, far too enthused about their tidings to realize they had interrupted. It did not matter; Kept-Us-Alive still gained her answer. Plays-With-Her-Earrings seemed for the first time all day to breathe.

"Straight Arrows shooed him away," volunteered Little Blackfoot.

"Like he was a coyote!" Among-the-Pines added.

"What of my father?"

"He has also left," answered Brought-Us-the-Book. The children had been chattering so excitedly, no one had noticed her approaching. "But we are glad you are here. You are very welcome in my dwelling."

"Thank you," the young woman mumbled, attempting to curve the corners of her lips. She continued digging, but once the little girls had scurried away, she made an effort to find her tongue. "It is not true— what my father said. Your son did not shame me."

"Why did he accuse him?"

"My cousin—Angry Man—lied. He told my father he caught your son forcing me but was too late to stop him."

"You did not deny this?"

"I...I was....afraid. He said I must m-m-marry him."

"Pretty Face?"

Plays-With-Her-Earrings shook her head, unable to meet the water-colored eyes.

"We know my son. We know he did not force you, but this Angry Man—he did?"

The girl nodded, catching her lip between her teeth to stop its quivering.

"But why did you not tell your father?" Small Doe prodded.

"I felt s-so dirty and a-ashamed, and then Angry Man's uncle asked my father for permission for him to court me."

"And he gave it?"

Again, the girl nodded. "His mother is my father's sister, and he is...was...my brother's friend. And even before I began to...to mound, my mother—Swallow Woman—noticed I had stopped going to...to the woman's lodge."

"And Angry Man knew your mother would soon suspect your...condition," finished Small Doe, remembering a conversation Pacing Wolf once overheard between Wild Dog and his cousins, "and your father would not withhold his consent."

"Y-yes," she choked out. "Mother insisted I accept Angry Man to keep our family from shame, but...but how c-could I? Then Pretty Face came."

Brought-Us-the-Book breathed in deeply, torn between a desire to protect her son and comfort Plays-With-Her-Earrings, who was in obvious pain. "And this heartless warrior blamed him?"

"Not at first. He was jealous of Pretty Face and angry my father encouraged him, but when your son did not offer for me, he saw a chance to keep my father's goodwill and still force me to consent."

"But if this Angry Man wanted you for himself, why did he come here and..."

"Pretty Face knows my potbelly is not his. Angry Man thought he would deny it and send me away—disgusted that I...that...." As the girl began weeping, Brought-Us-the-Book pulled her into her arms, rocking her as Old Quiet Woman used to do when she needed a mother's comfort.

"I also had my innocence stolen," murmured Small Doe, once Plays-With-Her-Earrings' sobs had quieted. "Though I gave my consent..."

As she told them how she felt the first night in the cave, Brought-Us-the-Book wanted to scream. She would like to have raced for her husband's war-club and bring it down firmly on Pacing Wolf's head; and yet, as she continued to listen, a small part of her also began to feel wonder. Her daughter not only offered Plays-With-Her-Earrings deeper comfort than she herself was able to offer but she also gently and clearly pointed her toward I-Am-Savior.

"Without Him, I think I might have thrown myself down ..." She stopped, realizing she could go no further without depicting the horrible place the girl's brother had died.

"I...I could not s-sleep for fear of Angry Man, but then your brother came. When he spoke to me of I-Am-Savior, I longed to meet Him, to know Him as your brother knows Him, and to let Him wash my dirtiness away. But I do not know where to find Him."

"He is here, little one," answered Brought-Us-the-Book. "You have only to ask."

Together they prayed, asking I-Am-Savior to create a new heart, a clean heart,[53] in Plays-With-Her-Earrings, a heart of flesh not stone,[54] and she asked Him to forgive her not only for the lies she had allowed her father to believe but also for all the bitterness she had kept tucked in her heart toward her mother.

As joy and relief spread over her young features, she also asked Brought-Us-the-Book to forgive her, confessing, "Your son is not obligated to marry me."

"He has already given your father horses."

"But I did not give him an answer. He is not bound. Only, please, do not send me back to them."

"We will not send you back, but do you wish to become my son's woman?"

"Yes," she admitted. "He is the kindest, most honorable warrior I have known, but I do not understand why he agreed to take me."

"We—you and I—will tell him what you have told us and ask him…."

"No…I…I could not. I could not bear to see the answer in his eyes."

"Do not fret," Brought-Us-the-Book whispered, stroking Plays-With-Her-Earrings' hair. She remembered how much she ached when Preying Eagle treated her only as his sister. "I suspect he has guessed much of what you have confided, but his father will talk with him privately, and we will let him decide."

So then you are no longer foreigners and without rights. You are brothers, blameless and of God's family.

Ephesians 2:19

Chapter 30

During the Moon When Everything Greens

"WHY DO YOU LAUGH?" asked Pretty Face. He was squatting beside his dun's front leg, running his palms over a swollen tendon.

"The Creator's plan for you offers much humor: you set out to avenge one woman and end up saving another."

Pretty Face grinned. "Plays-With-Her-Earrings never lacked appeal. Even as a child, I found her engaging. And you? I have seen you watching our sister's Blackfoot friend."

As the twinkle fled from Straight Arrows' eyes, he began stroking the dun's black mane. "I am not the only one who watches her. Have you not noticed Held-Back-the-Enemy? And her boy—he follows him as if he is his father. I would not lightly part them."

"If we follow her son's wishes, he might choose me. He still believes I am his angel."

Straight Arrows chuckled. "The boy's mistake saved our skins. He will soon see you are merely a man."

"And the Blackfoot? Can she not decide whose woman she wishes to be? Her eyes hold appreciation for his help, but she does not redden in his presence as she does in yours. And what of her daughter? She wishes *you* for her father."

"Little Blackfoot is much like her mother. Both display much courage and loyalty."

"Then why do you hold back? Do you dislike the thought of…"

Straight Arrows tilted his head. "Of what?"

"She has belonged already to two men. She is no longer untouched."

"Do you speak of my heart or your own—of Plays-With-Her-Earrings?"

Pretty Face let out a deep breath. "I wrestle mightily with this, but not as you say."

"What then?"

"I wish to kill him—slowly—the man who forced her. My heart wrestles as it did with Pacing Wolf, wishing to heap upon him all her pain."

"What do you intend?"

"Nothing." Pretty Face shook his head. "What can I do? The bond between our bands is like a rope a mouse has been chewing. The smallest tug may tear it in two. Besides, I-Am-Savior has taught me much during this past moon. Vengeance belongs to Him for good reason, and I will leave it where it belongs."

When Straight Arrows did not reply, Pretty Face glanced up to find the edges of his mouth slightly curving. "What?"

"I was thinking again of the Creator's ways—how far they are beyond fathoming. Would you wish your woman as she once was—dwelling untouched in the home of her mother?"

Pretty Face stood up, staring at his brother as if he had grown horns.

"If not for her foul-tempered cousin, would you have offered for her—the daughter of a family who has caused ours great pain? Wild Dog, not Pacing Wolf, tossed our sister into grief, and her parents have long openly opposed I-Am-Savior. If they could, they would treat us just as the Raven Enemies are treating our brothers and sisters."

As Pretty Face knit his brow together, a bevy of thoughts danced swiftly through his eyes.

"You would not have sought her," Straight Arrows answered for him. "In spite of her appeal."

"No," admitted Pretty Face, shaking his head. "Nor would our uncles have agreed to speak on my behalf. I felt stunned as you did, hearing myself claim her—and then I did not know what to do."

"And with parents such as hers, she is unlikely to have sought I-Am-Savior, and His Word is clear—light and darkness do not walk side by side."

Dropping his head a little lower, Pretty Face admitted, "That is why I did not consider asking for her while I was in their village. I was as surprised as our mother and sister to hear she wanted I-Am-Savior. But what of you? Does Last Woman's dead husband keep you from offering?"

"No."

"What then? What does the Creator tell you?"

"Nothing. He is just as He was with Corn Tassel—silent; and yet, for the last few moons, He has been stirring something in me."

Pretty Face's lips began to twitch. "The desire for a woman?"

"No," smiled Straight Arrows. "That has long stirred me. I am not able to give it words, even with Father. The Creator has been pressing on me, telling me He is about to act."

"How?"

"I do not know. I feel—expectant—as if something is about to happen, but what I cannot say."

"You need a wife. You already own too many summers."

Straight Arrows chuckled, but as he glanced across the horse's withers to the edge of the grasses, he lowered his voice. "We have a guest. Something large and bulky is moving through the bushes. See? Over there. In the sweet meadow."

"A bear?"

"No," replied Elk-Dog Man, their uncle. When he heard Straight Arrows' drop his tone, he had ambled over to peer at the place they were staring. "It is a man."

"An enemy?" whispered Elk-Dog's son, who had been with his father, tending their horses.

Neither his cousins nor father could answer until the warrior left the shadows of the clump to gain the taller trees.

"An Ally," declared Elk-Dog Man, renowned for his keen sight. "That unpleasant one who accompanied with Red Fox. He finds interest in our women. See—he is creeping toward the river. Go."

Straight Arrows and Pretty Face looked at each other then bolted toward the village, followed by their little cousin, their brother, and several other youths. "You go to the women," Straight Arrows told Young Deer, who looked severely disappointed.

"But..."

"Go!" snapped Pretty Face. "Take my woman to our mother's dwelling and find Father."

The youth had little choice but to comply while his brothers broke toward the trees; but understanding his task was also important, he ran with the swiftness that had earned him his name.

"Quickly," he told the small group of women and their daughters. "Go back to the village. You come with me." Grasping Plays-With-Her-Earrings by the wrist, he trotted as hastily as she could run, tossing the name "Angry Man" to his sister over his shoulder.

Small Doe took off in the other direction, dashing toward the herds grazing on the far rise. When she heard someone following, she whirled around and found Among-the-Pines. "Go home. Change into your doeskin!"

"But this is my favorite," the child whined, looking down at her elk-toothed blouse.

"You look like a Sparrow Hawk."

"I am a Sparrow Hawk."

"Do not argue. Go—now!"

As her stepmother hurried on, the child trotted back toward the dwellings, but Little Blackfoot seemed unable to decide whom to chase.

Stepping into the grass her mother's moccasins had just flattened, she turned to watch her unhappy friend.

Between several spindly horse legs, Small Doe spotted her husband's characteristic limping. Her chest heaved from dashing up the steep incline and the little potbelly on her back felt heavy as a boulder. "Angry Man..." she puffed. "He is back."

"Back...where?"

"I am not sure. My little brother came to warn us."

As Pacing Wolf turned to hobble toward the watching place, Small Doe caught hold of his arm. "No. Please—the dwellings—and I will warn the other Sparrow Hawks that they must hide also. If he sees you, he will alert Red Fox."

Pacing Wolf grinned at his woman, red-cheeked from the run. He would like nothing better than hole away with her inside their dwelling. "I am a warrior. Shall I cower like a scared rabbit?"

"No, but if Red Fox discovers you are here, he may bring a war party and endanger both of our peoples."

Realizing she was correct, Pacing Wolf complied. He would be of better use by concealing himself with his clansmen than by brandishing the ax his Lumpwood son had recently returned. As he limped toward the village, Held-Back-the-Enemy and Last Woman overtook him and put their shoulders beneath his arms to hurry him along; but just as they were rounding a grove of spruce, the surly Ally flew at them, knocking Pacing Wolf to the ground. Scrambling to his feet, Pacing Wolf took his stand, but Angry Man, hearing a rush of war-whoops, turned and fled. Straight Arrows, Pretty Face, and four other cousins tore past the two Sparrow Hawks, chasing their fellow Ally as if he, not they, were the enemy.

BEFORE DARKNESS DEVOURED the Moon When Everything Greens, the sentries once more spied a party of Allies approaching; but unlike the other party, this one was comprised of painted warriors. The meaning was unmistakable.

"Run!" Elk-Dog Man told his youngest son. "Tell my old uncles and your grandfathers a war party approaches!"

The youth did as his father commanded, enlisting his cousins, Young Deer, Eats-With-Two-Fingers, and little Follows-His-Shadow, to spread the word to the other three corners of the village.

"Grandfather!" Young Deer yelled so urgently that not only Running Deer but his three other sons nimbly slipped out their doorways.

"The sun is overhead," scolded Preying Eagle, flipping his eyes toward its zenith. "The little ones and their mothers are resting. What is so pressing?"

"Red Fox—he approaches with many warriors, all armed."

Running Deer and his sons exchanged brief glances, ducked back into their women's dwellings, and came out tucking weapons in their belts and slinging bows and bags of arrows across their shoulders. Several younger warriors nearly skidded into them, all dashing for their weapons.

"Where are they all running?" asked Among-the-Pines when her father, Bites-With-Dog, and White Belly sprang up from the game they had been playing.

"A war party is coming," answered her stepmother. "You have your knife?" The girl nodded, but before they slipped out into the bright sunshine, Pacing Wolf slipped back in. He grimaced as he sharply bent his legs, but Small Doe saw that something else was amiss. Following him with her eyes as he moved about her dwelling, she watched him snatch up his ax and bow and spotted bundled feathers poking up above his shoulder.

"I will not return," he told her, stopping to cup her face in his palm.

"You are my heart. Your father and brothers will care for…"

"No!" she sputtered. "You cannot…"

"It is Red Fox. He does not come for your father or your people; he comes for me. I cannot let him…"

Her lips so instantly twisted they could not form words, and his daughter, understanding her mother's burst of tears, began to cry. Seeing they had grasped his reasons, he leaned a cheek against his wife's cool hair and briefly held her for what they both knew would be the last time. Grasping the hands that clung to him, he trapped them against her sides, half clasping her, half placing her aside and then bent to caress his little girl's cheek before slipping beneath the flap.

Trotting as swiftly as his mending leg allowed, Pacing Wolf pressed through the gathering melee, but Little Turtle and Stands Apart, Red Fawn's husband, unexpectedly closed ranks at his sides and seized his arms so that he could proceed no further. Over the tops of several hundred feathered heads, they spotted Old Many Feathers' straight but wizened form and grew still as he offered Red Fox and his party a polite and proper greeting.

"I am Many Feathers, elder of the Allies, and have known most of you since you were boys running naked in and out of your mothers' dwellings. Why have you come to us boasting weapons of war? Is an enemy afoot?"

"The man who killed my son," snarled Red Fox. "Give him to me, and we will spare you, your women and children."

The old man peered silently into the faces of the mounted warriors. Several stared back boldly. Many dropped their eyes. He singled out a few, asking after their father's or brothers or acknowledging how valiantly they had fought by his side. Finally, he turned back toward Red Fox.

"I once pulled your father from the path of an enraged buffalo. You would not remember. You were still clinging on to your mother's skirt hem. Come. We will go to my woman's dwelling and talk as brothers."

"Brothers do not protect murderers," parried Red Fox while dismounting. "We know he dwells here. My kinsman saw him."

"Ah. The unpleasant man who was skulking around our village, spying on our women-folk. We chased him off, as we would any coyote."

As snickers echoed throughout the gathering warriors, mounted and on foot, Angry Man turned black with rage; but only after all grew silent did Old Many Feathers continue.

"It is true a few Raven Enemy are here among us. We have made an alliance with them. But your son's murderer—how did your skulking kinsman know him?"

"The embers he stomped out showed his face clearly," sneered Angry Man, curling back his lip. "I gave him the wound that makes him limp."

Old Many Feathers cocked his head and articulated slowly, "*You* gave him this wound. You stood so close, you saw his face, and yet you—alone—stand here before us. You—alone—left your companions. Did you return to see if they had fallen or did you leave it to others—to my sister's grandsons who happened by—to tend the wounded or honor the dead?"

As the entire gathering turned toward Angry Man, he located Pacing Wolf within the crowd. "He is the man! I followed him up to the cave's entry and pushed him from the cliff."

Pacing Wolf returned his glare, doubtful of his story. He had suspected the presence of a third warrior, but though his own breathing had been labored, he had remained attentive for sounds that someone followed. He had heard no one, and nothing but darkness had thrown him into the pines.

"Hand him over," demanded Red Fox. "You are our kin—why force us to harm you?"

As the edges of the crowd swelled with women and children, all wishing to learn what their Allies intended, Pacing Wolf wrenched loose of his protectors' grasps and hobbled forward. "I am Pacing Wolf, Sparrow Hawk of the Many Lodges."

"No," commanded Running Deer, nodding to Little Turtle and Stands Apart as they regained their grips and dragged Pacing Wolf backward. "Your vengeance quest requires a life for a life. Take mine."

As women within earshot gasped, Red Fox looked him up and down. "You are an old man," he sniggered. "Your life is almost finished. Hand me this Raven Enemy who killed my son."

"I will take his place," called Preying Eagle in a strong, clear voice; and while horrified eyes darted from Running Deer to him, Straight Arrows edged into the place between them.

"No—me!"

"No!" cried Pacing Wolf, struggling so mightily to break free that Stands Apart and Little Turtle needed the help of two more cousins to restrain him.

Red Fox slowly stepped past Straight Arrows to stand before his old friend. "From our youth, you and I have been like cousins. You were the one I chose to stand beside as we beat back our opponents in the games and the one who led my woman across my path, saving me from an evil fate."

His lips curved upward as he slid a glance toward Brought-Us-the-Book. It held such contempt, her spine began to tingle. As he tucked a hand beneath his buffalo robe, he stretched up so close to her husband's face, she fleetingly thought he might kiss his cheek. What Red Fox murmured into Preying Eagle's ear was too low for her to catch; but as he shrunk back down to his normal stature, he spoke in a clear tone no one could miss.

"You have brought evil to the Allies, turning hearts that were once hard as buffalo bone to soft pouches made of doe-hide. For many summers, I have hated you."

Without warning, he jabbed his hidden hand sideways, and Straight Arrows' eyes grew wide. Feeling a sharp pain in his rib cage, the young warrior slumped forward so suddenly that his father's childhood companion could barely support his weight. Withdrawing his bloody knife, Red Fox stepped backward, his gaze fixed on Preying Eagle as he allowed his son to thud to the ground.

"Now you, also, know how it feels to lose your son! I have my vengeance."

Two Bears grasped him by the throat, his large hand cutting off Red Fox's breath as it lifted his feet off the ground.

"Stop!" cried Pretty Face, grabbing his uncle's wrist while Last Woman rushed to Straight Arrows' side. "You avenge my brother and Red Fox's warriors will avenge him. When will it end?"

Two Bears fought hard to loosen his grip. Red Fox's face had grown the color of his name and his eyes had begun to bulge. Dropping the man abruptly, he strode away, the urge to finish the task broken only by Brought-Us-the-Book's shrieks as she weaved through the crowd. He could not bear hearing the lament she raised, as cadent as any woman born of his people; and he briefly feared that she, too, might pull out her knife.

As her wails rang toward the heavens, her daughter and Sparrow Hawk husband, now released, brushed by. Pacing Wolf gripped Straight Arrows' shoulders, shaking him and urging him not to die. Pouring forth his unworthiness for such a sacrifice, he watched as the young warrior's head lolled limply backward, declaring what all the others knew.

Small Doe flung herself atop her slain brother, adding to her mother's and her sister-friend's wails, though how the Blackfoot reached him first, she did not know. Elk-Dog Man, Little Turtle, and Pretty Face barely caught Pacing Wolf as he rushed past them toward Red Fox, who was still gasping for breath as he stumbled to his feet.

As Two Bears struggled afresh with his desire for justice, the tone of Brought-Us-the-Book's song of mourning began to change. She extolled Straight Arrows' courage and might, his unfailing accord with his father and grandfather, the love and wise guidance he had shown his brothers, and his gentleness toward his sisters. She then turned her praise toward the Creator, thanking Him for placing Straight Arrows in her womb, for gracing their lives for twenty-three summers, and for having written all the days of his life before any of them came to be.[55]

As she thanked Him for freeing them from revenge, everyone—mounted and unmounted—grew quiet. She rejoiced in Straight Arrows' friendship with I-Am-Savior, in his ardent desire to walk closely in His steps. With rhythmic reminders, she hailed his ready generosity of both goods and effort on behalf of those who could never repay him until a hush began to roll over the whole village.

Preying Eagle and Running Deer stood in stunned silence, unable to believe any man—particularly one they had called an ally—would snatch the life of a warrior who had done him good, not harm, who had washed the dirt and blood from his dead and ensured they would receive a proper burial. Angry Man had left Wild Dog to drop into the cave's belly and Walks-Behind-Them to rot. While Preying Eagle scooped up his firstborn's lifeless body, his own cadent grieving broke the silence. Only then, did Old Many Feathers or any of the others notice several of the mounted warriors tossing their weapons to the ground.

Red Fox slunk to his horse, keenly aware of the people's stares. Some held grief; many held anger; all held dismay. While he grasped the reigns to wheel his mount away, Old Many Feathers grabbed hold of his bridle. "My sister's grandson would want us to forgive you."

Red Fox hit the withered hand with his quirt, so startling Old Many Feathers that he withdrew it, and then galloped swiftly away. The war party he left behind seemed frozen, unable to follow such a man and yet unable to stay. Fearing Red Fox had made them a stench to their own kin, many began hesitantly to turn their mounts away, but Wooden Legs called out to them.

"Brothers, you have witnessed today the divide between light and darkness. It runs deep, like the canyons in the wilderness after the sun has baked the dry earth. We know you followed Red Fox ignorantly. I-Am-Savior bids you welcome. He would offer you water to quench your thirst, refreshment for the dry ground of your souls.

"Leave the bitter way of vengeance that dogs Red Fox, a way that will shrivel his heart until he can no longer feel affection or joy. For too long, I followed that same path, hating the Puckered Toes who slew my daughter, but then the Creator sent a fire-haired child, preparing the way for Brought-Us-the-Book to tell us of Him. I cannot fit you all inside my dwelling, and my dear woman cannot feed you from her grave, but there are many here who—like our savior—bid you welcome."

As he turned to survey his kinfolk, women began approaching one warrior or another to extend all the hospitality each had to offer. Some of the warriors turned away, riding in the path of Red Fox; some warriors stayed. No one would forget all he had witnessed that day.

Do not fear those who can kill the body but cannot kill the soul. Fear The One who can destroy both body and soul in hell.

Matthew 10:28

Chapter 31

"MAY I SPEAK WITH YOU?" called Last Woman. Constant weeping had streaked her cheeks, but though she respected Brought-Us-the-Book's privacy, she could stay away no longer. Watching a falling star's trail across the sky, she grew even more determined.

"I am here," rasped her friend's mother. "Is Little Blackfoot alright?"

"Yes. She is sleeping beside her brother. I wish to thank you for your care of her." Last Woman smoothed her hair, suddenly conscious it looked disheveled, but as she peered down into the older woman's face, she knew it would not matter. The flesh surrounding the water-colored eyes looked red and so puffy that even on this clear night she could barely detect their unusual color.

"She was no trouble, but you have already thanked me. You cannot sleep?"

"No. Can we walk—not far, but away from the dwellings? I wish to tell you something."

"Yes. Let me duck back inside to tell my husband."

Conversation was the last thing Brought-Us-the-Book wanted, but the tall Blackfoot's plea was so earnest, she could not bring herself to turn her away. Besides, until this day's sorrows, she had cherished a hope Last Woman might become another daughter, tying her to the little girl who had grown dear to her heart. Her eldest son had told her little, but she could not help seeing he stood erect when the Blackfoot happened to be present or that she turned bashful if she caught him watching. Little Blackfoot had also noticed and looked as if she might burst from happiness.

After Brought-Us-the-Book emerged, the two walked in silence, crossing the meadow to sit beneath the canopy of the ancient crabapple.

"I reached Straight Arrows before you did and cradled his head in my lap. As he was slipping away, he looked like no one—or nothing—I have ever seen, except perhaps the sun breaking through clouds that have spilled their torrents. His face was…was full of….joy! He raised his eyes to me only once, but he was smiling."

Pausing for a moment, she tried to control the quivering of her lips.

"I...I wished to tell you what he...whispered: 'When I awake I will...b-behold Your...face...'" She stopped, unable to keep herself from weeping.

"in righteousness?" his mother asked softly.

Last Woman nodded her head. "And...and be...be..."

"Satisfied with Your presence."[56] She peered toward the place where she had rushed to him, bright moonlight reflecting off the tears dribbling down her angular cheeks; but a look of peace, even rapture was spreading beneath them. "Thank you. This matters much to me."

The tall Blackfoot nodded but did not answer. Instead, the two remained as they were, lost in silent awe as they considered the joy of seeing I-Am-Savior face to face, a joy for which Straight Arrows need no longer wait.

As a tall dark form drew their attention to the edge of the meadow, they saw another emerging from a nearby dwelling.

"Preying Eagle," Brought-Us-the-Book murmured. "He may be concerned about me, and is that not Pacing Wolf's young friend?"

"Yes. Held-Back-the-Enemy."

When the two warriors reached the ancient crabapple, Brought-Us-the-Book asked Last Woman to recount her story, but she caught another dark figure out of the corner of her eye, searching between the dwellings.

"Is that our daughter?" she asked her husband, directing his attention to the increasingly frantic figure, and all four immediately hurried to Small Doe's side.

"What is wrong?" asked Preying Eagle, noticing his daughter seemed unable to keep her eyes still. They darted beyond him, over her mother's shoulder, and past her friends.

"Pacing Wolf," she fretted. "He is gone. I have searched everywhere."

"Go back to your small ones; we will find him."

By then, Pretty Face had joined them, plainly wearing questions on his somber face.

"Pacing Wolf," their father answered. "Go up to see if he is with the herds. I will search on the other side. Guide my woman, daughter, and her friend home."

The last he said to Held-Back-the-Enemy, who complied readily. He was anxious to return Last Woman to Little Blackfoot, who had ducked into his father's dwelling to say her mother had left and not come home.

While Preying Eagle headed toward the river, Pretty Face hurried up the rise. Once there, he spotted a low black shadow, though whether it was a man, a bear or just a large discarded bag, he could not tell. Cautiously approaching, he saw that it shook with what he soon would discover were involuntary heaves.

Pacing Wolf tried to speak, but his face so twisted that the sounds he made were barely coherent. "Me!" he cried, thumping his chest. "Red Fox should have killed *me*! *I* killed Wild Dog." Bursting into another round of sobs, his whole body seemed to jerk with sharp, rapid breaths. "Why…why did Straight Arrows step forward? I killed him!"

Pretty Face wrapped an arm around Pacing Wolf's shoulders, pulling him close as if he was a child. "Why did I-Am-Savior do the same? I was guilty. I killed him. He had no cause to die, and neither did my brother. They chose to die—both of them—so you and I could live."

Pacing Wolf could do no more than nod as fresh grief wracked his body; and while Pretty Face listened, the weight of his own guilt began heavily pressing in. Finally, he broke the silence. "If anyone killed him, I did." Pacing Wolf lifted his head, a puzzled frown wrinkling his brow.

"If I had not run to Red Fox, you would not have fled and he would not have gone after you. You could have waited until you were well enough to go alone, and when Red Fox came, it would be too late."

Pacing Wolf slowly shook his head. "That would have changed nothing," he rasped. "But it is as you say. We are all guilty, but the evil one—not I-Am-Savior—accuses us. I-Am-Savior's blood has wiped us clean."

As Pretty Face remembered that his sister was worried, the two headed down the rise, but they both stopped abruptly. Strange contours lay under the moonlight just outside the village, as if the ground had heaved into shallow ridges set apart by ruts.

"They look like warriors…bundled beneath buffalo robes," said Pacing Wolf when they grew closer. "I count nearly 40."

Just then, a tall dark form slipped up beside them. "They are from Red Fox's band," Preying Eagle told them. "Stands Apart and Wooden Legs have been talking with them. They cannot understand why my son gave himself for you, and they wish to hear of the Spirit who possessed him."

All three grew lost in private grief, but as Pacing Wolf stared at the rows of bundled warriors, he began to think of the mounds his people created when they planted their sacred tobacco. Clear as the star-filled night, I-Am-Savior's words burst like a war-party into his memory. "I tell you the truth: unless a seed drops into the earth and dies, it remains alone; but once the seed has died, it will bear plentiful fruit."[57]

He will swallow up death forever, and the Lord will wipe tears from all faces. He will remove shame from His people in all the earth, for The Lord has spoken.

Isaiah 28:5

Epilogue

August 10, 1847

Dearest Hides-In-Shadows,

I still cannot force myself to think of you as Annamary, even after three decades, and certainly not a senator's wife. It seems just yesterday we were hauling water to our families' dwellings while mooning over one or the other of our respective husbands.

I was overjoyed to see Nathanial, though sorry it took him such trouble to find us. I was also delighted to learn of the deep friendship that has sprung up between the two of you and my dear friend, Allison, and her husband, John, since you took up residence in Virginia. Who would have ever thought that my two closest friends would meet, let alone become grandparents to the same set of children?

Much has changed since you last visited and even since the events in this manuscript took place. Your father still grieves for your mother, and Old Many Feathers recently joined her and his beloved Quiet Woman and our grandparents in heaven. Running Deer is completely grey, and Two Doves has lost all sight.

I cannot believe you have been away nearly a decade, though I understand why serving as a senator's wife and the war with Mexico have been keeping you away. Besides, you have much back east to occupy your heart. How many grandchildren do you have now, seven? I have six, though I will leave them for Nathanial to describe, and an adopted girl who has just come into womanhood—but I will not tell you of her yet. You will meet her while reading the story you now hold.

I understand well the sorrow Nathanial said you are feeling now that Corn Tassels, Joshua, and their three children left for Oregon territory. How is Samuel? I want to hear all about his wife and their three. Your husband told us of them only briefly. I have my own joyful news on a similar subject, but again I will let you learn of it in detail as you edit.

Speaking of manuscripts, Nate informs me that you two have been beleaguered with questions about your time amongst "the savages" since the publication of my journal and the subsequent book about Light Bird. This last one has taken me so long to write, I am unsure anyone will still be interested in reading it. Pen and paper have been hard to come by, and frankly, parts of it were horribly difficult to write.

Nate told us of the trouble brewing in Congress, even his fear that fighting may begin to break out on the Senate floor! Though I am glad Garrison and his lot are working so valiantly to end slavery, I am deeply concerned about the repercussions for your family and for Allison and John's. Yet, as I write this, the Holy Spirit is reminding me that our hope is not in government but God. He knows the end from the beginning.

Returning to Corn Tassels, I have become so weary of parting with my loved-ones, I count loss among the reasons I look forward to heaven, which leads me to the news I have been putting off telling you. I can barely bring myself to pen it, but I must as I made Nate promise to keep it to himself until I told you. Straight Arrows is now home with Jesus.

You will read of the circumstances in this manuscript. As I took up the arduous task of quizzing persons present during this book's events, I found him at every turn. Do you remember his befuddlement, before you made your first trip to Boston, when you—or was it Two Doves—told him he was half white? I will never forget his laughter while he lifted his shirt for all to see that he was entirely one color.

Perhaps this was why God closed the doors of his and Corn Tassels' hearts to each other. We were all surprised, even dismayed at the time, but had they married, she would now be a widow. Without Straight Arrows, I cannot imagine she would have wanted to stay, but where could she go? Can you imagine her showing up in Washington with several dark-skinned, black-eyed, black-haired children? You and Nate would have loved them dearly, but not everyone back east would have been so kind.

He never married, by the way. He was deeply attracted to a captive Blackfoot, but as with so many prayers, a "yes" to ours would have meant a "no" to another's. Her little boy badly wanted her to marry a young Sparrow Hawk he—and we—greatly admire. In fact, you have met his father—the guide who brought Small Doe back to us during your last visit (you will understand as you read this last story). Happily for her son, the two married five summers ago.

Straight Arrows, with his last breath, he spoke of seeing the Creator face to face, and I confess part of me is jealous. Can you imagine seeing Jesus in all His glory, exactly as He is, unhindered by these dwellings made of flesh? I would not know how to act or what to say, though I'd probably be like John and fall on my face!

Recently, when I was reading The Revelation, I found myself wondering what he looks like now and what he is doing—and more so as I read First Corinthians' end. Do you remember? Paul speaks of the impossibility of guessing the glorious tree that will grow from a tiny seed.[57] If Preying Eagle were writing this, he could quote the verse by heart. He—like you—are much better at remembering Scripture precisely than I am. It says roughly: we sow a perishable seed but the body that springs up from it is imperishable,[58] and just as we bear the image of earthly man, we will bear the image of the heavenly one.[59] I cannot imagine how wonderful that must be—to be exactly in the image of I-Am-Savior—but then that was Paul's point!

While Preying Eagle was describing the ever-increasing number of settlers who trouble our hunting grounds with their wagons, I began to contemplate a verse I recently read in Isaiah. "When the righteous die and the merciful are taken away, no one understands: he is taken to be spared from evil. He will enter into peace and find rest on his bed."[60]

While I listen to our people voice fear of coming conflict, I sometimes wonder if Straight Arrows is not the most fortunate of my children. Though I know the Lord is the author of life and must, therefore, have His reasons for giving us grandchildren, I am ever more certain they will face perilous times. Yet, our holy, loving, and faithful God knows the end from the beginning and will cause Hisstory to unfold exactly as He planned. Indeed, when I grow afraid, I remind myself of a verse Nate quoted about my father's death: "Do not fear the ones who can kill the body but are not able to kill the soul; fear, instead, The One who is able to destroy both body and soul in hell."[61] Like Esther, God created us for this specific time and has His own perfect purposes.

When we were young and I thought of little but my longing for your cousin, death seemed so distant. You know how hard we endeavored to accurately reveal the Creator in all His glory to this beloved people, but life seemed so full of husbands and children and the happiness they offered. Now that we are older, I see how quickly life passes—like the blur of a fleeing animal running by or the tiniest of pebbles—not something for my heart to grasp tightly and hold.

I hope to spend every moment as I-Am-Savior did: going about our Father's business, not grasping for pleasure or comfort or even safety, though I am ashamed to admit how regularly I fail. I pray, by His grace, He will infuse the frail words I have written with His Spirit so that all who read them might draw closer to Him, ever mindful that intimacy with Him is far greater than anything this world may offer—and one day, He will come and take us to Himself, so that where He is we may be also!

I had better close. Please forgive my ramblings. They have woven in and out of each other in so many directions that I am no longer certain they even make sense.

Yours for eternity, with the deepest love,

Alcy Louise Callen

The Spirit and the bride say, 'Come!'

Let him who hears say, 'Come!'

And let all who are thirsty come.

Let all who desire drink freely from the water of life

*The One who testifies to these things says,
'Surely, I am coming quickly.*

Revelations 22:17 and 20

Even so—come quickly, Lord Jesus!

Endnotes

1. Acts 13:36
2. David, I Samuel 13
3. Matthew 6:34
4. Daniel 12:6
5. Romans 12:19
6. James 1:5
7. Psalms 27:1
8. Matthew 6:34
9. Psalm 33:4
10. Psalm 34:18
11. Hebrews 13:5
12. Hebrews 13:5
13. James (dir. Jacob)
14. Psalm 23:4
15. Isaiah 55:8
16. Romans 8:28
17. Psalm 139:15
18. Galatians 6:7
19. Mark 5:22, 34-43
20. John 11:3
21. I Timothy 6:6
22. Exodus 16:15
23. 2 Kings 4:2-7
24. John 19:26
25. James 2:4-19
26. Proverbs 26:2
27. Romans 12:19
28. Romans 12:19
29. Paul
30. Apostle
31. Philippians 3:8
32. Matthew 6:12
33. Luke 6:27
34. Genesis 37:36
35. Abraham, Moses, Samuel, David
36. Solomon
37. Ecclesiastes 4:12
38. I Corinthians 10:13
39. Annually, Sparrow Hawk warrior societies stole their rivals' wives
40. I Corinthians 15:6
41. Ephesians 5:29
42. Philip, John 12:22
43. John 12:26
44. John 12:27-28
45. Matthew 19:26
46. Psalm 51:10
47. Psalm 139:16
48. Psalm 133:1
49. Ephesians 3:20
50. Luke 12:23
51. John 3:19
52. Philippians 4:6
53. Psalm 51:10
54. Ezekiel 11:9
55. Psalm 139:16
56. Psalm 17:15
57. I Corinthians 15:37-38
58. I Corinthians 15:42
59. I Corinthians 15:49
60. Isaiah 57:1-2
61. Matthew 10:28

Meet the Author

Sydney Tooman Betts and her husband currently reside near the extensive cavern system that inspired the setting for several early chapters of this series' second book.

While single, Ms. Betts (B.S. Bible/Missiology, M.Ed) took part in a variety of cross-cultural adventures in North and Central America. After marrying, she and her husband lived in Europe and the Middle East where he served in various mission-support capacities. Her teaching experiences span preschool to guest lecturing at the graduate level and serving as the Sunday School Superintendent, Children's Church Director, or Women's Ministries facilitator in several evangelical denominations.

Before penning her first novel, *A River Too Deep,* she ghost-wrote several stories for an adult literacy program.

Thank You!

Thank you for reading Straight Flies the Arrow! I hope you found it worthwhile. If you enjoyed it, please consider leaving a review or rating on the site where it was purchased and Goodreads if you're active there. Writing a book is far easier for me than getting readers to know it exists, and your help in this gratefully appreciated. Reviews make a huge difference in helping new readers find the series.

You have taken the time to meet me (nothing could reflect my heart more fully than this series). Now I would like to meet you. If this interests you also, please drop by my Facebook author page: Sydney Tooman Betts. I have met many new and dear friends this way.

Made in the USA
Middletown, DE
18 November 2021